CRYSTAL MOTH

CONSPIRACY

ASH BORN

BOOK ONE

Written by: Konn Lavery
Edited by: Cara Flannery

STORIES

BOOKS

eBook ISBN-13: 978-1-990542-05-3
Paperback ISBN-13: 978-1-990542-06-0
Published in Canada by Reveal Books.
Photo credit: Nastassja Brinker.
Cover illustration by Lee Nielsen.
Book interior artwork and design by Konn Lavery of Reveal Design.
Printed in the United States of America.
First Edition 2023

Placed in 10 Award Programs:

- Gold Medal in Dan Poynter's Global Ebook Awards 2023, Fantasy/Contemporary Category
- First Place in Firebird Book Awards, Weird Book Genre: Canadiana Supernatural Thriller, Cross Genre, and Dark Fantasy Categories
- B.R.A.G. Medallion Honoree
- Second Place in The Book Fest 2023 Award, Fiction – Supernatural – Magic
- Silver Medal in the 2024 Author Shout Reader Ready Awards
- Bronze Medal in the 2023 Global Book Awards, Magical Realism Category
- Finalist in The Independent Author Network 2023 Book of the Year Awards, Fantasy and Paranormal/Supernatural Categories
- Finalist in the 2023 Readers' Favourite Supernatural Category
- Finalist in the 2023 N. N. Light Book Awards, Dark Fantasy Category
- Semi-Finalist in Indies Today 2023

AUTHOR MESSAGE

THE ROTTEN BIRTH

The Crystal Moth Conspiracy novel is the first book for a story concept I had floating around since 2008. Like any idea, it mutates over time and is almost unrecognizable from its origin. The setting stayed the same, and a handful of character types remained when I started writing the novel in 2020.

I waited many years before attempting this book because I didn't believe I had the ability to write it. It was a mix of confidence issues and wanting to do the story justice. There was no rush, and I kept putting it on the back burner. When the pandemic hit, I felt it was time to write the book since there was so much uncertainty within the world. We're here once, and you might as well chase your dreams while you still can.

This story is found within a shared universe I've housed all of my novels in. *The Macrocosm* spans across the fantasy-rich past, gritty present thrills and horrors, and the dreadful cosmic future. The Ash Born series blends those genres and makes clear connections within this universe through reappearing characters and lore.

Some examples would be the vazelead people and the Scalebane family. Kristalantice Scalebane is the protagonist in my dark fantasy series *Mental Damnation*. Abbygail and Bark Nose pay tribute to the horror novel *Cultivate: Seed Me Relapse Edition*. Lola Cabello's backstory is found within the thriller *YEGman*, which follows the events of Michael Bradford. Dasco Amoss and Yang Chen appear in short stories within *Beyond the Macrocosm*, while Tycho Flutcher has a role in the horror novel *Rave*.

The journey to complete this book has been a lifelong process, from building the lore through past novels and short stories, bettering my writing craft, and having the maturity to tackle some of the themes. I'm pleased to share this book with you, the reader, and I want to take you along the journey to see where the Ash Born series will go.

THANK YOU

I want to thank everyone who has followed my writing from the beginning. My writing path dates back to my childhood. I professionally started in 2012 with my first release, *Reality*. You all have read and watched a wide range of stories unfold within *The Macrocosm*. Thank you for the continual support, and cheers to the future.

Thank you to my mother, Brenda Lavery, for the countless years of love and support, giving life to this shared universe of stories. Thanks to my partner Lindsey Molyneaux for continually reading my work and hearing my endless blabber regarding the new book I am working on. Thank you to my brother for always reading my writing from the start and sharing his thoughts. Thank you Sarah Hein for catching those pesky plot hiccups in this book and previous ones. Thanks to Kit and those mentioned above for beta reading. Thank you to my editor, Cara Flannery for polishing this story. Thanks to my friends Nastassja Brinker for the excellent photography work and Lee Nielsen for the fantastic cover illustration in this book.

Last but not least, thanks to my family, friends, and readers who are exploring *The Macrocosm* with me.

TABLE OF CONTENTS

CHAPTER 1
NEW PRODUCT

Everyone is a media watcher, zombified by the screen and unable to see through its lies. Lola learned this the wrong way. Sure, she's been an outcast from society most of her life, but this isn't some goth club filled with posers wearing black head to toe, criticizing the masses for being sheep. This is rock bottom with roughnecks. No more fictionalized fantasies of how reality functions. No more ludic loops for dopamine kicks. Goodbye shock news on the tube. This is actual survival.

Mom would be so proud, Lola thinks, clutching her handgun with her sweaty fingers. *Mom. No.* She'd best pay attention to the man sitting across from her. The cartilage is misaligned, covered in red, from whence she pistol-whipped him earlier.

Cherry liquid drips from his nose, falling onto the unfinished wooden table, soaking into the grain.

Her mother, it's why she's here. It's why she dragged this man onto the second floor of the abandoned warehouse and zap-strapped him to the chair.

His narrow beading face tightens into a sneer under the clear lightbulb dangling by a chain. That's hate. He cannot see Lola's face as she hides behind the lamp, casting intimidation as best as she can.

"As you know, this ash stuff is taking the world by storm." The man says with an attempted tough-guy tone, reverberating in the darkness. His pitch is too high for the attitude he projects, but he tries. "And no one knows where it comes from. I still don't know where they got it or what the hell it is. Since that night, I just sell it. No way have I tried it. I'm clean now. My kid doesn't need a deadbeat father. Most of the time, I grind it up to disguise it, which makes it look like some charcoal or . . . ash."

"Okay, Chen, how much does it go for?" Lola asks, her voice faking a silvery calm tone. Truthfully, she's as scared as him. She's never interrogated anyone before. His pencil stash above his lip and tacky faded tattoos scattered across his arms make him less of a threat than some of the criminals she's encountered. Though, the white rag tied to his bicep represents the dangerous beast he comes from.

Chen says, "Well, a gram can be two-fifty. It depends on supply and where the cops are at." A pause. The moment holds. "Look, I told you names, everything. We change our meetup spot every time."

Lola slides her gun off the splintered table, away from the open black bag. She tucks the firearm behind her back and reaches for the black bag. The light hints at her pallid skin and the blonde wig that boils her scalp. Chen's eyes squint, trying to get a good look at her. Lola will reveal her face when she wants to.

Her hand goes into the bag and pulls out a flat, leathery, diamond-shaped object. She holds the ash into the light. The diamond is brittle along the edges, and some parts are about to flake off. The core is thicker, stretchy, and holds hydration.

"You said organic?" Lola asks. Despite the brittle edges, it's fresh enough that she can spin the ash between her thumb and index finger. *Amazing this was not around until the summer,* she thinks. *Changes my whole strategy.*

"Yeah," Chen says.

"A leaf?"

"Well, I don't know. It sure as hell isn't made in a lab."

"It's a scale," Lola says.

"A scale? Like a reptile?"

"Yes, dumb shit. You can have them as pets. They are in the wild?"

Chen shifts in his seat, upset that she is belittling him. He says, "Okay, lady, why hasn't the news said anything?"

Lola smirks, placing the ash diamond on the table. She drags the wig off, resting it on her sombre grey cargo pants beside the open burner phone. The cool air touches her sweaty, short hair as she pushes the light away, letting Chen get a good look at her.

He analyzes her up and down. His mouth hangs open, surprised at who she is. Maybe he expected someone older or a little more grizzled and not a girl kicked out of university.

Lola says, "The news knows, but they're part of the game. Everyone is fabricating this bullshit fairytale we live in. Give it time, and some leaks will find their way on the web."

"You're clearly not a cop. What do you want?" Chen asks.

She leans forward. Now, Chen's gaze locks onto the nasty bullet scar on her chest, underneath the left black tank top strap. Lola could have kept her jacket on, but she wants him to see. She wants this lowlife scum to be the message to his employers so they know she's coming for them.

"You street dealers have no idea how deep the Crystal Moths run," Lola says.

Chen doesn't blink, glued to the scar. "Hey, you're that girl, aren't you?"

Lola lets go of the light and sits still. The chain moves in a pendulum motion, casting sharp contrasts on her stone-cold face. Back and forth. Without looking, she grabs the burner phone and dials 911 with her thumb.

"Yeah," Chen says in a deep exhale. "You exposed the cops out west with the video. The Crystal Moth bust in Edmonton with that hashtagYEGman. Fuck me. I almost don't believe it."

"Believe what you want."

"I do. You're the reporter kid with that website people go to. Lola Cabello."

Lola tosses the burner phone onto the table while standing. She throws her leather jacket over her shoulder and clutches the wig. "Cops are on their way," she says.

Chen's face is frozen, looking at the phone. Now, he is aware of its dual functions displayed on the screen. One: dead center of the display shows the dialling of the police. Two: the recording text beside a flashing red dot and a microphone icon in the upper portion of the screen. His skin must be ice cold now, knowing how much he spilled.

She turns and walks towards the dark exit at the far end of the warehouse. With each step onto the cold concrete, the leather boots leave a high click.

"Hey!" Chen shouts.

Keep walking, Lola thinks, exhaling a wave of relief.

"Hey!" Chen shouts again.

She reaches the door, pushes it, and slips into the dust-covered stairwell.

"Don't go west!" Chen's voice is muffled by the door. "They'll kill you!"

She keeps walking under the night light shining through the broken glass windows. The distancing Chen curses her name. Lola's heart tries to climb out of her throat. She can't stop now, for she put this mess into motion. Chen isn't going to be alright. The cops are like the news with profound Crystal Moth influence. That failed recognition started the snowball she's frozen to.

Lola pushes the exit door and hurries down the alleyway, coated with fluffy snow. She slips into her leather jacket and tucks the wig onto her head. Sirens blare, increasing in volume throughout the night metropolis. She'll escape in time, and the cops will take Chen in. They'll hear the whole recording, and with a sliver of luck, an authentic law enforcer will get the evidence.

The probable scenario is a Crystal Moth plug will take care of Chen and the evidence, it's happened to her before, and that is okay. Chen isn't responsible for what happened in Edmonton. He is the message. Every one of these pricks is going to pay for what happened. Lola will make sure of it.

CHAPTER 2
FIRST CONTACT

Drug busts give an unmatched rush until you've done them a few hundred times. Even when the intel says this is a big one, on the East Coast in a bleak New Brunswick town, there's no adrenaline.

The province is peaceful to the untrained eye. To the keen, they see that it lacks direction from the government, leading to crime. More often than not, it's the typical things: no funds, drug abuse, domestic violence, robbery, and vandalism. These crimes are interconnected due to the recessive economy. The circumstances force individuals to make unhealthy choices, catching the cops' attention and resulting in busts and jail time.

Already the police task force surrounds the den from the

back entrance, the rotting front veranda, and the slanted side door along the cracked sidewalk. It would have been a nice house if it was upkept. These rundown slums are often owned by some lazy landlord who won't maintain the place. They offer rent at a good buck for these low lives because they're in on the drug market selling to their tenants. The druggies won't even know what hit them. When it comes to the law, they're going down.

It's a simple philosophy for Ricardo Iglesias. The thought is reinforced with a deep exhale, suppressing his relatable past. These are people, the types he grew up with. He doesn't care, or so he tells himself, as he guides his unit to the rear entrance with hand signals. The group of six stand alongside the door frame. His partner is behind him, with each RCMP officer breathing steadily, awaiting the next command.

Summer is hell out east. Sweat drizzles on Iglesias's forehead from the sun beaming above in the cloudless sky. Being geared in uniformed armor from head to toe doesn't help either.

Iglesias uses his free hand to command his team to bust the door open. One RCMP officer holds a black battering ram with both hands and hurries to the back entrance. Another officer swings the screen door open as the battering ram arches, colliding with the handle. It bashes through the rotting wood with a snap.

The unit swarms into the dark, wet room, their flashlights beaming into the hallway and stairwell leading to the basement. They can hear the front door burst open, then the side door. Trained RCMP officers each orchestrate their part according to Iglesias's command. It's a beautiful symphony.

"You first," mutters his partner.

"So thoughtful, Beckman," Iglesias says.

"Anytime." A smirk sneaks under Beckman's bushy mustache.

Iglesias heads into the wet room right behind his unit. At the end of the hall is a man running around the corner.

"This is the RCMP! Don't move!" Iglesias's voice booms, bouncing against the hole-infested walls. He inhales through his nose, conserving his breath. A sweet smell seeps into his nostrils. It's the typical scent that comes with a drug house. It's often mixed with piss and feces. This smell is accompanied by a metallic distinction.

"Left!" Beckman says.

Iglesias uses another hand motion, commanding three officers to go with them. He tells the other two to stand their ground, keeping an eye on the rear entrance in case anyone gets a wise idea of escaping. Iglesias guides them through the hallway, meeting with the side entrance squad. Now, seven officers move into the living room and kitchen.

He scans the lower cupboards, under the table, and behind the couch. Nothing. Footsteps stomp to the second floor. The sound is followed by the marching RCMP from the front entrance group.

Iglesias relaxes, keeping his gun pointed down, finger on the trigger. The mint green counter is covered with incomplete dishes. Tiles have fallen off of the backsplash by the sink and of course, more holes in the wall. The paint is chipping and stains trickle to the running boards. Yes, a buffet for the bugs and mice who scurry away.

They always smash holes in the wall, Iglesias thinks. A pointless thought due to his easing state. This is going to be a small bust.

There are trash bags on the floor, a copper-stained mattress on the corner, and dirt everywhere. Now, what's interesting is the yellow kitchen table. There's a glass pipe with a lighter. Beside that is a small baggie with spilled charcoal powder. To the blissful, this would look like smoked dope, meth or ketamine. Iglesias knows it's different. For one, there are no scorched white spots due to flame. The substance is a consistent natural grey.

"Well, this isn't much," Beckman says. "Why did we come here again?"

Iglesias sighs with equal disappointment. "We got the go-ahead from Sergeant Bando. The tip from the intel?"

"The rumour, you mean?" Beckman asks.

"Proving a waste of time," Iglesias says.

"Told you. We should have stuck on Cabello's trail."

"This was supposed to help."

Shouting comes from upstairs.

"Iglesias," Beckman says.

"Inspect the rest of the house," Iglesias commands the units.

He and his partner hurry from the kitchen, through the hallway, and up the stairs. Each step on the burgundy carpet creaks until they reach the second floor. There are two rooms on each side. In front is a bathroom with the lights off and a fresh excrement-funk scent lingering in the air.

The room to the right has the door closed, with two RCMP units standing by the frame, waiting for instructions. Four officers pin a middle-aged woman to the ground in the last room. Her sweat-drenched face is as worn and as dirty as her clothes are.

"He locked himself in," a brunette officer, Archer, says by the closed door.

Iglesias nods. "Get the battering ram here."

The metallic smell is more pungent on the second floor, and it's not from the bathroom. The sweetness is mixed in with rust and the strange fetor of a swamp. In fact, it sends Iglesias's mind a good decade into the past when he used to take his son and former wife to the pet store. There would be walls of aquariums with amphibians and reptiles. That subtle hint makes Iglesias clench his teeth because the memory serves no purpose. He suppresses it. Iglesias needs to keep his mind focused on the bust. Still, this is abnormal, and it is ever prominent in his mind, piercing through his years of training.

The woman shouts inaudible words. Her eyes are puffy and pink as drool seeps down her chin. Beside her is a pipe with smoke and charcoal powder spilled onto the carpet. Her head thrashes wildly. The frizzy hair dangles in her face as she howls like the animal she has become. She ends the fit with a maniacal cackle.

Creaks come from the stairs as the battering ram arrives.

Iglesias says, "Beckman, check the basement with the others."

"Good call," Beckman says before leaving.

Iglesias signals the unit to bust the door. Like the rear entrance, the battering ram slams into the door and sends splintered wood into the air. A frail man stands dead center in the empty room, looking at the closed curtains. His stained grey sweats are worn so low that his hairy ass droops underneath his hoodie. He holds a pipe and lighter in his hand with the flame mid-way to the bowl of charcoal powder. He looks back—a deer in headlights. The RCMP unit rushes in.

"Drop it!" shouts Archer, raising her gun.

He brings the pipe to his lips, flame to the powder, and inhales the drug. The fire morphs into a poisonous purple as his eyes flood with pink, skin somehow turning more blanched than it already was.

"Drop it now!" shouts the other officer, his gun pointed at the man.

The man listens instantly, releasing the lighter and pipe. The items tumble to the ground, and his muscles relax. The head dangles, eying the speckles on the ceiling. A gentle laughter rumbles from his stomach as he sways.

"Jesus, this new shit stinks," Archer says.

"Cuff him," Iglesias commands.

The male RCMP officer steps forward, holstering his gun, and takes his handcuffs. He snags the man's arms, bringing them around his back. The sudden motion tightens the doped-up man's face. The nostrils move upward with the cheekbones, forming a nasty snarl. Deep groans come from the bottom of his esophagus as his body thrashes violently.

"Pin him!" shouts Archer.

"I-I-can't!" says the first officer.

Iglesias holsters his gun and assists the two. The officer with the battering ram stands by the door, waiting to engage. The three officers immobilize the man as he tries to kick them. Their weight subdues him, and they slam him face-first into the carpet. Iglesias pins his shoulder blade while the man's gargling morphs into aggressive exhales, then watery screaming at the top of his lungs. Thick, stringy spit flies from his mouth, grazing the carpet blades.

Suddenly, he relaxes. The loose muscles give the officers the upper hand. They lock his wrists in. He bellows to the point his face turns red and his eyelids flutter.

"Jesus, what was that?" asks the second officer, getting to his feet.

"Meth heads," mutters Archer with disgust seeping from her words.

Iglesias doesn't respond to their comments. They sprout another memory that he crushes faster than an inhale. He doesn't stand, now noticing the crack pipe. He gets nice and close, looking at the powder that sprinkles the carpet. There's dark grey residue along the rim of the bowl of the glass. He grabs it while standing to examine it better in the light.

"Sir, I don't think we should—" the male officer says.

"Don't concern yourself," Iglesias interrupts, spinning the glass crack pipe in his hand. Sure, the warm tool is typical, small and easy to use. It's dirty from constant usage. The tar colour is different inside the chamber. Usually, there's an amber tinge. Not this one. It is a mixture of charcoal and swirls of purple. It's not the stained glass, either. Yes, indeed, that is caused by the strange substance that litters the ground.

He's careful not to inhale the ever-present metallic swamp smell. Iglesias is overtaken by his curiosity. His fingers approach the rim of the smoking bowl. He pauses, realizing that is unwise. His gut tells him this is a drug no one has encountered before.

His trance ends, and he hands the pipe to Archer. "Get this to forensics right away," Iglesias commands.

"Yes, sir," she says.

Smoke is the one word that enters his mind. He wants a dart to celebrate their successful bust.

At first glance, you'd think this was a complete waste of time, budget, and workforce. It's the kind of story you'd see on the news as justification for the police to be defunded. "Bullies," as the common civilian would say.

Their intel came through. Iglesias needs a follow-up chat for a clear explanation regarding this place. They've stumbled upon a new substance. The charcoal powder on the burgundy rug locks Iglesias in. His hair stands, feeling a sudden icy wind blow past his body, despite no open windows.

There it is: the rush he has failed to feel for many years. Looks like the decades in the RCMP Major Crimes haven't quite numbed him, and he is prone to feeling something other than monotony. It's thanks to a small ash-coloured powder. The workaholic lives.

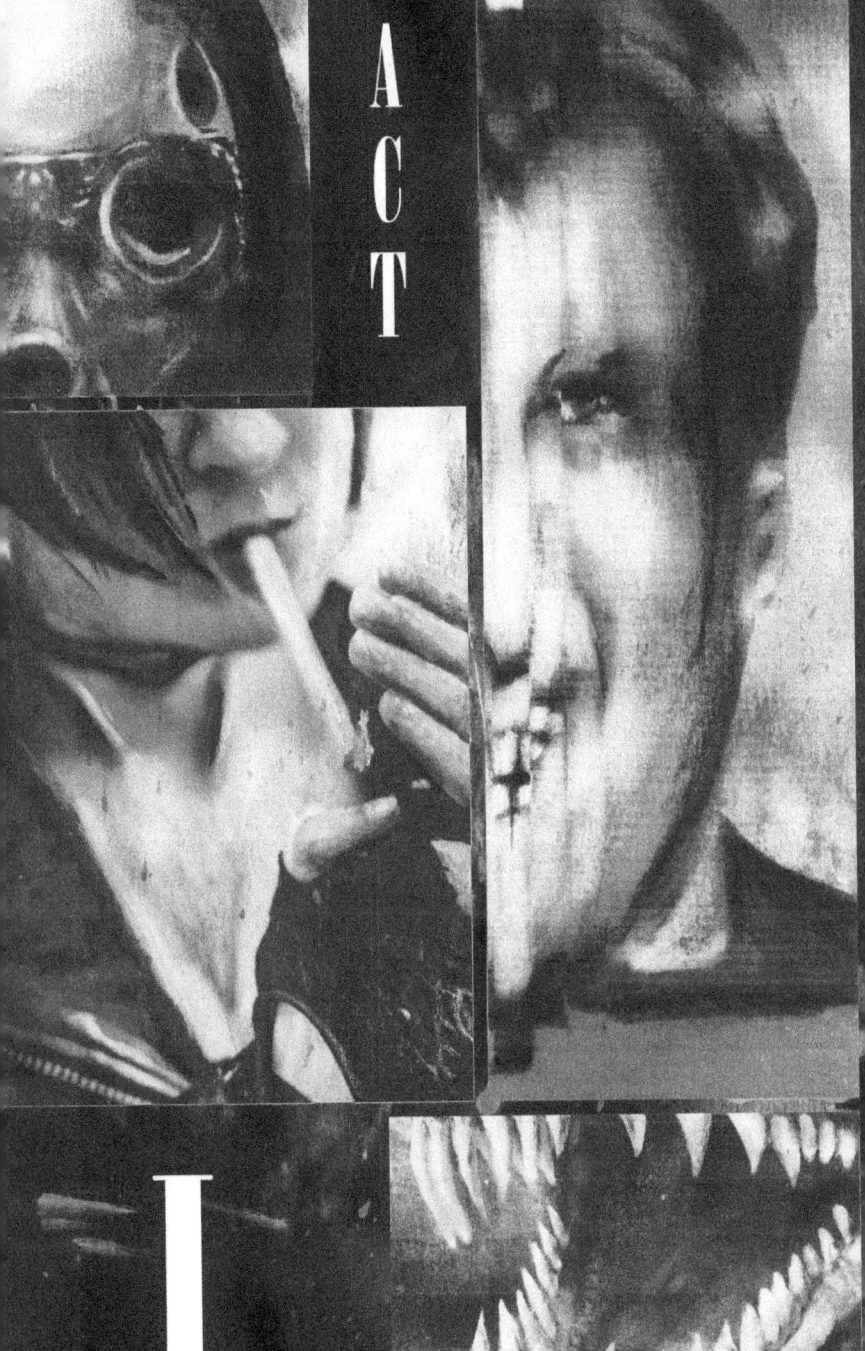

ACT I

ACT I
NOVICE
DEMORALIZATION

Good evening, and welcome to *CAMB News Now with Hucker Dime*. Believe it or not, it's been two years to the day since the horrendous November 5th, 2014, YEGman incident from Edmonton, Alberta.

YEGman, or Michael Bradford, was the poster child for police brutality. The Edmonton police had removed him from the force due to numerous offences of exploiting his power. That wasn't enough to stop the man. His mental health was not brought into check, for he had a corrupt sense of justice. Michael Bradford hunted people and attacked them.

His original act of supposed heroism was caught on camera, stopping a robbery. At first glance, it was just until it became clear he was feeding his need for violence. The assaults continued and escalated into numerous murders.

If you ask me, Michael Bradford was a deranged lunatic who enjoyed hurting people. His legacy didn't stop there because he had a protégé.

Michael Bradford's accomplice, Lola Cabello, was a journalist student at Grant MacEwan University. Her demented sense of journalistic integrity made her withhold key evidence from the law. Instead, Cabello uploaded her video to a blogging site.

I mean, come on!

As a legitimate reporter, I respect her attempts to make it big. Many want their shot at being on the air. If you're listening to this, Cabello, I gotta give you some credit for dodging the police this long. But, please, give it up. Tragedies happen, and we learn to move on in healthy ways. Keywording, healthy ways.

It was two years ago, and the law has spent enough resources playing cat and mouse with you. We all want to move on with our lives.

Do it for the people of Canada.

I, for one, can't understand why the police haven't been able to apprehend a university girl on the run. What are they doing with our tax dollars?

Speaking of budget, Public Health Canada continues to provide press statements urging caution with the use of street drugs. They discourage the usage of anything that isn't bought from a store or provided by your doctor. These PR statements don't help the homeless and youth taking drugs. Research shows from the West Coast to the east, we're seeing a twenty percent rise in substance abuse since July. Why the increase in usage?

Let's end it on a high note. Megastar Ashley Amber is making a comeback since her mental breakdown, filming in Canada for her next movie sensation alongside director Timothy Shepherd. The movie *Love, Play, and No Work* seeks local actors in Vancouver, British Columbia. Ashley Amber said, 'I love Canada so much. Maple Bacon and skiing is my favourite,' end quote. What a charm.

Thank you so much for tuning in. We strive to provide you with facts regarding the latest news at CAMB, stories that continue to evolve regarding you and your country. We keep you up to date with *CAMB News Now with Hucker Dime*.

We'll be passing you on to Justin and Danielle for the weather.

CHAPTER 3
REMEMBER

A potent sting of garlic seeps into the corners of the duplex, following a shout, "Lola! Lola! Is Becky staying over for dinner?" It's a familiar Spanish brogue belonging to her mother. Yes, mothers love you and care for you. At least the good ones do. Tell that to a teenager. They see the nagging as unbearable.

"Hello?" her mother calls again from the main floor.

Already it is clear to Lola that her mother is making gazpacho. She does so when there are potential guests. Her mom loves the cold soup more than anything, mixed with migas. The fried bread crumbs and bacon pair well with the tomatoey flavour.

"Hold on, Mom!" Lola shouts through the heavy kick drums

blaring from the portable speaker plugged into her smartphone. Distorted snares and modulated vocals create an unsettling, rhythmic dance pulse. In shorter words, industrial music, the iconic Canadian band Skinny Puppy.

"You staying, bub?" Lola asks, rising to face her friend, Becky, who sits cross-legged on the black sheet-covered bed.

"I don't know." Becky's voice is monotone. She's too occupied tapping away on that phone.

"Where else ya gotta be?"

"Well, nowhere, really." Becky's tone goes up a notch.

"Other than to some boy?"

Becky giggles. "Jealous, Lola Love?"

Lola smiles. It's a partial truth. Their inseparable nature is defined as a platonic, romantic relationship. It's simple, because they adore spending time with each other and boys take them away, not appreciating them right.

"Come on, stay for dinner," Lola says, grabbing Becky's ankle.

"I can, but I won't." Becky smiles. She hops off the bed, her red hair bouncing as she puts on her poofy green parka lying on the ground.

"Okay fine. I'll see you tomorrow then?" Lola asks.

"I won't skip math this time."

Lola rolls her eyes. "Sure."

The two girls exit the basement, leaving Skinny Puppy blasting as they close the door at the top of the stairs. Lola's mother is managing the stovetop in the kitchen with a spatula, stirring the minced garlic and onions into oil. Lola's stomach rumbles, ready to devour the signature meal.

Her mother smiles at the two girls, exaggerating the wrinkles on her thin, narrow face. The wrinkles arch upwards. They show many years of laughter and joy carved into her aging skin. The cheek-to-cheek beam guides you straight to the small nose bridge with a slight bump levelled with the eyes, no different than Lola's. Mix that in with the deep cupid's bow on her lip, and Lola's mother is a mirror reflection of what she will look like later in life. Except Lola has her father's silky, thick hair and not her mother's frizzy nest.

Lola's mother waves at the girls to come into the kitchen. She says, "Becky, you sure you don't wish to stay?"

"Thanks, Mrs. Cabello. I promised my mom I'd be home."

"Such a liar," Lola whispers into Becky's ear. Her warm breath makes Becky squirm in a girlish play.

"Stop." Becky smiles. "Thank you, Mrs. Cabello. See you soon."

"All right, tell your mother I say hello."

"Of course, bye!"

Lola leads Becky to the front door, and the girls embrace one another for a long hug. She gets a good whiff of Becky's natural peachy scent and ends the hug with a tight squeeze. Becky steps into the cool winter night to find whatever boy she's into. Her boots crunch into the snow with each step. Lola will hear about it tomorrow when they're in Mr. Weeb's maths class.

For now, Lola gets to have dinner with her family. Afterwards, she'll spend the night browsing the Internet to find disturbing online media to give herself a good spook. Creepypasta stories are a good search term to find unsettling campfire stories.

She shuts the front door and walks to the kitchen. Lola says, "Mom, need help with dinner, or can I go downstairs?"

There's no answer.

"Mom?" Lola asks.

Still, nothing.

"Dad, Bro?"

Lola enters the kitchen, and her mother is nowhere to be found. She's not by the sink, stovetop, or pantry. The garlic and onions are sizzling in the cast iron pan, starting to brown.

The lights shut off, leaving her in pitch darkness. The searing and boiling of the elements fill the silence. How odd.

"Anyone? The power is out," Lola says.

Red and blue lights shine through the backyard window with sirens ringing. Muffled male voices come from outside as the rear door thuds.

"Mom, Dad, Bro!" Lola shouts while hurrying to the door. "Where are you?"

"Freeze!" comes a man's voice.

Rifles fire, piercing through the windows. Shards of glass bounce off the tile as the door bursts open. Splinters of wood blows into the air. Bullets clack outside as smoke grenades soar into the house through the now-open window.

"Lola!" comes her mother's distant voice. There's a cough. Then an agonizing cry.

"Mom!" Lola calls. She starts choking on the thick air.

The bullets stop.

The sirens disappear as smoke envelops Lola's full view. Her breath is tight as she trembles to the ground. The room vanishes from the smog as she struggles for balance. As her spatial awareness spins, which way is upright remains a mystery. She calls her mom, even while coughing violently. Her first bark rips her throat. The second shoots hot liquid through the esophagus and into her mouth, and the third cough spews red into the open air. It splatters onto the tiles.

"Why did you abandon me?" comes her mom's voice. The tone hisses from the throat in a croaky whisper, lacking all forms of the motherly love she adores.

"Mother, I didn't. Mom I—"

"Why did you abandon me?" her mother shouts. The thundering tone throws Lola onto the floor, smothering her into submission.

"Why?"

The voice's sonic power splits Lola's skin and shatters the tiles.

"Mom!"

"Why?"

She sputters more blood. It flies up and back down onto her face.

"WHY?"

* * *

Lola gasps, looking upright. She's in a red and tan restaurant with rows of booths under fluorescent lighting. There's a poster on the wall beside her of megastar Ashley Amber posing with mini doughnuts. This is the Tim Horton's joint she stopped at. She blinks several times, rubbing the goop that built in her lids. It wasn't real. It was a dream. The memory of her previous life, mixed with night terror fantasies of regret, forged an event that never occurred.

Right, driving west, Lola reminds herself that she's in some small town, Hearst, if she recalls. *Just exhaustion.*

She's one of two people in the restaurant. The other is a older man in a dirty baseball cap and flannel jacket, gripping his coffee, staring at her under his sagging eyes.

"What?" Lola asks.

The man looks away, unthreatened by her harsh emphasis. He sips his coffee and watches the cars outside driving by on the dark morning highway. Speckles of snow swirl around in the wind.

Lola wants to vomit. A pain ruptures her stomach as the intestines twist, making her tighten her abdomen muscles to suppress it in any way she can. Stress, regret, and exhaustion can do a number on you. The dream's timeline was incorrect, mixing high school memories with recent ones. Her brother and father were around, but Lola was not there when her mother—

No. She can't bring herself to think about it anymore. There's no point. It's in the past, and she must keep moving.

She reaches for her cup of coffee beside the empty wrappers that once held her sandwich. She feels the paper rim. It is still hot, letting her know she wasn't out for long. Good. Then she can hit the road and stay on track for the first milestone, Winnipeg.

Lola clutches the black canvas messenger bag that rests on her lap. It should contain her laptop. Yes, it's there. It was foolish to pass out. Exhaustion is a bitch when you haven't known sleep in two years. The adrenaline from interrogating a guy will give you a hell of a burnout, mixed in with ten hours of driving. Her pass-out was justified.

She sifts through the bag, seeing the laptop beside a handheld audio recorder. It's the same backup recording device she had in her pocket when Chen sang.

Lola takes her laptop and powers it on to double-check her last line of communication with a man named Jack. He's the reason for the Winnipeg destination. Her computer's Internet connection has been disabled, reducing her chances of being tracked. Lola did take a screenshot of their last email communication using her fake name. It reads:

Jack Harris

To: You

Thanks for the deposit, Jamie. I got the envelope. This design will take a few hours, depending on how much you squirm. Then again, I haven't seen the final details of the art. Let's say a few hours.

400 Enniskillen Ave, Winnipeg, MB R2V 0J3

Don't be late. No BS. Don't bring anyone.

Jack

The last line is a good indicator of this guy's character. She won't bring anyone, for she is alone. A legitimate tattoo shop is too risky, and Jack's portfolio says he has the chops to re-create the message to her future self. Plus, tattoo artists can be particular with their rules, and this guy is too good to do it from his home, despite doing so.

She pulls the crumpled Tim Horton's receipt from her pocket with her scribbled notes, confirming she has the right directions and address. There are another thirteen hours of driving to go. She'd best get another coffee.

"Don't go west," Chen's voice plays in her thoughts as she fidgets with the paper. West, to Vancouver, which is the next milestone for payback. However, the warning haunts her. Crystal Moths kill. Chances are Chen is already dead. Perhaps he was an okay human and a father. He's also a small tooth in the beast's mouth, the same monster that ruined her life.

She crunches the receipt in a twitch of rage.

"You sure you're okay?" comes a croaky voice.

Lola lifts her head to see that the old man is watching her again with concern seen in his slanted eyebrows. Great, that's what she needs: people to acknowledge her existence. She needs to be stealthy, unseen, and unknown.

"Yeah, I'm fine, thanks," Lola says, closing her laptop and packing it.

"You remind me of my granddaughter," the man says.

"I'm sure I do." She stands, crumpling her sandwich paper and taking the coffee. It's time to go. That second cup will have to wait.

"Stay safe out there. The roads are slick in November."

"Thanks," Lola says, chucking the sandwich wrapping into the garbage. She exits the restaurant and lights a smoke under the dark sky, meeting a biting wind as she heads for her parked red Toyota Camry. Lola would prefer to stay for a little longer to rest. The older man ruined it because she couldn't afford to have anyone recognize her. Even with her wig, she isn't wearing enough cover-ups to hide her unique facial features. It's not worth the chance, and back on the road it is. She's off to Winnipeg to save a permanent message on her skin.

CHAPTER 4
VIRGIN LIPS

Civilization would be less confusing to the consumer if it functioned the way the media portrays it: a packaged series of events compressed into bite stories for the viewer on their daily commute to work. Lola would love the simplicity because it's a beautiful narrative with a clear story arch for people to understand. This theoretical civilization isn't reflective of the world, as Lola learned from her journalism school. At that time, it was her job to make it bite-sized. Life is messy and chaotic. You make one wrong move and will be on the run forever.

She drove twenty-two hours across the country after assaulting a man and tying him to a chair. She's changed her outfit twice to keep her camouflage fresh, blending into the upside-down, story-tranced civilization. Soon, she'll flip it right-side up.

Betting on black is a fool's dream. A backup plan is needed to succeed. Hence, she's getting a tattoo from a guy she found online as a killswitch for a potential future.

Mom would be so proud, Lola thinks, an echoing one from one night ago. *Not the time.* Mom cannot enter her mind. Right now, she'd best get the tattoo and the hell away from this scuz-house.

She's sitting in her new black jeans on a crooked metal chair right in the home's entryway. The walls are chipping. The floor creaks. Then there's the burning sweet plastic smell, which could be a meth lab in the basement. Her chair is placed under the flickering fluorescent light as an intimidation tactic. Good job, Lola.

"Yo, Jamie," comes a scratchy voice of a man. The guy is your stereotypical dirtbag in grey sweatpants and a stained white wifebeater. He appears from the shadows. Lola was too lost in her own misery to even see him appear. He walks across the cigarette-burnt carpet, barefoot, towards her.

This is Jack, the house-operating tattoo artist. Lola can't help but wonder if that outfit ever gets him laid or if he cleans himself. Or he slips an effective little pill into a girl's drink for an easy time. This is why she keeps the knife tucked into her left boot and her handgun in the other.

"Yeah," Lola says, flicking her brunette wig from her face. She wants to review her makeup because of the perspiration growing on her skin. She can't.

It's nerves, she tells herself, because her disguise is good. She double-checked it before leaving her car. He'll have no idea who the real Lola is, whose face is plastered over the news and the Internet.

"Cool, back this way," Jack says, waving her to follow.

She rises from the chair, causing it to squeak. They walk through the hall, passing a brown cloth poster with some Zen design and the word "peace" below it. It's not the decoration she'd pick for the place.

Onwards to the kitchen, Jack flicks the light on. It flickers several times, leaving an eerie hum and painting the room a cold blue. Black stains are on the corners of the baby blue walls and the blue-and-white tiled floor. The metal table is beside a rolling tray with the tattoo machine gun. It looks so sanitary. She doesn't dare examine that sink. All in all, this checks out to what she expected.

"Sit here, missy," Jack says, nodding at the table casually. He sits on a stool, prepping the machine, needles, and black ink on a steel rolling tray.

Lola walks across the table, clamping her leather jacket cuff tightly. She's nervous as hell. Nothing should happen because she gave him the deposit. Money talks, for the most part.

"So uh, you want this, right?" Jack asks while lifting a printed piece of paper with the design. There are dozens of squares and lines in black forming a collage in the shape of a pixelated heart.

"No. This one." Lola scurries around her pockets and takes a folded piece of paper. "I made some adjustments to it. Same design."

She passes him the paper, and Jack unfolds it. "Oh yeah,

moved some of the squares around," Jack says.

"That's it. Same thing."

"A QR code?" Jack asks.

"Not really."

"Looks like one."

"It's not," Lola says.

"Aight, whatever you say. Your arm?" Jack asks.

"No, I don't want it exposed, but easy to show flat," Lola says.

"Right," Jack says, walking to her and holding the design in front of him. He's eying her as if she were a puzzle.

"Stomach work?" she asks, pointing to her lower right.

Jack nods. "Sure. Think you can handle it, missy?" He grins, showing his crooked teeth.

Lola nods. "Don't forget the white ink."

"Yep. Get on the table then."

Jack drags a stool and the tray to the table as Lola hops up. The coolness of the table nips her stiff body. She's nervous, despite having a couple of tattoos already. They're small ones for fun. This tattoo serves a purpose. Look at prison tattoos, they're messages. This piece is no different, only more complex.

She keeps her coat on and lifts her black t-shirt, exposing her ivory skin with undertones of death. The sun is indeed absent from a life underground. Jack takes a damp paper towel and wipes her stomach with the cool antibacterial soap. It shocks Lola, but that's minor. If anything, Jack's sanitation process is impressive and not a reflection of his home.

He takes the new design, updates his tracing paper containing the linework for several minutes, and then places it onto her skin. After a solid press and wipe, Jack peels the tracing paper off, showing blue ink where the tattoo will go.

"How's that?" he asks.

Lola looks at the tattoo and deems it good enough. "Let's do it," she says.

The gun hums to life when Jack pushes the button. He leans onto the table, the needle going for her skin. With a deep breath in, Lola prepares her mind. She cups her hands together. The first sting strikes her stomach, and it twitches in reflex, blood rushing into her face as her heart rate increases.

Exhale, she tells herself. Steady breathing is vital. It's breathing, just like when your best friend dies right in front of you.

The pain amplifies.

Fuck. She can't send her mind to the depths of sorrow. She must breathe in through the nose and out the mouth. Driving for a full day doesn't help her energy levels. A smart person gets a good rest before a tattoo session. There's no time for Lola.

The sting lessens into a gentle hum with each focused inhale and exhale. There are some tingles, and a few pricks as the needle goes along the skin. The heart rate calms, and the blood evens throughout her body. Wonderful.

The buzz of the light mixed with the gun fills her ears, letting Lola drift into a strange form of meditation. She's uncertain how much time goes by in her trance. Eventually, Jack speaks.

"So what is this thing?" He squints at the piece of paper taped to the tray.

Becky. The thought is trampled by her will, and she says, "It's in memory of a friend," That's a partial-truth. She doesn't want to share its purpose or any details. The less he knows, the better.

"That's cool. What's it mean?"

"It's kind of an inside joke."

"I gotcha. I got plenty of 'em too."

Several moments go by before Jack talks again.

"I mean, you could have gotten this done at any shop. I do like the cash, though."

"I scoped you out. You don't talk, apparently," Lola says.

"Usually. It's odd to me." Jack uses the cool paper towel to wipe the tattoo and then presses the needle onto the skin.

"The tattoo?" Lola asks on an exhale.

"I like to know my clients. And your story sounds so innocent compared to how nervous you are and that wig."

Shit, Lola thinks. Jack isn't as dimwitted as she predicted. A sharp sting ruptures her stomach. She's losing focus on breathing. Her heart thumps as the bite channels throughout the nerves underneath the skin and around her torso. She was sure the wig was decent. Too bad for her. It looks like the cat is out of the bag, and her face morphs into a tomato.

"I thought you didn't talk?" Lola says.

"Well, don't worry. I've had all sorts of people come here. You're the cleanest of them. Pure in a way, no offence."

"None taken."

"I'm guessing you're new to this?"

"New to what?" Lola asks.

"Living a life you didn't choose."

"Oh," Lola says in a deep exhale. She doesn't want to get into it despite the man's persistence.

"It's a shocker," Jack says. "Survival is the name of the game. Whatever way you want to go about."

Lola doesn't reply, focusing on the cheap fluorescent light. Her nervousness fuses into the needling, increasing the intensity. With a dash of luck, Jack will shut up.

"I get it. You know? My upbringing wasn't horrible. Grew up in Wetaskiwin. You ever been there?"

Lola keeps breathing.

"It's a dead end. Crime is aplenty, and I didn't want to get a factory job. So, I was selling . . . jail . . . blah, blah, blah, you know? You gotta find ways to cope with life. Drugs helped. Thankfully, I had a nick for drawing and climbed out of my old ways."

"Crab in the bucket," Lola says on an exhale. "Got you."

"That's why I moved here to Winnipeg, to stay clear of that world. Unfortunately, my background followed me, and—"

Lola cuts him off, "We done?"

"Almost," Jack says. "So this friend of yours, who are they?"

"They died," Lola says.

"Bummer. Can I give you a piece of advice?"

"Why not?" Lola says.

"In this world, don't be so trustworthy."

Lola looks at him, saying, "No shit."

Underneath the tough words, her face burns, unsure if his statement is a threat. She could reach for her gun right now and cap him, not that she ever has. She likes to believe she could.

"Relax," Jack chuckles. "I'm giving you a forewarning. Not everybody is as easygoing as I am."

Lola can't help but smile. She's so on guard that she's failing to identify common decency. If that's what Jack is. She relaxes her head, looking at the kitchen from her upside-down view. There's that disgusting sink of greasy, meat-coated dishes stacked to the faucet. Moving beyond, closer to the stovetop, is a glass pipe and lighter. That's not unexpected. The surprise is a small little bag of charcoal-coloured powder beside it in a plastic bag. Jack looks too clean to be into that poison.

"You smoke that stuff?" Lola asks.

Jack stops tattooing, looking at the bag. "What about it?"
"Nevermind."

"Bullshit, spit it out." The tattoo gun starts, hitting another nerve. She twitches.

"Just surprised," Lola says.

"And why is that?" Jack asks.

"It's dangerous."

"Ash is like anything else. Remember what I said regarding coping with life? Not everything is gonna be squeaky clean, missy."

"Trust me, I know this." Lola is getting irritated. She didn't expect to get life lessons from a house-run tattoo artist. If you can even call him an artist with this sanitation.

"For some reason, I doubt that." Jack chuckles the words.
"Really?"

"Yeah, I don't think you've seen a damn thing."

Her nostrils flare. Jack has no clue what she's been through. For a moment, Lola ponders elaborating on her background, explaining how her friend Becky died, how Lola was shot, how she threw her life down the drain in a failed attempt for revenge, how her mother died, how she learned to survive on her own and why she went to see him. Then again, she knows she shouldn't get caught in a street cred dick-measuring contest with some lowlife. He could be fishing for information for his own gain. It's best to stay quiet and stick to the role of Jamie. She is Jamie with a wig.

"Tell you what," Jack says while leaning back and examining his work. "I'll give you a freebie of ash. Consider it an act of goodwill."

"You're giving me a sample? That shit is expensive." Lola smirks, amused that he's enticing her with drugs.

"I am. You need something to take the edge off." Jack brings the needle to the flesh and makes a few final touches.

"Trust me, I'm fine. I only want this tattoo of my friend."

"You don't." Jack lifts the gun and gives her stomach several wipes of the damp paper towel. He stands, indicating the work done. "My point still stands. Clearly, you've got a background. That type of suppression will build in you until you explode. It might not be today, tomorrow, or a few months from now. Just wait, it'll come at the worst time."

Lola ignores him, examining her stomach where a puffy four-inch tattoo rests. The line work is clean. It should scan once the red skin eases.

"White ink too," Jack says.

"Thanks," Lola says, rising from the table. Now she realizes how much she was sweating along her spine. She pulls her shirt down and finds the cash stuffed in her jacket pocket.

"Come on, give me more credit," Jack says.

"What?" Lola asks.

"Let's bandage that up first."

"Right."

Jack reaches into a lower tray, taking a transparent film aftercare as Lola lifts her shirt. He places the bandage over her stomach, patting it, and sealing the tattoo in a protective case.

"You've been on edge since you've got here. Personally, I don't like people who are untrusting of me and project negativity in my home."

Oh, wonderful, Lola thinks. This is taking a weird turn. She must read people better.

Jack finishes wrapping the design, and Lola pulls her shirt down. She fumbles through her jacket to find the remaining cash. Her search is victorious, and she hands the stack to Jack. It's more of a slam into his chest, which is another sign of nervousness.

He eyes the cash, then grabs it with his hands gliding against hers. He says, "And ash is the best fit because you're too strung up for a decent lay."

Her cheeks burn pink, ashamed that she enjoys the dirty man's flirting. It makes her feel normal again. "No, truly, this is all I wanted."

He says, "I agreed to do this work because I felt sorry for you. Ya seem like a good chick, then I started thinking."

Great.

Jack folds his arms, hugging the cash. "The wig was a red flag. I let it slide. Mind explaining why you got a gun tucked into your boot?"

Now, she's aware of the subtle bulge of her right ankle. What a fool. The damn jeans are a smidge too form-fitting. She will not survive if she keeps making these kinds of mistakes.

"It's for safety. I mean it," Lola says.

"I said no BS. Cops have been hot on my tail for a while, and then you come from nowhere. You wouldn't even tell me who referred you, another red flag. Still, I gave you the benefit of the doubt."

"Jesus, I'm not a fucking cop. See? I'm leaving." Lola storms towards the exit.

Her path ends as a behemoth of a man lumbers from the shadows. His broad frame consumes the doorway, and the bald head is inches from the top. The brows are flat. The thin eyes of a predator are focused on their target. Years of acne and drug scars run along the cheekbone to the frowning mouth. A white rag is wrapped around the tight muscles of his bare arm.

No, Lola thinks. The white rag is more demoralizing than the man's "I'm gonna fuck you up" glare. That simple little detail is the symbolic icon of the Crystal Moths. *Fucking die,* Lola thinks. They did this to her. They made her life this way. They're responsible for why she is here.

"This could get ugly," Jack says. "That's not my thing. I'm all for peace. This home is a safe haven."

Right, as if that's the case, with a goddamn Crystal Moth in the house.

Jack walks to the counter beside the bag of ash. "I need to know you're legitimate. If you are, take the ash, it will ease your troubles. If you're hiding anything, the trip won't go well, and old Ramon will take care of you."

"I'm not a cop!" Lola takes a step away from the Crystal Moth. She's pretty sure he has not blinked once. "I just let you tattoo me. I paid you. Christ."

"I've seen cops and their informants go through far more. You know why?"

Lola doesn't answer because Jack is going to tell her anyways.

Jack takes a dart and lighter from his pocket. "Because my home is a revolving door of the underworld. I'm, unfortunately, a vault of knowledge that they want to crack. Thankfully, they don't have dick on me. I move around, and my temple moves with me. I took pity on you, and I'm not sure why. Maybe I'm getting soft."

"How would taking ash prove anything?" Lola asks.

"Ramon," Jack says, lighting his smoke.

The Crystal Moth speaks, "Because they fear it like you do." His heavy, deep voice is tight with tension. It's the kind of pressure that says he's one word away from breaking her neck.

"I found you online, there was no referral. I told you this already." Lola swallows heavily, her throat closing, making her voice squeaky.

"I'm off the grid," Jack says. "So, how did you get my email? And your name sure as hell ain't Jamie." Jack exhales the smoke toward her. He takes the pipe, lighter, and the small bag of ash and starts loading the bowl. "I'm not asking for much. If anything, I'm being a very generous man."

"Please. I'm not an informant or a cop. I found you on some form thread. Your portfolio was there with your email. I swear. It was a shot in the dark."

"Sounds like another red flag."

They won't believe her because Jack has made up his mind. Lola could go for her gun. She doesn't know how to use it too well. She's played around with one at a shooting range and some video games. That's not like life. Her gun is an intimidation tactic. The knife could work, there are two of them.

Her mind fires off numerous scenarios of what could happen to her if she doesn't take the ash and if she does. How violent could this get? Will they kill her? Will they abuse her first? Is the ash a numbing substance, so she's easier to violate? Lola has no answer and no guidance other than her instincts. Instincts placed her in this scenario. Truthfully, they haven't been reliable.

"Prove it," Jack says, handing her the lighter and pipe filled with the charcoal powder.

Lola's hazelnut eyes lock onto Jack's bright green irises, neither one blinking. The single sound comes from the fluorescent light's hum. She has to think fast. She wonders how harmful the drug could be. Lola has had weed and coke a handful of times, yet they're not this heavy. There's a first time for everything.

She snags the pipe and lighter. "I'm no fucking cop." Lola brings the pipe to her lips and pauses before the glass touches her skin. She holds her breath, looking into the purple discolouring of the dirty chamber. There's no telling where this drug is going to take her. Her mind is buzzing with fear, and she's unsure how those thoughts will mix with the drug after she lights it. She'll be in this sketch house with a Crystal Moth and the scuzzy tattoo artist.

She's alone on this ride, or not. Wait, yes, a moment of genius enters her mind.

"You take it with me," Lola says.

Jack shrugs, saying, "Yeah, gladly. You have to go first."

"No way." She hands the pipe. "And he has to take a hit, too," Lola says, nodding at Ramon.

Jack licks his lips and lets out a hearty laugh. "Alright, well played. Ramon?"

The Crystal Moth shakes his head no.

"Ditch then. Come back later," Jack says.

Ramon's glare crunches inward further with disapproval.

"We're good," Jack says.

Ramon gives Lola one last stare and turns, walking clear of the light. His footsteps trigger the creaks on the stairs.

"Is he leaving, *leaving*?" Lola asks.

"Yeah. You and me, missy." Jack says.

A ruffling of a coat and the squeaking of a door comes from the lower level, followed by a relieving slam. Jack, she can handle, she thinks. A Crystal Moth, the size of Goliath, is a whole other ballgame.

"Light it for me?" Jack says, pressing the pipe against his mouth.

"Yep," Lola says, eager to get this done. She brings the lighter to the charcoal powder and flicks it, letting the flame scorch the ash. Jack inhales, burning the powder as the drug enters his lungs. He lets the smoke seep from his mouth while turning the pipe around for Lola.

"Your turn," he says gently. Already his eyes are turning red.

Lola takes the pipe and pauses, contemplating kicking Jack's ass. He may have more surprises up his sleeve, or Ramon is waiting right outside. In the end, you're as good as your word.

She decides to prove herself true and places the tip of the glass chamber against her lips and inhales, feeling the smoke kiss her throat and slither into her lungs. It's got a strange taste to it. She can't find a comparison. The ash tingles her tongue. Chicken? No, a pine forest. That's not right either. Mould, for sure. The smell is swampy, like the pet gecko she had years ago. It doesn't matter, for the drug is well into her system. There's an energizing hum growing underneath her flesh. The tingling is fast, rushing through her limbs. Goosebumps rise on her skin.

Jack is smiling, an authentic happy smile. His shoulders relax, wiping away his cool-guy attitude. "See?" he says.

Hold on, Lola is smiling too. Both of them are standing still, smiling at each other. She doesn't even feel the tattoo's sting. The word-based thoughts in her mind are melting. Their linear formations stretch into a perpendicular array of abstract ideas. Their vertical and horizontal expressions of emotions flood her psyche as she rises a foot from her body.

Hovering above her skull, she sees the knotted synthetic strands of hair on her wig. It stretches her smile further, cheek to cheek. She's giggling and says, "This wig is shitty."

"Totally." Jack starts snickering like a little boy.

The sensitivity knob is turned up in her ears with the fluorescent light hum taking the middle ground of the sound spectrum while the dripping of the tap in the sink rises higher. The wind from outside is a subtle treble. Her own breath holds rhythm. It's the orchestra of the world.

This ash is unreal, is the last true thought she has as she becomes the juncture. Her legs are liquefying onto the floor in slow motion. The body dissipates into some boneless creature.

Lola is on the tiles now, looking at the ceiling. Correction, it's an ocean of waves. She's underwater in this decelerating state. It's warm, welcoming. The vertical array of thoughts channels from her mind, projecting a rainbow of visual shapes like Jack's Zen poster.

The sea kitchen's sacred geometric patterns are everywhere. They meld with coral reefs ending in planets orbiting the sun. Above the star is a familiar older woman looking at her.

Her mother is here. The narrow face is recognizable. Lola blinks, and so does her mom simultaneously. The ocean dissolves the mother into more patterns, enveloping Lola's peripheral view. Jack's voice is near, laughing. It echoes. A hand reaches Lola's at one point. There's another limb. They're close. She's not alone, for she is a child of the universe. The visuals bloom brighter as the remaining bodies melt into golden amber, fusing the ash-dashers in an ever-lasting embrace.

"Home," comes a voice from no clear direction. It's not Jack's, and it isn't her mother's. The neutral tone must be the living earth. Lola didn't have to fear anything, for beyond the constructs of human civilization, past the media narrative, and distant from the dark underworld of the unwanted is the cosmos of eternal love.

CHAPTER 5
FROM FORGOTTEN

Meetings are essential for long-term relationships, both for business and pleasure. Gatherings occur on every level of society, including the darkest depths of the world, lost in the sands of time.

These secret agendas are where the forgotten find mutual ground. Over the ages, some have learned their outside perspective provides a unique angle. Others can offer rarities. Humans rule the world with an iron fist, yet these walking apes are unaware of who masters the gears of their reality.

The limousine driving through the mountain landscape showcases a secret affair. Its polished exterior's silver trimming and chrome bumpers glimmer against the clear blue sky. The windows are tinted, concealing the passenger. Its engine's steady roar proves it has plenty of upkeep. On the inside, most of the interior furnishing is complete with polished leather. It even includes a small fireplace for the passenger to enjoy as the chauffeur navigates them off the highway and onto a winding side road toward a gated mansion.

Both the chauffeur and the passenger keep silent during the exchange. There's no need for chit-chat. It is a business transaction. If anything, the patron is taken aback by having such luxurious services, let alone using a car. Her existence of the old world is one of raw truth: grit, survival, and the unforgiving.

Her black leather-bound legs are crossed, causing the wide boots to squeak against the seat. Her sombre grey gloves are clenched tight, pushing aside her personal opinions of the meeting she's been assigned to. There is little she can do because she follows the orders of her superior.

The limousine is cleared at the gate through a key fob. It pulls up at the curved, U-shaped driveway under the sheltered entrance supported by two roman-styled columns.

The chauffeur slides the glass divider to speak. "Your stop, miss." His voice is hoarse and old, despite being far younger than her.

"Thank you," the passenger's dry tone is muffled by the metal muzzle of the leather mask. Even under the veil, she can smell his fusty malodor. No amount of showering, deodorant, or cologne can hide the smell of humans.

She adjusts her hoods, ensuring the canvas cowl attached to the mask and her cloak's cover stay over her scalp. She opens the door and steps outside. Her goggles provide protection from the sun's unbearable rays rising behind the tallest peak of the snowy mountains. She hurries to avoid the fireball's death-strike, despite concealing any skin from exposure. It's misery to be in the light. As the mansion's wide, red oak doors open, she steps to the shade.

"Welcome to Mastema's personal mansion," comes a high-pitched voice of a thin, frail man in a deep brown suit and white tie. His lime green brows match the irises that lock onto the newcomer. He smiles, showcasing his pointy, bird-like teeth. "My name is Jekos, and I'm here to—"

He's interrupted by the guest. She says, "I don't talk to halfbreeds. Take me to Mastema."

"A little bit of courtesy wouldn't hurt," Jekos sneers.

She does not reply. This relationship is work-related, and she must remind herself to keep personal morality from the interactions. She's struggling. Damnit, it's difficult when coming face-to-face with abominations like Jekos. His disgusting mother and father merged two worlds that should have never interacted.

Imps and humans, she thinks. Her mind doesn't need to elaborate on the obvious any further.

Jekos takes the lead as the newcomer marches into the mansion's lobby, and she detects his potent firewood scent, reminding her of childhood. Their steps echo against the marble flooring of the dome-shaped entranceway. The matted white walls are lined with the same red oak as the front door, being far more luxurious than the stone cavern she's used to.

"Come. Mastema is this way," Jekos says.

The half-imp-half-human takes his new guest through a long hallway with mounted paintings. She doesn't examine them too closely. Their discoloration says they have a few centuries on them. She glimpses the side rooms they pass, seeing a maze of hallways until Jekos takes her to an open living room where windows overlook the mountain scenery.

Jekos opens the sliding glass door to the sheltered outside patio, where a man dressed in white sits at a round table, yammering away on his phone. His free hand stuffs his face with eggs, hash browns, and bacon on the plate in front of him.

His icy cool voice is low. Her hearing is better than his attempts to conceal the conversation. The man speaks, "It was sloppy. You should have known better than to revert to the sewers. Don't act like vermin. Ship her west to the abattoir plant."

"Master Mastema, your guest has arrived," Jekos says, taking a bow.

Mastema puts the phone down. He smiles and extends his hand to the empty chair across from him. "Lereif, what pleasure it is to have you join me." His hands push the pearl hair from his face, tucking it behind his ears. The strands dangle against his sharp jawline as he keeps chewing.

The visitor, Lereif, clenches her gloves. "My name——" she stops and says, "I thought you couldn't eat food?"

Mastema chuckles while grabbing a white napkin on his lap. He spits the food into it, crumpling the cloth, and tosses the used tissue into a small trash can beside his chair. He adjusts his white blazer, showing a glimmer of gold cuffs around his wrists.

"Observant," he says. "That's why you're a perfect fit. I can enjoy the flavour. Other than that, it serves no other purpose." He uses a toothpick to get some stubborn egg bits out of his symmetrical teeth and adds, "In fact, it will make me nauseous if I swallow."

"Master," Jekos says. "Is there anything more you need from me?"

"No, you're dismissed." Mastema shoos him away with his ring-covered fingers.

Lerief glares at the halfbreed. Thankfully, the mask hides the scowl of distaste. Jekos closes the door with grace and returns to the dark interior of the mansion. She's still clenching her gloves, holding the displeasure for the creature. She's here to talk with Mastema, nothing more.

"Don't mind Jekos," Mastema says. "He's a little skittish because he lacks a place in this world and the next. That is no different than the rest of us, isn't it?" He chuckles. "But you're an interesting case, climbing your way out of a burning fire."

Lereif steps towards the chair Mastema welcomes her to.

"How's the flight? I hope it met your expectations."

"Yes," Lereif says. "Truthfully, I have little knowledge of what makes a good flight. This whole luxurious life is alien to me. It's quite human."

"I embrace the times we are in, while wishing to change them. Please, please, do sit down. And do remove your mask. Whom am I to judge?"

Lereif listens to the first request. She sits across from him in a slow and controlled manner, keeping her eyes on the man, not that you can call him that. "You know I'm best not to take this off. Which is why I requested we meet at night."

"Right, that long history of your people and the sun. It's quite unfortunate. We're misfits in the new world of man."

"Which brings us to why we are here."

Mastema nods and takes another mouthful of food, chewing it and grabbing a new cloth napkin. He spits into it and tosses the mess into the garbage can. "That's right. It will change, and your people will no longer have to scurry underground like cave creatures. I won't need to possess this human body. We'll both experience liberty." He rattles his gold cuffs.

Lereif's stomach sinks. It takes a lot to ruffle an emotional reaction from her while on an assigned mission. She knows what Mastema is referring to. He's a lion in a cage, waiting to unleash his jaws onto those who oppose him.

She says, "Desperate times and common goals can unite the unlikely. I would have never thought I'd be sitting from the First, let alone you owning a mansion."

"Agreed. You come from mud, and I come from smokeless flame. Our worlds shouldn't mix. You also shouldn't have been born in Dega'Mostikas's Triangle. Times have changed, and we'll rise from the forgotten, my dear Lereif."

She clamps her jaws. Before she can get a word in, Mastema continues.

"Speaking of our unity. I need more ash."

"Yes," Lereif says.

"I've asked multiple times and have not been given a clear answer."

"It's in the works. The demand is growing far faster than our supplies, and it's impossible to synthesize."

"Perhaps we need to bring in the right chemists to break

down what makes it tick on the molecular level."

"No one's been able to emulate anything from the old world after its collapse."

"Human sciences are making impressive leaps and bounds. Perhaps they need to scan your DNA."

"That's above my pay grade."

"As if money is your concern. Nor is it mine."

"You do enjoy the perks of it," Lereif says.

Mastema lets out a satisfying chuckle. "Of course. Ash is a small component of what the Crystal Moths do. Right now, ash is on a lot of people's forefront. Those that want it need it, and those that resent it are captivated by it. It's a form of currency, opening new doors for us that we couldn't access."

"So increase the price."

"And raise the clientele. Getting it onto the street is to build interest. I presumed your people could make far more, much quicker, and we'd poison the cities. It would have turned the right heads. Now our hands are tied, converting it to a luxury drug."

"For whom?" Lereif asks.

"Anyone willing to pay. Politicians, the famous, or businessmen. Anyone with deep pocketbooks and powerful words. You're forcing me to change the sales pitch."

"My people are doing what they can."

"And when can I expect more, Lereif?" Mastema asks.

"It's a scale, look, the scales grow fast in terms of skin. It's not meant for this demand spike. We have to make sure that the Nine don't die either. You want top-quality scales, right?"

"That is correct." Mastema crosses his legs, pushing his food aside. "That is, if we have to start targeting the upper class."

Lereif says, "Give us more time."

"And why don't you breed more? Aren't there enough females of your people?"

"It's complicated."

"Not so. It's the most natural thing the Creator gave. You're what? one of another dozen or so of the remaining vazeleads, and none of you can put two and two together that it is for the survival of your species?"

"No, it's . . . the Nine are different, and you know King."

"All right." Mastema raises his hands. "I won't push it any further. I understand. Pride can be difficult to manage, and it's best left between you and King."

"And what of you and your people?" Lereif says.

"I'm sorry?"

Lereif continues, "The humans are starting to notice. The law and their broadcasting are fast. With your connections, do you have any way to stop their interest?"

"I'm diverting it. I have good actors in both realms."

"There was a capture in Toronto with a Crystal Moth and ash. Something regarding a rogue human hunting the drug. Should I be concerned about it?"

"I thought you were above human media." Mastema grins.

"What's the old saying? Keep your enemies closer. I have to understand them. In some ways, I must think like them, no matter how much I detest their kind."

"We are of similar minds," Mastema says. "These are luxuries that the majority of their people dream of. My perks aid me in entering their thoughts to recruit humans that will serve without question. Do not worry yourself with the news and the police. I have that side covered." He taps the table. "Now, when will King meet me in person? We had one introduction so long ago I am beginning to forget his face. With yours behind that mask, I feel I am talking to ghosts."

"King doesn't leave his throne," Lereif says. "It's no different than you and your over-the-top mountain mansion. It's the ego thing."

Mastema nods in agreement. "Quite observant. My home is my sanctuary, and it is beautiful here, do you not agree?"

"It's cold, vacant, and too bright," Lereif says.

"Precisely."

"Is that why you chose Canada?"

"You've answered your own question, my dear. It's vacant. Unlike you and King, who look for ties to the old world, I prefer being somewhere fresh and unlikely. It's far less suspicious when avoiding humans and other old world beings."

"I cannot deny your strategy, considering you've positioned yourself as a crime lord over the centuries."

"It's one of the longest-lasting businesses that stands the test of time. There are a few others in my position who enjoy the spotlight. Far too public for me." Mastema leans forward. "Now, Lereif, it's wonderful to see you again. I'm pleased that we get to work together, and your dedication to King is admirable."

But, Lerief thinks.

"But I know you're far more than a loyal soldier. Tell me, Lereif, what is it that you want?"

She clenches her fists again. *It's Scalebane.* "We didn't come here to talk about me."

"No, we did not. You need to know that breakfast meetings are intended to be semi-casual. You talk some business and a little of yourself. It creates stronger bonds. Humans do it."

"If you forgot, I'm not one of the soft skins."

"And that's why I want to know what you want. I know what King wants and his dear wife. Not so much as a son. The Nine don't count. Your sister is obvious, aligned with King. But you, you're the feral one. What is it that you want?"

"It isn't important right now. I work for King, and that's all you need to know."

"Such a good pawn, aren't you, Lereif?"

Rumbling reverberates from the depths of Lereif's core, rising to her throat. It ends in a rattling hiss.

A clownish smile spreads across Mastema's face from cheekbone to cheekbone. "There's my breakfast, that delicious pride you can't let go of."

Lereif closes her eyes, taking a deep exhale, attempting to neutralize her emotions. She should have foreseen Mastema trying to feed off her sin. It's what his kind does. They're leeches that benefit from the suffering of others. She cannot give him the upper hand again. She needs to keep her wits about her. Mastema is an ally, though he is no friend.

Mastema leans back. "Our relations are new, and I would prefer to meet King directly. I understand his comfort level and caution of leaving his throne in a world of hostility."

"If you feed off him, it will be your grave."

"No, no. I did this to see what made you tick. You've got a tang to your pride. It's refreshing."

"It won't happen again."

"The taste is enough. I have a better sense of you now. I do it to every new Crystal Moth member. It's a simple procedure in my books."

"I'm not joining your people."

"But you're working with me, and I consider you part of the family."

"I wouldn't consider the Crystal Moths a family."

"It's what we are. Or, if you prefer the more neutral term, an organization. And I have to manage it with a keen eye after a major slip-up in Edmonton two years ago."

"Yes, I heard that. Before that exposure, there were no suspicions from the humans. Which is why I asked about the incident in Toronto."

"If you wish to look into it, go ahead. Know that we are expanding far beyond Canada. A small scenario like Edmonton or Toronto doesn't matter as much anymore. The global affairs mean I must leave this country to hire new recruits and attend to the other markets."

"The red market?"

"It's quite lucrative."

"Because of that, I am appointing my trusted worker, Erol Terzi, to spearhead operations with ash. You may have heard of him since you are fond of the news."

Lereif shakes her head no.

"You'll be accustomed since he will be working with you."

The patio door clicks open. An acrid scent follows as a man dressed in a slate grey suit with a white shirt steps onto the balcony. His dress shoes click as he approaches. The man extends his hand to Lereif, showcasing a ceramic marble ring.

"Hello, I'm Erol Terzi. I'm very much looking forward to working together," the man says in a thick Eastern accent.

Lereif, or Scalebane as she prefers, is sitting, looking at the human's hand. She doesn't wish to shake it and could dismiss his welcoming gesture. She is also building business relations with the Crystal Moths and her employer, King. Mastema was cunning by poking at her personal bonds, making her blood rise, and this, human, adds a whole new level of complexity. Here she thought she would be working with the First on ash distribution. Now, sitting across from Mastema, she sees that her arrival is another gear in the machine that King and Mastema are building. She's a pawn, no different than this Erol Terzi.

She smiles under the mask while standing to shake the soft skin's hand. She is not naïve to the irony of working with a human. You need to keep your enemies close.

CHAPTER 6
RATS CAN SING

Some new fad always pops up in the war on drugs. When you get the upper hand on those black market sons-of-bitches, they invent a new and often more dangerous product. Krokodil, Molly, Flakka, designer drugs, you name it. The game does not end. Once upon a time, LSD was a new, radical invention with great promises until people could make it from home. Bad folks got a hold of it, the media went insane, and it was stamped illegal. Taking something away fuels people's interest. The clever dealers work around the system and continue to move new enticing products, making a quick buck, endangering the public, and feeding their empire.

The latest in the game is ash. Who would have thought that

such a potent product could exist? Hell, Iglesias has been busting operations for a good couple of decades. He has not seen anything like this. A man at his age doesn't need this kind of a stretch when raising a son. The street thugs get more intelligent, and drug lords more cunning, pulling new people into crime. Good luck keeping any of them behind bars. The crooked law is alive and well.

Late nights, takeout food, cigarettes, and coffee. Iglesias's fuel combo is consumed daily, stuffing it into his tire and getting ahead of this drug. Then there's Lola Cabello, a key witness withholding evidence. It's a new morning, past ten, and he's already gone through one-third of a pack of cigarettes. It's time for another smoke.

Staring at the computer screen to find some clue into the ash distribution line fuels the nicotine desire. His skills are better on the street, interviewing people and going to the crime scene. Unfortunately, the ash cases have been slim. The Crystal Moths started with a boom in the summer, and now they mask who gets ash. Today there are only rumours.

Iglesias stands outside the station, sucking his cancer and watching the frosting fall streets. His mind travels to the first encounter with ash in that New Brunswick den. It was mind-boggling. They didn't know what they were dealing with, so the law couldn't even bust the two druggies who had it. The item didn't fall under any category, and the two were set free. They weren't going to talk either. End of the story.

Since that summer day, there have been a good thirty or more ash busts in Canada and the US. Iglesias and his team keep in contact with law enforcement across North and South America to uncover where the hell the Crystal Moths are getting their ash product. He can't even reach his intel, who introduced him to this mess. It makes the days long. Work hooks like this is why his former wife married the bottle.

"Detective Iglesias," comes the flat voice of Beckman.

"Detective Beckman." Iglesias imitates the formality.

"Mind if I take a dart?" Beckman says.

"What will your wife think?"

"Come on," Beckman says.

Iglesias smirks while handing him a cigarette and lighter. Beckman lights it, and they stand in silence, puffing away. Both are lost in their thoughts, wanting some break from this ongoing investigation.

Beckman speaks, passing the lighter. "You hear it's spreading to the UK?"

"No surprise."

"One case. I think the Crystal Moths are international," Beckman says.

"We've had our suspicions," Iglesias says.

"Think we'll be involved for much longer?"

Iglesias ponders the question. Yes, likely, the Canadian Forces Military Police will want to interject. The US is also trying to get its hands on Canadian affairs. Then there's the UK. He says, "We will, just not in the big leagues if this thing blows up. The CFMP love sticking their nose into our work. The FBI boys south want to take over."

"Wrong country, pal," Beckman says.

"I know, right?" Iglesias says.

"Well, we have something they don't, that ash diamond. The

very first. Oh, and the lab got back with the results."

"Yeah?" Iglesias stands straight.

"They put the report on my desk bright and early today."

"And?"

"Turns out it's lizard-related," Beckman says. "Most of the sample is of an unknown origin, so a new suborder of reptiles."

"We had that hunch already, and Chen confirmed it in the recording. What kind of lizard are we talking here? Is it like toad licking?" Iglesias asks.

"Toads are amphibians. Think iguana."

"You can't get high off that," Iglesias says.

"That's the funny thing," Beckman says. "The lab results show traces of the, the, uhm, they called it the squamata order, I think. It's the largest reptilian group. They don't know what type of animal it is, other than having relations to the lacertilia suborder. That's a small trace."

"What gets you high? Is it like meth?"

Beckman sighs. "It was a lot of chemistry talk. They're still breaking down the molecular compound. Most of it appears to be new enzymes. There's relations to the coca family. Erythroxylaceae. The lab says it doesn't make sense because this is a scale, not a plant. Plus, the coca family branched off from other plants one-hundred and twenty million years ago with no other relatives."

"Okay?" Iglesias chucks the butt of his cigarette.

"In short, we don't know. Maybe it's laced with plants and lizards. It might be a Frankenstein's monster," Beckman says. He finishes his cigarette, putting it in the ashtray. He's too clean-cut to throw it. "They did find that bufotenin is a prime culprit."

"Which is?"

"Psychedelic. 5-HO-DMT. That toad licking you mentioned was the thrill in the nineties."

Iglesias doesn't know how to reply. If anything, the answer pisses him off. It doesn't tell them anything, and they're no closer to understanding where ash comes from. He says, "Suborder of reptiles. Lacertilia?"

"Yeah, the scaly ones like snakes and iguanas."

"That explains the diamond," Iglesias says. "But the plant relation?"

"This was the first full sample we've gotten. We didn't confirm it was a scale until we found Chen in the warehouse. This species branched from the rest of evolution long ago."

"So the Crystal Moths got their hands on some magical new species."

"Or messed with bioengineering," Beckman says. "We know organic and animal. It was, it was, what was that term?"

"Reptilia class," Iglesias says.

"Yeah, that. Lizards. Christ," Beckman says. "Now we know it's lizard-like and new."

"Right," Iglesias says. "Does Sergeant Bando know?"

"Not yet. I'll share the info in the next War Room meeting. He's busy enough, and we have little on Cabello, which is what he wants."

"True. Christ, reptiles."

"Hey, we'll be credited for a new species."

"I doubt it. We're cracking down on the substances, and biology is supposed to help. The scientists will name it."

Beckman laughs. "I haven't studied animals in decades. High school, I think. It's kind of fun."

"The lab results are supposed to give us an idea of what region it comes from. That's it."

"They got nothing," Beckman says.

Iglesias fiddles with the lighter in his pocket, distracting himself as they head into the station. Each time they get one step further with the ash case, there's a new roadblock and another mystery to solve.

Beckman is correct. It is good news. The law can categorize this drug as an illegal substance. If it is an unknown suborder of reptiles, then the animal is not categorized to be within the country, alive or consumed. Take that legal loophole.

Iglesias speaks. "We were waiting on those results for a few days. How the hell did it take them that long, and tell us nothing?"

Beckman raises his arms in defeat. "What can they do? They couldn't analyze it due to backlog, so they moved it to a more experienced lab. It got put on the waiting list due to their limited resources."

"Right."

"They're as clogged as we are. Funding has gone down the shitter since this political bull—"

"Right. I get it," Iglesias says, pushing the elevator button.

"The lab is doing what they can," Beckman says. "We've never seen anything like ash before. We have to keep it confidential to the unit. No one can know about this until we get a better understanding. We'll come across as incompetent."

Iglesias hits the elevator button. "I agree. It'd give Sergeant

Bando a reason to pass this case on to the CFMP. Damnit. This keeps getting weirder and weirder, you know? Chasing that girl wanna-be vigilante, gangsters who don't want to talk, now reptiles."

The two step into the elevator and head to their floor.

"On the bright side, we get to keep that Crystal Moth from the Toronto warehouse right here in the station."

"That so?" Iglesias says, surprised that they transferred him to Ottawa. "It's the best news we've had in a while."

The elevator door opens, and the two step out. "Well, next to the actual recording itself. I mean, we can hear it from the horse's mouth," Beckman says.

"We'll find out how much is true and what is being set up by the Crystal Moths. They're always feeding their own kind to us to test their people."

"Exactly," Beckman says.

"Speaking of the recording, we got the highway patrol on alert, right?"

"Done. Reyna took care of it."

"Good, Lola Cabello is heading west based on Chen's recording," Iglesias says.

"And we can see what else this lowlife has to say. Archer is in the interrogation room with him. Want to join?"

"Yes, I do," Iglesias says.

"I knew that'd make you happy," Beckman says, taking a step to leave. "Lemme get my stuff."

"Same."

This, indeed, has been the best news in weeks. Ever since the Crystal Moths had their hiccup in Edmonton, they've run a tight ship. Then this ash drug arrives.

A reptilian. Who decides it is a good idea to take reptile skin, grind it, and smoke up? It's ludicrous. Well, kids sniff glue and rub lip balm on their eyeballs to get high. Wait until they're adults. They will take more dangerous consumptions to chase that limited joy. One thing Iglesias learned in his youth is that the high will end, and you're left with a dump-of-a-life. That's what separates him from those that abuse. He got out.

The reflection on his past jolts his fatherhood mind, and he whips out a smartphone and taps on the screen to text his son, José. The message reads:

> (You: hey, looks like it is another late night.
> There's a pizza in the freezer.
> 8:45 PM)

"Sir?" comes a female's voice, smooth, deeper. Identifiable as Officer Reyna.

"Yeah?" Iglesias says, finishing his texts. He hates leaving his son like this.

"We have results of the ash forensics from the lab."

"Beckman filled me in, thanks."

He hears her walk away and finishes staring at the phone. He didn't even look at Reyna. The interaction was rude. Still, his son comes first. Iglesias puts his phone into his pocket, takes his documents on Chen's case, and marches to meet Beckman at his desk. His partner gathers the rest of his papers and nods at him.

"Ready?" Iglesias says.

"Let's roll," Beckman says.

The detectives head to the interrogation room, where a

narrow-faced brunette is standing. Detective Archer is at work. She's looking through the one-way glass at a skinny guy with tattoos and a black pencil moustache, if you can call it one. His face is down, and he fiddles with his thumbs. The Crystal Moths don't like rats. They'll have him dead in a ditch if the RCMP doesn't protect him. They will if he sings beautifully.

"So this is him?" Iglesias says.

Archer folds her arms and says, "Yang Chen, the Toronto local authorities found him in the warehouse with his arms tied with zap straps to a chair."

"And how'd you get him here?" Iglesias asks.

"It wasn't hard with the chopper."

"You got one? And kept him from the local jurisdiction?"

"Isn't that why you have me, sir?" Archer says with a smirk, exposing her far too perfect white teeth.

Beckman says, "To think you're a phase one."

"I'm almost full phase two detective like you old geezers."

"Old?" Beckman jokes.

"Good work," Iglesias says, keeping them on track. "That's a nasty hit to the nose."

"Yeah, a pistol whip," Archer says.

Beckman says, "So, how do you want to handle this?"

"Let me start," Iglesias says. "I want to go in alone."

"Really?" Beckman says.

"You know I can relate to these guys better than you. I've been in their shoes."

"All right, lone wolf," Beckman says.

Iglesias ignores the offhand comment, leaves the viewing station, and enters the interrogation room. The door clicks open, echoing in the empty space. He closes it with force, causing Chen's eyelids to twitch. Iglesias strolls to his chair, pulling it back. He sits and drops his sheets of paper on the table with an exaggerated slap.

He looks deep into the criminal's brown eyes. Chen's brows flatten, and his lips press together. He thinks he's pulling off that cool tough guy look, but his ears are pulled backwards. He's a scared animal ready to fend for his life.

"So, Yang Chen, am I saying that right?" Iglesias asks.

"True that," Chen says.

"And they found you tied to a chair in an abandoned warehouse?"

"Yeh, yeh," Chen says.

Iglesias stares for too long at Chen's dirty green tank top stained with dried blood. "You like working for the Crystal Moths?"

"I don't work for them," Chen says.

"Don't try and pull that on me. Cut the act, and let's talk about what happened."

"I want a lawyer," Chen says.

"We're looking into it. Until then, we have you here. We found you with a bag of ash in your pocket and a full diamond on the table where you were handcuffed. Mind explaining why you had a white rag tied to your arm too?"

Chen keeps quiet.

"This isn't looking good. Drug possession and dealing the ash drug."

"I wasn't dealing," Chen says.

"That so? That whole recorded chat says otherwise."

Chen's face morphs white. The guy is stressed out. He's running every scenario through his head, scheming how he will escape or if he should. It's unfortunate for him; there is no way out other than what Iglesias decides. This is his game.

"Listen, we've got your options tied up." Iglesias can't help but smirk at the stupid pun he made. "That girl who kidnapped you kept the phone on the whole time, and you squealed. What do the Crystal Moths think of that?"

"Why the fuck do you wanna talk to me, eh? That Edmonton Spaniard trash bag tied me up! She's got the intel."

That's the attitude Iglesias wants. The silent game doesn't interest him. He wants heat and aggression because anger is a powerful emotion. It makes people act impulsive and spit new information.

"I want to hear it from you firsthand." Iglesias leans back, pushing the papers aside, ready to listen to the bird's song.

"About what?" Chen says.

"You need to start talking if you want to get off easy. That recording of you is a valuable piece of evidence, a confession, against you. You ever want to see your kid again?"

"Yes," Chen's voice chokes. Some tough guy. Iglesias understands his pain. Unlike the moth, he can control his emotions.

"Okay, you need to work with me."

"I just distributed the drug on the street. That's all I did. I swear I didn't take it. You even listen to the recording? It's the bosses that control it. The girl interrogated me. And my boss's boss said ash makes a Frisco Speedball look like child's play. That's my sales pitch to these lowlifes who buy it. Done and done."

"Mastema, that was his name, right?"

"Yeah, you know he's gonna kill me?"

"Don't worry. As long as you're with us, he can't reach you."

"Right, you could be a Crystal Moth." Chen laughs. "They have plugs in the law."

"This isn't Edmonton. This is on a federal level. We will protect you," Iglesias says.

"Edmonton was the start of this. When that bitch uploaded her video, the game changed."

"I am well aware of the girl. In the recording, you accused the girl of being Lola Cabello, correct?"

"Yeah. It was her. I saw that bullet scar. Besides, who else would pistol-whip a random stranger and tie them to a chair in some warehouse to learn about ash? She's got motive, man."

"You were wearing the white rag," Iglesias says.

"Of course, I was going to meet my customer."

"Well, there you have it. She's after you and your kind."

"No shit," Chen says.

"Did you get a good look at her?" Iglesias asks, leaning closer.

"Just that scar. She kept the lighting dark and wore a wig."

Iglesias fiddles with his pen, considering the authenticity of Chen's statement. There's the off chance it wasn't Lola Cabello and another Crystal Moth was faking the interrogation to test Chen. Then again, they analyzed the recording closely, and it sounded like Cabello.

If the moths were testing him, then there is a crooked RCMP officer in the station who will get Chen out of this mess. The Crystal Moths aren't afraid of sacrificing their lower-level members for the greater good of their business. There's the off chance that Iglesias is overthinking it and the Crystal Moths aren't that clever.

"And what of your direct boss? She still in Toronto?" Iglesias asks.

"As far as I know, she hasn't been around much lately. She gets her assistance to distribute ash to us."

"And do you meet around the docks?"

"Sometimes. As I said, the location changes all the time. Since I'm here, I'll miss the next drop, and they won't like that."

The door opens, and Beckman appears. His eyes are wide, stroking his graying mustache. "Iglesias."

"What?"

"We traced a new phone call from Donnie Morris's phone."

"So?"

"You're going to want to hear this." He enters the room with a tape recorder and places it on the desk.

Iglesias eyes Chen and then Beckman.

"Him too," Beckman says and presses play.

Static comes from the recording, followed by a "hello?" It's Donnie Morris. Then, a croaky feminine voice says, "H-h-hey."

A moment of silence.

"Who is this?" Donnie asks.

"Don't play stupid." The girl laughs, masking her nervousness.

"What do you want?"

"I, I just need someone to talk to."

"We can't be talking."

Chen strokes his neck, saying, "That's her."

Iglesias listens to the full conversation. He heard the recording of Lola Cabello and Chen. This is the same girl. In this new tape, she sounds desperate, sad, and well over her head.

He'd take pity if it wasn't her own damn fault. If she didn't want to get into this mess, she should have provided the evidence to the police in Edmonton instead of uploading it to a blog and ruining her life. Journalists are bad enough. Mix that in with the naivety of a gothic punk, and you end up like Cabello, thinking you can take the law into your own hands.

Now, her charges keep stacking. Assaulting a man and interrogating him is another to add to the list. Lola Cabello better watch herself, because Iglesias is onto her and always cuffs his criminal.

CHAPTER 7
WE'RE HUMAN

The higher you rise, the greater the fall. This is why wise Buddhists focus on neutrality. The rest of us fools are riding the elastic highs and lows. Fall too far, you'll spring up eventually, right?

The aftermath of ash is far worse than anything Lola has encountered. Blissfulness ends for the ash-dashers as the real world seeps into their minds. Then there's a headache of astronomical proportions.

She did not plan on partaking. Then again, she didn't think she'd be among the scuzzbags of the world. Here she is, on the filth-coated bathroom floor of a drug house in Winnipeg. Her tongue is stuck to the roof of her mouth. The inner lips are glued to the gums. The eyes are fused shut, and peeling them invites a shredding sensation against the cornea. Clear signs of extreme dehydration.

Lifting her head proves it's transformed into a cement block. It's top-heavy on her neck. She musters the strength to pull her eyelids and look at the sunlight attempting to shine through the once-white curtains. They're a light yellow now.

There's a drizzle of vomit caked onto the side of the toilet bowl beside her. Some of the bile has dried on her chin too. Her muscles have been reduced to raisins, tight and minuscule. Further in the flesh, her bones are brittle enough that it feels as if they're ready to snap at any moment.

A groan comes from the bathtub. The creeping recent memory of taking ash with Jack crawls into her awoken mind in non-linear blips, reminding her that she had to prove she wasn't a cop in a hogwash right of passage. Well, bravo Lola, you've passed the test.

She gains the courage to sit upright, lifting that concrete head. The room becomes a carnival ride, spinning a little too fast, despite the ride ending hours ago. Vertigo. Damnit.

Her body reeks of sweat, and her mouth of sewage. Her clothes are still on, and the wig is a slanted, knotted mess. She pats her body, checking if she has her belongings. The gun is tucked in one boot and the knife in the other. Her car keys are hidden in her bralette. The wallet with the fake ID and cash is in the jacket. She's in one piece.

Jack's disposition prove he isn't complete dirt, and the Crystal Moth did not return. The hot presence on her stomach reminds her she got the tattoo. The nightmare is over on the post-ash day, thus being a win.

Lola adjusts the wig and brushes strands off her face. She can't imagine what her makeup must look like. She attempts to stand. Frail bones and weak, inflexible muscles force her to rest on her knees. With all her might, she rises with a grunt. The wall helps her gain balance to her feet.

The memory of last night isn't clear. Most of it is a muddled mess of visuals and emotions blipping at once. They weren't normal thoughts, more so moods within her mind bringing her to peace at the height of the trip. At one point, she swears she was back home with her family before everything went to hell. Beyond that, she felt connected to the living world. She was contacted.

There are brief flashes of her and Jack acting like goofy kids in the kitchen. They ran to the bathroom and back, laughing, and even went outside at one point. The recollections are fragmented and don't paint the entire night's picture. Ash is what it's talked up to be. It takes you somewhere else, somewhere better.

Nonsense. She has stayed clear of drugs while on the run. She has to stay sharp, except when she pounds a bottle of whiskey to drown her misery at the end of the day.

Jack's dirt-coated foot is sticking out of the bathtub. His face is smeared against the side, and he is drooling. He's out, and it is time to book it. Lola creeps from the bathroom in stiff-and-janky movements, past the kitchen and to the front door. She opens it a crack, not looking back, and slips into the brisk morning air. Freedom at last.

It has to be mid-morning based on the sun's position. She

increases her pace, with little limberness. The houses are a mix of war-time bungalows and larger houses from the sixties, made with cracked and slanted stucco exteriors. Garbage litters the ditches of the road, and the lawns are dead with dirt patches.

A few blocks down, she wipes her chin of the dried vomit and pauses against a tree. She closes her eyes and exhales relief. Lola takes a deep inhale, composing herself. She can relapse to the previous night and the risks she took. She's taken dicey moves before, and it doesn't get easier on her nerves. She's not cut out for this and feels the need to cry, though her body is too dehydrated to offer.

Some reporter is her first clear thought since ash. She exhales a juddering breath, the closest thing to tears she's going to get.

No time to reflect upon her poor sob story. She got herself here, and she'll swallow the repercussions. Lola will clear her name and deliver fairness wrapped in the fury of vengeance. It will be the kind that wasn't given to the Trinity of Souls.

To Mom. To Becky. To Michael.

With one more deep breath, Lola pushes the justice-begging ghosts from of her psyche. She marches clear of the neighbourhood and to her car, covered in a soft layer of frost, parked by a small park.

She reaches under her shirt and into her bralette for the keys with her icy fingers, then opens the door from the passenger's side. The driver's keyhole is busted, making it a game of musical doors. She unlocks the vehicle, gets in through the driver's side, and starts the engine. The old beater hums to life with a sputter, getting a good taste of the fresh morning Manitoba air. She doesn't wait long for it to warm and puts it into drive. Lola can leave this freak episode in her past. She got the cryptic tattoo, and her next stop is British Columbia, on the other side of the country.

The Camry's engine generates a steady purr as it merges onto Highway One, heading through the prairies and to the mountains. It's a long drive and the single option. Even with a fake ID, flying is too risky with the security guards and the cameras. Facial recognition technology has come a long way, and the curves in her stupid cupid's bow and nose bridge's angle have been described as 'rare beauty' features. It also makes her an easy target. She'll pass on the cameras.

Pressing the gas pedal is straining while both of her clammy hands hold the wheel. More perspiration is coming from her forehead and pits. Basically, sweat is everywhere despite the raisin body. Goddamn drug. Like most, she's researched it to uncover what the hell it is. Her interest piqued because of the Crystal Moths.

People died because of Lola. Thanks to her naivety in maintaining journalism integrity, it's her fault. Lola didn't think that would be her downfall. She should have gotten good at writing top ten articles regarding celebrities and lip injections. Then Becky would be alive. Her mother wouldn't be six feet under. The foolish girl didn't realize justice is one of those beautiful theories on paper. In practice, money talks, and power is the prime motivator.

Despite keeping her eyes on the road, her mind keeps falling into the past, reliving each event that got her here today. Her knuckles are white, and the muscles move in spasms in her biceps. It's a flood of moments and feelings where no single one stands out. They work as one symbiotic organism, eating her motivation and rendering her worthless.

She doesn't mull over her past much anymore. There's no reason to. She's always on the go, planning the next move. Similar to the tattoo incident. The exterior events and liquor let her suppress the inner turmoil she has not acknowledged. You must be tough in this world.

Now, alone in this humming car, she cannot control it. Sadness is the single emotion she feels in this hollow, brittle body. Yes, this has to be the ash hangover. It's the only explanation. She's fighting to keep herself together. The past is written, and she must look forward.

The highway takes her out of the city, close to Brandon and near Saskatchewan, the next province over. She'll stop in the first big city, Regina, for gas and to gather herself. She needs to keep driving away.

Leaving Winnipeg gives her some relief from the unsettling night. Jack had a damn Crystal Moth there. She can't help but wonder if the man knew who she was. The Crystal Moths are everywhere, infecting everything and everyone.

Both Jack and Ramon knew "Jamie" didn't exist. It's time to change things up.

Lola pulls into the shoulder lane, parks, and pops open the trunk. She exits the car and pulls off her wig, then shuffles through the duffel bag. It contains various disguise items: wigs, makeup, and clothing.

She swaps her coat for a windbreaker, new tank top, and puts on a longer brunette wig. With luck, this one won't be shitty, as

Jack put it. With a cloth and makeup remover, she wipes the former Jamie for a new lighter variation. The resurrected Jamie is alive.

Paranoia strikes her, and she double-checks if her belongings are in the trunk.

Laptop, yes.

Bag of documents and cables, yes.

Ammunition, yes.

Change of clothes, yes.

Burner phone, check.

The mobile telephone is for emergencies. It's a medium of communication to contact the people from her former life. An example would be her family, who no longer speak to her and for a good reason. Then there are her once-had friends.

Donnie is the first name that pops into her head. She needs to talk through her feelings.

No.

Her emotions are getting the better of her, thanks to ash. Her stomach starts to twist. Cold sweats against the wind make her tremble. This life seizes Lola's inner self, for she cannot keep being a fugitive forever. She could turn herself in. The system could win.

Vengeance is a reckless thing, anyway. Who cares about moral integrity? It's a waste of time. The world has been this way forever. Lola isn't the first to attempt exposing the evil that rots society. She's some punk with a key interest in journalism and got in over her head, like any true journalist these days. It's why none of them write anything meaningful. They fear for their lives. Most write what the people want, get paid, and call it a day.

Water trickles onto her cheeks. Oh no, Lola is crying. Her body did have enough liquid to give. Her lips shake while snagging the burner phone. She starts dialling Donnie. Lola has his number memorized even though calling is a downright foolish thing to do. The last thing she needs is his smartphone tracing this call. It's too late. The phone rings.

She should hang up.

The phone keeps ringing.

She can't. Lola longs for a familiar voice to know there's a life for her to go to when this is done.

The phone keeps ringing.

Lola checks the time. It's after three.

The speaker clicks, and a croaky voice says, "Hello?"

"H-h-ey," Lola says with a slight stutter.

There's a moment of silence.

"Who is this?" Donnie asks.

"Don't play stupid," Lola can't help but laugh. It feels like old times.

"What do you want?"

"I, I just need someone to talk to."

"We can't be talking."

"I know. I just, I fucked up last night."

Silence.

"I, I'm scared, Donnie."

"Don't, you know they track this phone."

"I know." Lola freezes. She's not even sure what to say. She needs to hear hope. Calling her brother or father would be suicide. They'd remind her of her mother and how it was Lola's fault. Donnie is hope.

"Are you in a safe place?" Donnie asks.

"Yeah," Lola says as a semi-truck roars by, heard by Donnie.

"On the move?"

"Yeah, it's the new normal, hey?"

Dead air.

Lola speaks. "Look, I'm sorry. I didn't ever think about you when we—"

Donnie interrupts. "Stop it. We've been through this, and it happened."

"I took ash," Lola says.

"You did what?"

"I had to. There was no other choice."

"Jesus. What are you doing?"

"I, I don't know."

"Are you fine?"

"N-o-o." Lola begins to sniffle as a tear worms out of her eyelid. "It's getting into my head. I, I—" *I want more.* The thought surprises her. People weren't lying when they said ash was a slippery slope.

Donnie speaks. "We can't be talking. You're sure you're safe?"

"Yes, I'm fine. I just needed to talk to someone."

"And this is a smart way to do it."

"I know. Just on the move."

"Don't take that junk again," Donnie says.

Lola exhales heavily. "I know." It's like talking to her dad in high school, getting scolded for smoking dope for the first time.

"I've got to go," Donnie says. "Look, they aren't all working for the gangsters. The cops helped me, and I'm in the clear. You still have his card?"

"Yeah."

"Call the detective. He can help."

"They won't give me the same treatment as you, not after so much time has passed."

"You don't know. Listen, I can't talk to you. Call him," Donnie says.

"Bye." Lola hangs up the phone. She knows damn well that she shouldn't have dialled. He's on a tight watch with police logging his calls.

Idiot. She let her emotions get the better, jeopardizing her past two years of hiding. Mistakes happen, like taking ash. Life is survival of the fittest, and Lola must rise to the occasion. No more ash.

"Come on, you've got this," Lola mutters, slamming the trunk shut. She pops the battery out of the burner phone and chucks it into the grass fields before getting into the car. The ash hangover isn't forever. She can push the strange emotional buildup out of her mind. She'll make it west, thanks to Chen's info. That's where ash comes from.

Lola must expose the Crystal Moths and the toxicity they've injected into the world. She will be free, and Donnie will be too. The death of her mother and friends will have their day of right.

These are hopeful thoughts that Lola tells herself numerous times on the long drive. Deep down, she fears that it is in her head. With each move she makes, she fails a little bit more, and hope dwindles below. Another bump of ash would ease the pressure for the budding ash-dasher.

CHAPTER 8
SINCERITY

True friends are hard to come by. Lola accepts this reality. Survival is the name of the game. Bring it down to brass tacks and everybody's out for themselves, meaning you'd best fend for yourself and amplify the echo chamber of selfishness.

The encounter with Chen in Toronto gave her plenty of insight into what the Crystal Moths are doing. The ash drug in diamond form was crucial. She prays to anyone listening that the diamond landed in the right hands. Then she won't be so alone.

Damn Donnie, he took the coward's way out. He was there when Lola uploaded the video and article. The simple submit button served as the domino effect destroying their lives.

Donnie bent over and took it from the crooked law. He is aware that the police are part of the problem. Most of them, if not all of them, work for the Crystal Moths. Lola is sure of it, and her scar is a clear reminder. It's why they did what they did.

Even if Donnie wants to be a cur, why couldn't he have her back? Then again, he blames her for ruining his life. He doesn't even want to know how deep this thing goes. Lola would love to share what Chen told her.

Road rambles, she tells herself.

The twenty-nine-hour ride from Toronto to Regina in Saskatchewan is killer. The pitstop to Winnipeg didn't help. It'll make your mind run in circles. She has no music to listen to, and her niche tastes make her detest the radio. She tunes into the Canadian All Media Broadcasting station to silence her mind. CAMB covers hockey season, pipelines, and tax budgets. At least until Hucker Dime is on. He rambles his opinions on reports and trash talks Lola. No honest reporter would do that.

Lola's ass is numb, and her back is stiff in her determined travel. Her eyes burn from the lack of blinking. She has to watch the night streets and needs a reasonable distance before taking a break. She regrets the senseless call to Donnie. It's too late now.

Even in her ash hangover, Lola knows that the police are tracking Donnie's phone. They got her exact location. To her advantage, they don't know her car or her disguise. The license plate is under the Jamie persona, and no RCMP vehicles on the highway have stopped her.

In Regina, Lola fills the car with gas, pays inside the convenience store, and notes a tabloid stand by the cashier. For once, she's not on the front page. Instead, there's megastar Ashley Amber and her new movie filming in Canada. They show two photos of her, the first being last year with her famous breakdown when she lit her hair on fire, chasing a paparazzi with a broken wine bottle. The second image is her from this year smiling for the camera. It's unimportant. Gossip is a great time sucker for the passive. After paying, Lola parks the vehicle at a dingy two-floor motel. Driving throughout the night, morning, and afternoon is rough, and she deserves this.

There are a few trucks and a van parked in front in the U-shaped motel, none of which are suspicious. Lola takes a wad of cash from her bag in the trunk. There's not a lot left, and she can't keep doing motels. They are expensive. She pays for a room under another fake name. Right now, she needs sleep in a warm bed away from the looming Canadian winter. A shower would help too.

Lola takes her duffel bag of clothes, notes, and the messenger bag from the car and heads to the second floor of the motel room. Lola pauses with the key in hand, looking across the street to a liquor store under the evening sun.

Donnie, she thinks and retreats into the motel room, flicking the light on.

Liquor will come at a later day. She knows Donnie's email and has Chen's recording. The foolish Crystal Moth didn't know the burner phone was recording on her lap. He also didn't know there was a second recorder poking from her pants pocket.

Does Donnie need this recording? Lola thinks, already knowing the answer. She plants herself on the bed with her messenger bag while taking out a handheld recorder. She wants to hear

Chen spill. It will remind her why she's driving to the opposite end of the country.

What she learned in Toronto wasn't like anything else. Chen was special, unlike a usual street dealer. He saw something. Lola needs fuel for her soul, so she rewinds the recording and presses play.

"They get a lot of their shipments from overseas, from what I understand," comes Chen's voice from the speaker. "Vancouver gets shipments from Japan, India and China twenty-four-seven. Then they bring it here. Hell, along the west coast and into the US and Mexico. Think about it. Slip in some loyal plugs within the shipment business, and you build a network to distribute both ways. Trains, boats, easy stuff. Drug lords have been doing it for decades."

A pause comes in the recording.

Chen continues:

* * *

Really, that's as far as I know. West is the big game. You'd think it was here in Toronto. I mean, that's why you're here. The first ash case the cops found was in New Brunswick further east. But nah, I'm telling you, it's out west. The supply chain is good at keeping this hidden. It confuses the law. And well, you heard what they said in the sewers, shipping that thing. Go West. You'll find answers. Every Moth knows something. Why do you think Mastema screens each one?

As for me? Well, I haven't ever been caught. Fuck, until now. Truly, I hate dealing. I've been doing this since I was a little brat, and it's way more work than the payoff. Each day we put our lives on the line in hopes we can get a bump up the ranks and a sweet pay increase. I don't have many options. In this "organization," I've gotten the hint that the bosses aren't gonna give us anything more substantial. We have a role to fill, and they aren't interested in sharing the profits. Bosses need workers, and druggies need the product, and the "company's" pocket gets thicker.

Let me tell you, when a new shipment comes in, it's time to hustle. This particular shipment came in at around, like, two AM, which is common. We don't know what day or the specific time. Your phone will buzz, and you better stop whatever you're doing and get there to get your piece of the goods. If you don't, tough luck. The rest of the street-crew will take it and sell it. At times, they'll despise you for it too. Other times they're glad to take the cash. It depends on the drug, the amount, and people's workload. The game is: sell the drugs fast, so the bosses don't expect you to front the cash. If you don't, say your goodbyes to your loved ones.

I was half-tanked this specific evening, playing pool. My girl came and visited me later and stayed the night. She has no idea what I do. I like to keep it that way, way less headaches. When you get a phone call at two AM after a drunken mattress tangle, she starts to raise an eyebrow. Maybe I'll tell'r one day so she stops thinking I got a side piece.

So, I sobered up, got dressed, remembering to tie the white rag to my arm, bosses get pissed if we don't show loyalty. What kind of name is Crystal Moths, anyways? The rag symbolizes a moth, I think. Whatever, it doesn't matter. They're the biggest players in the game and have work. Most people would, and have, killed to be a member of the Crystal Moths. I don't ever want to lose my gig, no matter how much I bitch about it.

The drive over wasn't long, yes, still getting sober. Even though Toronto doesn't sleep, you can get to the docks from North York fast if you know the roads' ins and outs. I'm no fool and parked my car a few blocks away. I suppose if a police bust happened, I'd be screwed. If I had the car closer, they would get the plate. Eventually, I got to the docks to meet the rest of the Crystal Moths. Our direct boss, a couple of goons, and a higher-up that I haven't seen in a long time stood with six street crew members. I was the last to arrive, on time too.

All of them had some representation of white clothing. Shirts, bandanas, suits, you name it. This superior, his name is Mastema, which I doubt that's his real name. Seriously, think it through. What kind of name is that? I was raised in a hardcore religious family and remember a thing or two. If you weren't, look it up.

I know the street crew pretty well. We're all hungry to feast ourselves onto whatever goods there are. The boss has been stingy on the smack and coke, and that stuff sells for top buck. I know enough junkies who are dying to get their fix. Well, that changed after this night. There are worse products on the market than junk and lines. Plus, this is another job, another paycheck to me. We have bills to pay, and you have to fend for yourself. Not to mention I got to pay for my kid's child support. Don't get me going on his mom. Whatever she likes to say, my work is no different than some corporate sleaze climbing their way to the top, squishing losers into poverty. I'm just squishing junkies.

Our boss was quiet, her hands cupped together, face cold. Like Mastema, who was pacing back-and-forth, she was wearing a full white suit. What makes this pickup more interesting is that Mastema was there. I think the last time I saw the guy was when he recruited me. The Crystal Moths are frugal with who they hire after that incident in Edmonton. It involved some hotshot vigilante and the exposure of our plugs in the police. Since then, Mastema screens everyone who is involved with the business.

Mastema kept his eye on us. I can't think of a time he didn't look sharp, dressing in expensive suits, long hair. His skin is so pasty, and his eyes are so bright, they look white. Hell, the guy looks like a vampire if you ask me. I'd never say that to his face. There are stories of him gutting people that say the wrong thing. Not that I have witnessed it, but I prefer not to find out.

He looked tense, fiddling with his golden rings. This wasn't like him. There's no point in saying anything because Moths stay quiet until a boss talks. I'd have loved to have a smoke too, ask the other street dealers how they're doing. We're semi-close. I keep them at an arm's reach, with my kid. Small chat would have to wait for another time.

The warehouse doors were open, where two other guys came out, wearing white dress shirts. They were holding crates. It must have been from overseas. The two Crystal Moths dropped the wooden boxes in front of Mastema and took their place with the other goons. One of them holding a crowbar. Mastema stopped walking in front of the crates.

"We have something new," he said in that creepy, calm voice

he has.

His words gripped my attention.

"In these two boxes, we have a particular product that is going to revolutionize our business."

A few of us exchanged glances, having no idea what the boss-man was getting at. I looked at our direct superior, whose gaze was on Mastema. Mastema nodded at the man with the crowbar. The guy leaned into a box and cracked it open, handing Mastema a black plastic vacuum-sealed bag.

"This," Mastema said, "is the future. No one else has their hands on this product, except for us."

"What is it?" a street-crew gal, Sierra is her name, asked. Way bolder than I am, as I stayed silent during this whole thing.

Mastema chucked the bag at her. "Crack it open and pass it to your colleagues. Understand that because we have exclusive access, no soul anywhere has had it before. You will need to persuade our clients. Lace it. Taste it with them. Use any method you prefer, as long as you move it."

Sierra peeled the bag open, taking a palm-sized charcoal diamond chip from inside. She passed the bag around as each street-crew member grabbed a piece. It was my turn to take out one of these new drugs. It was brittle along the edges but had more of a leathery texture in the centre, like a leaf losing moisture. This was organic for sure.

"It's quite addictive, so be careful. However, I encourage you to familiarize yourself with our new product."

"What's it do?" Sierra asked.

A devilish grin painted Mastema's pale face. "It makes a Frisco Speedball look like child's play."

We were staring at these strange diamond-shaped drugs. I had never seen anything like it. The street-crew, including myself, had so many questions, but most of us were too afraid to ask. I heard of Frisco Speedballs before. I don't know if the others had.

"Some of you are so young," Mastema sighed. It was a weird thing to say because the guy looks no older than the rest of us. It's the way he talks, though, it's like he's had past lives. I'm not spiritual anymore but just telling you.

"Ever shoot up a concoction of cocaine and heroin as you're about to peak on a tab of LSD?" Mastema asked.

Silence.

"It's an exultant ride," he said.

You have to be ballsy or fucked up to want to do that. I haven't, despite my abuse background, hence the child support, and there was no way in hell I was going to try this, this . . .

"Ash," Mastema said. "It's similar, but more cohesive, more addicting, and a lesser burnout. We don't know the long-term effects yet, but that's why we're selling, isn't it? You grind it until it is a fine powder, self-explanatory. Snort it, smoke it, lick it, or whichever creative method works for you. The effects will vary." Mastema grabbed another plastic bag and raised it. "This is a historic moment, and you have the honour of being a part of it."

One of the street-crews, Bari, smelled the ash he held. He said it had no odor. Well, at least until you light the damn thing. "Where does it come from?"

"Not for you to know," Mastema said.

"People are gonna ask, whadda we tell'em?" Bari asked.

"Get creative. I don't care," Mastema said.

After that, we chatted prices and split the drugs. Two crates of this stuff. We were pioneers embarking on something no one had heard of. It was the last time I laid eyes on Mastema too. I'm sure he's off handling the business.

As you know, this ash stuff is taking the world by storm and no one knows where it comes from. I still don't know where they got it or what the hell it is. Since that night, I just sell it. No way have I tried it. I'm clean now. My kid doesn't need a deadbeat father. Most of the time, I grind it up to disguise it, which makes it look like some charcoal or . . . ash.

* * *

Lola stops the recording. A part of her feels ashamed for feeding Chen to the cops. He says he cares for his family and 'job' but sure was quick to talk. That's his problem, and it's info Donnie and her family need to hear. Truthfully, the world does.

She's not uploading the recording to a blog post again, not yet. She powers on her laptop and gets to work, prepping a cryptic email for Donnie and her brother. Her brother and father will dismiss it. Donnie, on the other hand . . . after a good night's rest, it's back on the road.

CHAPTER 9
WELCOME TO THE FAMILY

O vercoming hate for a higher purpose is no easy task. Control and regulation are what Lerief Scalebane tells herself, no matter how many generations of hate are boiled within her DNA.

She is no different than any of her people who resent humans for what they have done. The baffling arrogance of the soft skins eludes her. Centuries have passed without the humans even being aware of the damage they have caused. They will in due time. All of them will pay. At present, Scalebane has no other choice other than to work with a soft skin. King's word is to listen to Mastema. Mastema has ordered her to work with Erol Terzi.

Scalebane is standing on the same balcony she had during the previous morning's meeting. She's here far earlier than prior, and the sun has not risen past the great Canadian Rockies. It leaves the sky dark blue with hints of an orange lingering underneath. The cool air against her bare face is refreshing. The mountains are an impressive range, encompassing the entire view on the mansion's balcony. It reminds Scalebane of her past life, before the old world's collapse where the legendary Mount Kuzuchi resided. It was once known as the largest mountain until it too vanished. No different than every aspect of her culture. She takes a good whiff of the mountain air, letting the atmosphere kiss the black scales along her nostrils' rims. The sharp sting of the pine trees below swirls in her nose. It mixes with the richness of the humidity, creating a concoction of natural enjoyments that are far more welcoming than the industrialized crud created by the soft skins.

A gentle wind brushes against the white scales of her face under the cloak's hood. She often wears that metal and leather mask to conceal who she is. It also serves as protection from the sun. As does her leather armour. The cloak hides her physique, for her tail screams otherworldly, and the legs are not human. Thus, her usual method is to coil the tail around her leg.

Not now. She is alone, letting her tail sway side to side.

A new smell arises, much closer. It's coming from the mansion as the balcony door slides open. The odour reeks of human filth. Scalebane cannot distance herself from them, for her people live in their world now. The stale aura overpowers the natural scent of nature. It is accompanied by clicking dress shoes as a visitor walks onto the balcony.

Her tail retreats below her cloak as she slides her mask down, strapping the leather buckle against the skull below her scalp-feathers. The black cowl drapes against the back of the helm to her shoulders. Scalebane is concealed once more.

Erol Terzi walks to the edge beside her and grips the railings with both hands. He's dressed in his suit as he did the day before, complete with the marble ring. A gold ring lives on his ring finger, indicating marriage.

"I did not take you to be an early bird, Lereif," Erol says.

"My name is Scalebane," she says. *Soft skins*, she thinks. Scalebane didn't presume her morning would be interrupted by having to entertain Erol Terzi. She will speak to King regarding the arrangement Mastema has made. She did not expect this when he ordered her to work with the crime lord.

Erol takes a slight bow and says, "I apologize. I presumed it was your name because of what Mastema called you."

"He did. He has a way with words."

"Is Scalebane your true name?"

"It's my last name."

"I see. We have pride that we protect closely. I have no problems respecting your choice."

"Good," Scalebane says with little enthusiasm. She folds her arms. The tail coils around her calf to the ankle in a tight grip, controlling her boiling emotions. She's beginning to wonder if she can even work with Erol. Her thoughts slip. Slavery. Banishment. These upright apes infected the world and decided they were superior. Now she must manage to cooperate with one.

Erol speaks. "I, too, am an early bird. It's ingrained into me from running CAMB for a good fifteen years. Even before, working for them a decade prior."

"Is that how you got roped into this?" Scalebane asks.

"Yes." He chuckles pointlessly. "Mostly. I was a reporter before I was promoted through the ranks and became CEO. I wanted to cover the news. I learned how none of that matters, does it?"

"The Crystal Moths' influence is everywhere."

"Indeed. My eyes are open now," Erol says.

"Was the previous leader of this, CAMB, involved with the Moths?"

"I don't think so. There was some scandal that forced him to retire. Either way, here I am, juggling a second life with my partner."

"Lovely," Scalebane says.

"My personal life? Yes, quite. However, he doesn't know what I do here, and I feel two-faced, betraying him. I envy you, the way you don't have to fake it."

What do you want? Scalebane thinks. She takes another sniff, letting the warm skunk of human odour in. Her sense pushes past the exterior smut and descends into Erol's blood. The metallic liquid is hot, rising in his tense muscles. It bites his natural aroma. To her, a trained expert in smell, this is recognized as fear. The man is afraid of her for a good reason.

She taps her metal mask with her charcoal claw that extends from the leather glove. "I do fake it, soft skin."

Erol's lips smother into one, feeling embarrassed for his

foolish words against the obvious. It's no surprise. Soft skins are arrogant to their limited lens.

Scalebane continues, "How much do you know about what you're involved with?"

"Quite a bit, actually."

"And Mastema? You must know what he is."

Erol clears his throat and says, "I know who and what Mastema is. I am aware of what ash is and where it comes from. I know who you are and what you are. So I'm clear on most things under the Crystal Moths' umbrella. They operate in the organ market, the drug market, and some legitimate businesses as well. Otherwise, why would the media need to be involved?" He smirks as if the answer is evident.

Scalebane nods, wishing he didn't know what she was. She uses the mystery of her being to invoke terror in those around her. Erol's fear is present. He controls it. Proof of it is in his bold action to speak with her. Still, Erol has not seen a photograph of her people. They were long gone before its invention.

"And what of yourself? Why are you here?" Erol asks. The man doesn't know as much as he has been leading on.

Scalebane's wrapped hands squeeze her biceps. "If you know what I am, then you know why I am here."

"To oversee the operations for King, like an ambassador?"

"I prefer the term foreman," Scalebane says, freeing her arms and brushing aside her cloak. Her exposed leather-bound torso showcases the belt on her waist, housing two sai. One is sheathed on each side of her.

Erol says, "Sai, that's an unusual weapon."

"My people have stayed hidden in Asia for centuries. Naturally, we adopted some of their tools. Sai work better in pairs and in fast stabs. It suits my preferred fighting method. Swords and daggers are clunky."

"Firearms?"

"I have no interest in long-range combat," Scalebane says.

"Face-to-face. Admirable. I have a feeling we will work well together," Erol says.

"If I get my way. I'm here for King, not you nor the Crystal Moths. King's word is my action. If this was any other circumstance, I wouldn't hesitate to kill you."

"I expect nothing less after what you have endured. Being what you are can make my life quite difficult at CAMB. However, because we are working together, we do know that the exchange goes both ways. Please, stay away from human eyes and cameras."

"I've done so for this long."

"It's a word of caution. That's business talk. The fast pace of information exchange makes hiding more difficult than ever. Scalebane, do you like art?"

Scalebane shrugs, leaning against the railing. "I understand the deep historical notes that art contains. They communicate the culture of the time. They're a resource, as far as I'm concerned."

"Fine art?"

"Not my specialty. My people used to construct impressive statues and architecture, influenced by your people's ways centuries ago."

"Then you may be a fan of my partner's upcoming show.

There are many references to what you are familiar with."

"I'm not here for tourism. Quite frankly, you should know I can't go to an art exhibit."

"It would be during off hours. I would love to give you a personal tour of his work."

"If you insist," Scalebane says.

"You will not be disappointed," Erol says.

"And how do you know that?"

"His work is quite astonishing. Plus, it will give us a chance to establish our newfound relationships. We can coordinate our efforts. I cannot work with a colleague that I don't know on some personal level. A personal touch gives me my edge."

"We have our differences already. There's no reason to mix personal and business," Scalebane says.

"That's where I disagree. The two should very much be married. Otherwise, purpose becomes split with harsh conflicting contrasts."

"Like how you're living a double life right now?"

"That I cannot agree more on," Erol says.

"And how do you know I won't do anything to your partner, his show, or him?"

"I don't. Even if you hate my kind, I'm taking a leap of faith."

"Letting loved ones so close to your work is dangerous, Erol."

"Do you have a family?" Erol asks.

"I do. It's unfortunate my sister is involved with the Crystal Moths. At some point, you'll meet her. Our numbers are small, and everyone must pull their weight under King's rule."

"I have to say, Scalebane, we are involved with this whether we like it or not. There is no escaping the Moths. Even the passive consumer plays a key role, unaware of the world that once existed. They are guided to the light under the Moth's wing because they have no personal dreams. Sheeple is the term."

"I'd prefer if my sister was not involved. This is our life, though."

"Right, she is assisting on the eastern side. I hope to meet her soon. Then again, you and I will be quite busy keeping this ash business going."

"Or family, as Mastema likes to call it."

Erol chuckles. "Even I feel that is a bit of a stretch."

"Good to know. The business sounds straightforward. We ship the ash here in the west, and you take it from there?"

"That's the trick. We need to make sure that the source of ash remains hidden. It is catching the media's attention from independent sources found on the Internet. Rumours are flying everywhere, and the law in several countries is working together to dissect what ash is. There are a few cases where street dealers lose their supplies, letting it fall into the wrong hands. CAMB must report on it now. It has made its way into our southern neighbours, the United States. We aren't ready to enter other nations until we have upped our production."

"Understood. We already knew this was going to happen. With your people's technology, they will learn the organic material of ash is from a new species. At least to their modern knowledge."

"That's as far as it needs to go. It's a new animal, no offence. The Crystal Moths are the ones who have it. End of the story.

Sweet and simple."

"I question the longevity of such a narrative."

"As you should, my friend. We, humans, are curious creatures. A do-gooder will feel a need to expose ash and what the Crystal Moths do. I have men working on keeping those that talk silent. Whether it is within CAMB or from outside sources, they will be removed. The public will know it's from a reptile."

"And what happens when Mastema and King initiate the next phase? Will you have control over your people, soft skin? Or will you even live long enough to see it?" Hints of mockery slither from Scalebane's tongue. Soft skins don't live long, and she's heard King and Mastema go over high-level thinking. Erol won't live to see it.

Erol speaks. "Ah yes, time will tell, won't it?"

"Indeed."

"For now, we focus on the present."

"Which I prefer. My people provide ash, and you sell it," Scalebane says.

"And the Moths will protect your kind. We gain funds and influence to build the New World Order."

Before Scalebane can reply, Jekos, the half-imp, appears from the balcony doorway leading into the mansion. He rubs his skinny, pointed fingers together, pressing his palms against his vest. The lime-green eyes fixate on Erol. He says, "There's word from the Ontario wing. It's Kye Pung."

Scalebane constricts her tail around her own ankle, controlling her pent-up distaste. It was enough to discuss with a soft skin, and Jekos has to be here. *Abomination*, Scalebane thinks.

Erol asks, "What is it?"

Jekos says, "One of the original street dealers of ash was caught by the girl, and she passed him to the cops."

"Where?"

"In Ottawa."

"Kill the street dealer. No risks of anyone talking," Erol says.

Jekos nods and takes a bow. "Of course." He hurries into the mansion. *Good riddance.*

Scalebane asks, "Girl?"

Erol extends his hand to the mansion doorway. "How about we have breakfast?"

Scalebane freezes for a moment, taken aback by his level of chivalry. His personality is far more tolerable than she presumed.

The forced relationship is sprouting. Scalebane will do her damnedest to keep her mind open. It's for the bigger picture of their people's survival. As Erol's graceful words stated, everyone is under the Moth's wing, flying to the New World Order's light.

CHAPTER 10
MORE THAN A CHEERLEADER

Why am I doing this? Lola asks herself on repeat while driving west. Her resilience has kept her going for two years. The normal is hiding and hopping from city to city to unravel the Crystal Moths. She can't abandon the ghosts haunting her mind. If she does, then the Moths win. The Trinity of Souls must be avenged.

The stress, the worries, it went away with ash.

No. She's better than this and cannot give in. That was one use! The street word holds truth; ash is an alluring drug. Lola does not have an addictive personality that she knows of. Coke never did anything for her. Liquor is a fun substance which never got in the way of her grades.

Two days since her consumption, and her mind is clear once more. Well, at least that is what she likes to tell herself. Her goal must be front and center.

Step One: Get to the west coast, Vancouver, almost complete.

Step Two: Find a temporary base. The car works for the first couple of nights.

Step Three: Find the Crystal Moths' shipments Chen mentioned.

Step Four: Learn where their supply chain originates and document the Crystal Moths' whole system. Feed the intel to the law, government, and online. She can put a bullet in a few mobsters on the way. Liberation.

Lola has not been along the west coast in years. She was far younger during the last visit and was going to underground nightclubs. Chasing shows is so trivial now that she's on a path of vengeance. Technically, she knows people in this city thanks to her background in the gothic industrial music scene. Like hell, she's going to get in touch with them. She can't trust anyone. No soul needs to know that she is here.

One short stop for a rest, and Lola makes it to the coastal city. The bug-eyed drive is over. Vancouver is filled with ships and porting docks. Cars buzz on highways and over bridges, and glass skyscrapers fill the downtown behind the seashore under the cloudy sky. Lola parks the car on a downward hill off Main Street in a residential area. Finding a place to set up base is her next immediate step. To do that, she needs the web.

She checks her makeup and wig, then exits the car. Like a good criminal, she has the gun and knife, one in each boot. She tucks them in deeper to avoid any evident bulges. Jack spotted them too easily. She puts on a fresh swab of deodorant for precautionary measures. With her messenger bag around her shoulder, she lights a smoke and heads onto the strip. A sea of people swarm into bars, coffee shops, and restaurants. Too many people are on the streets looking for a good time at this late hour for her newfound taste of hate.

Right, Friday, Lola thinks, realizing the day. They mean little to her now.

A block up is a hole-in-the-wall bar with a painted sign stating *The Pig's Gut.* It's got a wi-fi decal on the window; they must be desperate for customers. Lola chucks the butt of her drag onto the street and heads inside.

The interior booze and mould worm their way into her nostrils as she steps on the creaking, scraped, dark wooden floor. She was once so particular with her *dark n' spooky* aesthetic that she would not be found in a place like this. Fashion, interior design, music, her whole world had to match the dark criteria. Her clothing and venues were the kind you'd see at a Sisters of Mercy or a Combichrist show. Reflecting on her narrow tastes, Lola sees her past self as privileged and naive. It didn't help that her friends at the time were of the same nature. Breaking the law and running from the cops is an effective way to humble your ego. It will broaden your perspective on life.

There are a dozen patrons under the amber lighting, laughing and drinking with friends. The normal things that she remembers once doing. People are compliant and unphased by the impending threat of the Crystal Moths. Two clean-cut guys at the bar do a doubletake of Lola as she approaches, undressing her with their perverted eyes, even in her simple attire. They're too typical to be cops or Moths. Therefore, it means nothing.

"What can I get you?" the husky, old bartender asks. She's cleaning a glass while examining Lola's exhausted face.

"A shot of whiskey and one on the rocks," Lola says. She can't get sloshed but needs to take the edge off. During the drive, she couldn't stop considering that drug. Mental resistance can wear out the willful. She is in a metropolis, meaning it would be effortless to get another scale. Vancouver is known for its accessible drugs. *Shit, I should have never had that ash.*

"What's the wi-fi?" Lola asks.

"There." The bartender nods at the chalkboard behind the bar with the info written beside some pizza deals.

"Thanks."

She pours her the shot and a glass of whiskey with ice while Lola pays with cash. Lola throws the shot into the back of her throat snags the second glass. The two guys at the bar smile playfully, watching as she finds a dark, unpopulated corner by a mounted pig skull. It's far enough away from the rest of the crowd. The perverted lose interest as some other gal in tighter clothing walks by. The simple-minded are easy to please.

Lola exhales through her nose, feeling the liquor's warm embrace. The booze allows her to become quiet in the white noise of nightlife. The whiskey's burn is soothing, calming her nerves.

She pulls out her laptop and powers it on, logging into the

wi-fi and ensuring she has the VPN proxy enabled. The last thing she needs is her laptop to connect to this bar's Internet without security. It'd be a giant beacon for people to find her. Next, she'll search for some dives to rent on a week-by-week basis. It has to fit into her budget too. Cash is tight.

Step Two-and-a-half: Get some cash. How?

First, Lola reviews her email for anything. It's been a few days since she's checked it. Other than sending Donnie and her brother the recording, sometimes she gets encouraging emails from her site. Even after that fateful upload, she's kept her freelance journalism site afloat. Overseas servers and cloud caching mirroring keep the website alive regardless of what Canadian law or hackers do. It keeps that original article and video live with that tech routing. She can also share any new ones she chooses to. The views on her blog have been steady for two years, meaning people want to know the truth, Canadian or not.

These followers aren't allies. They're more like cheerleaders who want to encourage the 'heroes' because they are too fearful of partaking. She can't blame them. Look at her situation. The supporters do send her fan email, boosting her drive. Others are a little more foul-mouthed.

She loads a web browser. It's open-source software that avoids data collection, another layer of protection, and she cruises through her email. There is a lot of spam and trash. There's some fan mail based on the titles like:

<Amiga009s: You're brave.>

<Sab34: You're my inspiration to get out of my dead-end job. >

<0V3RR1D3: I hope you're okay. You're exposing the deep state! Viva La Revolution!>

Right, deep state. It amuses Lola because she has not even thought of the US. This chaos is right here in Canada. The country where most presume the people live in igloos, watch hockey and drink maple syrup, then say "sorry" to you for no goddamn reason. Most of these people couldn't find the region on a map even if they tried. Still, the letters are warming.

And to no surprise, there's hate mail. The typical slander is like, "just kill yourself, you waste of breath," and "great use of tax money, you dumb shit." Or "I'll skullfuck your dead body, you whore." The emails are original craftsmanship. The hateful and kind people find her thanks to the contact form on her website. It's her smoke signal on a stranded island, hoping aid will come. The thought is a fool's dream because she's been alone for years.

Some do donate money via third-party currency exchange services. The cash is not enough for her to rent a place. She can eat at least. The rest of the email is worthless, and she closes the browser to open a second one. This software is used to cruise the dark web. It's accessible through another port, like changing the radio channel. It is where the goods, or devils, are. Lola's no fool and has already dabbled into alternative networks while in journalism school.

On this secondary Internet, Lola has another email account for safer communication. This account has slim mail. The address isn't public like her main email. She uses this dark web address to communicate with people like Donnie, who has not replied to her, or finding people like Jack.

Look at this, she thinks, sipping on her whiskey.

One new email is in the inbox. It comes from an address oldworldshadow@wi7qkxyrdpvr.onion, with a time stamp from ten minutes ago. The title reads: That was a long trip, hey?

It pushes her heart into her stomach acid. She takes a swig of her drink, hoping to numb her gut. Lola glances around the bar to spot anything abnormal.

I have my gun, she reminds herself and opens the email:

<oldworldshadow@wi7qkxyrdpvr.onion>

To: You

Lola,

I hope this email finds you well. Then again, knowing how your life is going, you're in the biggest mess you've ever gotten yourself into. I must say, I am an admirer of your courage, and your actions are honourable. It also shows the naivete of your nature.

I don't want to be known, as you can conclude from this letter's delivery method. My colleague aided in finding your address. They're able to maneuver this dark web effectively. I've watched your steps since you published your video and article in Edmonton. Let me tell you, you don't know what type of world you're getting yourself into.

I want to meet, as I am sure you are finding yourself alone right now. Few people are willing to be a whistleblower for the ever-expanding mould in your people's system. I appreciate the determination and could offer you some valuable insight or assistance if our goals align.

Please reply before you get yourself killed.

- S

Lola stares at the email, reading it over and over again. A part of it is nice to be complimented for what she has done, and the other is insulting. She knows she is naive. Her mom bit the dust because of it. Her father and brother won't talk to her, and her friends have died too. Her choices are for some foolish journalism integrity.

What if this oldworldshadow character is an undercover cop? Or a Crystal Moth? This person could be dangerous, like a gun for hire who wants to lower her defences for whichever party pays the most. On the flip side, Lola is in over her head.

She takes another drink to suppress the brewing excitement. Hope, fear, and worry rise again from the corners of her mind. The sinister emotional triad compliments the three grim souls ever haunting her. The six slither from her mind, to the throat, and into her gut, twisting the organ around.

"This ash," Lola mumbles, rubbing her face. The long drive and drug consumption give her emotions command of the self. It'd be nice to ease the tension, like with Jack. She can't. Drugs are a slippery slope of temporary freedom.

This email has her hooked on the screen, leaning into the pixels. She could ignore it, return to her plan, or see where this email takes her. At some point, she is going to have to return to Step Two. The mystery person could be speaking the truth, and there is no vindictive motive. Her concerns are the choice of words in the email. No one talks or writes in a formal manner unless they're a psycho.

"Hell with it," Lola whispers while pressing the reply button.

You

To: oldworldshadow@wi7qkxyrdpvr.onion

Hey,

We should chat. IM app first. BoomChat?

Lola

The popular consumer's app is not secure in the least. Lola can use it as a test. She has a smartphone simulator on her laptop to use BoomChat, keeping herself encrypted. Referencing the app will fish how much knowledge this 'admirer' has. This person did navigate the dark web and found her email. They claim they had aid. Anyone interested would know that the surface web, like BoomChat, is not wise. Data is mined at every level of the standard Internet. If they don't pass her screening, she'll disregard the email.

Lola presses send and stares at the email.

"BoomChat?" a smooth voice says from the shadows to her left.

Lola sits straight, her skin turning pallid. She lifts her foot to snag her gun as a dark-clothed, hooded man appears beside her table.

"Back off," she says.

He raises his bone-white eyebrow under the dim yellow lighting. The beam brushes against his smooth complexion. The man says, "Really?"

She doesn't blink, unsure what to say. Lola is too focused on keeping her gun-wielding hand from shaking.

CHAPTER 11
SPILLING GUTS

The stranger's purple eyes are relaxed compared to Lola's wide gaze. She is speechless, pointing the gun at him under the table. Other sounds in the bar dampen by the suffocating grasp of fear. Her dilemma: should she be prepared to kill the man or listen to him?

"You stalking me?" Lola asks, putting on the formidable, silvery voice that she did for Chen.

A crooked closed smile forms under his hooded face. One hand holds his whiskey, and the other grasps a small laptop tightly. No hidden weapons appear from his ankle boots tucked under the black pants. His zip-up hoodie beneath the leather trucker styled-jacket is worrisome, for anything could be concealed under it.

He points at the spare stool across from her. "May I?" The confidence is troublesome, thinking he controls the whole situation.

Cocky prick, I got a gun right on you, is what Lola tells herself to not lose what little command she has.

"What do you want?" Lola asks, closing her laptop with her free hand.

"I see you got my email," the man says, sitting on the stool and placing the notebook on his lap.

Lola says, "Yeah, clearly."

"You can cut it with the gun under the table," the man says before taking a sip of his whiskey.

Lola doesn't listen and instead observes his movements.

"You have a little more attitude in person than I expected."

"I bet you know why," Lola says.

"Yes, I'm aware. Which is why I'm an admirer of yours."

"So you say."

The man says, "I don't blame you for your hesitant nature. Even then, you're like an open book. Tense, fearful."

Lola swallows heavily, scared beyond belief. Usually, she can hide her emotions for a brief time. Now she feels vulnerable. Her head is foggy, her eyes scratchy, and her bones are brittle. The mighty campaign across the nation, blended with ash, is taking a toll on her willpower.

"Please, relax," the man says, his smile opening. His teeth are too white, like his skin, which has a natural oval undertone. He has to be in a basement daily, scurrying around in the dark web, never getting sunlight. The well-formed frame and clean-cut clothing say otherwise.

"My name is Synarion, and I know yours is Lola."

"Synarion?" Lola can't help but snort.

"Yes, something funny regarding that?"

"The purple eye contacts, pasty skin, bleached eyebrows, hoodie, and you go by Synarion? Seriously, are you pulling some kind of a joke on me? Then that email address?"

Synarion removes his hood, revealing medium-length bone white hair, slicked back with gel, buzzed on the sides. His ears are damaged, and the cartilage along the upper portions is scabbed and bumpy. The creep must have had his day in fistfights. Beyond that, his entire face could have been carved by the heavens.

He must be five or six years older than Lola. His eyes say otherwise. Their steady gaze would say he has seen a lifetime's worth of travel, unglazed and unsurprised. This man is an example of what happens when you spend too much time in the world's underbelly. It ages your soul.

"Can you remove the contacts too?" Lola asks.

"Usually, I do wear contacts. Not this time. I'd prefer you see me as me to build your trust."

Trust, Lola thinks. Sure, Synarion, trust isn't won by charming talk with Lola, not now. The man isn't leaving any time soon, so she decides to listen to the stalker and tucks her gun into her boot. Sitting straight again, she says, "Purple eyes. You're a rare bird."

"Yes, one could say such a thing." Synarion takes another sip of his whiskey. "I didn't bring any weapons. I only brought this portable computer." He raises it again, showcasing a missing index finger. "You realize that you are close to opening Pandora's Box?"

"I'm managing," Lola says, tucking her laptop into the bag in case she needs to jet. Not once does she lose eye contact with him.

Synarion says, "You're doing a piss poor job. Look how easily I found you."

"You're also some pasty dark web stalker with creepy friends."

"Full of rude comments, aren't you? You haven't even been in this real world for very long, let alone scratched the surface, and you're more jaded than most I know."

"I've lost a bit," Lola says, looking at her empty drink. An uneasy mood makes one drink too fast.

"Can I get you another?" Synarion asks.

"No. Tell me why you're here," Lola says.

Synarion takes a swig of his. "All right, you read my email. You know why I'm here, to give you some advice. Also, I'd like to offer some assistance if you are willing."

"Assistance? For what?"

"For the situation you find yourself in. You have the Crystal Moths hot on your trail, and the law wants to get hold of you. Both of them stem from tainted roots. How long is it going to be before one of them finds you? They have this country tied up, and you've exhausted your resources."

"I've got evidence. If the cops don't listen, I will take it south. The States."

Synarion guffaws, a deep one from his belly. "You don't think the States are any different?"

"I can take it elsewhere. People will find out. Look at what my video and article did. It created this. People online want the truth. Imagine if I expose more dirt on these assholes. I'll clear my name, make it right."

"Bold but reckless," Synarion says.

"Really?" Lola asks.

"Really. Think about what you're doing. You're attempting to take apart one of, if not the largest, operation the modern world has ever seen. The Crystal Moths have gotten their hands on a unique product. One that is so cutting-edge it puts them in a new category. A drug renaissance, if I may. With their connections, it is distributable and far more addictive to their users than any other drug. We don't know the long-term effects of it or where they're going with it."

"I know this." Lola scratches her arm under her jacket. *Ash.* He had to mention it. One puff, and she can't stop pondering it. Lola isn't this weak, no way.

Synarion raises his only hand with an index finger wrapped in the fingerless leather glove. The right hand rests on the table, with a stub where the longest finger should be. "Yet, you think single little Lola can figure it out and collapse the entire system? Even before you published that online article, you knew that the government had plugs from the Crystal Moths. That was one city and one police force. You didn't stop to think that they had more? Others that are higher up?"

Lola doesn't say anything. She has an answer. It's not the best, but she prefers learning what Synarion is leaning towards.

"I'm not here to criticize you for what you've done. As I said, I'm an admirer. Because I appreciate the work you've put in so

125

far to expose the outer layers of this system we're in. The Crystal Moths are the start. I want to know." He leans forward, not blinking. "Why did you do it?"

"I've made my statement on the website."

"Yes, yes. It's not the same. I want you to tell me. Written words crafted for public relations can be so cold and unauthentic. What are your emotions? I want to know the thoughts that drive your heart. Why did you publish that article with the video? You could have simply handed it to the corrupt police and moved on. You're a smart girl and knew the dangers."

Lola contemplates the answer. No one has asked her face-to-face so calmly. The cops, her parents, and Donnie are the others who have asked her about the video and article. The Internet swarm spits many words from its hive-tongue. They are just noise.

"Anger," Lola says. "The phone was tucked in my boot."

"Yes, much like how you keep your weapons there. Old habits die hard," Synarion says.

Lola bites her lip. "You've heard it. Everyone has. It's why I published it in the article. I was with that vigilante Michael Bradford. At the time, he was the biggest story in the town. Edmonton was, and still is, going through shit with the Crystal Moths, and I wanted to make a difference."

"Michael Bradford, the infamous Hashtag YEGman vigilante."

"Yeah. It's pretty self-explanatory." She folds her arms.

"But they got to your friend."

Becky. She looks away, suppressing the surge of collapse

evident in her trembling lips.

"I'm sorry, Lola," Synarion says.

"No," she says, gaining her composure. "Becky and I made a mistake. Michael Bradford wanted to fix that corrupt city."

"He was quite the courageous man. A little unscrewed in the head, but aren't we all?"

"Michael was a true hero, and I wanted to help him. I wanted to get revenge on the Crystal Moths. So I published the recording online, trusting the people that it'd work out."

"Sounds like you've rehearsed this answer."

"The recording says it. Nothing else matters."

"Nothing? Only anger?"

She smirks. "Boy, it was anger. Becky. I—" she pauses, considering why she's telling the man her inner thoughts. *The hell with it.* "After I published the article, Mom learned on the news back east and flipped. I got threatening phone calls from the Crystal Moths, the police, and random numbers. My family called me and would have slapped the hell out of me if they could. What got me was when both Moths and cops came for them. My m-o-m." Lola chokes. "I-I- didn't know it would turn into this nightmare."

"How could you?" Synarion says, leaning back.

"You just said I should have," Lola snaps. The sadness feeds the vengeful fire scathing her soul.

"Yes, if you had any experience. You don't. Neither did your friend, Don?"

"Donnie."

"Right. You and Donnie's naivete have caused you to stumble into a world you can never return from. Donnie took the easy way out."

"No shit. That wasn't the end of it either."

"I have no doubts. Tell me, why?"

Is this guy a personal shrink? Lola thinks.

She is opening up to him without any second thought. The information is old news. The past two years are hers to keep. His voice is soothing, and the confidence in his mannerisms is welcoming. He's the sounding board she's been lacking since she raised hell.

The aggravating thing is the man's magnetism. His sharp angled face and gentle, direct tone are commanding, even seductive. Lola doesn't need to think in such primal ways. She has no idea who he is. Even in her tangled emotional mind, she knows she is weak. Too much has happened too soon, and she is breaking. Comfort is what she needs.

"Mom," Lola's face scrunches. "The fuckers. Mom's heart couldn't take it."

Synarion remains silent.

"Before that, I brushed the whole thing aside, like Donnie. We were playing it cool. Then Becky, Michael, and my mom. My brother and dad won't talk to me. I was kicked out of university. The Crystal Moths took everything for me. My entire life, my family."

"You don't have any others?"

"What? Family? No, not really. Not now. They wouldn't dare get in touch with me."

"Of course," Synarion says. "Are you sure you don't want another drink?"

Lola touches her face. Willful tears drizzle down her cheek.

She wipes them, smearing some of the cheap makeup. The dead raccoon isn't trying to impress him anyways.

"I'll get it. Then tell me why you're here," Lola says, standing. "Perfect."

She snags her bag and heads to the washroom, deciding to clean herself from the tears. She relieves herself, washes off the runny makeup and places on a new quick eyeshadow, blush, and eyeliner. The true Lola must be hidden. She is Jamie, even if this Synarion knows. Next, a drink. God, she needs another after exposing her heart to the stranger.

Synarion, what a name.

Lola gets another whiskey. The two bros from the bar show no interest. She returns to the table where Synarion sits cross-legged with good posture, looking at the pig skull mounted on the wall in front of him. Seeing him from afar, she gets a clear view of his frame. His proportion is perfect. She didn't think genetics could make a person so flawless. The cauliflower ears and his missing finger are the two things that aren't. It's odd for a dark web cruiser.

"Okay," Lola says, sitting down. "You've dissected my brain enough."

Synarion shrugs. "I asked you some questions. You chose how to answer it."

"Let's cut the bullshit. Who are you?"

"As I said, an admirer."

"No. It's obvious you're capable of finding me even through my layers of security. Why do you want to give me advice?"

"I'd hate to see you fail after how far you've come. The Crystal Moths aren't an organization that I'm fond of. They're advantageous, lack morale, and have invested into something far darker."

"Obviously."

"I'll clarify. They have no morale of any kind. The things they've done and their roots aren't a traditional gang origin. Their agenda is inflamed by allies of ancient hate."

"Enlighten me."

"Are you sure? Once you know this, you can't step back ever again. The world you know will dissolve, and you will see things for the way they are."

"I can't walk away from where I am now, so I must go forward, right? So open Pandora's Box for me."

"Right you are," Synarion says. "Is your phone off?"

"It's turned off in my bag."

"Good, and your laptop, based on the brand, doesn't have a camera?"

"No, it doesn't." Lola is intrigued by the secrecy. She glances around the bar, on guard, considering she didn't even notice when Synarion came in. It looks like there is the same number of people. The nineties rock music is blaring, and the people are enjoying their time, unaware of the secrets that are to bloom.

Synarion speaks, "I'm going to ease you into it. Otherwise, you'll think I'm a lunatic."

"We're already past that, buddy. Stalking girls online?"

Synarion looks around the bar once and then leans onto the table, his voice lowering. "The Crystal Moths are far older than the date of this country. They have been around for centuries, waiting for their time."

Lola listens, sipping her drink. Synarion is off to a good start.

"Their organization is managed by others, not of your species."

Not of your species, Lola thinks. It's an interesting phrase. Lunatic is right.

"Like aliens?" Lola asks.

"Not quite," Synarion replies.

Lola takes another drink. She'll need more brain lubrication to sit through this.

"That's the reaction I expected. You should be on the defence. How can you take such words seriously? I assure you, what I am telling you is the truth. I can show you a testament to my words. However, the Crystal Moths are from a much older world long forgotten. You humans have eradicated Earth's true history, claiming it a dangerous threat. Then it was rewritten."

"I'm going to stop you there," Lola says, leaning in. "You humans? You want me to buy that the Crystal Moths aren't human?"

"There are a lot that are humans. I'm referring to the superiors. Their origin and their allies are age-old. Ever think of where they get their ash from? Do you even know what it is?"

"I know it's reptilian."

"Exactly. It's not some animal you'd find on a remote island or in a desert. It comes from something intelligent. Something ancient. A relic of the old world."

"Old world? Okay, you've officially entered the loonie bin. Got anything to back this up? Or I'm walking."

Synarion looks around the bar and reaches into his inner jacket pocket. He takes out a plastic bag containing a full ash diamond and slides it on the table. Lola presses her lips together, feeling her heart stop.

Relief. Lola could grind the ash, smoke it, and relive that fantastic release in Winnipeg. It's sitting right there. She can resist. Focus. Lola grabs it, examining the diamond. She can't stop.

"Not so high, under the table," Synarion says.

Right. The scale locked her in a trance. One-hit weak Lola wants another drug fix to forget her mess. She wishes to wash her brain away after listening to this nonsense. She's no ash-dasher, not yet anyway.

Synarion says, "That is a reptilian scale."

"I was able to figure that out. Same with a lot of other people."

"Yes. Why do you suppose that is?" Synarion asks.

"The scale? People take all sorts of idiotic things to get high," Lola says.

"No, what do you suppose a scale that size belongs to?"

"I'm presuming some big lizard. A scale this size would protect the animal."

"Not a bad guess. It's vague. For example, what kind of reptilian is it? What part of the world does it come from? How did the Moths discover what ash does? If the police made a public announcement regarding this drug's origins, people would lose control. Society isn't ready to interact with non-human persons, not anymore. These beings that the scale comes from know this and don't want to be found."

"Are you telling me what I think you are?" Lola raises her eyebrow.

"Which is?"

"These scales come from non-human persons? Reptile people?"

"Correct. Their history breeds hate for all."

Lola raises her drink, tucking the scale into her pocket with the other hand. "You've lost me and have until I finish this whiskey to convince me that you're not batshit."

"And so casual in taking that ash?" Synarion says. He is deflecting her threat. Well played. "I saw your jittery nature when you sat in the bar. I'm sure some of it is nerves. Most of it is a withdrawal of ash. I've seen people consume it. I know the sinister minds behind this and their probable motive. I've seen everything, Lola."

"Uh-huh. Because you work for the Crystal Moths?"

"See any white on me? I know where they get the ash from. That scale comes from the reptilians, distributed to the Crystal Moths directly."

"You mean these intelligent reptilians know the scales are a drug?"

"For humans. It doesn't work on me."

"Now you're telling me you're not human?" Lola cannot withhold a laugh riddled with pity for the man. He's reaching with great effort.

Synarion reaches into his pocket again and reveals a handful of photographs. They're old. Some of them are from the eighties, sixties, and twenties. They're brittle, no colour for most, saturated and laminated, indicating they are authentic. The others are a couple from decades before, based on the discoloration.

"Please, be careful with them," Synarion says. "I cherish each and every one."

Lola takes a large gulp of whiskey, finishes it, and brings the first photograph closer to spot any fraudulent clues. This image is from the eighties based on the written timestamp below. Synarion looks the same with his slicked-back white hair and purple eyes. He's at a concert, wearing a T-shirt from the band Eurythmics. He's even wearing a fanny pack. It's ridiculous.

The following photograph, from the sixties, is another musical event. This one is outside, with plenty of people in ragged clothing, bell bottoms, and beads. There are buses, bongo circles, and people holding hands. Even in the saturated photo, Synarion is clear to spot from his crooked smile and cauliflower ears. His hair is dyed black in this one. He's mid motion, dancing with a pale brunette girl with large canine teeth. Woodstock in New York would be the educated guess.

No way, Lola thinks.

The saturated brown photograph from the twenties showcases a man sitting in an old Ford. He looks identical to Synarion with his signature ears and the same sharp angles on his nose and jaw. The hair is shorter and brown here. The vehicle has the classic thin wheels with white rims of Ford's first model. The ride is complete with a fabric convertible rooftop. It's a two-seater with another brunette gal in the passenger seat, smiling with the same sharp canine teeth. Both figures have the face of the two from the sixties. They haven't aged one bit.

The oldest photograph, made of torn pieces taped together, is a portrait of a man in a peacoat and scarf. Here he has long, bone white hair tied in the back with some strands tucked behind scarred ears. He's standing beside a man in a top hat holding a strange cane with a skull and raven claw strapped to it. To his other side is a brunette girl with the same thin frame as seen previously. Even in the black-and-white photo, the highlight of his purple eyes is evident. The text written below the photo states 1905, Illinois. This can't be.

"You wanted proof? There's the best portable proof I have," Synarion says while finishing this whiskey.

Lola doesn't say a word. She keeps staring at these photographs, reviewing each one closely. He is fooling her.

Intelligent reptilians are nonsensical. The photos must be doctored. She can't be baffled by smoke screens. The man wants her to trust him. She's already made plenty of mistakes and can't trust random Internet stalkers.

Then again, on some off chance, what if Synarion is telling the truth? What if he is the man in these photographs? Does that mean he isn't human? Without a doubt, that would make Synarion right. It would be an introduction to a world she cannot unsee. Pandora's Box is open.

CHAPTER 12
DATA HEAD

The evidence is obvious, yet Lola cannot buy the idea that the man in the photographs is the same person sitting across from her. The reason doesn't add up. The images range from the past hundred and twenty years (or so), and Synarion has not aged a bit. If his mad rambles are true, then Synarion is not human, and his age is unknown. Lola is tempted to ask him. She also doesn't want to buy into his story. If he is right, the world she knows will collapse.

"These are doctored," Lola says. She isn't convinced of her statement. Her cocky words are an attempt to break him.

Synarion shrugs, taking the photographs. "It's evident right there."

"Come on, some fake photos? That's how you expect me to buy your conspiracy of reptile people?"

"Can I provide you with advice?" Synarion says.

"That's why you wanted to meet me," Lola says.

"You need allies. There's no chance in hell you'll take the Crystal Moths on your own."

"And I suppose you're going to be this ally?" Lola asks.

"I can be. If we align and if you're willing to trust me."

"Let's say I trust you, and what you say is true. What would an ally offer me?"

"Inside information. Ash is part of the old world." Synarion stands. "Ponder on it. I don't expect you to make ultimatums now, let alone trust a stranger you met on the Internet. In this case, I would suggest you do."

"Right."

"And if you want more proof, we can arrange another meeting. I can guide you through this uncertainty. I can also ensure you don't end up dead."

Lola ponders her response, feeling her head spin. More proof is what she needs. She plays with the idea that Synarion's words aren't lies and how deep this 'real world' goes. The obscurity is too much right now.

"Be careful with that," Synarion says, eying her jacket, indicating the ash. Then, the man, or whatever he is, leaves, disappearing into the night crowd. Lola watches until he exits the pub and is out of sight.

Suspicion grows inside of her. He let her keep the ash. Drug dealers give samples to bait people in. A pusher is what the cauliflower-eared man is. Diamonds are a generous-sized sample. Because of this strange interruption, she did not bother with Step Two: finding a base.

Wait, she thinks. It's a wild plan, as is everything in her life.

Lola guzzles what little droplets remain of the whiskey, clutches her bag, and hurries into the dark and raining streets. She spots a hooded man moving through the crowds, his hands in his pockets. She dashes to catch him.

This is crazy, she thinks and says, "Wait!"

She reaches for Synarion, touching his bicep. He turns to face her. There's a frown under the scruffy beard of a worn face.

The stranger says, "You okay, miss?"

Lola takes a step back. "Yeah, I'm fine. I thought you were someone else. Sorry."

The man turns and leaves. Lola spins around a few times to spot Synarion. He vanished in the same method he appeared. She's not ready to take a hostel, for they are too public. A motel is the best option. With any luck, she can get ahold of Synarion again.

Not human, she thinks. It's impossible. The Crystal Moths using intelligent reptilians for ash sounds like a half-baked idea on a late-night documentary show. She has time to ponder over the obscurity later. For now, she needs to recoup.

Lola returns to her car, starts the engine, and drives to the first available motel. The city streets never sleep. Day and night, cars are buzzing around bumper to bumper. Police patrol the road as pedestrians, homeless, and the scuz walk under the cloudy sky. Her grip on the wheel tightens each time a cop car drives by. Are they looking for her? Her paranoia is eating her. A tiny dose of ash will help her sleep.

The drive takes her to an old motel with its blue paint chipping off. The shingles are a discoloured pink indicating it's good and cheap. She parks the car and enters the lobby with her belongings. As a routine, she checks in with a fake name, pays with cash, and proceeds to her room. It's on the second floor. The door creaks as she pushes it open.

A flip of the light switch brings the flickering, dim bulb to life. It stabilizes after a few pulses and settles into a warm yellow. The room's interior is what one would expect from the exterior. The tacky floral pattern carpet pairs well with the yellow-stained walls. At least the bed sheets appear clean. Bring a UV light in here, and guaranteed, bloodstains and other body fluids will emerge. It's the kind of place one would take a sex worker for a night of fun or murder. One night in this dump works as a base until Lola plots her next move.

Vengeance is what she desires. The complexity of her yearning grows with each new clue unravelled. Synarion has plastered on another, creating more questions and concerns. It would explain the diamond ash she saw in Toronto and the one in her jacket pocket. As it is, there's no explanation for why the ash diamonds are so large, or what she and Chen heard.

Liberation is accessible. Lola bites her nails while staring at her jacket lying on the bed. Then again, she doesn't have a pipe. That wouldn't be too hard to find, not in this city. There's a spoon. No.

Lola ignores the temptation, settling into the motel room and taking off her wig and makeup. She gets a solid look at herself in the mirror to see the bags under her eyes. She's not some badass ninja of the night like that Synarion character. Nor is she a top-notch reporter busting evil. She isn't even close to Michael Bradford, the infamous YEGman vigilante who fought criminals with his bare fists.

Sad girl on the run. Pathetic. She looks away, knowing it's not doing her any good.

Lola reaches into her jacket for smokes, and her fingers glide over the pocket with the ash. She can't. The shaky hands fumble around until she finds a cigarette and lighter. Lola hurries outside and lights the drag, inhaling several times with big puffs.

It hasn't stopped raining under the cool air. She hugs her bare arms. Life feels like a constant bad dream. Normality is a fairy tale she will not return to. In a twisted sense, she can't help but think Michael, Becky, and her mom got the easy way out through death.

Keep it cool, she reassures herself, for there is no room for weakness in the criminal world. Darkness is real. Evil is everywhere, and the biggest fish wins. She cannot be gobbled up and focuses on her dart, sucking away fast and hard in hopes of freeing herself of the stress. Lola could use a harsher substance. The cigarette is gone before she knows it, and it's back to work.

In the motel room, she takes her old, cracked smartphone with an overridden OS. The last thing she needs is some device tracking her location. Thankfully, before Donnie alienated her, he showed her a thing or two about computers. You can learn a lot from online message boards too. It's time to see if this cryptographic tattoo is effective.

The situation with Jack could have ended so much worse.

Online claimed he had the skill and didn't ask questions. That was a lie. He was asking her a range of questions, and then that ash nonsense. She didn't even get a chance to test if the tattoo worked. If it doesn't, she has some botched squares collaged on her stomach.

The information from Chen and her previous evidence to date is far too valuable to place on her freelance journalism site or on a thumbdrive. The dark web was an option. It's not as secure as a hidden port leading to a gated intranet cloud, accessible with a decompressed algorithm. In lament terms: her heart tattoo is the key to her stash of evidence.

Lola takes off her shirt and the bandage, exposing her tattooed stomach. The skin is red and irritated. She takes a damp cloth to wipe off sweat and blood. Next, she swipes the phone screen, enabling the motel's wi-fi connection, and activates the same VPN she uses on her laptop.

Lola opens an off-the-market camera scanning app and peels the tape off the lens while walking to the mirror. She flips the device around, letting the lens face her skin and taps the scan button on the app. From the mirror, she can see the screen aligned with the tattoo.

Several seconds go by with the scanning app reading. The screen switches from a SCANNING to an UNABLE TO READ.

Lola taps the scan button again. Several more seconds go by, and the application fails once more.

Shit. Jack botched it. Lola puts the phone down and snags her bag beside the bed. She scurries around to find the original printed paper. She knew it worked because she tested the paper version before getting the tattoo.

She shuffles through her bag again, looking for the printed paper. It was in here. She showed Jack the drawing before she got tattooed.

Jack's house. Goosebumps rise along her lower back and arms. She had left Jack's house in such a hurry she had forgotten the printed design. Jack has a copy of her cryptic key and, therefore, a copy of the data.

"God damnit!" Lola shouts. Frustration boils thanks to another mistake added to her ever-progressing list of errors.

Lola pulls her hair while pacing across the room.

Good job, fucking idiot. She wonders if Jack is even smart enough to do anything with it. He knew it was some kind of QR code. He doesn't know what kind. The app to scan the artwork isn't right off the shelf. You need to know where to download it on the dark web. He liked his drugs and hippie philosophy, which works in her favour. His intelligence didn't seem good enough to crack it. There's not much she can do now. She can't drive back to Jack's house. She can hope that Jack buys the tattoo being a memorial piece.

Third time is the charm, she thinks. Lola snags the phone and repeats the process of scanning her stomach. Several seconds go by before green text appears, SUCCESS.

Lola exhales a grizzled sigh of relief.

She spins the phone around to operate the device. The app decrypts the key with two windows on the screen. The left side transcribes the design into data with a progress bar, feeding into the second window displaying a folder structure. The folders and files come in one by one. The file type is in one column, and the file size is in the next. She feels her skin start to sweat, watching each file appear on the list.

So far, so good. Videos, audio, photos, and written notes. Her work appears to be here. She taps a few of the files to double-check. No files are corrupt, and each is transcribed from decryption off the intranet.   The first she opens is the audio file from her interrogation with Chen. The next is the original video from Edmonton with Michael and Becky that created her newfound hell. Following those, she opens some written notes. The evidence has not grown much since Chen because Synarion's crackpot story doesn't count, yet.

The left window projects new text above the progress bar, stating, UPLOADING TO CLOUD MIRRORED SERVERS FOR PUBLICATION. Perfect.

Lola terminates the command. Now isn't the time to have the files populate the public web. Her evidence to date would go live on dozens of servers, blogs, and onto her sleeper social media accounts, along with her primary journalism site. It's her last resort if she gets caught. A quick scan and the evidence to date will go live to the world.

The tattoo working is a small victory.

With that, she crashes on the bed. If she ends up dead, the data can be extracted from her corpse. One way or another, Lola will bring the Moths to her light. She's not sure how or whom to share this information with, despite what Synarion said. Lola will fight to the bitter end. She will be free and the Trinity of Souls will have their day.

ACT II

ACT II:
REGULARITY DESTABILIZED

Good evening, and welcome to *CAMB News Now with Hucker Dime*. We're living in a time when information is instant, and demand is higher than ever. People and organizations can't stay hidden forever.

For example, the east coast local media are the first to report on a crazed new drug called ash. Its grey powdered form is in high demand on the streets. It's believed to be distributed by the Crystal Moths, our country's own mob.

The government's PR statements on drug safety and the police tell us that ash is a threat. They've kept their knowledge under close watch since the summer until they had sufficient information to warn the public. Ash is deemed dangerous and addictive and should be avoided at all costs.

Personally, I've never seen this drug. I've never been offered it. Ask yourself this: have you ever seen an ash-dasher on the streets? Are your kids talking about it?

Again, information is instant, and things snowball. I question if it's buzz and no substance. The government tells us otherwise. At the end of the day, I report the facts. It's up to you to determine how they affect you.

In other news, Prime Minister Stéphane Trudell is thrilled to have Vancouver host Canadian art sensation Dasco Amoss's new set of paintings. His work is world-renowned for revolutionizing fine art. Prime Minister Trudell states, 'we are honoured to offer Canada's iconic painter our finest gallery. Everyone should make a point to visit the show after the opening. It's history in the making.'

Dasco Amoss, Ashley Amber, the province of British Columbia is booming right now. Maybe the federal government will share some of the tax collections with the rest of Canada. Just don't waste it on the law or PR statements.

Thank you so much for tuning in. We strive to provide you with facts regarding the latest news at CAMB. Stories that continue to evolve regarding you and your country. We keep you up to date with *CAMB News Now with Hucker Dime*.

I'll pass it to Justin and Danielle for the weather.

CHAPTER 13
CONSPIRACY

Long shifts at the office are difficult for a family. You have twenty-four hours a day to complete your tasks. Wake up early, shit, shower, have coffee, and drive to work. The accumulated time of the morning ritual is at least an hour, depending on how quick you scrub and how merciful the traffic is. Once you arrive, the grind begins.

You'd presume work would last eight hours as is agreed upon with the employer. Good luck with that. On a federal level, in Major Crimes, people don't leave work after standard hours. There is too much to do and not enough budget. The law enforcers don't operate within the realm of time. They work within cases. The cold penalizing nature of the clock comes into question when these legal workers must return to their off-duty lives.

For Iglesias, work drags on for twelve to fourteen hours. Well, more like every waking moment, unless he is pulling an all-nighter, which is cutting down his lifespan. Iglesias knows he can't keep this routine going with his age and family.

Iglesias keeps people safe. The system needs him more than ever with ash rampant on the streets. He also finds a personal satisfaction when doing good for his country. The war on drugs does not go away, but goddamnit, he isn't going to let them have the upper hand.

Unfortunately, Iglesias's rigorousness requires sacrifices. His son doesn't see him in the evenings since he stays late in the interrogation room with a Crystal Moth named Chen. He stands with his colleagues Beckman and Archer, eying the gangster through the viewing room. They're good workers. These two understand the importance of the job and not the time. That is why they have questionable lives outside of their work.

"I think we squeezed everything we can out of him," Beckman says, arms folded.

Chen keeps his head low. The criminal is exhausted like the rest due to the waves of questions. They've listened to the recording. They've asked Chen the basic routine questions to see if he's lying. "Who do you work for?" and "where were you on the night of . . . " Also, "how did the assailant find you again?" Let's not forget the "describe the assailant to us." These are the usual mundane questions. Chen's answers are consistent.

Then, Beckman had to walk in with the new recording of Donnie Morris talking to Lola Cabello. They're going to have to question that Donnie Morris kid once again. He knows more than he is leading on. Right now, the three detectives need to focus on what's in front of them: Chen.

Archer sips her coffee and says, "I think I'm tapped out."

"And we can hold him for the night?" Iglesias asks.

"Yeah, we have enough on his file the keep him around," Archer says. "He's not of much use right now either."

"What if we cut him a deal?" Beckman says.

"Get him to work for us?" Iglesias asks.

"Precisely," Beckman says. "The guy cares for his family and puts them first. His boss's boss, this Mastema character, is said to be ruthless."

"They'll kill him. His family, too," Archer says. "We should keep them here."

Iglesias wipes his moustache, staring at Chen. It's an interesting dilemma. The Crystal Moths are disturbing with their awareness. On one hand, they could keep Chen here and squeeze any last bit of juice from him. On the other hand, they could train him and send him into the wild to see what he can bring back. It would run the risk of him being murdered.

"Christ," Iglesias says, wiping his eyes.

"No one says we have to figure it out tonight," Beckman says. "We still have him here."

"That's not a bad point," Archer says. "We're exhausted. We'll think far clearer in the morning."

"The night shift is already on duty," Beckman says, looking at his smartphone. "Yeah, it's past midnight."

"I'm calling it," Archer says.

Iglesias raises his brow. "You're calling it?"

She smiles. "Seriously."

"My wife is already pissed," Beckman says. "We were supposed to see some new movie."

"Ashley Amber's new one?" Archer asks.

"Yeah. It got good reviews."

"She's making a comeback since burning her hair."

Iglesias exhales heavily. "Focus, you two. We'll look at this in the morning. Get good sleep. Both of you be here early in the morning."

"Yes, boss," Archer says.

"You got it," Beckman says.

The two are quick to leave, as they've hit their physical and mental limits. For Iglesias, he can go a little longer. The mind is a muscle he's exercised well, which is why he is a workaholic. It needs constant stimulation, and the RCMP Major Crimes provides that. Likely, it's why his wife's divorce ended so poorly. Hindsight is king.

Iglesias stares at Chen, scheming to see if there's anything else he can learn from the man tonight. He taps his finger as his brain runs through scenarios until he decides to check Chen's story one more time.

He's worked with these criminals for years, for he was one in his youth. Cutting a deal with his intel is a perfect example, and then he introduced Iglesias to ash. Tycho Fulcher, that damn flaky intel prick. He has been unreachable since he sent Iglesias and his team to New Brunswick in the summer. A good couple of months have rolled by. The guy is likely dead, scared, or the

Moths silenced him.

Iglesias enters the interrogation room, and Chen lifts his head at the sound of the door opening. Iglesias sits down, placing one hand on the table. Chen's squinted face expresses confusion and exhaustion. Not Iglesias—his eyes are firm on the man, his face is stone, ready for another round.

"Tell me again," Iglesias starts, "how did Lola Cabello find you?"

"I already told you, she jumped me outta nowhere." Chen's left eye twitches.

Yes, Iglesias thinks. That's the emotion Iglesias wants. He knows there's more to the story. The man is cracking.

"Out of nowhere. You have no idea, eh?" Detective Iglesias asks.

"Yeah, I was on my way home after doing a deal. I wanted to go see my kid the next morning."

"It's confusing you'd say that," Iglesias says.

"Why?"

"Look at it from her situation: why target a random Crystal Moth? That first time you saw ash was in the summer. It's November and she just happens to attack you of all Moths."

"I don't know. Bitch crazy! I told you multiple times, man."

"What could a street dealer know?"

Chen's face is frozen.

"You happen to be there when the first distribution deal happens with the ash drug. There's no way Cabello could have known before."

"I got lucky! A test rat, I suppose."

"With a player as big as Mastema there?"

Chen swallows a thick lump of saliva.

Gotcha, you prick. Iglesias can see the man is nervous now. He's scared of his boss's boss. Archer and Beckman were begging to leave as Chen was going to lose his persona.

"Cabello knew you had a relation to the ash. Either you are important or did something. That's why she targeted you, isn't it?"

Chen is silent. It's no concern to Iglesias because he's got more cards up his sleeve.

"So you're telling me she assaulted you outta nowhere. You let some young broad attack you and take you hostage?" Iglesias says. "Seriously? You let a dainty mid-twenties Latina girl beat your ass?" Iglesias laughs, playing the role. He's not misogynistic in the least. This tactic can get under Chen's skin by belittling his manhood. The guy needs to prove himself, clearly, with those pencil-drawn-styled tattoos.

Chen's nostrils flare, taking a deep breath.

Come on, you want to defend yourself. Iglesias continues, "We both know that isn't the case. I bet the reason she got the jump on you is that you weren't paying attention. You were part of something bigger or distracted by something because you're not just some street dealer, are you?"

"She jumped me. I didn't see her," Chen says.

"You told me that. With your life on the streets? There's no way a brittle little university student could get you. What happened?"

"Man, he's gonna kill me. You know that?"

"Mastema?"

"Yeah, no shit!"

"You have already sung. What else do you have to lose? Mastema will have his way unless you make friends quickly."

Chen collapses his head into his palms, the cuffs rattling. He takes a big inhale. *There we go. Break, little man, break.* Iglesias watches, puffing his chest in success thanks to his words stripping the pride of this man's mental barriers. Chen breathes heavily with staggered breaths. It's a beautiful trumpet of victory to Iglesias's ears.

"You gotta cut me a deal," Chen says, lifting his head. His eyes are red, glistening, looking at Iglesias for help.

"I can agree to that. We can massage the details later."

"I want a lawyer."

"Yes, you'll get one."

"How? When?" Chen asks. "If I play as your snitch?"

"I don't like bullshit. I don't think you do either. Let's talk real before we get lawyers or the rest of my team involved. One-on-one. Clean and simple. You have my word, and I will trust yours."

Chen sits back in his chair. "What can you do for me?"

"My partners and I were talking. We can keep you safe and clear some of your past charges. We haven't decided. I want you to talk because if you're withholding information, that's another charge on your head."

"So, what do you have for me? How can I trust you?"

"You have a son, correct?"

"Yeah. Why?"

"I do too. It's tough. You share custody?"

"Yeah. His mom and I couldn't make it work."

"We have that in common. My ex preferred the bottle. I

know what it's like being a single father. I don't want to take you away from your kid, so you have my word. You'll be protected. It's not much for you to go on, I understand. We can discuss the details with clear heads tomorrow. If you tell me who you are and what happened that night before Cabello assaulted you?"

Chen clenches his hands into fists, looking away. He's biting his lip and shaking his head. He is distressed, reliving whatever he saw or running through the consequences of saying anything more. Come on, Chen, work with Iglesias.

"You gonna put me in a nut house, man," Chen says.

"Why is that?" Iglesias asks.

"I want you to promise me that first. Man-to-man? One-on-one? If you stand behind that, I want to know that I will not go into the nut house."

"Deal. Just you and me."

"Cameras?"

"Those have to stay on. I promise you won't be locked away in that sense."

Chen presses his lips together. The moment passes, and he says, "That Lola Cabello gal got the jump on me because of what I saw. I think she was following us for a bit. It wasn't like any other pickup. We didn't meet at the docks like the first time. This was some underground chamber. We went through the sewers. It smelled like shit."

"Sewers in downtown Toronto?"

"Yeah. It was abnormal. None of us liked it."

"There was more of you?"

"Some of the street crew from the first go. Three of us. Ash is in high demand, and we're having trouble keeping up. They wanted to get the stuff out quickly, that's why they led us there."

"Is that where ash is made?"

"No, I wish it was that simple. This was desperation to push more product."

"How many of you were in there?"

"Bari, Sierra, and I were led by our boss, Kye Pung. She and a couple of her personal men led us blindfolded in a van. They guided us from the vehicle. We heard running water, and the smell of funk grew. Eventually, the guards took the blindfolds off in the sewers. I had no idea they went so deep. The Crystal Moths treated me good and all—still, this was creepy, you know? The tunnel led us to this chamber. I really don't know how else to describe it. It's larger than one room, there are many rooms and floors, but we stayed in this chamber. It looked like it was for the maintenance crew managing the water system. Hell if I know."

Chen continues, "I think they trusted us because they don't let any street dealers join them. I think we were the first. Again, we try to keep up with the distribution. The money is good. Kye had her guards stop us at the entrance. They had their guns out, ready for us to do anything. I could see a little bit as she walked towards this assembly line of fold-out tables that they had going on. There were plastic drug bags, crates, and fresh ash, with one large table in the center. It looked like a temporary surgical operation with the steel tools, wrist and ankle cuffs. The sounds, man, the sounds."

"Go on," Iglesias says.

"I got a glimpse of it. Kye came back quick. She knew that we weren't supposed to be down there. Again, she trusted us, or she did. She sure as hell won't trust me now. The sounds were hissing. Like, not the type of hissing of a car or anything. It was an animal. An alligator or crocodile's sound when you piss it off. Each time there was this plucking sound, a yelp ending in a hiss." Chen imitates the sound with a loud smack noise from his lips, followed by an attempted crocodile hissing sound. "*HIIISSSSSSS*. Something smashed on the table and snapped. It got the guards' attention. There was some shouting and a cry. I got bold. I don't know why. Maybe it was fear and curiosity. I stepped a little closer to take a peek. The guards were walking towards the table and didn't notice me. What I saw, I can't explain."

"Try me," Iglesias says. "I know that ash is a reptilian scale."

"This ain't no regular lizard. It was like us. I saw it for a moment and didn't know what I saw at the time. Legs, like ours. Scaly, with the calves bending like a bird. The foot ended with three-toed claws, man. Smooth, white, scaly skin ran along the legs to the foot. There were thicker, blacker scales on the shin and on top of the foot. Come to think of it, the larger ones look like ash. The tail flailed around wildly. It had dark ash scales on the spine. The Moths had it chained, and it spoke."

Iglesias stiffens his posture, listening intently.

"See? Crazy. But I was there. Bari, Sierra, Min, and her men. The tone is close to a person. I know it wasn't. People don't hiss like that. It had to be gagged cuz the sound was tough to hear. I think it said words. Like a *cuh, cuh-ing*. Ending in an *ing*. *King*? I don't know."

"And?"

"They eventually got the thing under control, and the guards returned. I don't think they ever saw me, and I want to keep it that way. Our boss returned with distributed packets of ash, full diamond shapes. They were warm. After, business continued as normal. I heard it shout a muffled *fuck* before Kye and her guards put blindfolds on and took us to the surface."

"And that's when Cabello assaulted you?"

"Yeah, I was so spooked. I wasn't going to go meet a client. I lied to you. The whole walk to the surface, I was sweating balls, man. Like, what was that? I don't want to go to the crazy bin, yo. I know what I saw. It was real, a fucked-up whack reptilian humanoid thing. I hear crack monkeys talk about reptilian overlords from the underworld, and now I talk like them!"

Iglesias strokes his goatee. The information is a lot to process, and he can tell the man is sincere, unlike before with his partners. Chen's hands have been open the whole time, pointed towards Iglesias. His eyes are wide, and the tone of his voice is up a notch. It's the sound of a desperate man. He wants to be believed.

Chen is confident in what he saw. Is it accurate? That is another question entirely. Major Crimes knows that ash is a reptilian scale, and it could be some new species based on what Beckman told him, despite the relation to the cocoa plant. Iglesias isn't buying the humanoid component of the story.

"That's all you saw?" Iglesias asks.

"Yeah, that's it. Bari, Sierra, and I gave each other that look, knowing what we heard. We knew it was real. I was the one that saw it, but we couldn't gossip. Crystal Moths are watching. Sierra sent her supply to New Brunswick like the first time in the summer, Bari retired after that, and I was walking home doing business as usual. That's when Lola Cabello assaulted me. How she knew about this deal and the sewers is beyond me."

"Cabello chose you over Bari and Sierra."

"I'm the lucky asshole. I saw the thing. That's it, man. I'm no special superior or anything. Just some guy who saw the wrong thing at the wrong time."

"Could you take us to this chamber?"

"No way, I have no idea where I was. Those blindfolds were on. It was strange, like why didn't they give us the ash from the van? I don't know. Maybe it isn't easy to get the scales off those reptilians. They were in a rush and were sloppy from their usual presentation. The makeshift tables, the boxes. I think they were packing up?"

Or they planted Chen here, Iglesias thinks. Chen could be a giant distraction to occupy the cops and Cabello, while the actual method of ash remains a mystery.

Chen says, "I have a funny feeling Cabello followed us into the sewers. I think she saw me see that thing in the chamber. That's why she assaulted me."

"Did you tell her?"

"Yes, that was the first thing she asked. I assume that wasn't on the recording?"

"I wish I was being coy with you." Iglesias stands, adjusting his blazer.

"You don't believe me." Chen shakes his head. "I knew I should have kept shut."

"I never said I didn't," Iglesias says. "This sounds like a make-believe distraction." Iglesias leans on the table with his fists. He says, "We're being man-to-man, and I'll give you the benefit of the doubt. I can tell you're telling your truth this time."

Chen blinks.

"I'll make sure you're protected. You and I will work closely together, and no one will get their hands on you. Understand?"

"Yeah," Chen says.

"Good," Iglesias pounds the table. "We'll get you to a holding cell where you can rest for the night. See you in the morning bright and early."

"Aight."

"How do you like your coffee?"

"Uh . . . whatever."

"Great." Iglesias leaves the interrogation room. Finally, that was the type of information Iglesias needed. His colleagues and Chen broke under the pressure of time. Iglesias doesn't. This is why he is the best. He gets the information he needs.

Reptilians, he thinks. It's not what he would have ever predicted ash being. This underground chamber, the temporary operating table, humanoid. It's a lot to process. Iglesias will be chatting with Chen more frequently. He'll even get one of the sketch artists to draw what Chen saw. This is a significant breakthrough.

Iglesias stops by one of the night shift officers, checking that Chen is taken to his cell. Then, he leaves the office. He gets into his black SUV and starts the engine. Iglesias checks his phone to see if he missed any calls. There aren't any. José must be okay. Iglesias told him what to have for dinner. He's also a teenage boy, and Iglesias is a single father. He won the court case against his ex-wife to keep his son back in the day. Now, with this ash, he isn't the shining example of parenthood. Iglesias doesn't know how much time he has spent at work today.

The drive home is quick on one highway. There are a few cars parked near the house. Iglesias checks the time to see that it is almost two in the morning. He parks his vehicle in the driveway, seeing the lights are on, far too many for this late hour. The subtle sound of bass thumping pierces through the walls.

"Goddamnit," Iglesias sighs. He knows what's going on here. Iglesias exits the vehicle and enters the house. The door is unlocked.

A handful of people are visible from the kitchen with open red plastic cups and bottles on the island. The sonic electronic club music is far louder now, projecting from the living room.

Iglesias strolls to the kitchen. A teen boy walks by him in the hallway, hair far too shaggy to see where he is going. Iglesias extends his arm, hitting the boy in the chest. "Get out of my house," he says.

The boy's face says he was punched. It was a light bump from a forearm. *Kids these days: bitches.* Now Iglesias is being grumpy. He works too much, and his son disobeys him. His patience is thin.

"Beat it," Iglesias adds.

The kid ducks under his arm and hurries to the front door. One down, many more to go. A good party killer is stopping the music, an obvious choice. Iglesias shifts his focus to the stereo. Bingo, the living room. There are kids on the couch, talking. A couple of pairs are making out.

Rage simmers inside Iglesias, this is his home. He keeps his cool and marches to the sound system. He presses the button on the stereo, stopping the fun. The conversations die as soon as the kids spot him.

"Everybody out!" Iglesias shouts. "Party's over!"

The kids on the couch stop sucking faces. These party teens are stiff as deer in headlights.

"Come on, go before I decide to arrest all of you," Iglesias says while eying the red plastic cups on the coffee table.

One by one, the high school kids leave. There are a few drunks that stumble on their feet while their friends help them move. None of them should be driving by the looks of it.

All the partiers leave except for one who comes from the kitchen. A thin boy with dark, messy skater hair, wearing designer jeans and a graphic T-shirt. His lips are pressed together while looking at Iglesias. His hands are in his pocket. José, son of Iglesias, is in for it now.

CHAPTER 14
LOST SHEEP

Relationships are a rapid river to navigate. Erol insisted that Scalebane and he share breakfast together to build a stronger bond. Business breakfasts are not what she is here to do. Clearly, Erol and she have opposing methods, and she already foresees future conflicts arising. Erol is too personal and casual, while Scalebane has teeth. Communication should be to the point. She remains professional and cooperates with Erol's request for the sake of King and her people.

Mastema's mansion does have impressive food, despite being incapable of eating. The meal consists of slow-roasted pork with red velvet waffles as a side. The coffee comes from Ethiopia. Most likely, slave workers gathered the beans. Scalebane understands the irony in humans enslaving others for cheap labour.

Erol eats a bit while Scalebane watches. She isn't going to take off her mask in front of this human. Besides, her hunger can wait. Meat isn't her forte. Thus, the mask is left on as she stares at the man chowing down.

"Please," Erol insists to no answer.

The awkward exchange doesn't last long. Erol attempts small talk, such as, "tell me about your sister." And, "my partner and I met years ago, after he finished art college." "Do you have anyone, Scalebane?" Then the easiest of all, "what food do you enjoy?"

His questions are met with short, deflective answers, killing the topic. They're far too personal for her. "She is my twin." No response. And, "I have my sister." The last question is the single hint of personal information Erol gets: "I used to butcher meat for a living. I don't eat it." The man detects her mood and drops his napkins on the partially finished plate.

"Let's get a start on the day, shall we?" he says.

"I'd prefer," Scalebane says.

Erol grabs his belongings from upstairs. Scalebane has what she needs, for a hunter travels light. She presumes the Crystal Moths, in their lavishness, will supply any extras. The wait isn't long. Erol must have pre-packed, returning with his black messenger bag strapped around his suit. He holds the handle of carry-on luggage with the other.

"Ready?" he says.

"Give me the grand tour," Scalebane says with a streak of sarcasm.

Erol doesn't pick up the underlining hint. He smiles at her. "Excellent. Mastema wants to show you the whole procedure behind the Crystal Moths, not just the ash. Of course, with the different businesses, that takes some time. We will get you familiar with the immediate. Mastema and I want you and King to trust our abilities to create a more cohesive alignment."

"Okay," she says, folding her arms as the man blabbers diplomatic nonsense. The true scenario is Mastema wants to put pressure on Scalebane, moving it up to King, so they will get more ash.

Scalebane has not decided on his intelligence level. Erol might not even know the true play, as he is too go-lucky. The two factions' true tension is the lack of ash, an issue more profound than the Crystal Moths know. The lack of ash is due to the lack of vazeleads. The simmering breeding matter is for her people's knowledge only. Right now, it's the last thing Scalebane wishes to ponder.

"Where is Mastema?" Scalebane asks.

"Mastema will not be joining us," Erol says. "He is to take care of screening new recruits. As you know, since that whole Edmonton fiasco—"

"I'm aware of what happened," Scalebane interrupts.

"It's a shame because I think Mastema could give you the greater vision of where everything will go with the New World Order. You and I are pieces of the bigger picture. King and Mastema are the visionaries."

"A type of vision."

"Mastema and I would love to get together and understand your people's needs better. Strengthening bonds is my specialty."

"In time," Scalebane says. "King isn't keen on travelling."

Dress shoes click from the far end of the marble hall, where Jekos walks towards them. Even the way he moves irritates Scalebane. His frail body sways in subtle spasmodic motion, with his legs jolting forward with each step.

Jekos is accompanied by two Crystal Moths fashioning white blazers and black shirts on each side of him. Their sunglasses cover their expressionless eyes. These are the usual goons that the public is familiar with: characterized gangsters. It's not their looks that make Scalebane's claw twitch, ready to draw her sai. The blood of a thousand bodies lingers in her nose. Any normal being would miss such a minor detail, for the rustic foulness hides under their skin. These aren't men.

Vampires, Scalebane thinks. Upon close examination, their canines are too prominent under their top lips. The skin is too pale. These details the common observer would overlook. Unlike Scalebane, they can hide in plain sight. It makes her wonder how these old world beings can tolerate the sun. Her people share a vampire's weakness.

The three newcomers stop in the hall, and Jekos takes a bow. He says, "The helicopter is ready."

Jekos leads the four from the mansion's front entrance and around the side, following the stone pathway surrounded by circular-trimmed bushes. Trees with twisted roots and trunks shroud the sun. One of the vampires walks in front of Scalebane and Erol while one follows behind them. It keeps them neat and orderly.

The half-imp leads them past the garden, descending a hill,

and towards a helicopter pad in an open, grassy field. The small plant blades dance from the spinning chopper, ready for takeoff.

Erol looks at the clearing sky and says, "I apologize that we have to do this during the daytime. I know of your people's condition."

"I'm not surprised. Human arrogance flourishes."

"Arrogance?"

"Crystal Moths are no different than any other soft skin. Even with a head like Mastema or these vampiric guards. The First has embraced your people's culture and is no different than you. It's why you're dealing with the Edmonton girl."

"The girl isn't an issue. We've got it taken care of."

"I question that. Mould grows from a small spot and is underestimated until it takes over the whole fruit."

"Poetic," Erol says. "We're already on her tail. She will be dead within the week, just like the street dealer who shared far too much with her and the police in Toronto. It's been a pain to manage the media on that front."

"Proving my point," Scalebane says.

Jekos extends his hand to the open helicopter and gives a toothy grin, showing his sharp fangs with wide separations between the black gums. "It's yours, Mr. Terzi."

"Thank you, Jekos," Erol says. He steps aside, letting Scalebane in first.

Jekos watches her for a little too long as if expecting a thank you. She is tempted to lunge at him. Ultimately, Scalebane is civil and boards the helicopter. Erol and the two vampires follow. Then, they take flight. The pilot maneuvers them high over the snowy mountain tops, heading for their next destination.

Scalebane shouts through the spinning blades, "You're certain the street dealer will be dead?"

"We have key players within the police, and I have a hitman on the girl. They will be gone before you know it. I assure you."

"It better. We're in the infant stages of our relationship, far too soon for anything to unravel regarding the old world."

"I assure you, everything will be fine."

"If it's not, I'll handle it myself," Scalebane says.

Erol says, "Of course, you're the foreman."

The loud engine and blades of the flying machine fill the remainder of the flight. Shouting a conversation is far too much of a breath. The aircraft soars past the mountains and beyond the forests to the flatter regions, closer to the ocean coast. Far in the distance is the great city of Vancouver.

The helicopter descends, and the metropolis disappears behind a rocky peak of a mountain. They hover over a pad near an ocean beach beside an industrial complex made of concrete and metal. Several docks are by the ocean leading to the building. Seacans are loaded and unloaded from a large cargo ship at one of the ports.

The helicopter lowers onto the pad. The four leave with the two vampires behind Erol and Scalebane. These bloodsuckers follow them like watchdogs. It irritates Scalebane because she isn't a child needing caretakers. She reminds herself to play nice with her new business partners.

"This, Scalebane, is Allen Shipping Solutions." Erol extends his hands to the concrete building with a puffed chest.

The four march on the docks and towards piles of seacans resting on a blue cargo ship. Dozens of workers move onto the ship and into seacans with pallets and forklifts. They take the goods off the boat, down the docks, and to a semi-truck line. A crane does the heavy lifting of moving larger containers off the ship.

As the four approach, workers take double glances at Scalebane, baffled by the black-cloaked figure. She can't blame them. It's not a usual sight, along with three Crystal Moths in full suits. Thankfully, her reptilian features are concealed. Her clawed toes are in custom, wide military boots. Her finger-claws are retracted into her leather gloves. The metal muzzle and leather mask hide her face while the hood keeps the feathers from view. Her tail is coiled around one of her legs, with the cloak keeping her tailbone concealed. Of course, there's nothing she can do regarding the formation of her calves. They are without a doubt reptilian. The long fabrics draping her body to the ground will have to do.

"Ah, perfect!" Erol says, pointing at a row of seacans as they board the ship.

He leads the group to the last seacan. The doors to the container are open and crates are unloaded by busy workers. There's a stack of six crates at chest height in front of three workers loading them onto a forklift.

"You there, sir, may you open one of these?" Erol asks one of the workers.

The man, a leather-skinned old thing with a scraggy beard, turns around. He takes a double glance at Scalebane and says to Erol, "Yes, yes, sure, Mr. Terzi."

"Thank you very much," Erol says.

The worker cracks one of the wooden crates, letting Erol sift through packing peanuts. He pulls out a boxed dragon statue and takes the foot-tall sculpture from the package. Erol holds it with both hands, presenting it to Scalebane. Her nostrils flare, understanding what the winged beast represents.

"Really?" Scalebane asks.

"Leave us," Erol says to the worker.

Once they are alone with the babysitters, Erol speaks. "Yes. This is where we put the ash once your people provide it. It's our newer method now that we're marketing to the higher-ups. The street ash gets sent in the plastic bags when we have spare supply."

"But a draconem? Of all things you could have chosen? Let me guess, that was Mastema's idea?"

"I believe so." He eyes the statue. "Is there a problem with the dragon?"

"You truly don't know what you've got yourself into, do you?"

"I understand that there were once winged serpents, draconem. If I recall, they looked very much like a dragon. Thus, mythology was born."

Scalebane folds her arms. "Our people and the draconem share common roots. Even our name, vazelead, comes from the ancient draconem tongue, meaning Drac Men. Did Mastema share that?"

"And your people don't like to be associated with them?" Erol asks.

"Draconem were horrific monsters. These intelligent and

sophisticated tyrants ruled the world for thousands of years. It was far before my time, but it was the primary reason your people and mine have a violent history."

Erol lowers the dragon statue, his face frozen with embarrassment.

Scalebane continues, "Humans believed we were in allegiance with the draconem. It's a long tale of war and misery. The short version is that humans enslaved and banished us from the surface world. It created a new war, fueling a burning hate that exists to this today."

Erol says, "I'm so sorry. I had no knowledge of this." He looks at the dragon statue and exhales. "This is a symbol of evil, then."

"Very fitting for Mastema and his love of pride. This stings our ego more than anything."

"I'll see if there's anything we can do with changing the form for future shipments. The idea behind the dragon statues was to have a symbol representing the strength and uniqueness of the ash drug to the clientele. Dragons are a powerful one. It made sense. I understand I was misled."

"You were," Scalebane says. "May I?"

"Of course," Erol says while passing the dragon statue.

Scalebane inspects the charcoal-scaled statue, feeling the clay texture. One knock confirms it's semi-hollow, and she grips the neck of the dragon, breaking it open. Inside is a pointed edge of an ash scale poking out of the darkness.

She brings it closer, lifting her mask by an inch to get a good sniff of it. *Which one are you?* she thinks while dissecting the smell of the scale. It's been sitting inside the dragon statue for too long. The factory clay, human stench, and ocean funk make it impossible to detect the unique scent of a vazelead.

"Ash has no effect on you, does it?" Erol asks.

Scalebane passes the dragon statue. "No. It's for humans and a few others. It surprised us when we learned humans could use our scales as a recreational activity."

"It would be a strange thing to discover." Erol passes the dragon statue to one of the vampires. "Please, stay here. I want a moment with Scalebane alone."

The one Moth takes the statue with his ever-expressionless face.

"Walk with me," Erol says, moving off the ship. Scalebane follows, and the two stroll to the far end of the dock, overlooking the ocean. The wind rises, blowing Scalebane's cloak, forcing her to hug it tight to keep her reptilian features hidden from the nearby soft skins.

"Allen Shipping Solutions doesn't only ship ash at this small port. Yes, they work for us, but they are an international organization owning many businesses. They provided the dragon statues from their Lang Enterprises company."

"See if they have anything else."

"We will. Those boxes of dragon statues you saw contain the last ash we received. It's far less than the previous ones. It's making expansion quite difficult."

"I am aware," Scalebane says.

"We would like to grow if King is as willing as he said he was. It's vital to get the drug into human hands, grow revenue, and build connections. We understand that you can produce a specific amount. King said there are methods to increase ash production. We want to explore them."

Breeding, Scalebane thinks. She knew this topic would arise and didn't want to discuss it with Erol. She asks, "Are you trained in combat?"

Erol lets out a hearty chuckle and says, "I heard you were more hands-on."

"Yes. Are you?"

"You want me to prove my worth to you?"

"It's a simple test. Tasting blood builds trust." *Discussion avoided,* she thinks.

"I'm much more interested in the information. Our technology is moving humanity into a new era, and I believe the extension of consciousness is our media."

"Is that so?" Scalebane asks, keeping him off topic.

"Media is potent to the human mind. I have been fixated on how our senses absorb information from a young age. Radio is audio only. The newspaper visual. Television combines these two senses passively. How people obtain their information is critical to how you present it to them."

"A symbiotic relationship with the mind," Scalebane says.

"Precisely. I read many papers by philosophers and experts in the field. It inspired my career in broadcasting. Fists and blood do not appeal to me, despite being involved with a ruthless group of individuals."

Scalebane says, "So you're not going to get your hands dirty?"

"If I must prove myself, I'll give you a dab of my blood."

"Funny. I'm no vampire, unlike our two comrades." Scalebane snorts.

"They're a bit intimidating, aren't they?"

"No. I mention hand-to-hand combat because it's a primal bond, and you're keen on bonding. If we're not going to fight, tell me why you are involved? I see the way you treat the workers and the way you treat me. You're living a double life with your partner. The sadness behind your eyes regarding that dragon statue was clear. You're too empathetic for this. Why are you here?"

Erol gazes into the ocean. "Like many people in the upper class, I can make a change for the dying world. We know of the global catastrophes that are happening around us. These occur thanks to worldwide politics, war, environmental issues, and markets built by communication and the distribution of economics. I don't think it's done anyone any good. This old world you're from is gone because of past mistakes. My people had their time to shine and make the world better. We've failed. We've brought destruction and misery to the Earth and ourselves. Our population is growing, the planet is weakening, resources are dwindling, and people are divided despite being more connected than ever. It's saddening, and I wish to make a better world."

"And your partner? How much does he know?"

"Dasco is not ready. He is delicate, despite his artwork. I'm warming him up to it."

"So you wish to make a utopia?"

"Money is no longer an object when you're given immense power. The basic needs of survival are washed away, and your life's legacy enters the forefront. There are three ways you can go with that amount of power. One: act as a humble being. Take the money and disappear, living a life of peace. Two: you become drunk with the power, feeding your pride. This is why Mastema prefers to rub shoulders with the upper class. Then, the third: a small amount of the elite don't go mad with their power or escape from reality. These people understand the influences they have and know they can navigate the world to do good. If their intentions are such, their power can make a better place for everyone."

Scalebane nods. "You consider yourself one of the third, a bold and humble diplomat here to replenish the world?"

"At this level, you must make harsh decisions that affect hundreds if not thousands of lives. Individuals will suffer. Each person cannot win when making the world a better place. What matters are ecosystems. You will save people long-term if they are restored, both in the environment and human-made versions."

"I've been around for a long time, Erol, and that is a daunting task. It will take generations for your people."

"I'm willing to initiate that change for the New World Order."

"And working with Mastema, you do know you're betraying your own kind? You've aligned yourself with an ancient evil."

"In short, Scalebane, humans are misguided sheep that need a shepherd. Evil is questionable."

"Broad thinking. I admire your reasoning. Now, as a soft skin, do you know how far this thing will go? You know that Mastema is the First, how those cuffs bind him to that temporary body, and who else hides in the shadows?"

"Yes, or what you and King are. I'm not aware of the details, like your people's history, clearly. I'm aware enough and know others have their own agendas on where the world should go. It's why the Crystal Moths are so careful with their methods."

"Mastema is systematic."

"He is. I hope there will be mutual understanding with people from most walks of life. My people need to know all-out wars cannot happen anymore. It's what got us here, to begin with, and feeds the hate-riddled past."

"There are other fools like you who believe in utopia." *The balancer,* Scalebane thinks, reflecting on her past.

Erol smiles. "My turn. Why are you and your sister involved? I know you like to keep your personal life protected, yet you and your sister are in Canada. Are both of your agendas as one-sided as King's idealism?"

"Hate is a powerful motivator for our people."

"I hope to get to know the person behind the mask of hate a little better," Erol says.

Scalebane shifts her focus to the sea, watching seagulls soar above the sharp waves underneath the wind. If she can keep mediating the Crystal Moths' expectations of ash, she will not have to 'get to know' this soft skin. She can perform her duty, be done with this cold northern country, and return to her people. It's where she and her sister belong.

CHAPTER 15
A NEW ANGLE

A nother few days go by, and Lola has no luck finding a better place to rent for her time in Vancouver. This motel is the best place, despite the revolving door of questionable truckers and sex workers. There are also a few other unique characters of shady legal statuses that come and go. Lola keeps her head low and goes for a smoke. The shadowy beings don't engage with her, and she doesn't bother them.

The wi-fi connection is a pleasant surprise. She can surf the web with her encryptions protecting her location and find updates about herself on the media. Her searches regarding the Crystal Moths and their shipments require a hands-on approach. According to Chen, the drug comes from overseas.

She also has to decide if she wishes to get in touch with Synarion again. Her cash will take her to a point. Unless she gets a side gig to get more and keep living here. The night she met Synarion, she was going to ask if she could stay with him. It was a senseless thought. The mysterious bastard is in her mind throughout the day. She wants to know who he is. His tale is bogus, and his true agenda is yet to be uncovered. She was too burnt from the drive, the ash, and didn't have her guard up. In the days after, she realizes how ridiculous his claims are.

Then again, what she heard in Toronto counters the dismissal.

Lola steps out of the shower, drying her hair. Even after a few showers, she feels a layer of filth seeping from her pores. It's the ash.

Take it.

The diamond she keeps is tucked in her bag in case she needs it. She shouldn't. Her goal keeps her focused, distracting her from the desire to have another hit of the reptile scale. Ash is reptilian. Intelligent? Nonsense.

Synarion's wild stories keep her thoughts occupied, pushing the desire for liberty clear of her mind. What he said at that bar offers parallels to what Lola experienced in Toronto. She doesn't want to admit it because she is practical.

For her own sanity, Lola pulls out the recording device she used when capturing Chen. This one she didn't share with the police, and for a good reason. The first portion of the recording is for her to keep. Not even Donnie got it. This version starts when she first discovered Chen and the other street dealers getting into a van. Lola rewinds the entire cassette and presses play. It rests on the bathroom counter as she dresses and preps a brand-new disguise as Jamie.

The recording starts with static white noise, followed by the busy streets of Toronto. Cars buzz by, and people talk. Lola's voice is louder. She says, "Toronto, Ottawa, on November 5th, 2016. Three Crystal Moth dealers are led by two men and a woman into a van. A white one, go figure. I'm following them now."

A car engine starts and hums for several minutes as Past Lola explains which streets she goes down. A turn here, then another there, until the car engine stops.

Past Lola says, "The van parked near a sewer entrance on the outskirts of the major metropolis sector. The three street dealers are blindfolded, being led by the others past a gate, into the tunnel."

The cocking of a gun is next. Keys jingle, and a car door closes gently. Footsteps and nearby birds fill the void until a liquid stream arrives and a soft creak from a gate. Subtle breathing follows as Past Lola goes deeper into the sewers.

"They're close," she whispers. "They are going in far."

I should have bought a camera, Lola thinks. She can remember the whole event clearly, and her statement isn't good enough without visuals to support the audio.

More footsteps and breathing come from Past Lola. The occasional dripping water and stream of sewage are in the background, with sounds textured by a vast reverb due to the hollow space. Past Lola stops as new voices arise. It's too far for the mic to record clearly.

"I'm going to amplify the signal," Past Lola says.

The sound gets a little bit better. The devices are not complex for distant recording or spying. Lola recalls being a good twenty meters from where the three street dealers stood with the two suited Moths. Their higher-up went into an open chamber within the sewers.

Lola couldn't see anything in the chamber. The recording detects the loud streams of liquid. Underneath the booming liquid layer, the Crystal Moths discuss shipping *it* west, and a little lower are growls followed by the snapping of a whip. The sound of rattling chains, snarls and a muffled inaudible word ending in an *ing* makes Lola stop putting on mascara.

"FHMM-ING" the smothered voice shouts in the recording. "HSSFM-ING" Its tone ends with the hiss of a snake.

Lola swallows saliva, feeling goosebumps kiss her bare thighs and spine. That voice wasn't human. The other two street dealers stood frozen as bold Chen moved closer to the underground chamber.

"They're coming back," Past Lola says. Her voice is shaking, and her breath stutters. Lola recalls being horrified as she rushed out of the sewers and into her car parked under a bridge.

"The five are exiting the sewers. Blindfolded street dealers. They are hopping into the van. I'm going for one." Her keys jingle, the car starts, and the engine hums. "Out of years of stalking Moths, it led to success," Past Lola mumbles to herself, reflecting on following the first ash case in the New Brunswick drug den, supplied by the street dealer Sierra. Then Chen saw the thing, making him the prime target.

Lola fast forwards the recording, aware of how she followed the van until they dropped off the three street dealers. She picked Chen when he was alone, pistol-whipped him, and dragged him to a warehouse she had scoped out. Abandoned buildings are handy to keep on file.

She presses play, and Past Lola speaks. "What did you see in the sewers?"

"You wouldn't believe me if I told you," Chen says.

"Try me."

"Jesus Christ."

"I heard a snake or animal. What was it?"

"Yeah, a reptile, okay?" Chen says.

"Someone spoke. It was muffled. Were they kidnapped?"

"I don't know! I saw a reptile. That's it. Okay?"

"Right. That's where ash comes from?" Lola asks.

"No way. It can't," Chen says.

"Why the sewers?"

"That was new. We didn't meet there."

"Where then?"

"The docks are more common. They get a lot of their shipments from overseas from what I understand." Lola pauses the recording. The adrenaline of kidnapping a man overtook her thinking, and she dismissed her paranoia about the reptile as the sound of scraping rocks or a gangster yelling. At least, until Synarion arrived.

He could be right, Lola thinks.

The Crystal Moths' web of confusion grows. She'll review her evidence after getting herself a proper coffee to start the day. Caffeine is one of the few accepted drugs in society you can use to alter your brain, unlike ash.

Lola adjusts the bangs on her black wig, and the new Jamie

persona is complete. The brown eyeshadow and subtle pink lipstick help hide the real her. She tucks her gun into the back of her cargos and throws on the leather jacket.

Outside, Lola looks for anywhere to get a cup of joe. The day is long over with the sun riding the skyline, and it's Remembrance Day in Canada, meaning fewer shops are open. She prefers the night anyway. Darkness is when evil lurks freely, more suited to her mission.

The proof is evident as she moves under the rain, looking at every face she passes. Those shoes are white on the man passing her. That woman is wearing a white top. Over there, an unsuspected older man has a white polo shirt. Each person cannot be a Crystal Moth. Because the gang doesn't own white.

The liquor store across the street would help. She could buy a bottle of whiskey and numb the constant paranoia.

I'm just a civilian, Lola reminds herself while finding a café on the same block. There's no need for her to overanalyze the concrete jungle.

She needs to get to work and get cash fast. Lola could pick up a side gig. The dark web is full of odd jobs to keep her afloat for the next few weeks. She orders an americano, black, and leaves, not looking at the bright, minimal furniture of the interior, or the customers.

Lola walks past two men in white dress shirts, catching a blip of their conversation.

"Scales and all?" asks one.

"I don't want to go," the other groans. He lights a cigarette.

The two pass Lola, and she stops. *Moths.*

"They hot?" the first asks, taking a swig from his flask.

"You're dead."

The two laugh and turn into an alleyway. Curiosity piques Lola's interest, and she strolls behind them. This is no ordinary conversation. Besides, opportunistic Lola can rob them for cash. It's a win-win. The question is, can she take both?

"Go West. You'll find answers. Every Moth knows something. Why do you think Mastema screens each one?" Chen's words echo in her mind.

Lola glances around and deems the coast clear. She walks to the Crystal Moths, who are unaware of her presence. Their conversation and the flask is of far greater interest. The alleyway is shrouded in blackness with dumpsters resting against each side, creating a zigzag formation obstructing the view. Perfect. It's discreet and unnoticeable to anyone walking by.

One turns around, showing his youthful face covered in patchy facial hair. He says, "Hey, yo, check this out."

Lola pops the lid of her coffee cup, enough so it rests on top of the rim. She brings her voice to a nasal pitch. "Hey, do you guys have any coke?"

"Who's asking?" says the other one. The light from his cigarette highlights his wrinkles and bad acne scars.

The Moths mutate into wolves, approaching her from the left and right. Their movements are synchronized, ready for the kill. Lola is no lamb. There are fangs underneath the gentle exterior of Jamie. The street dealers are a meter away and stop on each side of her, naïve to the danger. All they see is a piece of candy.

"I'm asking," Lola says. "Going to a party, and I need a

bump."

"We have ash," the young one says. "I could get you coke at my place."

"Hmmm," Lola says in a playful tone.

He says, "Ash is way better."

"Is that so?" Lola says.

"So."

Lola has them. She takes one inhale through her nose, gaining balance and focus. She glances down the alleyway; they are alone, making this her best chance.

Old one first. Likely more experience, Lola thinks.

The older one says, "You gonna buy or what, missy?"

"We could give you a sample," the young one says. "If you want to party." A perverted grin spreads across his face, showing his cracked tooth.

"I like a party," Lola says with a smile. The gangsters lower their shoulders for a split second. She flicks the lid off her cup, chucking the steaming hot liquid at the older Crystal Moth. The coffee collides with his face, scorching the skin on impact.

He backs up, yowling as he wipes the scathing liquid from his eyes. Steam flies off his flesh as Lola lunges at him, throwing a swift punch into his gut. He slams into one of the dumpsters. The younger Crystal Moth's eyes widen in shock. The slow fool forms fists and swings wide at Lola.

She ducks and frees her gun, aiming it at the man. The chamber is a foot from his face. The young man freezes under the moonlight. He's no man. The lunar beam reveals he's a kid, no older than eighteen.

"Want to die a hero to save your friend?" Lola asks.

The boy raises his hands and takes a step away. "No funny business," he says.

"Beat it," Lola shouts.

The Crystal Moth glances at his friend for one second and then books it. He shouts, "Bitch!" while dashing to the other end of the alleyway.

Lola flips the gun around, holding it by the chamber, and uses her classic pistol whip on her prey's skull.

"Argh!" he cries as Lola snags his neck with a harsh clasp. She pins him against the dumpster as her other hand flips the gun, bringing the chamber's tip to his chin.

"Whadda ya want, lady?" he asks. His face is bright pink from the burning liquid. His watery green eyes squint from the pain.

"Who do you work for?" Lola asks, inches from the man's bumpy skin.

"Nobody," he mumbles.

Lola slams him against the dumpster again. "Start talking. You mentioned scales." She presses her gun against him.

The Crystal Moth gathers a good-sized spitball and horks it onto her face. It splatters right on her nostrils, sliming down. She smacks him against the noggin with the gun's handle.

"Don't test me, piece of shit," she says.

"And whadda ya gonna do?" the Crystal Moths snears.

"Start talking. Who do you work for, and where do you get ash from?" Lola asks.

"I'm not afraid of some broad," the Crystal Moth says.

Lola hits him again with the end of the gun. She glances at both sides of the alleyway. She's uncertain how much time she has. That kid could be getting help, or a civilian could have heard them. She needs to make a clean exit.

What am I doing? Lola thinks.

"If you ask me, Michael Bradford was a deranged lunatic who enjoyed hurting people," Reporter Hucker Dime said on the radio. Michael had a reason for his attacks, and so does his protégé.

Cash. His phone. The drugs. These are the things she can use. She doesn't need to interrogate another Crystal Moth. Subtlety is key.

"That's as hard as you can hit?" the Crystal Moth says.

Lola gives him one final smack against the noggin with the gun, making a blunt *thwump* sound and freeing his consciousness. His weight falls onto Lola's hand. She drops him. The body slides into the pool of water.

She tucks her gun behind her belt and searches the man's trouser pockets, then the blazer. First are keys which aren't much use. His wallet is in the front pants pocket, housing five hundred in cash in fifties and twenties. His phone is in the blazer's inner pocket, accompanied by a small bag of cocaine. She powers the phone off, preventing anyone from tracking her to the motel. It has to have helpful information. She checks his other pants pocket and finds a pipe. She doesn't need it and takes it for reasons she won't admit to herself.

The deed is done, and Lola hurries out of the alleyway, opposite of where the Crystal Moth kid ran. She zigzags through the streets, taking a roundabout way in case anyone is following her. For her own sanity, she does slip into a liquor store and gets a bottle of whiskey with her newfound cash. The adrenaline needs to be suppressed. Then she returns to the motel and locks the door securely. The ambush was a success.

Lola releases a deep sigh and slinks to the carpet, resting her skull against the door. Her heart pounds against her ribcage as her hand trembles, lifting the bottle. The poor girl has not adapted to the rush that violence provides. Her aggressiveness brings haunting reminders of the original character who got into this mess: Michael Bradford, the infamous YEGman. Little by little, she's becoming more like him. She has her version of justice, like he did. Unlike Michael, her sense of right comes from a personal vendetta against the damn Crystal Moths.

Time for that reward.

Lola's unstable hands unscrew the lid from the whiskey. She takes a chug before tucking it between her thighs. Getting tanked isn't the plan. It's only a little bit. Besides, her coffee was expended on burning the man's face. Lola must remain sober, focused on her new priority: removing the SIM card from the phone. Those tiny, little chips make phones trackable, even when turned off.

Lola gets up and hurries through her bag of supplies. She finds the small pin used for removing SIM cards and pokes it into the phone's tiny hole. A small card slides from the device's side. She takes it out and bends it once. The chip snaps in two.

Next, she'll have to crack the operating system to go through text messages, caller history, photos, and other helpful information from the device. That phone is far better than scouring the streets and the web for evidence of Crystal Moths. These two street dealers had an exciting conversation. Further discussion must be in the phone's logs. There must be more clues to validate the information from the sewers and the words of her supposed ally, Synarion.

Lola should meet that man, or whatever he is. She can approach Synarion with a clear mind. She sits at the desk, placing the whiskey beside the computer. She turns on the laptop and navigates to the dark web email to send him a message:

You

To: oldworldshadow@wi7qkxyrdpvr.onion

Hey,

A second date?

Lola

It's time to crack the cell phone. She's no master at jailbreaking phones to get into the goods. Lola knows enough to be dangerous. She also has access to the most extensive library of knowledge in human history: the Internet. The web will have information on how to pierce through a password.

She works away with her computer, some cables, and the phone. An hour of research goes by. Many articles with technical terms are new to her. It's daunting. Now Lola notices her fingers are still shaking. She needs to calm her nerves first and slips outside for a smoke.

If Donnie— Lola stops her thought. She can't reflect upon those who have deserted her.

Lola puffs on the cigarette, watching the highway streets. A man one floor below across the way is having a smoke too. He isn't wearing white and is no threat. By the lobby, some young couple, both in matching grey sweatpants, checks into the motel. There's a spring in their strut. Lucky them. Lola cannot imagine having such spirits. Even in her past life, she was an outsider, gravitating to the underground. Normies. They live in a strange alien existence that she will never be accustomed to. It matters little. This is Lola's life. Alone.

Becky and her poor mother were faithful to her. Michael was honest. Donnie was once a friend. Her brother's and father's resentment still stings. They'll blame her for Mom's death. There were others who weren't quite as impactful. Each of her ex-boyfriends, co-workers, and acquaintances abandoned her. They threw little stabs into her heart. As a mass entity, their weight is immense.

Time is working against her, and she needs to make progress. The Moths are faster. Her stress from a life on the run and crime isn't helping her emotional state. She has a substance to ease the tension.

Inside the room, Lola grabs the bottle of whiskey and takes a big swig of it. She needs to numb her emotions and focus. The lubricating potency of liquor can't wash away what's crawling in the back of her mind, unlike the diamond-shaped item in her bag. It's so willing to ease everything. Yes, this is the thing she wants. Despite fighting it, Lola is on a slippery slope.

Just a little bit.

Jack gave her quite the hit the first time. With a little smoke, or even a nibble of it, she can elevate herself gently. Mastema did mention you can eat ash. Lola also took the pipe from the Crystal Moth.

"Fuck," Lola sighs while scurrying through her purse. It's over. Her mental resistances have collapsed. What does it matter? It's one night. It's not like she's made any progress on the phone. She's been working around the clock non-stop, travelling, fighting, and running. This night can be for Lola.

It is for Lola, comes a thought in her mind. She's unsure if it's her own.

Her shaking hands go through the bag to find the diamond-shaped scale in the hidden compartment, tearing off a small piece. On the desk, she uses her gun to crush the brittle material into a fine powder. A piece of paper works to scoop the dust into her newfound pipe. With a flick of a lighter, she ignites the ash and brings it to her lips. Lola pauses for a moment, watching the flame burn the precious purpling deliverance of peace. *Don't waste it, Lola.*

Lola inhales. Smoke runs through the chamber and into her mouth, seeping into her system. She wobbles and sits on the bed, exhaling slowly. Purple-tinted smoke rises in the air.

Paranoia strikes her while sniffing the swampy air. This was a mistake. She glances at the door to see that it is locked and chained. She's safe. The high is going to occur whether she likes it or not. She should have another hit.

It doesn't take long for the drug to take effect. Like the first time with Jack, she gets a heightened sense of humming throughout her system. Her heart rate increases, and a tingling sensation buzzes through her skin. Her once-clouded mind of fear expands from linear thoughts.

The experience is similar to the first. The fear is different. It's the paranoia of being alone. She's in a safe place and can let the drug wipe away the stress.

Embrace the real world. These foreign words command her action. The lighter and pipe slip from her hands, tumbling onto the carpet. She lies down on the bed, staring at the ceiling. Within the dim lighting, pieces of information form in the stucco ceiling. They're maps. No, they're circuit boards. Wait, it's both overlapping and connecting together. This is the joy of the drug. It's psychedelic and met with a rush of adrenaline and awareness.

The remaining sober worried thoughts seep from her brain and float into the air. Words and visions of her past hover on the ceiling, letting her process the situation.

Crystal Moths. Synarion. Michael Bradford. Her past life. Her fear. This array of thoughts happens at once, firing from different directions. She can examine her problems together.

The emotional state she can learn to cope with, as many do. The brave heroes of her past will be her role models. If she doesn't, this new underbelly will devour her. It's time to get thick-skinned. Her mom didn't raise a wussy-ass loser who gets eaten by her enemies. After all, her foes are responsible for her mother's death. Lola will defend her family name. If she doesn't, what good is she?

She will make new allies. There is no other option because she can't do this alone. This leads to her next epiphany. Synarion, the mysterious stranger. Lola isn't a fool; what she heard in Toronto is real. The growling, hissing, and that voice are not of human origin. The tale of a fictional world is unrevealing itself.

Cash? Solved for now. A place to rent? She has the motel. Synarion is an option when he replies. Ash-dasher Lola is the unpaid consultant for Sober Lola's issues.

She stands and paces back and forth. This wasn't what she had planned when taking ash. She hoped for a simple release, like marijuana, to ease the tension. Instead, her mind is firing a million thoughts a moment. Her trip is not like the one with Jack, where they acted like baboons. Right now, no one is around to influence her high. Lola is driven.

At one point, she goes to her laptop and the phone. She taps away on the keyboard, opening several pieces of software she has not used before. The ash-dasher must have just downloaded them. Lola can't remember. Her mind is moving on so many different levels that she isn't even conscious of her actions.

Lola is a passenger inside her own body, watching the heightened mind move through strange new code on the screen. She presses a button, sending a signal to break open the phone.

The first attempt: fail.

That's okay. She can troubleshoot and decide where to go next. More typing and another software download later, she makes a second attempt: success. The device's data opens in a new window on her computer. The folder structure showcases the phone's hard drive and the data it holds. It's jailbroken.

Lola lets out a childish giggle as a wide grin spreads from cheek to cheek. She did it. Better yet, the ash did it for her. There is an otherworldly component to this drug. Clearly, Sober Lola's mind was limited to a box, trapping her true potential. She can learn faster with the drug, her new tool.

Text messages, phone records, credit card information, photos, and contact cards are in the folders. She has found a treasure trove. Lola skims through the most recent text messages. It reads:

(Ricky: Seven Days, Dasco Amoss's show.

We need bodies.

Monday, November 10, 2:36 PM)

(You: Time and Location?

Tuesday, November 11, 5:13 PM)

(Ricky: North Vancouver Gallery

of Modern Prestige on Lower Lonsdale.

7 the guests arrive. The Prime Minister

is there and expecting. Get there at 6.

Tuesday, November 11, 5:22 PM)

(You: Is one of those reptiles going

to be there?

Tuesday, November 11, 5:18 PM)

(Ricky: Ya

Tuesday, November 11, 6:04 PM)

(You: Duck

Tuesday, November 11, 6:55 PM)

(You: Fuck

Tuesday, November 11, 6:56 PM)

Lola continues to smile, and then laughter rises from her belly. Ash is otherworldly. This was a tiny hit. Imagine if she kept going. Instead, she should pause because the drug is beginning to wear off. It's not as euphoric as the first time she took it. Her sober thoughts are an anchor, pulling her into the box of realism and closing the mind's multidimensional array.

Boundaries are how people live. Hell, the matching normy

couple is in a box. Again, Lola judged them based on their exterior. That's no way to live. People have so much more depth than what's presented on the outside. They're authentic people, like her, finding their way through life.

I should be kind, Lola thinks. She recalls the Crystal Moth kid who has no idea what he is dabbling in.

Christ, Lola, these are hippie idealisms nonsense brought on by the drug. Crystal Moths are the enemy. The trickling stubbornness of her ego is returning, resurrecting the rage. Her repressed frustrations and anger are her reality. She is hate, nothing more.

Lola closes the laptop and flicks off the lights. Paranoia makes her double-check the door, ensuring it's locked and the windows are sealed. She is safe in this motel room for another night. She cracked that phone and unlocked a goldmine. Today was a victory, and she crashes onto the bed, embracing triumph.

CHAPTER 16
HIDING IN THE SHADOWS

Drifting into a peaceful sleep offers weightless joy from the horrors of life. Lola has not had this deep rest since hell rose in 2014. Two years is a long time to experience irregular sleep, resulting in lasting effects of poor judgment, slow reflexes, and reduced recovery. This heavy slumber is the best feeling Lola has ever had. Praise the ash!

She had a minor hit, and the effects are potent, rising fast and wearing off on a gradual decline. Lola didn't even know she had drifted into sleep. The motion happened after she unlocked the phone. Her thoughts melted, and her adrenaline spike fell to zero as her fingers glided against the bedsheets.

Dreams flourish in her newfound state. They're blips of memories. Her loved ones and the childhood home. She's in her basement bedroom, laughing with Becky. The girl had a warm smile. There's no telling how much Lola will remember when waking the following day. It doesn't matter. Lola is here in the present and at peace.

Rattling rises from silence.

The audio does not sync with the visuals of her Becky bub. It's distant and sharper.

Another jingle comes from silence, a click, and a twist. An elongated squeak makes it clear the sound projects beyond the dreamscape. It wakes Lola. She's groggy and is unable to comprehend the situation. It sounded like a door. *Her* door.

Lola's head is filled with marbles. Her eyes peel open, scraping against the cornea. She's had this dehydration side-effect before and lifts her cement head, swaying in the process. The room is too dark to see anything other than the open door leading to the night streets. A humanoid silhouette stands by the doorframe, watching her.

She lifts her frail hips, fumbling to snag the firearm tucked in the back of her belt. The silhouette dashes forward. Lola snags her gun, flicks the safety off, raises it, and pulls the trigger twice, creating ear-shattering bangs. It flashes the room with sharp beams. A bald man with powerful arms and a white tank top darts to the bed. One arm is held high, holding a knife. It plummets down.

Lola rolls out of the way and onto the carpet, shoulder first, as the knife stabs the mattress, and she stumbles to her feet.

The attacker moves around the bed, swinging the blade in a wide arch. The knife slices her bare arm as she fires again. Her bullet grazes the man's leg. His other hand punches her gut.

She drops the gun as her eyesight blurs. The knife's handle slams onto her head, knocking her into the wall. She slides to the floor sideways. Lola reaches for the double-visioned gun. Either shock or the ash has numbed her body, for the pain has not sunk in.

The man curb stomps her ribs, reminding her she isn't invincible. She yelps. He kicks again. The boot smashes her chin as Lola snags the gun, firing and hitting the ceiling. He descends the knife, missing her heart by inches. The sharp tip rips through her skin, sinking into her clavicle. She cries, attempting to punch him with her good arm. He immobilizes her legs with his knees against her thighs and snags her gun-wielding arm, pinning it to the floor. He rips the knife free from the wound and raises it. She's locked in place and has nowhere to go. It's been a good run.

A high-pitched swoosh blips by, and the man gasps. His body tenses. His eyes freeze, lips relaxing. The eyebrows slant in confusion. He looks up, dazed, and drops the knife. His body tumbles onto Lola with a heavy thud. He smells of sweat and of cheap cologne. The weight is unbearable, pushing out her breath.

Lola can't lift him. She pushes again to roll the man off. His deadweight is too much for her wounded body. She coughs and groans, fighting to push the dead flesh off, wondering what happened. A second intruder saved her. People don't spontaneously die.

Footsteps come from the entranceway as a silky voice speaks. "You can't even hold a fight." It's Synarion's.

"Get this fucker off me!" Lola wheezes. Liquid drizzles from the top of her skull to her jawline. A surge of heat accompanies sharp stings rising throughout her body. The pain is settling in.

Hands snag the dead man's shoulders, and the corpse rolls off her. Synarion's purple eyes stare at her as the night streets cast sharp shadows on his all-too-perfect complexion.

"He would have had you," Synarion says.

"No shit," Lola says. Her vision moves in circles as she catches fresh air in tight wheezes. The motion ignites the pain in her ribs. Lola sits against the wall, panting.

"Let's take a look at that wound. It doesn't look threatening." Synarion kneels down, taking a closer look at the stab wound beside the strap of her tank top. He eyes the nasty scar on the other side of her chest, remnants of Michael Bradford. Synarion would be well aware of how she got that if he's her fan.

Synarion leans back and says, "Oh no."

"Oh no?" Lola says, looking down to see a decent flow of red oozing from her open wound.

"Yes. This is threatening. It could have gotten an artery."

Lola forgets to breathe for a moment, raising her voice. "I need a doctor," she says. "I'm bleeding." Her voice slurs.

"That you do," Synarion says. "This is manageable."

"Don't call 911. Please, it's over then."

"You think I'm a fool? Perhaps a little, but I'm nowhere quite as foolish as you have been."

Another criticism from Synarion is not what she needs right

now. Lola feels herself sobering with each passing breath, lessening the wondrous reality-numbing effects of ash.

"Pl-l-lease don't," Lola repeats.

"We won't. Stay with me."

"Where, where did you come from? I've been trying to get a hold of you," Lola says. Her logic is failing, as she had emailed him hours ago.

"Don't worry about that," Synarion says. "I need you to focus on staying awake. Can you do that for me?"

Lola takes deep breaths. She stares at the dead man on the floor, looking at the white tank top and the scar on his face. She has seen him before at Jack's house. Jack called him Ramon.

"Ramon . . . followed me," Lola says.

"I can see that. He knew where you were," Synarion says while walking to the bathroom. He returns with a damp cloth.

"That's not going to help. I need a doctor," Lola says.

"You were hit on the head. Let me aid you."

"I-I-I need a doctor. No hospital."

"You're looking at one," Synarion says. He places the cloth onto the bump forming on her head. The fabric is cold on her hot skin. "Hold that, please." He uses another cloth to wipe the wounded clavicle.

Lola follows his instruction, holding the cloth in place. It stings. She keeps staring at the corpse, noticing a thin circular blade in the back of the man's skull. Spikes line the rim. Synarion uses throwing stars. Of course, he does.

"Christ!" comes a man's voice from the doorway.

"Get lost," Synarion says.

"She okay?" the man asks.

"Yes, and you won't be if you don't leave."

A woman shouts, "Call 911!"

"We need to hurry," Synarion says. "Just do as I say."

Lola nods. "His name is Ramon. I met him in Winnipeg before I, before . . . I drove here." Lola pants heavily, controlling her breath through the sharp pain. She's been beaten and shot before, making this familiar territory. It doesn't make it any easier. She needs to manage her breathing. It will keep her awake.

"He must've followed you for a number of days then," Synarion says.

"Uh-huh. . ." Lola can't understand why Ramon took so long to attempt the assassination. In speculation, he wanted to see if she had any more value or to confirm who she was. Her head is scrambled, and it is pointless to ponder. She can't stop thinking. The man found her. Synarion found her. Her stealth is as good as dirt. At least the cops haven't located her. None of it is adding up. Lola should focus on breathing. In the end, Ramon is dead, and Synarion saved her. She has no choice other than to surrender herself to him.

"There's a body, Syn-Sssynarion," Lola says, slurring.

"Gee, I did notice that," Synarion says.

Sarcasm is written into his DNA, like her. She's being serious and has no idea what he's doing or how much blood she has lost. Lola doesn't dare look. She has the one job of holding the wet cloth on her head. Her mind's distorted state keeps attempting to piece the facts together. Where did Synarion come from?

Synarion fumbles through his leather coat's inner pockets and to the buckled pouch on his thigh. With his fingered glove, he takes some medical bandages and leaves from the bag.

"Chew on this," Synarion says while handing her the leaves.

"Whuh?" Lola says.

Synarion pushes the leaves into her mouth. "Chew them. I need them to be crushed into a pulp."

Lola opens her mouth and chows down. The plant releases a sharp, bitter taste with each crunch until it is ground to a paste. Meanwhile, Synarion unwraps the medical bandages. He extends his hand for Lola to spit the pulp into his palm. He examines her work and deems it right.

"This is going to sting," he says.

Without warning, Synarion jams the pulp into her open wound while pressing his palm over her mouth. His fingers poke around in the hole, coating the flesh with the paste. Fire flares around the wound and through her veins, kindling her torso. Her limbs turn to ice, feeling sweat seep out of her from head to toe. She wants to scream. Synarion puts pressure on her mouth as she drops the damp cloth. Her legs kick in spasms.

"Stay with me a little longer," Synarion says. He lets go of her mouth as Lola's head sways. He wraps the medical bandages around her wound. Her body is liquid, and he is forced to hold her.

The room darkens. The fiery sting from the plant escalates inside as her exterior continues to freeze. Lola's head flops sideways, and her eyelids flicker.

"Come on, Lola," Synarion says.

Sirens blare from outside. Despite her best efforts, she cannot fight the body's desire to pass out. The pain lessens, taking the heat with it. Coldness remains.

Synarion lifts her rag doll body as if she were a kid. He wraps her arm around his shoulder, holding her legs with his forearm. He snags his throwing star from the man's skull and hurries to the desk. With his other hand, he flings a strap around his arm. Next, he hurries around the room. Lola can't keep track anymore. A gentle whoosh soars around Lola's ears. The lights are too bright, and she closes her eyes, hearing more sirens from the highway. Footsteps pick up in the rain.

"Don't worry, Lola, we're in the clear now," Synarion says.

"Copsssss," Lola groans.

She surrenders herself to her saviour. Thoughts of worry dissipate as her breath guides her into a gentle sleep. This is a similar slumber to what she experienced earlier. Now, it's deeper. She needs to get beaten to near death each night, and then she can enjoy a decent rest. Goodnight, Lola.

CHAPTER 17
A REAL MAN

Parenting is no easy career. Sometimes Iglesias wonders if his day job with the RCMP Major Crimes is less work. At least you can predict patterns with a criminal. Unlike his teenage son, who is a wild card. One moment he is straight-laced and going to school, then the next, he's throwing parties with drunk 'n' horny kids.

"Dad," José starts.

Iglesias raises his index finger, silencing his son. "I'll do the talking, understand?"

José puts his hands together, holding his phone, which keeps buzzing. One can presume its texts from his friends, which Iglesias will deal with later. Right now, he needs to give his son a lecture regarding responsibility. José is a Iglesias whose history is filled with crafty and resilient individuals from day one. He doesn't enjoy treating his son as a lesser.

In the back of Iglesias's mind, he can't help but reflect upon his own past. He, too, would have done the same thing as José, thrown a party with friends. That's for starters. His son has not gone down the dark path he once did. They have a good home in a safe neighbourhood with a good school. Even the kids at the party were like-minded. They were clean and wanted some fun.

"Did you know I would be coming home?" Iglesias asks.

"Yeah," José says softly.

"I texted you, telling you I'd be working a little bit late."

"Until two AM?" José says. "By midnight, you end up staying at the office regardless, so why does it matter?"

"That doesn't mean you can start acting like a wild animal."

"It wasn't crazy. There were eight of us."

"I know. I'm here," Iglesias says. He grabs one of the plastic beer cups, raising it. "And this?"

"Mom didn't mind me drinking."

"You think her letting you drink was justified? She abandoned you for this shit." Iglesias shakes the cup. "Who the hell brought this?"

"I—" José stops.

He doesn't want to rat on his friends. Iglesias can't blame him. If anything, that would explain the constant buzzing of his phone. His friends are either threatening or begging him not to squeal, presuming that his friend circle got the alcohol.

Iglesias sighs. A part of him wants to forget what his son did.

The other side knows he needs to be a strong father and make this a lesson. It's late at night, and he has to be at the office in the morning. Picking your battles is a part of parenthood. Each new challenge presents a difficult choice with consequences. It doesn't help that Iglesias makes these choices without a partner.

José's phone makes another hum. He checks it from the corner of his eye, and a slight smirk grows on the corner of his face.

"You're popular," Iglesias says. "Who is it?"

"Nothing," José says.

"You're not in a position to stand your ground here. You know you're going to be in a lot of trouble for this?"

"Dad, it's just a few friends."

"Eight."

"Whatever," José says, looking at his phone.

That's enough. Iglesias doesn't need his son ignoring him for some stupid screen. He marches to José, extending his hand. "Give it to me," he says.

"No," José says, taking a step away.

Iglesias is faster, snagging it in one fluent motion, leaving his son petrified, for his life was taken away. The phone's screen shows an open text messaging program. There are messages from a few boy names within the past ten minutes. The top name catches his eye, a girl named Hailey. Iglesias skims through the first few messages from her.

> (You: Hey hot stuff, u coming over?
> Tanner and Leah are here.
> 11:13 PM)

(Hailey: Check your door dumbass ;)

11:42 PM)

(Hailey: Hope your dad can

fuck you as good as I can.

2:25 AM)

A swift swipe reveals a stream of more messages going back days and weeks. Iglesias won't snoop into his son's personal life. He has been oblivious to José's world. The last crude text would be funny to a teenage boy; to a grumpy father who wants to go to bed it is irritating. Surprisingly, Iglesias doesn't feel rage. Guilt sinks his chest for not being present in his son's life.

"How long have you been seeing her?" Iglesias asks.

"A couple months," José says.

Iglesias didn't know his son had romance in him. He has caught José taking a look at women, sure, but he didn't know José would be dating so soon. It's safe to say that his son is a man after that last text message. Is sixteen too early? It wasn't for Iglesias, but this is José!

Iglesias is no better than his son's mother: absent. He should spend more time with his son and stop obsessing over this ash case and some runaway university girl. He has a good team working with him and should take a holiday.

"I like her," José says. He stands straight.

"I can see that," Iglesias says. He hands José his phone. Iglesias is tired and feels more shame than anger. His son is growing up before his very eyes with facial hair that he overlooks day-to-day, wishing the boy was still a toddler. High school is such a short window, and José is halfway through it. As for Iglesias, he's been doing the same thing for the past twenty-odd years: spending time with dirtbags and low lives. Nice job,

Iglesias.

"That's good," Iglesias says. "Look, clean this mess up and forget it, okay?"

José's face says he got a get-out-of-jail-free card. "Totally."

"And I'd like to meet her," Iglesias says. "We can have dinner."

"Yeah, sure," José says. His voice rises a notch as if he's somehow dodged the death sentence. In his world, he has. His father has shown a weaker side in his older age. Such a hiccup would have not passed a few years ago.

The last thing Iglesias needs is anyone learning that his son threw a party while drinking underage. Then the kids drove home. He's the lead detective for the drug unit at Major Crimes. He doesn't even want to ask if his son had other party supplies tonight. Even though weed legalization is right around the corner, the less you know, the better. At least this one time.

"Great." Iglesias places his hand on José's shoulder. "I do have to get to the office early tomorrow. When I'm awake, this mess is gone, understood?"

José nods.

"Good, no more parties here." He pats José's back and leaves, heading for the bedroom. Iglesias likes to think he played his cards right. He's human, and his son is becoming an adult. He has to treat him like one.

My son's first girlfriend, Iglesias thinks. He can't help but smile while crashing onto his bed, proud of his boy. There's no way he could tell that to him right now. He must pretend to be disappointed. Parties and girls, the life of a teenage boy.

* * *

The ringing alarm of Iglesias's cell phone frees him from slumber. Sluggish, he rises from the claws of tempting sleep. He washes, dresses, and is ready to head out. He goes down the stairs to a spotless, squeaky-clean main floor. Excellent job, José. That's one thing off Iglesias's plate.

He needs to spend quality time with his son and get to know this girl. It's a delicate balance raising a teenager. You need to be there for them while stepping aside and letting them find their own way.

In two years, José will be a legal adult and can party across Canada. That fact has not sunk in for Iglesias. He prefers to put it aside and think of his boy as the kid who used to draw crayon portraits of his dad in the RCMP. He still keeps those drawings in his desk drawer.

José is already having a coffee and cereal at the island counter, looking at his phone. The kid couldn't have gone to sleep at all. Tough for him because it's a school day. The mornings are their one time to talk before the day spirals out of control.

"Morning," Iglesias says.

"Hey, Dad," José says.

Iglesias makes a quick cup of coffee from their pod machine before heading to the doorway. "Want a ride?" he asks.

"It's okay," José says. "Tanner's picking me up."

Iglesias turns around. "You sure? It's on the way to the office."

"It's all good. Thanks, Dad."

Iglesias nods, standing without anything to say. He's played his one card and will spend time with José later. It's not going to happen this morning. The weekend is a good time. Correction: he has to take care of some paperwork from an old case. The evening will work if he doesn't have to work late, but that isn't going to happen. They are hot on this ash case. Damnit, Iglesias, figure it out.

"Great, see you tonight?" he asks.

"Sure," José says.

With that, Iglesias leaves the father version of himself at the door. His mind tunes into the case, reflecting on the previous night's events with Chen and the valuable information he got. The squealer shed the most obscure information regarding the ash case to date. Iglesias isn't buying the bullshit story, reptilian people. Come on.

Ash. Reptilian scales, Iglesias thinks, gripping the SUV's wheel.

They know that much. He'll keep the team keep researching different reptile species. Knowing Beckman, he is already on it. Iglesias will chat with forensics to see if they have any new DNA insights. It's probable that Chen did hear a reptile in the sewers. The rubbish part comes from the anthropomorphic being speaking in the story.

Hopefully, Chen had a good rest and can think more clearly. Time and the lack of sleep break people, and he had to have exaggerated the story. Chen and Iglesias have a deal to not send him to the crazy house. They can push it a little further. Chen could be their eyes and ears into the Crystal Moths.

Iglesias will see what Archer and Beckman say. He has to tell them about the new information. Chen can help them discover which sewer tunnel it was. Unlikely, but Iglesias is willing to try.

He parks the SUV, takes his coffee tumbler, and heads for the station. He enters the lobby, into the elevator and to his department. The doors slide open, revealing a busy floor of officers racing. Flustered faces and frowns are everywhere. Team members are being interviewed by another department in suits. He has seen these guys before. They're internal investigations.

"What the?" Iglesias mutters. He exits the elevator and walks through the rows of desks.

He finds Beckman and Archer standing by the interrogation room, arms folded. There are suits with gloves on, running prints on the entire room. Iglesias pieces it together. His partners look at him with sagging faces.

Beckman speaks, "Chen is gone."

Iglesias's mouth hangs open. He's not even sure what to say. There's the obvious: What the hell happened? Have you checked the security cameras? Who was watching him last night? Those are questions that internal investigations will ask. Chen is no longer here, taking their one advantage with him.

The weasel did not tell them where the other street dealers from the sewers were. Chen would have been willing to stay if they could have persuaded him to work with them last night. Unless Chen didn't go willingly. The Major Crimes drug department could have a Crystal Moth plug on their hands.

CHAPTER 18
HUMILITY

A wholesome smile spreads across a young woman's chalk-white face. Her black and red dreadlocks dangling in front. The bright white room fades to black as rough, stubby fingers slither around her slim neck. The smile melts into shock as the hands grasp tight, squeezing ever more until her neck jerks and her spine breaks. The girl's head dangles to the side with her mouth wide open, making room for the handgun poking out from her esophagus. It fires with a loud bang. The bullet soars straight into a clavicle.

The skin absorbs the metal, bubbling into the soft, wrinkled face of an older woman. It boils again, and dreadlocks sprout from the older woman's forehead. More carbonating of the flesh mutates the elder's jaw into a chiselled chin covered in whiskers. A deformed scowl rests above. The Trinity of Souls is fused into a single entity of misery on Lola's chest. Becky, Michael, and Mom.

The eyes of the woman melt away, leaving fleshy holes leading to pitch blackness. The mouth elongates, showing razor-sharp teeth. The forked tongue slithers out with a bloody heart balancing on the end of the tip, pumping rapidly. The motion accelerates until it makes a sudden stop. The organ crushes inward, spewing a fountain of blood from its valves.

"No!" Lola shouts, reaching high. She's covered in sweat, and a throbbing ache ruptures from her chest. She falls onto the mattress, damp from her intense sweating. This is no ordinary slumber. It's fueled by nightmare ghosts who will not rest until her vengeance is complete. The ghosts, or demons, are her will whether she likes it or not. It doesn't matter how many times she has been stabbed or beaten. Lola couldn't move on.

"Easy there," comes Synarion's voice. He's sitting by a table with a pile of mechanical junk on one side, papers and jars with plants resting on the other in front of a closed cabinet. The laptop he is typing on is dead center.

They're in a dingy, dark studio apartment. Short-and-wide windows are near the ceiling, coated in dirt. There are two lamps on opposite sides of the loft space projecting a warm glow onto the cracked concrete walls and splintered wooden front floor. Based on the lighting, it's nighttime. Synarion knows how to live.

"Where the hell am I?" Lola asks. Her voice is croaky, and her head weighs a ton with a hot sting coming from the top of her noggin. The combo of ash and the blunt end of a knife leaves one stupid. Stack that with her stomach, ribs, and clavicle wounds, and she'll be limping for far too long.

"Welcome to my humble home," Synarion says, scooting his rolling chair over to her.

"It sure is roomy," Lola says, looking at the bareness of the space. One corner has the fridge, sink, and stove beside a doorway leading to the bathroom. The second corner has his table of junk and the exit door. A third is where Lola is with his bed. The fourth is bare.

"No, it's not much. Live as long as I have, and you realize you don't need materialistic things."

"How enlightening." Lola cannot help the sarcasm. She's in pain, and his advice is irritating while she wishes for the misery to go away. If her mess could disappear for one day, she'd be a new woman. Unfortunately, that's not the case.

"You took quite a beating," Synarion says.

"I have to thank you," Lola says, sitting.

Lola scoots against the cool concrete wall, sending a pulse of pain into her torso. Synarion aids her, pulling her gently. She closes her eyes, attempting to ignore the hot agony. There's no change in hell. It hurts like a bitch.

"Thank you," Lola says again.

"You would have passed on to the next world, wouldn't you?" Synarion says.

"Yeah, I thought that was it." She hugs her knees, looking at his alien purple eyes. She has many questions for him. Yet, her mind is focused on the pain. Another hit of ash could help numb it. That cannot be. Lola has been through this cycle once before, and it ends now.

"And you said you know the man?" Synarion asks.

"He was a Crystal Moth in Winnipeg before I came here."

"Where you got that tattoo? It's quite fresh," Synarion asks.

He saw it? Lola thinks. Now, she realizes she's wearing her bralette and cargos. Her stomach is wrapped in medical bandages around her clavicle to her lower rib. There's also one around her forehead, above her flushing cheeks.

"A cryptographic tattoo. I must give you more credit. I did not expect you to be thinking so forwardly," Synarion says.

"Yeah, well, I did."

"You must forgive me. I did scan it and examined the files."

Lola's eyes widen, saying, *you did what?*

"Do not fear. I terminated it, clever girl. If that key on your stomach is activated, your evidence will become visible to them. Ten seconds later, they will broadcast onto sleeper accounts and stand-alone websites. The brief script timing delaying the publication is brilliant."

Lola sighs, feeling relief rush over her. The release of her information would have been catastrophic. She's not ready to publish any of her evidence. It's too vague and incomplete. She would be doubling down on her initial video. Lola needs hard evidence to free herself of crimes and break the Crystal Moths for good. If her information is released too soon, the Crystal Moths will pivot their behaviours. They did in Edmonton. It set her below ground zero.

"Is your big plan to polish your data and publish a world-class report on the Crystal Moths, clearing your name and collapsing their empire?"

"Yeah," Lola says with hesitation. His words cast doubt into her mind. "It's as good as I got for now." *My laptop*, Lola thinks. "My things, where are my things?"

"I got most of them. Well, as much as I could while carrying you. The police arrived and my escape window was limited. What I got wasn't much." He rolls his chair over to the table of junk, pushing the jars and papers aside to grab her linen messenger bag. He snags a second large plastic bag and rolls to the bed. He passes the two bags to her.

Lola opens the linen bag and sees the laptop is there, along with her recording device, her phone, a few notes of paper, and her stack of cash. The plastic bag has her gun, the phone she took from the Crystal Moth, her sheathed knife, and a few clothes and makeup. Thank God.

"That's it?" Lola asks.

"Plus your jacket. It was a juggle sneaking out of there."

The Jamie persona will have to retire. Her other belongings are in the hands of the cops: the disguises, spare weapons, ammo, some notes, and her car. Losing her goods is disappointing, and she forgets how Synarion killed a man, repaired her critical wound, and then carried her and her things without being caught.

"How did you find me?" Lola asks.

"Last night?" Synarion says.

"I sent you an email before the attack, and then you show up before I'm going to die?"

"When we met at the bar, I could tell you were being watched. I couldn't leave you for dead."

"How did you know I was being watched?" Lola asks.

"Call it keen senses," Synarion says, tapping his ears. "They may be scarred, but they work well. Not as well as they once did, still better than yours."

"What does that mean?" Lola asks.

"It means I can hear a lot better than you humans. I can see far clearer and further than you. That Crystal Moth has followed you since you got to Vancouver, waiting to strike."

"I've had plenty of vulnerable moments," Lola says. "Why did he choose that night?"

Synarion shrugs. "He was investigating you. Or a Moth gave him the final order to kill you."

"And you didn't think to tell me?"

"The Moths didn't know I knew. That gave me the advantage of ending them once and for all. Now you're in the clear."

"You sure cut it to the last minute," Lola says, putting the bag down. "Well, thank you again."

"Of course. Unfortunately, your DNA is littered over the crime scene with the body in the motel. We already know how the police will pin you in their books."

"Great," Lola says. She reflects to the point before she was unconscious. Synarion held her with one arm and exited the motel room. "How did you get us out of there?"

"My little secret," Synarion grins. "One I cannot perform frequently. There's a lot for you to learn about the real world. I must say, you've done a good job at covering your tracks. We need to fix your combat, though. You're helpless."

"I'm working on it," Lola says. "I'm not that terrible. Look." She takes the phone she stole from the plastic bag. "I got this from a Crystal Moth and know where their next big ash sale is."

"Do you?" Synarion asks.

"Yes. I downloaded the call logs, texts, and contacts from the phone."

"Impressive. I outsource that."

"Well, I know a few things." *Ash helps*, Lola thinks. The drug enhancing her mind is a minor detail Synarion doesn't need to know. Criticism would follow. The ash is also why she got her ass handed to her by the assassin. She says, "I had my guard lowered at the motel, unlike how I got this phone."

"Alright, no need to be defensive," Synarion says.

"The phone logs mentioned an art show in over a week. The Prime Minister is going to be there."

"With the Crystal Moths?" Synarion asks.

"Yes."

"It's what I feared."

Lola looks at her bandaged torso. "And with this, I . . ." Lola isn't good at asking for help anymore, not after the years she has had. She isn't sure how to continue.

"You need help?" Synarion asks.

"Yes. Except I don't trust you," Lola says.

"Understandable."

"If you claim you want to help me, and I thank you, really, why are you so evasive?" Lola asks.

"I don't follow?" Synarion says.

"Okay. You said I needed allies. You're right. I know I can't do it all. You come and go as you please, share bits of batty information, and, and, I'm afraid." *Damn ash,* Lola thinks. Post-ash Lola is vulnerable, like when she called Donnie for no good reason.

Synarion says, "I have to protect my own interests too. It's why I can't share everything until you're willing to trust me."

Lola swallows a lump of saliva, pushing her ego down. Whether she likes it or not, she's in no shape to persist on her own. She needs to adapt her plan or die.

She says, "Listen, I want to work with you. Please. I need your help."

Synarion smiles. "That's splendid to hear. Quite frankly, it can get lonesome on my own. I mean, there are a few others. They're not as concerned about the Moths as I am."

"Others?" Lola asks.

"My," Synarion says, "we sure have a lot of work to do with you."

"Okay, where do we start? I can't move much."

Synarion leans back, pondering the question. "Now, that is a compelling question indeed."

Lola leans forward, grunting. Her stomach must be bruised badly. She's too interested in this strange man not to get closer. "How about you start by telling me who you are, what you are, and what any of this has to do with you?"

"An excellent beginning," Synarion says.

Bingo. Lola is getting somewhere. She has an ally, no longer alone in the underbelly of the world. Her mysterious saviour will unravel his cloak of vagueness.

CHAPTER 19
OLD WORLD ORDER

There's safety in conformity, protecting individuals in the machine of group thinking, and strengthening the instrument's voice. Lola is willing to leap from the machine's protection for an individual right. Go beyond the societal apparatus, and you tumble into a world of monsters and evil. Freaks, crime, and every form of horror you can imagine live in the shadow of the civilized automaton.

"I'm not like your kind," Synarion says, returning from the kitchen. He holds a tray containing a black pot of tea with two complimentary square cups. "It'll help ease your pain. These herbs are miracle makers."

"Thanks," Lola says while taking a cup. It's far too hot on her fingers.

Synarion places the tray on the bed and hops on. He sits cross-legged beside her. It's the first time she's gotten a whiff of his pine scent. The smell is soothing. It's like she's in a ravine. The man is a walking forest filled with a sharp sting, sap, and bark tingling her nostrils. She wants to get a good noseful of him. Right now is not the time to embrace. His calm manner eases the tension in her muscles. Being near a body is a blessing. Anyone she's been close to is due to violence. Donnie was the last person she was this close to since that fateful submit button.

"You were saying?" Lola runs her fingers through her hair, pushing her basic needs aside.

"I'm not of your people," Synarion says, sipping his tea, unaffected by the heat.

"No shit," Lola says. "I gathered that from the photographs."

"And yet you don't believe me."

"I didn't, sort of. I mean, I saw a thing. More so heard something in Toronto. It brought me here to Vancouver to find the Crystal Moths." Lola sips her tea, letting the heated earthy maple flavour run along her tongue. She thought it would taste like dirt.

"And what is that?" Synarion asks.

"I interrogated a Crystal Moth in Toronto because he and two others were led into the sewers. I heard hissing. It was an animal growling in pain. The Crystal Moth saw it. When I had him tied up, I could see it in his eyes and hear it in his voice. He was scared. I got it on the recording. It's in the cryptographic tattoo when you scan it."

"I didn't have time to examine the files."

"I'll show you. It's why I believe you, sort of. I heard that muffled voice in the sewers speak clear English."

"Of course," Synarion says. "So you fear the truth."

"No," Lola says. "It's such a far-out theory. If you've spent any time on the Internet, you'd know this kind of stuff is never perceived well."

"I've had my share of the information highway."

"Then you know how obscure this sounds? I mean, after two years of this hell, running from the RCMP and gangs, I thought I'd seen it all. Obviously not."

Synarion pats her knee. "We will change that."

Lola jerks from the movement. "Thanks. Those photos of you, they're so old. I want to know they're fake."

"They're not."

"Right."

Synarion reaches into his pants and pulls out a golden ring. He takes the jewelry in his hand, showcasing its carved vampiric fangs containing a deep red amulet. The craftsmanship is impressive. Intricate vines are around the band.

"How's this for some evidence?" he says.

Lola raises an eyebrow.

Synarion puts the ring on his single index finger and forms a fist. He closes his eyes. A couple of seconds go by, and nothing happens. Time tick . . . tocks. After several heartbeats, the ring vanishes before their eyes.

Lola double blinks, wondering if she missed a part of the trick. No, her gaze is indeed on his hand.

Next, Synarion's finger fades to his knuckle. There's no bone, blood, or flesh in place of the stump. The space is blurry. It's as if Lola's view is smudged. He releases his fist and exhales heavily, with sweat building on his forehead. The finger and ring appear from the cloudy space.

"A magic trick?" Lola says. She won't admit the disappearing finger is remarkable because she needs to grill him for her sanity.

Synarion says, "How do you think I got you out of the motel?" He takes the ring off and spins it around his fingers. "Invisibility takes a lot of energy from me and time to recharge. It wipes me and anyone I hold from smell, sight, and heat."

"Let me see it," Lola says, opening her hand.

"This never leaves me."

"Let me guess, a special artifact from the old world?" Lola asks.

"No. It's from someone dear to me," Synarion says.

Lola shakes her head. "Who are you?"

"That is where we left off, isn't it? Well, I'm not human. You could tell by the slight differentiations between my kind and yours."

"No. I can't. The eyes are strange," Lola says.

"My ears too. Finer details like the bones, muscles, and skin also hold truth. My people are an ancient race, and I fear I am the last."

"Which are?"

"Nymphs."

"Okay." The conformity machine wasn't so bad.

Synarion continues. "There used to be hundreds of thousands of us. There were others too. Many other races were found on the lost continent in the old world."

"Pause for a moment, lost continent? Old world and other races?" *Christ,* Lola thinks. She barked up the wrong tree. Then again, the recording leans into the madness. She is stuck here healing and should hear him out.

A mischievous grin spreads onto Synarion's face, showing his symmetrical white teeth. He says, "I told you there's a lot to unbox."

"Fine," Lola says. "Let's start with you."

Synarion says, "Wonderful. I forget how young you humans are and how limited your lifespan is. Stick around for even a few centuries, and you glaze over details that mean nothing to me and a world of difference to you. We'll get your toes wet first. It will keep us focused. Eventually, we need to find the ash growery. If what you say is true regarding Toronto, then they are making the drug here. My suspicions are proving true."

"Which are?"

"One thing at a time, right? Nymphs. These are my people. I am the last to the best of my knowledge. I've searched as far and wide as I can. I even used your information highway to a private port where we old world beings communicate." Synarion shrugs. "Even then, no luck. I am the last. Nymphs are similar to you humans. However, look closer, and the details will bloom. We're stronger. We can hear better, see better, and age far slower. The ears and eyes are the most blatant." He taps on his ears. "I had to do that on my own to blend in with your kind. As our numbers dwindled and the old world dissolved, humankind was on an all-time rise. Paranoia grew and they killed others and burned the evidence of the past. They even eradicate their greatest collection of information prior to the Internet to bury the real history. I bet you can guess where."

"I am not in a speculating mood," Lola says.

"The Library of Alexandria was the last true archive of history. Records after have been a lie. Religions and history books were rewritten. They adjusted timelines, names, locations, everything to put reality into the realm of mythology."

"Let me get this right, this old world vanished when the Library of Alexandria burned?"

"The last of its knowledge. The collapse of the lost content happened hundreds of years before. It was a gradual extinction. For me to survive in this world of man, I had to be less conspicuous. The eyes were challenging before you people made those clever contact lenses. My ears, my poor ears, I had to cut most of them off. They were beautiful, believe me. Long and pointy, bouncing like a rabbit. I do miss them."

"Sorry," Lola says. She's unsure what other words would be applicable.

"Don't be. I've mourned over them plenty of times. People presume I'm a Swedish basement dweller with a case of cauliflower ears. Nymphs don't absorb the sun like your kind. Then the rest is history. I've lived under many names and locations, and here I am, living amongst your people now."

Lola plays along. "Okay, so you're an ancient person. How old are you?"

Synarion pats his knees, eyeing the ceiling. "Well, that is something I haven't thought of in a long time. Living so many lives and watching friends come and go in the passage of time makes it easy to forget when you were born and where you belong. I digress. I believe I'm in the realm of twenty-four hundred."

Lola takes another sip of tea, processing what he said. "Two thousand and four hundred years old?"

"That is correct. Memory has a strange way of dissolving over the centuries. No matter how much you train the muscle, the brain can't retain all facts. Ever notice how memories of your childhood dissolve or mutate into a half-baked version when you're an adult?"

"Gotcha," Lola says.

"I should have kept a personal journal covering what I've experienced. Yet, I have been too busy keeping up with your people's amazing inventions. Electricity? Astonishing. Then we get to computing, you and I have a kink for those. I enjoy electronics and have delved deep into the technological era of your people. Perhaps that's why my memories are foggy as of late."

Lola ponders the age. It's tough to grasp. Synarion could be a loony, as her first instincts concluded. Lola would default to that conclusion if she didn't hear what she heard in the sewers. The photos are also convincing in retrospect.

Two thousand and a half years, Lola thinks. She has dozens of questions to ask him. Indeed, knowing what the different time periods were like would be high on the list. Synarion could have met historical figures. This lost continent is of interest too. As he says, it's a lot to unbox.

Lola says, "Now you hang out in a battered old apartment? With your worldly background, I'd think you would have old money, living life to its fullest."

"I'm not like some of the other old world beings. They have 'old money,' and I resent their embracive nature. They have an exploitative advantage over humans and insult their own people's origins. These beings have wormed their way into the roots of your people's society, and quite frankly, it is a disruption of nature."

"What do you mean?" Lola asks.

Synarion says, "This makes an easy transition, doesn't it? Many others survived the final death of the old world at around fifty BC. We've endured the crusades of man by blending in with civilization. Those that have physical traits too different from humans went underground or to the mountains or the forests. Those unfortunate souls have had to change their entire life."

"Like these intelligent reptilians?" Lola asks.

"Precisely. Those that can live with humans have taken thrones of power, manipulating the global market and political agendas to their will. One group you're familiar with."

"Crystal Moths. They've been doing this ever since?"

"Essentially, yes." Synarion takes a drink from his cup.

"This sounds like some heavy conspiracy shit. Next, you're going to tell me the Earth is hollow."

Synarion lets out a hearty chuckle.

"Seriously?"

"No, no, not at all! There is an underworld. Impossible to get to now. It played a role in humans believing the Earth is hollow. Most conspiracies and myths stem from a seed of truth. Humans have a funny way of throwing in a dash of fantastical elements into their beliefs."

"And the world is run by ancient old world beings. Great. And what? They're satanic baby eaters too?"

"That's ridiculous. Not all elites are old world beings. Some are of your kind, allied with them. Then there's countries and economic gains, splitting the Earth."

"Including the Crystal Moths?" Lola asks.

Synarion nods. "There's no single government."

"And you're so humble that you don't see a point in joining your old world buddies?"

"Funny girl. I have an oath I swore centuries ago. You see, the nymphs were much like your people: divided. Unity is the most difficult thing for living things. My people, or a group of them, were ancient protectors."

"Which means?" Lola asks, taking a sip of tea.

"We kept the balance of nature. Not too often did we interfere with the affairs of Mother Nature. Our people watched closely, observing how the world took shape. Unfortunately, we didn't foresee the tragic events that eradicated the old world, leaving humanity as the last. I hold my oath, keeping balance in the world."

"Like some superhero who deems what is right and wrong?"

Synarion says, "I'm not that arrogant. I look for equilibrium in nature which is a cluttered mess of grey. The concepts of right and wrong are philosophical ideas that were created for survival purposes. It binds us to nature and helps us understand where we need to go as an ecosystem. Humans morphed from small groups into empires of war, with mass production damaging Mother Nature's Earth. I am one balancer."

Lola asks, "How do you decide when to interfere then?"

"I interfere when I am needed and am able. Mother Nature is a willful beast. She thinks long-term. Not in fifty years, a hundred, or even a thousand. She has good means of keeping balance on her own. Every once in a while, she needs a little push. This is where I come in."

"And the Crystal Moths are disrupting the balance of nature?"

Synarion nods. "Yes. The Crystal Moths and their supplier of ash."

"Intelligent reptilians?" Lola asks.

"Intelligent reptilian is a derogatory term, isn't it? It's not wrong and not accurate. It is like calling you an intelligent mammal. Vazeleads is their proper name."

"Vaze-leads?" Lola raises her eyebrow. "That's what their people are called?"

"Yes. It's from an ancient language meaning Drac-men."

"Okay. So in Toronto, what I heard was a vazelead. The Crystal Moths have one?"

"Yes, or all of them. Whether the moths captured them for their own benefit or the vazeleads provided ash is yet to be determined. This is what we need to find out."

"That reptilian I heard wasn't working with them willingly."

"Vazelead." Synarion takes a drink.

"Right," Lola says. "And why interfere with this? If the old world is gone, why do you care for some vazelead?"

"If I can rescue this one vazelead, I'm hoping they will provide some answers. I can then save the others or reason with their leader. You see, the few vazeleads that survived the old world are closed off. They are a bitter people with justified hate towards humanity. The Crystal Moths shouldn't be re-introducing them into the new world of man. They already had one war. They don't need a second. That's one problem."

"The other?" Lola asks.

"The Crystal Moths know the dangers they're dabbling in. In that case, they are scheming a sinister plan."

"Care to share?"

"I have a few hunches, nothing concrete. Either way, I don't think it's good for humanity."

"In short, you want to bust the Crystal Moths' ash growery? I'm in."

"Patience, Lola. Did you forget you were beaten and stabbed a day ago? You are in no situation to go guns blazing into a rescue mission."

Lola finishes her tea, shifting herself to lean against the concrete wall. "And you aren't able to stop the Moths yourself?"

"I'm afraid not," Synarion says.

"Come on, even with your throwing stars and your mysterious stealth ability to appear whenever you want?"

"Amusing, and I suppose I could. It would get messy." Synarion raises his four-fingered hand. "Things don't always go as planned."

Lola is tempted to ask him about the finger. She decides to leave it. There's already enough information to absorb.

Synarion continues. "Chances are the Crystal Moths will know who did it too. I can't fight an army of them. An ally with deep knowledge of this organized crime will do me good. Plus,

I must admit you are an interesting specimen, Lola."

Lola smiles. "I'm an interesting specimen? Like some experiment?"

"Not exactly. Forgive my words. After living for centuries, your people are a blip of existence in my eyes. It's like watching ants. They're alive one day and gone the next."

"Great, I'm an interesting insect in your farmhouse called Earth."

"Don't take such offence, Lola," Synarion says. "Humanity is far more able than a bug."

Lola doesn't respond, despite wishing to bite back. It's not worth her energy. Synarion's age, if it's true, has desensitized him to other points of view. Lola knows she has value because she's given herself that power. Before this, she brought love to her family and friends. She gave people unfiltered news on her website. In her new life, she'll do the same with more truth and a harsh hand of justice that was not delivered by the law.

Lola asks, "Why don't you call an old world friend to help you?"

Synarion says, "As I said, many of them have embraced their advantages, exploiting them. Many have lost hope. Others run for the hills. It's tough to find people you can trust."

"And you will trust me? Didn't humans eradicate your kind?"

"Those were people of another time. I cannot blame modern man for the faults of their fathers. There is good in humanity, like there is in all races." Synarion chuckles. "Good. such a funny concept. Anyways, yes, I saw your initial publication with the video and article. I paid attention to the news to see where you would go. From there, your case became more fascinating.

Your face is on the news while you maintain your online publications. I see you are unravelling something grand."

"Yeah, the Crystal Moths. I want to get these bastards for what they have done to me and what they have done to everyone I care for."

"Vengeance can be a powerful motivator. It can also blind you," Synarion says.

"Thanks for the dash of wisdom," Lola says.

"That is one thing I have a lot of." Synarion claps his hands together. "There's my elaborate backstory. Do you feel more aligned? Do the pieces of the grand narrative of the world fit together now? Are you fulfilled?"

Lola can't help but smile at Synarion's strange mannerisms. It must be a side-effect of living for so long. She has to admit she has plenty of questions. Vazeleads, nymphs, the Library of Alexandria, and what happened to it all.

He paints a fantastic story. In actuality, she is recovering from a stab wound from a man who attacked her. She is rational and has her doubts.

"Satisfied for now," Lola says.

Synarion hops off the bed and takes Lola's cup along with the tray. "Excellent, because you need to heal. We need to rescue ourselves a vazelead."

"Look, I want to work with you," Lola says.

"Great," Synarion says.

"You've followed my case."

"Yes," Synarion says.

"Then you know why I'm after the Crystal Moths."

"That I do," Synarion says.

"Then you understand that I document what we see. That includes this vazelead and you. People have to know."

Synarion's face lowers into a frown. "Yes, I understand revenge for your family is the goal. You want to clear your name. Sharing videos and photos of me or the vazeleads isn't going to do that. It will raise anger."

"And what will then?" Lola asks.

"Dismantling the Crystal Moths," Synarion says.

"I know that. If I can get enough information on their operations, higher-ups, and where they are, I can give it to the genuine police. Then I can do right for the terrible things that have happened."

"You're hotheaded, Lola. It makes you naive. Don't upload anything we do."

He's right. Lola is eager for revenge. Even in today's world, a recording of the vazelead wouldn't be enough for people to buy the truth. The world of CGI effects, motion capture, deep fake face-swap technology, and the notorious godless immorality of the Internet means the videos won't go anywhere without physical evidence cross-checked by other sources. She has to keep her head on straight. Lola can't crash too soon because she acts on her first impulse. She has to be cunning and strategize her moves, like she did with the failsafe cryptographic tattoo. Or how she followed those Crystal Moths from New Brunswick to the Toronto sewers. She must be patient.

Lola says, "If we're going to work together, I'm recording everything. In case anything goes south, my work will be published."

"Alright," Synarion says, his tone stern. "Let me be a

curator."

Her heart pulses pain from her injuries. The tea is good, yet not enough to stop the misery.

Synarion speaks. "Now, get some rest. We do have a lot of work to do."

He heads for the kitchen, and Lola lies down, absorbing the knowledge Synarion shared. Old world, lost continent, and ancient beings, it's such lunacy. At least she's not alone. She has a supporter despite their end goals differing. There will be tension, and Lola must protect her interests.

The rabbit hole keeps going and going underneath the machine of conformity. What would her mother think? Would she tell her to turn back before it's too late?

CHAPTER 20
FROM THE SOURCE

Every officer: interviewed. Every security camera: double-checked. Every detail of the station: swiped for fingerprints. The list goes on because people don't walk out of jail. It's even less common if they're a high-profile witness to a case.

Iglesias is dismayed as to how Chen escaped. He talked to the officer, Miguel, who led Chen to his cell before he left for the night. Iglesias knows the guy, and his statement is accurate because Iglesias was there. There is no motive for him to free Chen either. For Christ's sake, the man has a wife and kids. He's not a crooked cop that was paid off.

Iglesias grips his armchair tightly, sitting in the interrogation room, the single fluorescent light beaming on him. There's humour in this scene. He's sitting on the opposite side of the table and being questioned by the police, which Iglesias did to Chen less than twelve hours ago.

"To confirm, it was you, Archer, and Beckman who were with the suspect last night?" asks the internal investigations officer. She's writing additional notes on a pen and paper with a grip as tight as her hair held in a bun.

Iglesias knows what they're doing. They're taking notes of his posture, stress, mannerisms, and how he replies to the questions. The flashing red dot of the recording camera also provides a closer analysis of him.

He says, "That's correct. The two of them went home, and it was myself and Chen."

"And you kept the security camera recording while it was you and Chen?" the officer asks.

Iglesias nods. "That's correct. Otherwise, I'd have to talk to security to disable them."

"And you didn't go into the security room?" she asks.

"No, I did not."

"And what time did you go home?"

"Passed two AM in the morning."

"Can anyone confirm this?"

José, Iglesias thinks. He squeezes the armchair, knowing his son can confirm his statement. José also had an underage drinking party. That opens a can of worms he doesn't want to get into, considering Iglesias let it slide. It's not a good example for a father or officer. His cards are played.

"I can. My son happened to be awake when I got home." It's

not the whole truth and not a lie.

"Okay, perfect. Can we get in touch with them?" she asks.

"Of course, his number should be on my file."

"And you're certain that you left the security cameras on?"

"Yes, why?" Iglesias asks.

"Because there's a gap in the time stamp as soon as Archer and Beckman left you alone with Chen."

Iglesias feels his back turn ice cold. "Excuse me?" he asks.

"The security footage clips before you step into the room with Chen and after you say you left the office."

"Only this camera? Or each of them? The parking lot?" Iglesias asks.

"All of them."

Iglesias wipes his face. "What did the night shift say? They saw me leave alone."

"Yes, we will be interviewing everyone. We're not pegging you, as there's no evidence leading us that way, if that's what you're thinking."

"Of course. That's not my concern. I think we share the same worries."

"Yes, and we will be interviewing each officer twice."

"Fair enough. If there's anything I can do, let me know."

"We will. Thank you, Detective Iglesias. You may go." She opens the clipboard of her binder and changes to a new page, preparing for her following interview.

Iglesias exits the room, heading through the hall, passing the line of officers to be interviewed.

I can't believe this, Iglesias thinks.

"Iglesias!" comes a strident voice belonging to Sergeant

Bando. The man waves his index finger, summoning him. He is standing by the door frame to his office, holding a cup of coffee.

Iglesias strides over, and the two enter Bando's office.

"Yes, Serg?" Iglesias asks. Neither of the men sit.

Bando says, "Your ash case just blew the roof off Major Crimes."

"Yeah, I can see that."

"You have to get this under control," Bando says.

"I know. We're working on it," Iglesias says. He puts his hands on his hips.

"The CFMP will get involved if we don't get some answers soon."

"Yes, I know," Iglesias says. "The Crystal Moths are proving far bigger and more complex than we thought."

"The Department of National Defence is starting to ask me questions."

"I figured. The Moths are international, as we've learned."

"Thus, the military will take over." A pause. "I don't want that. You don't want that."

"Our whole department doesn't," Iglesias says.

"Look, you and your team are good, but your resources are limited."

"Tell me about it. It took weeks to get more DNA info on the ash scale."

"Any idea where it comes from?" Bando asks.

"Not yet."

"Proving my point. I can keep the CFMP and the DND at bay for now. You have to give results, though."

"I understand," Iglesias says.

"An escaped criminal right in our office doesn't look good. The news will be on it before we know it."

"Yeah."

"If we need the extra manpower, tell me, Iglesias," Bando says.

"Manpower as in the military?"

"It's our next shot. I can't get you any more budget. That's a whole political mess on a federal level bending to social demands."

"Yep," Iglesias says. He's lost interest and means no disrespect to his sergeant, this conversation is pointless.

"Get on it," Bando says. He sits at his desk, turning his focus onto his computer.

Iglesias storms out of the office, losing his cool. He exits the department, goes to the elevator, and heads outside for a smoke. He didn't think it would be possible within his own department. He has heard plenty of stories of Crystal Moth accomplices within the law. Not to mention Sergeant Bando is breathing down his neck.

He can deal with Bando. They've worked together long enough. Regarding Chen, the security footage was manipulated to hide who freed him. Internal investigations are at a dead end with film. They need forensics to process the fingerprints, if that will even provide any clues.

Whoever did this is a professional. Iglesias has been in this for long enough to know the amateurs from the real deal. The Crystal Moths aren't reckless enough to break into the RCMP station and free their fellow gangster. Chen had value. Now Iglesias is the one knowing his statement. Internal affairs will want to know eventually.

Iglesias lights a smoke and sucks on the dart repeatedly. It's troublesome. Iglesias can't stop thinking that one of their own is working for the Crystal Moths. He cannot trust anyone, for they are all suspects.

They are going to hear about this for weeks. It's an embarrassment to lose a key witness, which will tighten security throughout the station. He can't let it ruin his case. There won't be any goddamn military. Iglesias must focus on finding Lola and the Crystal Moths' ash distribution. These pricks are a daunting foe. Any evidence of their progression must be kept close to prevent the plug from squealing to the gang. Iglesias can trust a few officers.

Beckman exits the station and lights a smoke, looking as terrible as Iglesias. No sleep and stress take years off your life. Stack that with betrayal and fear, and you'll be springing grays. They don't know how deep the Crystal Moths go into the law, let alone their own hierarchy. The gang is a master puppeteer.

"So," Beckman says while puffing on the drag.

"So?" Iglesias asks.

"I know what you're thinking," Beckman says. "Same here." Both officers suffer from paranoia.

"Yeah," Iglesias says. "We're not the only ones either."

"No," Beckman says. "Tension is going to divide us. This isn't good."

"No shit," Iglesias says. *Do I tell him?* he thinks.

The two finish their cancer sticks and head to the station. The entire office is tainted with an infestation of moths. It makes Iglesias want to squirm. They have to press on; it's their job in

RCMP Major Crimes. Professionals push their emotions aside for the greater good.

The two detectives step into Iglesias's office and close the door. Now is as good as any time to share Chen's tale. He's uncertain how much to tell. It sounds loopy. Then again, these are Chen's words, not Iglesias's.

"They got my statement, hey?" Iglesias says.

"Yeah, they got mine already," Beckman says. "What do we do about this?"

"We keep on the case and let internal affairs figure this out. I have nothing else to give them."

"Sergeant Bando talk with you?"

"Yep."

"What happened last night?" Beckman asks.

Might as well, Iglesias says. For all he knows, Beckman set Chen free. It is doubtful, considering his wife could verify his story about being home. Beckman is Iglesias's partner. If anyone understands crazy talk from criminals, it's him.

Iglesias says, "I stayed longer than you and Archer. I couldn't let that asshole get the better of us. I knew he was hiding information." Iglesias proceeds to tell his partner about the discussion Chen and he had the night before. Chen not wanting to go to a nut house, the potential of making a deal, and the obscure situation of how Lola Cabello targeted Chen. Toronto, the sewers, the underground chamber, and the ash growery. He excludes the reptilians part for now. Even saying this much makes Iglesias feel like a crackpot. Unstable people talk about secret underground bases.

"Huh. That's quite the story," Beckman says.

"It is," Iglesias says.

"And then you passed him to Miguel?" Beckman asks.

"Correct," Iglesias says.

"You believe Chen?"

"I believe he thinks that's what he saw. It was genuine. I know I got through to him. I think he would have worked with us."

"So Chen didn't know he would escape?"

"I don't think so," Iglesias folds his arms. "You saw him last night. You tell me if that was the face and voice of the next Houdini. The guy is a loser who stumbled into an event bigger than him. Crossfire damage. He's valuable now. I don't think that is what he wants from life. He's a family man."

Beckman shrugs. "Yeah, the guy ain't too swift, eh? It's clear that he is a street dealer. He had to have had help to get out of here."

"Unless he didn't go willingly."

"Captured? Why last night? He's been passed around the police since he was found tied up in that warehouse."

"I know," Iglesias says, putting his feet on his desk.

The two sit in silence, pondering the situation. None of it adds up. Being betrayed by your own kind is a new feeling of violation. God knows how long the Moths have been infiltrating the operations. It explains why the law can't dismantle them.

For the time being, Iglesias and Beckman have no leads to work with. The internal affairs team will sniff through the computers then document and interview the team. Twice.

Beckman kills the silence. "I talked with forensics again about the ash scale. That technical gibberish with squamata and lacertilia reptile orders makes up a large portion of this scale."

"So there's a chunk that's unknown, then?" Iglesias asks.

"Like ninety-six percent is known DNA. The rest is unknown. This is a new beast."

"Kind of like we're ninety-nine percent ape. Interesting."

"Humans are fifty percent banana. Most things share the same DNA."

"What of the coca plant? And the DMT?"

"Lucky we got that full ash scale. They determined the plant traces are part of the molecular structure. The scale isn't laced. The speed-like effects of cocaine are natural to the drug. The same goes with the bufotenin giving a psychedelic feeling. The lab dug deeper and found a chemical compound similar to diamorphine."

"Heroin."

"Like heroin," Beckman says.

"Fentanyl?"

"That's synthetic. This variant is organic, stemming right from the scales. Like the other components."

"Okay, so let me get this right. The scale has the speed of cocaine, the hallucinatory of DMT, and the high of heroin."

"And more."

"Great," Iglesias says.

"They said this scale is complicated with many layers. The lab is taking their time peeling away each component."

"Any idea what the four percent is?"

"They don't know," Beckman says. "It's above Forensics's pay grade. They're passing it on to a couple different labs. One specializing in zoology and the other in substance analysis."

"How long will that take?" Iglesias asks.

"They didn't say," Beckman says.

Footsteps come from down the hall, and Archer knocks on the door. Iglesias waves her in. She enters and folds her arms, standing by the second chair.

"Fuck, this is fucked," she says.

"And?" Beckman asks.

"I'm clear. The bar confirmed me being there," Archer says.

"What do you think of the whole thing?" Beckman asks.

"It's fucked," Archer repeats in an exhausted laugh.

"It makes me want to act," Iglesias says. "I can't sit here and watch."

Archer says, "We can keep drilling on Cabello's location. I think we have good information on her after that call with Donnie Morris."

Iglesias says, "Yeah. We have to revisit Morris."

"We could take a flight," Beckman says.

"That's possible. I'm thinking more local, like that sewers chamber."

"Chen was blindfolded, right?" Beckman says. "We'd be trying to find that location for days, if not weeks. Have you seen the schematics of the city sewer system?"

Iglesias says, "I know."

"Sewers?" Archer asks.

"Long story," Iglesias says. "I don't want to stick around this office. I'd rather be on the street than sitting in here and watching the internals sniff through our office. This place is tainted."

Beckman says, "I feel you. I need to get the hell out of here too."

Archer says, "I've got some work to do. Follow up on a new lead."

"Oh?" Iglesias asks.

"There's a murder in Vancouver, in a motel. A guy named Ramon Blackwell was found dead with a gunshot wound to his leg and a stabbing in the back of his head. Based on what he wore, he is a Crystal Moth."

"They're dying all the time," Beckman says. "Gang violence and initiation processes. What's special about this?"

"We think someone was wanting to kill him in his unit. A girl that matches Cabello's description was there. I'll update you when I have more."

Iglesias says, "Perfect. We're out."

Beckman asks, "Where to?"

"A small drive over to Toronto."

"Thinking the intel?" Beckman asks. "I thought he's been vacant."

"He has. That bastard has been avoiding my texts and calls since the summer."

Archer says, "Doesn't he contact you?"

"I don't care," Iglesias says.

"He'll be pissed. That's not the agreement you two have," Beckman says.

"We have a plug in the station, the ash scale is of unknown origins, and somehow Tycho Fulcher knew about the first use in Canada. We're going to pay a visit."

Archer says, "Don't anger him. He's valuable."

"Yes, boss," Iglesias says.

Archer smiles at the sarcasm. "We also don't need any

attention from the news."

Iglesias says, "Think I'm an amateur?"

Archer shakes her head, leaving them to their business. Iglesias needs to keep focused on a task, and getting the intel to talk is an excellent first step. With that, the two detectives exit the station and hit the road. They take Iglesias's SUV and head onto the highway for their long road trip. They leave at noon, driving for four hours to get to the core of Toronto from Ottawa.

Iglesias has been to his intel's place a handful of times, respecting their mutual agreement of communicating when *he* gets in contact with Iglesias. This time, it's different. Fulcher has been silent, dodging Iglesias's calls, and Iglesias wants answers now.

They drive into an old, worn-down neighbourhood, parking the SUV on the crooked pothole-filled road. The wartime-era houses have chipped fences and overgrown plants in the yards, with plenty of broken stucco and collapsing decks. Grass and weeds sprout from the cracks of the pavement.

"Let's make this quick," Iglesias says. "He doesn't need any attention from the community."

Beckman says, "You got it."

The two detectives exit the SUV and head to the front door of the Fulcher's home. Iglesias knocks on the pastel redwood with a heavy hand. Beckman checks the windows. They're covered by knitted curtains. Several moments go by, and Iglesias knocks again. His patience is wearing thin.

Rattling comes from inside as bolts and shackles move, and the door opens a sliver with a gold chain holding it to the frame.

Through the crack, the room contains a couch, TV stand, and a brown rug in between while the hall leads to the kitchen further back.

"Not supposed to be here," comes a deep voice behind the door.

"Fulcher, you need to talk," Iglesias says.

"Nah, man. I'm good." Fulcher says.

"This ash thing is getting wild. You introduced it to us from that bust in the summer in New Brunswick. You need to talk now."

"Man, get off my property. People have eyes on me non stop."

"Open the door, and we'll be out of sight," Iglesias says.

"Showing you was a mistake." Fulcher goes to close the door as Beckman places a firm hand on it. Iglesias takes one look around. The coast is clear and he slams his shoulder into the wood, breaking the flimsy chain holding it to the frame. The force is enough to knock Fulcher back, and he stumbles slightly, almost falling on his ass. The two officers step inside, closing the door behind them.

Beckman says, "Was that so difficult?"

Fulcher scowls. "What is wrong with you? I said I didn't want to talk. I thought we had an agreement."

Iglesias says, "Things have changed." He adjusts his blazer and extends his hand to the couch. "Why don't you take a seat and start telling me why you've been avoiding me for months."

"I told you too much." Fulcher folds his arms. "I should've never told you about ash. Aw shit, you would have figured it out anyways."

"You dangled the carrot in front of us," Beckman says. "Now we need you to talk."

"I told you what I know about ash," Fulcher says.

"Bullshit," Iglesias says. "I've let you slide many times in the past, Fulcher. You can keep your pathetic drug ops going here, but you have to give us the info."

Fulcher shakes his head. "I can't tell you any more. The Moths are too dangerous, man."

"You work with them now?" Beckman asks.

"I don't. I don't work with anyone other than myself."

"That's why you take some of their goods and distribute them?" Iglesias asks.

"It's the street dealers. That's who I talk to. They gimme the goods and shit rolls downhill from the distribution line. That's it. You know they'll kill me if I talk."

"We know a bit of that," Iglesias says. "They're in the office. They took one of our suspects right from under us."

Fulcher begins to squeeze his arms, rocking back and forth. His voice trembles as he says, "F-u-u-ck man, it's already started."

"What started?" Beckman asks.

"Nah, no, no. The Moths guide us all, man. They've been working towards this for a long, *long* time. The distribution chains, not only the drugs, the red, the legal, all of them!"

"Meaning?" Iglesias asks.

"The Moths are bringing us to the light. The days are coming to an end. There are signs in the sun and the moon and stars, and on the earth dismay among nations in perplexity at the roaring of the sea and the waves!"

Beckman extends his hand. "Okay, take a deep breath."

Fulcher continues, breathing rapidly, "Man fainting from the fear in the expectations of the things which are coming upon the world; for the powers of the heavens will be shaken. Then they will see."

Iglesias and Beckman exchanged looks. *A Bible quote*, Iglesias thinks. A Catholic upbringing came in handy.

Fulcher continues, "They're looking to make people useful in civilization again, man. Shit. They are the light that lets the little Moths fly. They're rising from the shadows. Naw, they don't mess around. Don't let me talk any more, please."

Beckman asks, "You high?"

Fulcher begins to snicker. "Am I high? What kind of professional do you think I am? I've got work to do and can't get high off my own supply. The shit's real. The Moths are a force to reckon with."

Iglesias says, "If it's already started, then it's too late. Spit it out. We can stop them. It's why you work with us anyways."

Fulcher nods. "They've changed the whole game. They've been around for so long, dormant."

"A part of you believes we are the good guys," Iglesias says. It's a stretch, but he's lacking negotiating options.

Fulcher sits on the couch, resting his head on his palms. "I first heard of ash from some of the guys I used to party with out west in Prince George in British Columbia. It was no Crystal Moth street dealer who told me."

"Who told you?" Beckman asks.

"An old party friend. Prince George isn't that far from Vancouver. It's also a hub for drugs. The West Coast is great to distribute with the ports."

Iglesias asks, "Can you tell us their name?"

"Hell nah. He dead," Fulcher says.

"Name?" Iglesias asks.

"Chris Lance. OD'd a month ago," Fulcher says.

"From ash?" Iglesias asks.

"No clue," Fulcher says.

"Family?" Beckman asks.

"No clue, man."

Iglesias says, "Did Chris say how he heard about it?"

Fulcher says, "Look, I didn't even know ash was the Moths' at first. Chris said something new and big was brought into the country. That den in New Brunswick is famous for experimenting, and they got their hands on it first."

Iglesias says, "From where?"

"Dunno, man. It's imported from overseas. That's what Chris said. Moving goods to the other side is a good way to keep you distracted."

Iglesias says, "You knew this and didn't tell me?"

"No, I pieced this together. Chris knew a new drug coming from the west, and then word of the den came out. I had a hunch but tell you the good stuff, you know?"

Beckman asks, "Back up a moment, Mr. Sober. What do you mean by the end of days?"

Fulcher lets out a chuckle. "I stay clear of the Moths, man. This has been going on longer than we've been alive." Fulcher licks his lips, checking around the house to ensure they are alone, even though they are because the guy had the place locked and all of the curtains closed. "Look, I heard crazy things in Prince George regarding ash. Crazy talk, like talk of reptilians."

Beckman guffaws.

Iglesias remains silent, listening.

Fulcher continues. "Not a metaphor like krokodil from Russia or nothin'. True, crazy, Illuminati shit. Like these reptilians can talk and walk among us." He raises his hands, waving them around, chuckling to himself. "Just crazy shit."

"And you couldn't be bothered to share that with me?" Iglesias asks.

"Want transcripts from every party I go to when I fly home? Get real. Listen, the Moths have always been here. As far as I know and from what folks say, they're far more public than at any other time in history. They want to be seen now. They've got a plan to take down the man."

Beckman and Iglesias exchange looks, unsure what to make of the riddles Fulcher is spilling. Neither one knows what to ask him next, and they can't stay too long, for there are many long noses in the neighbourhood.

Iglesias points at Fulcher and says, "Stop ignoring me when I call you, got it?"

"I call you, remember?" Fulcher says.

"We're changing that. This is serious with ash and the supposed end of days." End of days is a stretch. It'll speak to the man, though.

Fulcher nods. "Yeah, I will. Man, after telling you about the den, I've been on the low for a while. Seeing ash appear on the news and that girl trying to stop them, things are starting, man. I wanna sell goods and be left alone."

Iglesias says, "Right. We'll be in touch."

The two officers leave the house and head to their SUV. Iglesias starts the engine, and they drive clear of the neighbourhood, leaving their intel in his safe little bubble.

Beckman says, "He had to have had some crack before we saw him. Those were some kooky ramblings. End of days and reptilian people?"

Iglesias says, "I'm not too sure."

"And why is that?"

Iglesias grips his wheel tightly. *I have to tell him,* he thinks, reflecting on his last conversation with Chen. The entire recording is missing, meaning that Iglesias and Cabello now are the two that know what Chen saw in that chamber. Reptilian people are off the deep end.

"You ready for an actual crack story?" Iglesias asks.

CHAPTER 21
MORALE

Scalebane complies for the sake of King. She follows Erol and his two vampiric Crystal Moth bodyguards throughout the rest of the Allen Shipping Solutions' dock. The grand tour showcases how Crystal Moths distribute ash, and other drugs, from the seacans on the freight boats. It's as she expected: the ash is disguised before shipment; they arrive from overseas and are sent throughout the country.

The reason Erol is showing her firsthand is to demonstrate how little ash is coming off the boat. There's obvious tension between the two parties. Scalebane can hope that King can increase the production without breeding. His choice won't involve her, nor her sister, despite his pressure to carry on the vazelead people. Maybe King will choose to leave the Moths entirely. She can hope.

Erol takes Scalebane to a small building off the side of the ports near the helicopter pad. It's a humble office with a cheap desk, a grey interior, and fabric chairs. There's a map behind the desk showing pinpoints of where Allen Shipping Solutions takes various supplies.

Erol raises his hands and says, "That is what we do with the goods you provide us."

"And are the employees of Allen Shipping Solutions involved?" Scalebane asks.

"The company is owned by the Crystal Moths. Most of the workers are unaware. What they don't know doesn't hurt them," Erol says.

"The dock workers?"

"They understand certain details and remain quiet for their own safety," Erol says.

"That's a weak point," Scalebane says.

"No process is perfect, my friend, not at this size. Now, I come to this office quite a bit when conducting calls for the Crystal Moths after overseeing the seacans. It's a satellite base with that double life I live. You can use it as your office too."

Scalebane eyes the desk with a computer monitor on it. She says, "I prefer to be more hands-on with my approach. Sitting idle does not appeal to me."

Erol says, "This is a business, regardless of the product. We oversee the operations. Others do the grunt work for us."

"I'm not a businessman, Erol."

"Right, the foreman."

"That's the title we'll work with. I have not embraced this new world, unlike the Crystal Moths." Scalebane pokes the monitor with her claw. It scrapes the plastic encasement, leaving a mark. "This is foreign to me. I've never touched any computer, and I don't know how to operate an automobile."

Erol says, "The world is moving on whether you like it or not, Scalebane." His phone buzzes from his blazer's inner pocket. "One moment, please, sorry."

Scalebane eyes the two vampire Moths. They still have their shades on, standing by the door. Their cheap, tangy cologne is potent in the confined space. It doesn't hide their stolen blood. She can smell the death of countless humans on them.

"What?" Erol says, speaking on the phone. "The news is reporting on it? Local? What of the girl? They have his body?" He wipes his face. "Okay, okay. No worries, run the story. For the safety of the people. If it's a hot topic catching wind nationwide, we should get some ratings too." He hangs up, slipping the phone into his pocket. He presses his hands into fists on the desk.

Scalebane asks, "What was that?"

Erol says, "We'll get to that. Just some minor hiccups with broadcasting. Now, I have a gift that will please you. Consider it a welcome present for us working together."

"What?" Scalebane asks.

"It'll put your hands-on specialty to use." Erol leads Scalebane and the guards out of the office.

The group walks on the wet gravel road to a warehouse further from the other storage facilities. Behind it is the helicopter pad with a second landed chopper. Scalebane didn't think there was enough room for two. She is also amazed at the flying vehicles coming and going under the Crystal Moths' eye. Mastema's pockets run deep.

Scalebane asks, "And what is it?"

Erol slides the warehouse's doors and lets them in. "We flew in a particular individual and his family that we need to set an example of. Your specialty is hands-on, isn't it?"

"You flew them in by helicopter? Isn't that costly?"

"Money is not an object, Scalebane. You should know this by now."

The vampire Moths slide the door shut, and the four move deeper into the dark warehouse, where several lamplights shine dead center on a kneeling man with black tattoos on his bare arms. His pencil-thin mustache sits above the red-stained rag in his mouth. He, a woman, and a small girl are tied with blindfolds and ropes around the ankles and wrists. Their skin is red and raw from the tightness of the constraints.

There are two more Crystal Moth goons beside them, with a woman wearing a full white suit. She stands in the middle of her two accomplices.

"Well done, Kye Pung," Erol says, stepping into the light.

Kye Pung says, "We got him as soon as you gave the order, sir."

"What is this?" Scalebane asks for the second time now.

"Remove the blindfold and let them speak," Erol orders.

Three of the four Crystal Moths grab the captives and remove their blindfolds. Watery, red eyes struck with fear look at their captors. Next, the gags are removed, letting their cries fill the space.

"*Run, daughters!*" Scalebane blinks, pushing away the strange verbal memory. The family in distress is resurrecting the voice of her mother. She has not thought of her in so long. Her heart consists of her sister, Namsruc, and no one else.

The human on the floor says, "Come on, man. Leave my girls outta this."

"Silence, rat," Kye Pung hisses.

"Would you like to go first?" Erol asks, extending a hand to Scalebane.

Scalebane circles the group, standing clear from the light. "You go first."

"Why thank you," Erol says while reaching into his blazer. His hands return equipped with a studded, spiked leather glove. "Jump in whenever you'd like, my friend. This is part of the job, punishing those who have not obeyed the critical rule of the Crystal Moths: never expose our secrets." He stops in front of the man. "And that is what you did, wasn't it?"

The man says, "She would have killed me. I had to. Please leave them outta this."

Erol's face shrinks into a hateful scowl. He lands a swift backhand across the man's face. The small metal spikes shred across his cheek, ripping the flesh open. The little girl wails as the mom attempts to cover her face with her head. It's no use. The girl had already witnessed the horror. The man would have toppled over if it wasn't for Erol holding him by the skull.

Erol says, "You've committed the worst act known to a Crystal Moth. You're lucky that Mastema isn't here. He would have decapitated you right here and now."

Kye Pung says, "Our methods tend to be a little elongated.

We trusted you to be among the first to distribute ash."

"It won't happen again," the man says.

"And this is how you repay us, Chen?"

The man says, "Please, it was one time."

Erol throws another smack against the man's face and another. Blood splatters onto the concrete floor. The little girl is a watery mess with snot dripping from her nose, her cries filling the sound between each fleshy smack from Erol.

"Go! I love you," comes Scalebane's mother's voice. Her bright, squinting eyes flash from memory. They were in pain.

Kye Pung points at the girl and mother. "Make them watch."

The two human Moths snag the little girl and her mom, dragging them further from the man. The Moths lift their heads and pull their eyelids back, forcing them to watch Erol land another metal-spiked smack against Chen's face.

"Please, stop!" the woman begs.

"We have to go!" Scalebane had said to her sister. She held her with one clawed hand. Her other reached for a stranger's. Those purple eyes were the Scalebane sisters' hope to escape hell.

Scalebane stops on the opposite side of the mother and daughter. The little girl looks at her with wide, pink eyes.

The gaze stabs Scalebane deep in her psyche, pulling the memory of her mother into the forefront. This little girl is some spirit of her past, reminding Scalebane of her horrific upbringing. Scalebane's mother fended off the multi-limbed flesh abominations from hell. Their rotting skin drooped from their exposed muscles as she hacked into them with her claws. Scalebane's heart was crushed that day, dragging her sister on the red dirt to safety.

"I love you!"

She snaps out of the trance once Erol drags the spikes along the man's face. It peels the skin from his eyebrows to his chin. Chen screams, attempting to wiggle free with no success.

Kye Pung says, "You'll be the prime example of what happens to a traitor." She spits on Chen's bald and bruised head. Erol throws a fist into the man's gut, and he coughs blood.

"Please! Where is your humanity?" the mother cries.

"Don't watch!" Chen manages to groan through the constant beatings.

"Daddy!" the little girl begs.

"I love you, baby!"

A growl rumbles deep from within Scalebane's throat. It rises into a rattling hiss as she steps forward. *Humans*, she thinks while unsheathing one sai. The three-bladed chrome weapon glimmers in the light. Her boots echo in the warehouse as she approaches Chen.

The sounds catch Kye Pung's and Erol's attention. They step away, and Erol smiles. "Good, the smell of blood brings you forward."

"Move," Scalebane says.

The two Crystal Moths obey. Chen's body plummets onto the concrete. Scalebane grabs the back of his skull, holding him. She moves the sai under him and throws his head forward. His face plunges past the side prongs and shaft and into sai's saki (tip), piercing into his eye socket. The weapon descends deep into the hole, past the brain, and against the inner skull.

The room's cursing and sobs hush. Scalebane frees the sai and wipes it against her shoulder before sheathing it. Chen falls, blood drizzling from his punctured eye and mixing with the pools of water on the concrete.

The little girl bursts into uncontrollable screeches and elongated sobs. Both of the Crystal Moth goons let her and the mother go. The mother presses her daughter's head against hers. The nightmare is over.

Erol's voice croaks. "Scalebane, you ended it so quickly? It is a surprise for one who hates humans so much."

"No need for senseless violence," Scalebane says.

Erol sighs. "Kill the mother. Let the girl go. The media loves a survival story."

Scalebane says, "No. The mother and the girl live."

Erol squints into Scalebane's soulless black goggles. "Let her live?"

"The mother and the girl live," Scalebane repeats.

"She has seen too much. She knows who I am, you, and where we are." Erol says.

Kye Pung says, "It's a risk we don't need."

Scalebane uncoils her tail from her ankle, whipping it into the air and unleashing a loud snap. She snarls, extending her claws toward Kye Pung. The Crystal Moths take a step away, unable to believe their eyes that bear witness to the flailing tail of a reptilian humanoid. Never before have these humans seen such a foreign being like a vazelead. Kye Pung's mouth hangs open, dumbfounded by Scalebane's presence.

Erol nods several times. "All right, no need to turn on each other. We're allies here."

Scalebane says, "Throw them into the streets of the nearest

town. They will find their way home, and you will get your news story regarding survivors."

Erol points at the mother and daughter and then at Kye Pung. "Make sure they don't say anything."

Kye Pung nods at her Crystal Moth goons. They snag the girl and mother and leave the warehouse while the two vampire Moths look to Erol for further instructions. One of them makes a faint snarl, exposing his fangs. It's obvious they are unsure of what protocol to follow. Their training has not prepared them for Scalebane.

Erol says, "Scalebane, I don't understand?"

"Death is a part of life, Erol. Killing is needed in self-defence and to end one's suffering," Scalebane says, paraphrasing a childhood memory. *Mother,* she thinks. It was necessary to establish dominance and save the mother and daughter. Scalebane would have preferred to keep her vazelead features hidden.

Erol swallows a thick lump of saliva, understanding the line Scalebane has drawn. She will hear of this from King. Scalebane cares little of the scolding he will give her. Her mother's words of wisdom are her law of life. Mercy is among them, unlike humans who lack a sense of humanity.

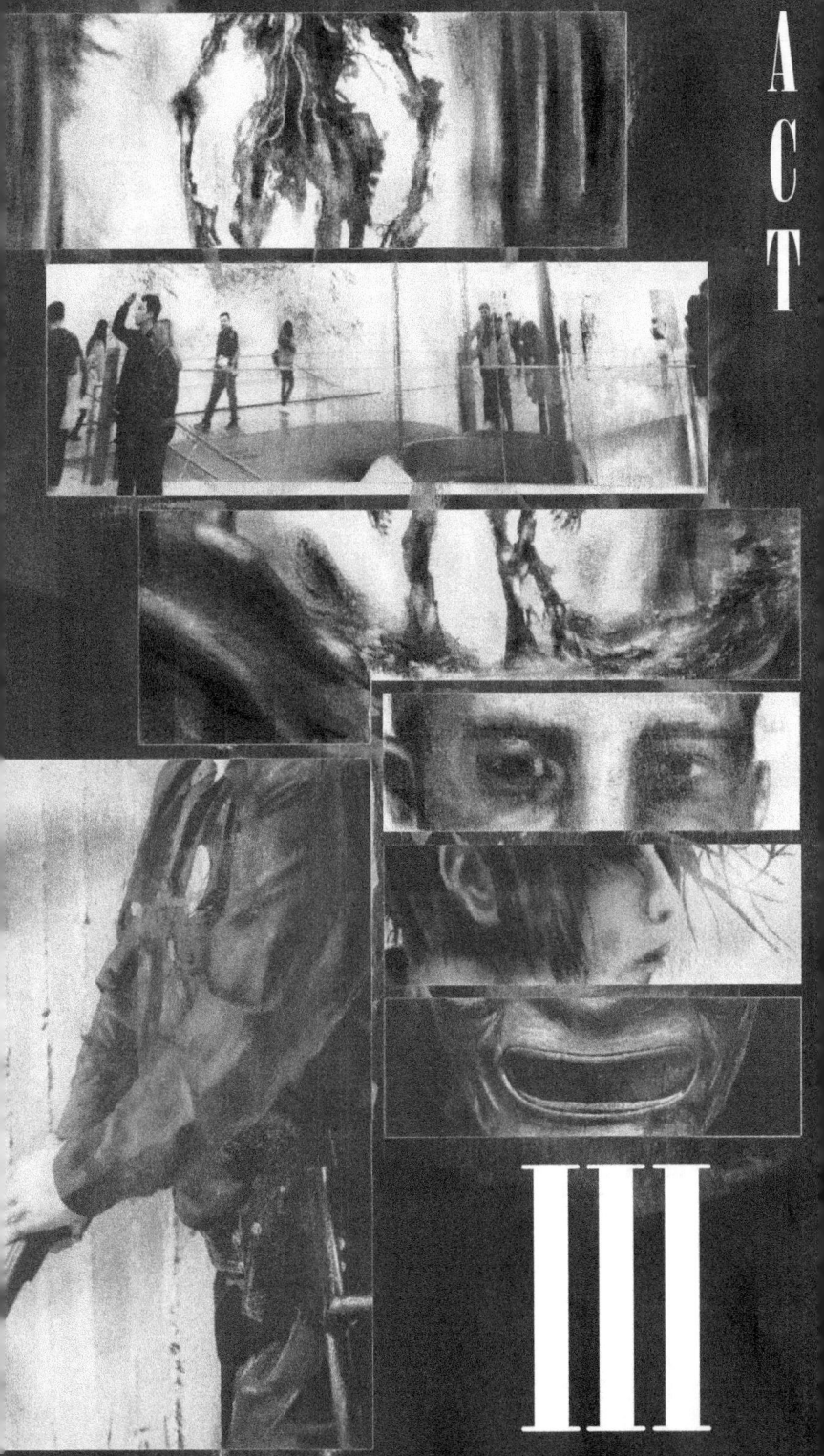

ACT III

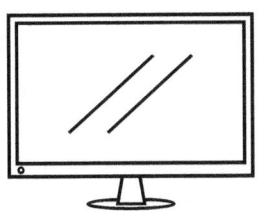

ACT III:
TRICKY CRISIS

Good evening, and welcome to *CAMB News Now with Hucker Dime*. There's nothing but violence everywhere we go in this country. What are the government and those funny red coats doing to keep us safe?

Well, I can tell you they're spending our coin on finding an escaped member of the notorious Crystal Moths. Yang Chen was a key witness regarding the whereabouts of the infamous Edmonton vigilante Lola Cabello. Chen happened to walk right out of the RCMP Major Crimes' head office earlier this week. Isn't that what prison cells are for? They should shift the budget from excessive force and buy some locks.

Sergeant Bando of the Drug and Organized Crime Department says they are searching for Yang Chen. The police are asking anyone who has seen him to come forward.

The Crystal Moths are becoming a hot topic everywhere, as is Lola Cabello. She has made disturbing progress in Vancouver, British Columbia. A man named Ramon Blackwell died in his motel room a week ago. Traces of Lola Cabello's bullet shells and fingerprints were found in his room, along with her car and belongings in the parking lot. Ramon was loved by his wife and kids, working for Allen Forestry Solutions in northern British Columbia. He was coming home from his two-week shift and stayed the night at the motel. His son, daughter, and wife were expecting to have him drive home in the morning. Police are looking for any sort of relation to the Crystal Moths regarding Ramon Blackwell.

It's a tragic turn of events since many outliers believe Cabello to be a hero. Is murdering a family man heroic?

Famous painter Dasco Amoss's grand opening at the North Vancouver Gallery of Modern Prestige is one week from today. This will be a historic date for Canadians for years to come, thanks to the artist's era-defining work.

Prime Minister Trudell is pleased to share that many Hollywood stars are making a memorable trip to Canada for the event. Megastar sensation Ashley Amber announced she will come to the opening to enjoy a slice of Canadian culture. What a gal!

Thank you so much for tuning in. We strive to provide you with facts regarding the latest news at CAMB. Stories that continue to evolve regarding you and your country. We keep you up to date with *CAMB News Now with Hucker Dime*.

It's back to Justin and Danielle for the weather.

CHAPTER 22
CELEBRITY STATUS

No matter a damaged soul's resilience, the itch of desire creeps into the cracks. Willpower is a solid antidote to deflect addiction. Learning to "suck it up" is insufficient to quell the longing. Distance is the single option. Some don't wish to rise from the shadows of their tampered spirit. This kind descends further into the depths of their psyche, suppressing, forgetting, and seeing where desire takes them.

Lola tilts towards this darkness, scratching her arms as her leg bounces. She's sweating from her pits down. The comedown isn't as intense as the first day with Jack in Winnipeg. It's relieving that she has the energy to twitch, considering her recent physical health. Synarion's magic tea works wonders.

"And you unlocked this on your own?" Synarion asks.

He sits beside her at his table full of junk, looking at her laptop screen. Lola operates her computer, skimming through the files of the street dealer's smartphone that's plugged in.

"Yeah, I have a thing for computers," Lola says. *Ash helps*, Lola thinks. It's a troublesome secret. She is ashamed of the insight it provides. The drug is related to the Crystal Moths, her sworn enemy. When she succeeds, yes, *when* her access to ash will be gone forever, she will no longer have deep insights and increased ability.

"I'm impressed," Synarion says. "I know simple computing, like changing the port to access a new Internet or executing a Trojan key from a USB stick. That's as technical as I get. Beyond that, I outsource to a colleague of mine."

"If he's good, why not?"

"Yes, he or she is quite talented."

"You've never met them?" Lola asks.

"Anonymity is the beauty of the Internet. One day I hope to meet them. They're quite elusive. Eden Breaker is their name. Speaking of, I requested a new ID and passport for you from Eden Breaker."

That's such a typical hacker name. Lola smirks. "ID? Thanks. I do need a new persona."

Synarion says, "As long as you're with me, my resources are yours."

Lola raises the unlocked phone. "I went through the texts briefly. The street dealer was talking to some guy named Ricky. It was a text message from November tenth and on Remembrance Day, saying they need bodies at an art gallery in seven days."

"May I see?" Synarion asks.

"Of course," Lola says.

Lola navigates the computer files and finds the text message from the phone. Synarion leans closer. It makes Lola wonder if she reeks. Her cheeks even turn pink, feeling shy beside the near-perfect specimen of a man. It's a foolish thought. She shouldn't be ogling over the man who, in theory, kidnapped her, and isn't human at all.

Synarion says, "North Vancouver Gallery of Modern Prestige. Even the Prime Minister is going. Impressive."

"And?" Lola says.

"Vazelead," Synarion mumbles into his face. "*One* of the vazeleads."

"Think it's the one you're looking for?" Lola asks.

"Hard to say. It's not impossible to have her shipped from Toronto."

Lola says, "The fact they had a growery hidden in the sewers says a lot. Chen said the shipments come from overseas."

"They're struggling with supply," Synarion says.

"That's what I figure. The Prime Minister? That's big. He must have knowledge of these reptilians. Vazeleads, sorry."

"Hard to say. The Moths have thrown in many wild cards lately. Anything else of value on here?"

"Not that I could see. I haven't scraped through the data yet."

Synarion rises. "You do that. It will give you time to recover from your wounds and your ash adventure."

Lola folds her arms. "Where are you going?"

"I think this show is worth looking into. I'm going to go pay it a visit. Seven days from the tenth would make the show on November seventeenth. Let me get some tickets. We're going to an art opening."

"I don't know if I'll be recovered for it."

"Keep applying the paste I supplied and drink the tea. Looks to be doing you well."

"It's amazing. It's like magic."

Synarion chuckles. "Magic. True magic expired a long time ago. This is Mother Nature's blessing."

"From the dark web?" Lola asked.

"Close. Another port for the old world. It has access to many things."

"Thank you again for saving me."

"You would have been dead," Synarion says.

"I know," Lola says.

"Get rest, and do look through that phone. See you soon."

"Later," Lola says.

Synarion points to a jar in the kitchen. "I got a spare set of keys hidden there. Only use it if you have to. Please, stay here and keep a low profile. You're popular on the news."

With that, the man—or nymph—leaves Lola alone in his dump of an apartment. She watches him depart, eyes gravitating to his behind. A pinch comes inside her stomach as her heart warms. Instantly, Lola knows this type of feeling. It is a terrible cliché and welcoming. The classic crush. She can't fall for the stereotypical knight in shining armour.

Upon reflection, Lola isn't his prisoner. He lets her wander through his belongings. Perhaps her guard has shielded her for too long. Perhaps she is experiencing a sense of attraction due to her ash withdrawal. Or, maybe, just maybe, her mind is mangled in fighting the urge to do more. Perhaps Synarion is telling the truth, and there is an old world with intelligent reptilians. The bouncing leg has not stopped.

Lola makes herself a fresh pot of the strange tea and applies another layer of the paste onto her torso, bandaging it anew. Unlike Michael Bradford, fighting crime on the streets is not her specialty. It's time for her natural skill: some classic reporter investigation.

Lola cruises through the street dealer's smartphone for the next while, digging through text messages, photos, videos, and phone logs. Unlocking a phone and looking underneath the operating system is a tedious task. There are dozens of folder structures with endless clicking. You have to know what you are looking for. Otherwise, it looks like a gibberish mess. Most of the data is foreign.

Reptilian people, Lola thinks. She hears about scaly humanoids on late-night streaming videos of madmen rambling. Back to the dilemma—is Synarion telling the truth? It wouldn't be the first time she heard conspiracies surrounding ash. Chen was concerned. She finds the original MP3 recording of him. Scrubbing through the audio file, Lola finds the spot where Chen explains his employer.

He says, "This superior, his name is Mastema, which I doubt that's his real name. Seriously, think it through. What kind of name that is. I was raised in a hardcore religious family and remember a thing or two. If you weren't, look it up."

"Thanks, Chen, I will," Lola says.

She hops onto the web using her VPN. Before she even

presses the first key, her eyes wander to the home screen of the search page showcasing the local news. Her heart sinks, and her fingers coil into her palm. It's not the ash aftermath. The first headline reads:

Motel Murder Near Surry Linked to Edmontonian Vigilante Craze

Damnit, Lola thinks. She clicks on the article to reveal a complete mugshot of herself with her name underneath it. It's the photo used when she was first brought into custody by the police in Edmonton. There aren't any photos of her since.

The article reads:

The body of a man was found in a motel north of Surry. Ramon Blackwell, a father of two and loving husband, was assaulted. DNA evidence at the scene links to Lola Cabello, who was involved with the YEGman incident two years ago in Edmonton, Alberta.

The police found the assailant's abandoned car in the parking lot. Police believe that Cabello attacked Ramon Blackwell in the middle of the night.

She has refused to cooperate with the law since 2014.

Anyone with information on her whereabouts should immediately come forward to their local police. If anyone spots Cabello, they are not to engage with her. She is considered armed and dangerous.

"Pure bullshit!" Lola says. She doesn't intend to get so enraged. She can't believe how the news reporters are spinning the story. One scroll shows the following news site from the supposed credible CAMB, where night host Hucker Dime reports on Lola and Ramon Blackwell's death. Several other news sites source the same information regarding the murder in the motel.

Synarion was right. Once again, there is no going back for her. She sold herself to the dark world of crime once she pledged revenge. There's no chance in hell she will ever see her brother, father, or Donnie again. On that note, her email has no reply from any of them. No surprise.

Lola switches to the search engine, dismissing the articles and her family ghosting her. She types the name "Mastema" in the search bar. Results of biblical quotes sourcing from the Book of Jubilees appear.

One of the outcomes states Mastema: the persecutor of God.

Lola catches a slight shiver and adjusts her seating.

Some more digging reveals that Mastema is the name of an angel who carries out God's punishment. He tempts humans and tests their faith. This character is mentioned in the Book of Jubilees, the Zadokite Fragments, and the Dead Sea Scrolls. These predate King James's Bible, the most common version in the modern world. The further reading states Mastema is an angel of disaster, the father of evil, and a flatterer of God. His name shares the same root as the Hebrew noun for hostility. He is the first angel and becomes a fallen angel and is removed from the scriptures at around two hundred BC.

Written out, Lola thinks. Synarion mentioned the old world being erased from the history books. The Library of Alexandria was founded around two hundred and eighty BC. There could be truth to Synarion's mad tale.

More history sites cover Mastema, digging into the biblical references, stating the Jewish faith didn't have a prominent satanic character. Mastema was the first adversary of God in religion. There is plenty of fan art within the photo sections as well. Beyond that, he is a relic of the past.

Lola closes the browser and sighs. She rubs frustration from her scalp with her nails. The idea of a fallen angel ruling the Crystal Moths is as ridiculous as Synarion's tale. Chen is on board the crazy train.

If she had kept the gangster a little longer, she could have asked him who Mastema is. She was too scared. Interrogating a man was new to her, and she was focused on giving the police clues to work with.

The front door rattles and Synarion steps in with a paper bag full of takeout food. Now, Lola realizes how many hours have gone by with her cruising through the web. She loves getting lost in her research and uncovering information. It's the true nerdy her coming to life.

"Welcome back," Lola says.

"Thank you. I have brought us food to eat." Synarion places it on the kitchen counter and opens the bag. He pulls out the two bowls of ramen.

"Great," Lola says while standing. She walks to the kitchen, rubbing her arm, fidgety from the ash. The comedown doesn't give her much of an appetite. Still, for her recovery, she needs to eat and gain strength.

"Both of these are the same, chicken ramen."

"Thank you, that's wonderful. Did you look at the gallery?"

"Yes, I did. It's quite lovely under any other circumstances. For us, it's the grand opening to Dasco Amoss's new series of paintings."

"Dasco Amoss?" Lola asks.

"Yes, a Canadian icon of postmodern art. A character you should know. I got us both a ticket from a scalper. It wasn't cheap, considering its importance."

"Great, so we have a date."

Synarion smiles. "Looks like we do. Since this grand opening will have the Prime Minister, normal security will be increased. The moths are there too. We have to change your attire."

"All my clothes were at the motel," Lola says. "I have some cash, I think."

"We'll doll you up and conceal your unique features."

"Speaking of, the motel murder is on the news. They've pegged me for it."

"Predictable. The Crystal Moths are watching, and I didn't leave a trace."

"Well, I don't have weird old world nonsense to stay hidden."

"I've become good at remaining in the shadows. We'll improve your skills. You're new to this. Anything useful on that phone?"

"Not quite. He was a street dealer. He made ash and coke deliveries, but I need to review the contact logs more. It did remind me of a particular Crystal Moth I researched."

"Who?" Synarion asks.

"Does the name Mastema mean anything to you?" Lola asks.

"I can't say it does. How come?"

"The Crystal Moth I interrogated in Toronto mentioned he is in charge of the Crystal Moths. Mastema is also the name of a fallen angel. The first angel."

Synarion's lips press together.

"And that name means nothing to you? The old world?"

"There's a lot of history to remember. It spans beyond time. A fallen angel does ring a bell."

"Okay, so the Crystal Moths are ruled by a guy named Mastema, who is a fallen angel, according to what I read. Your tall tale gets more insane by the day."

"You think I'm lying?" Synarion asks.

"I mean, well, yes. Sort of." Lola feels sheepish, confronting him about his story. Synarion has been so kind in giving her hospitality, and she's challenging him. "I'll show you the recording of Chen."

"Sure, show me. Then let's go on a field trip for actual evidence. It will convince you," Synarion says.

Lola squints, wondering what this could entail. Rambles of old world nonsense mean little to a practical woman. Tangible evidence would change her mind entirely.

CHAPTER 23
FIRST IMPRESSIONS

❚❚ Huh. Reptilian people?" Beckman asks.

Iglesias raises his arms in a shrug. "That's what he said last night. Then the Moths took him."

"Presuming it's the Crystal Moths," Beckman corrects.

"It's them or a gun-for-hire working with them. Chen said a lot, and he's gone."

"Reptilian people. That's something. Fulcher mentioned it, then Chen. Who is next?"

"No idea," Iglesias says. "We should take it into consideration."

"Really?"

"What they're saying. Not actual reptile people. It's either symbolism, a nickname, or these are big lizards that somehow no zoologist has discovered."

"Did you tell Internal investigations?" Beckman asks.

"No. They know I was the last to talk to him before Miguel took him to his cell."

"Does Archer know? Or anyone on the team?" Beckman asks.

"No. You're the first I have told. It happened last night, and after this morning, I'm not ready to share."

"Internal investigations will want to know."

"I'll work on that. Let's try to keep this quiet until we know who we can trust," Iglesias says.

"I think it's best. It's a vague connection at the moment."

The detectives drive to Ottawa to make sense of the new info on the ash case. In Iglesias's mind, he knows Chen is already dead. He's frustrated that the Crystal Moths have them on a wild goose chase across the entire country, and now Fulcher claims they are on the West Coast, which was an oversight due to having no evidence pointing to British Columbia.

The rest of the week is filled with tension at the station. None of the officers enjoy having internal investigations asking the same questions over and over. The officer looks at the other with a sheen of distrust in their eyes. They are wondering the same thing: who is the Crystal Moth plug?

Corruption is everywhere, seeping into society. The office can't pretend life is normal when their department is tainted. Sideways looks, tight tones, and no collaboration are common. The station is supposed to be where Major Crimes works as a team, collaborates, and eliminates trouble. Iglesias can't let evil persist. There's no chance he will raise a son in a world with these scumbags. He'll do everything in his power as a father to ensure his son is safe and becomes a good man.

During the week, internal investigations call each officer in for their second interviews. They have already called José and confirmed Iglesias's story. Iglesias's is on a Wednesday afternoon, where he recites the exact events he told them previously.

Internal investigations don't mention José's party. Thank God his son is bright. He knows better than to tell cops about the evening. Then, Iglesias shares his discussion with Chen. He is weary of sharing and decides to exclude the reptilian humanoids. He elaborates on the finer details. The chamber in the sewers, Lola Cabello assaulting him, and the deal Chen and Iglesias struck are on file. That is the end of those suits for now.

Friday rolls around, and Iglesias leaves work early, drowning in discouragement from the loss of Chen. He must shift from a detective into a father. It's his first priority. Tonight is a special occasion: he will meet his son's first girlfriend.

José had been seeing this chick for two months, and Iglesias didn't know. Two months is like a lifetime in high school, meaning they're married. José likes her, and Iglesias is going to be supportive. He wants to be a good parent, unlike José's mother. She put a strain on the family and another ten years on Iglesias's life. José doesn't mind because he knows his mother is a victim of drinking. Thus, he stays with Iglesias.

A positive energy hums inside Iglesias as if he's opening a present. He gets to meet his son's mysterious girl. Tonight is the best thing in his life right now. The rest of it is stress, annoyance, and worry.

You have to learn to cook well when you are a single father. You can't eat frozen meals and TV dinners throughout your life. That packaged cardboard called *food* doesn't sit well in your stomach and will plaster on the pounds. Iglesias is a master of quick meal recipes full of nutrients. José doesn't need to find his father having a heart attack. The takeout food doesn't count. Tonight's dinner is special: red wine, marinated rabbit, asparagus, and forbidden rice. There's also that delicious family salad with the secret carrot oil-based dressing. He has perfected it from his late grandmother. This will be a delicious dinner to remember, or so he hopes. He has no idea what José's girlfriend is like. Girls are picky.

The television is on, showing news throughout the nation. Hucker Dime with CAMB News Now is going on his usual rants. Even though Iglesias is not at work, he can't stop pondering over Lola Cabello and ash. Reptilian humanoids.

His phone buzzes on the island counter. Iglesias ignores it and continues sifting the sauce, and stirs the rice. His phone buzzes again and then a third time. He can't shrug off the repetition. It could be important, and he takes a peek at his phone. It's a text from Archer, reading:

(Archer: turn on the news.

6:30 PM)

(Archer: I'm getting intel from

the homicide department at

Vancouver police.

The news got to it first.

Fuck I'm slow.

6:32 PM)

(Archer: We've got her location.

Ready for a flight?

6:38 PM)

Iglesias doesn't reply but fixates on Hucker Dime's signature bewildered gaze into the camera. Iglesias's mouth hangs open. Beside Dime is a mugshot of Lola Cabello. Once again, she's headline news. He increases the volume as the reporter speaks.

". . . as is Lola Cabello. She has made disturbing progress in Vancouver, British Columbia. A man named Ramon Blackwell was found dead . . ."

Iglesias's phone buzzes again. The message is from Beckman, telling Iglesias to turn on the television. Archer texts again.

(Archer: Police are cooperative in Vancouver.

I'm talking to them on the phone now.

They have a lot of evidence on Cabello.

She left her belongings, ID, car, and wigs.

Eyewitnesses say she exited the motel

with a man. We've got a lot to work with.

6:39 PM)

Iglesias grabs the phone, and his thumb pauses over the call icon.

No, he thinks.

He can't be in work mode. He has to be a better father. José is his first concern; he is not chasing adrenaline rushes and a runaway goth girl. Iglesias puts his phone on silent. The father returns to cooking dinner.

The interesting news is promising, and he listens to Hucker Dime on CAMB. It shows a mugshot photo of the man who died. Dime mentions a potential connection to the Crystal

Moths. The rest of the report isn't helpful, as eyewitnesses said, "She vanished." The commentary from the reporter that follows is sensationalism at its finest as far as Iglesias is concerned. Dime's offhanded comments are as famous as his facial expression. Next, Dime talks about painter Dasco Amoss and megastar Ashley Amber, losing Iglesias's interest.

Cabello escaped to the West Coast. She didn't stop and visit Donnie Morris on her way unless he was hiding it from them. Iglesias and Beckman will pay him a visit while heading to Vancouver.

His first instinct says that Cabello didn't murder the man in the motel. He has many questions regarding this individual and the nature of the encounter. It'll have to wait until tomorrow or Monday. Iglesias is in father mode, cooking dinner for his son and girlfriend. He is the master, juggling several elements on the stovetop. The chef orchestrates the meat, vegetables, and rice with heat.

A car rumbling comes from the driveway. The front door jingles. Iglesias looks at the clock to see that it's past seven. The two must have been hanging with friends. That's okay. Iglesias said that they didn't have to arrive until dinner. Now he can meet this girl.

"Welcome!" Iglesias says over the sizzling of food and clanging of metal pots.

"Hey, Dad," José calls from down the hall.

"Dinner is almost ready. Salad is prepped."

"Thanks," José says.

Footsteps come through the hall, and two kids stand by the kitchen's island. José is in front of a short blue-eyed girl standing behind him. She's shy. Her attire is clean: skinny jeans and a black long-sleeved shirt. Her dyed pastel orange hair is in a messy ponytail. Her face has a little too much eyeshadow for one her age, which isn't as distracting as the chrome septum piercing.

"Dad, this is Hailey," José says, putting his arm around the girl.

"Nice to meet you, Hailey. I'm José's dad." Iglesias nods at her while juggling the elements on the stove.

"Hi, Mr. Iglesias. It's nice to meet you." Hailey puts on a closed smile.

"Come, sit down. Dinner's almost ready," Iglesias says.

Hailey whispers into José's ear that Iglesias doesn't catch. Lovebirds. Iglesias focuses on the meal and turns off the elements, grabbing plates, napkins, and cutlery to prep the dinner table. Then, the salad for his guests. Next, he brings the main course of rabbit, asparagus, and rice drizzled with chilli oil. He places the plates in front of the kids and then his own at his seat before sitting down. Sweat beads on his forehead from standing in front of steam for too long.

"You know what would make this great?" Iglesias says.

Hailey is stiff, staring at the plate. José has a polite closed smile. This is unlike the usual ravaging animal that José is during dinner. He must be nervous.

"Some wine," Iglesias says. "And you can't tell me neither you have drank before." He winks and brings his index finger to his lip, hoping to look cool. He has no idea if it's working. Hosting isn't his specialty. His armpits have sweat stains too. This is silly. They are kids, one of them being his own. Either way, Iglesias gets a bottle of wine from the cabinet and pops it. A Pinot Noir will pair well with the meal. He pours three glasses and brings them to the table, then sits and raises his glass. He says, "To introductions."

The two kids raise their glasses before taking a drink. Iglesias sips the wine and takes his utensils. "Please, dig in. We're not religious or anything. Have at it."

"Dad, did you get my text?" José asks. He cuts some of the rabbit meat. Hailey isn't. Oh no.

Iglesias pats his shirt's front pocket, then his pants. Where is his phone? "I think so. You said you'd be a little bit late."

He glances at the island counter to see the phone is there. In the heat of the cooking and the concerning news report, Iglesias must have left it. He is confident he saw the last message from his son.

"No, after that," José says.

Iglesias scratches his head. "Is there something I missed?"

Hailey strokes her neck, eyes slanted back. "I'm vegan," she says sheepishly. "I'm sorry, Mr. Iglesias."

Iglesias stares at her dumbfounded. He feels like a goof, stomach tightening and yes, his face is a little red. It has to be the wine. At least, that's what he wants to believe. Deep down, he knows he made a mistake.

"No, no." Iglesias stands and reaches for Hailey's plate. "This is my mistake, and I do apologize. I must've missed the text. Is the salad okay?" That's such a cliché thing to say to a vegetarian, vegan, or whatever she is. Iglesias is scrambling! He's not like this. Is he experiencing embarrassment? Seriously? These are kids.

"I'm fine. Don't worry about it," Hailey says.

Iglesias scoops the rabbit off the plate and snags more rice from the pot. His mind opens the cupboards and the fridge to think of anything he could give Hailey. Kids these days have the strangest dietary choices. Meat is suitable for people. Veganism is practical if you want to starve yourself to death. There's no protein, calcium, or iron. Damn it. Iglesias had to miss that last text from José. It's too late now, and he's on damage control.

Iglesias returns with the plate and sits down. "Nonsense. I hope that will do?"

Hailey smiles. "Thank you, that's nice."

José looks at her and grins. This is okay. Iglesias will remember it in the future. "I'll get you some of those plant meats next time."

"Thanks," Hailey says.

Iglesias takes a chug of his wine, pushing the embarrassment aside. "So, tell me a bit about yourself, Hailey. You know that I don't pay attention to my phone. Must be the old age."

Hailey giggles as a clear sign of nervousness. Even then, she's intimidated by him. She must have a shy nature. "Well, I go to the same school as your son."

"Taking?" This isn't a police interview. Iglesias needs to remind himself to be casual.

"Um, I like biology. I kind of want to see what I can do with animals after graduation."

Iglesias nods. "Excellent, that is great. How did the two of you meet?"

José says, "Math class."

"We both hated it," Hailey says.

"That was never my specialty either," Iglesias says. "That's wonderful, and it's two months now?"

"Yeah," Hailey says. She reaches for José under the table. Iglesias hopes it's his hand.

"Glad to hear, and your family? Are they here with you in Ottawa?" Iglesias asks.

"Yeah, my mom and dad are both working, so that's quite nice. No offence. I mean, um, my dad is a lawyer, and my mom is a dentist. They work a lot."

"Those are good careers, and you were not interested in following their steps?"

"No, I am drawn to animals and nature."

"That's great," Iglesias says. *Animals. It's a far fetch,* he thinks. "They teach you much about reptiles?" *What am I doing?*

"Biology is broad. I'm hoping to specialize in ecosystems."

"The environment needs people like you in the field."

"I want to make the world better," Hailey says.

Iglesias is surprised that his son is interested in her. She's got a hippie heart. José has taken plenty of glances at the classic cheerleader girl type. The popular, dominant, and controlling stereotypes appeared to be his thing, and here he is with Hailey, who is none of that.

Hailey has passed his initial screening process: a good family and ambitions and looks at his son with caring eyes. José is doing well. The vegan lifestyle is the odd thing about the gal. Iglesias can live with that because he considers himself open-minded with the youth. At their age, he was into far more dangerous activities. Gangs, fights, graffiti, and dealing aren't anything his son does. That's all a father can ask for.

CHAPTER 24
TITANS

Our pattern-seeking minds cause most people to fall for some form of conspiracy to the unexplainable, whether as harmless as ghosts or as unreal as intelligent reptilian people from the old world. Lola isn't an extremist. She can't accept reptile people. A reporter finds the facts. That's what she's doing right now.

It's been three days, Monday, since Synarion rescued her and claimed he can provide her tangible proof of the old world. Following a mysterious man claiming to be of an ancient race is a good nominator for disqualifying her journalistic integrity. The man, or nymph, didn't even flinch when listening to the recording of Chen. It's as if he expected Chen's words.

He enters the apartment unit holding a mail envelope with various stamps covering the paper. He passes it to Lola. She takes the envelope and examines it closer. It's been moved to many countries across Europe and to Canada.

"What is this?" Lola asks.

"Your new identification and passport from my dear Eden Breaker," Synarion says.

"Nice. Thanks."

"From now on, you are Talia Marquis."

"Fair enough." Lola opens the package. Inside is a passport and an ID card with her face on it. Her hair is short like it is now, and the documents contain a complete profile of her features. "How did they get a recent photo of me?" she asks.

"I don't ask. Eden Breaker provides. They are well aware of your previous fake ID and made sure the photo wasn't identical."

"Concerning," Lola says. "I need glasses to drive?" She digs deeper into the envelope and finds a pair of glasses.

"It's better to hide your nose."

Lola pulls a credit card from the envelope with her new name, Talia Marquis, right on it. "How much is on this?"

"Not much. Five grand."

"Five grand? Talia doesn't exist. How did—"

"Eden Breaker finds a way."

With Lola healed, the two are ready to embark on Synarion's field trip. Synarion leads Lola from the apartment's burgundy-rug staircase and into the rainy streets. She gets a good sniff of the ocean-side air, realizing she has not been outside in three days. Further down the road are docks, ports, ships, and industrial buildings with a few apartments like Synarion's. On the side street, to the ocean, is an abandoned warehouse with boarded up windows covered in graffiti. To Lola, they're handy to make a note of.

"Over here," Synarion says while crossing the street towards a silver Hyundai hatchback. There's plenty of rust on the vehicle's body, and the tire treads look well past their prime.

"This is what you drive?" she asks.

"Yes, it's quite reliable and effective on gas."

Lola stares at the crooked side mirror while opening the passenger door. "You don't care for nice things, do you?"

"Nope. It is a means to an end," Synarion says.

"Your balancing purpose?"

"Precisely. The world needs me more than ever." Synarion gets in the car.

Must be nice to think you're so important, Lola thinks, hoping in and buckling her seatbelt. A part of her wants to tell him that. She decides it is best to not piss him off.

Synarion starts the engine, and it sputters to life with loud rumbles, indicating the muffler is dead. He says, "If I could, I would have some other form of transportation. Vehicles are the way to cover vast distances."

"Oh, right. The pollution."

"The use of oils and gas is not ideal. What else can I do?"

"Beat the system from within, eh?" Lola asks.

"It's what I've concluded. From my experience, Mother Nature's Earth is massive, with many intricate moving parts making it impossible to change head-on. You have to work within its existing constructs and adjust portions and regions before we can take on the whole scope of the planet. It's what makes the environmental crisis such a complex thing."

"Because there are many moving parts? I don't know about that. It's pretty straightforward."

"How is that, then?" Synarion asks.

"Greedy rich assholes. This has been a problem with people forever. It's not just the environment. It's every aspect of our existence. War, famine, health, everything is dictated by the rich."

"A shadowy group of people that control the world? Come on. I'm the one convincing you of conspiracies. There isn't a council of greedy humans."

"Perhaps not, but there are a lot of billionaires that have a lot of power and influence. They build organizations with enough pull that countries bow to their demands. They can destroy the environment by threatening countries they'll leave, killing an economy."

"That's a simplification, brainiac," Synarion says.

"It's one example. Poverty is another one that I'm too familiar with."

"Your family wasn't well off? And you went to post-secondary?" Synarion asks.

"Sure did. Drowning in student debt. Like that matters now."

"It does not because what you are involved with is far more important."

"Apparently. Where are we going anyways?" Lola asks.

"To the Lower Seymore Conservation Reserve north of Vancouver here."

"A giant park?" Lola asks.

"A reserve. They keep the plants and animals safe, protecting them from human intervention. I have a friend who lives there. He will give you what you need to see."

"Can't wait," Lola says.

Synarion tries to start a conversation several times during the long drive with no success. He asks, "And you have a brother?" and "What does your father think of your situation?" and "Canada is a beautiful country. Have you seen much of it?" along with, "Have you been to the reserve?" Lola isn't interested in maintaining small talk concerning her upbringing or the regions of Canada. She would prefer more rest. Her ribs ache, and the clavicle is tender, sending a sharp sting when she moves her arm. The sooner they can see this proof, the sooner she can decide if she should move on or stay.

They reach the Lower Seymore Conservation Reserve, and Synarion parks the vehicle in an empty slot. A handful of other automobiles are here on a Monday. Cameras, hiking gear, and families are aplenty. A few are having picnics close to the parking lot.

A large info sign by a primary path showcases a map with trails. According to the map, a river runs straight through the middle, dividing the reserve into two sections.

"We have a bit of a hike. I'll do my best to slow down," Synarion says.

"I'm not that injured," Lola says.

"You don't have my agility. This is a natural place for a nymph. As a balancer, our home used to be in the forests where we can connect with Mother Nature."

"You're quite the tree hugger," Lola says.

"I know my roots, and you humans have long forgotten them."

Synarion leads the way from the map, following the gravel path. They walk over a wooden bridge and trail off the main road onto a dirt footpath descending into the forest. It winds through lush vegetation underneath trees standing at least fifty feet, shrouding the cloudy sky. Under typical scenarios, this would be a relaxing hike. For Lola, she wants proof. Being covered in sweat, panting, and following a madman into the woods isn't Lola's idea of a good time.

Synarion takes her far deeper into the greenery, following a twisting dirt route, turning off onto another one, and moving off-path. Their journey through the undergrowth takes them to another river in a more secluded area with no human structures or man-made roads.

They step on the rocky beach near a cliff. Lola wipes the sweat from her forehead, wishing she could dry the black tank top of the visible dampness. Synarion shows no evidence of strain.

"He likes to come around here," Synarion says.

"A hermit?" Lola asks.

"In a sense, he is." Synarion walks up a steep hill by the cliff. Lola follows, and they reach the top of the ten-foot incline and walk to the edge. Synarion kneels down, closing his eyes.

Lola asks, "What are you doing?"

"Being silent," Synarion says. "Join me."

"And this is where you kill me?" Lola asks while kneeling.

"Don't be ridiculous. He does not appear when there's noise. He can sense you and needs stillness to pinpoint us."

Lola obeys, staring at the man whose eyes remain shut. The ruffling leaves through the wind are met with the gentle chirps of birds. Splashes of the river against the rocks come from below. Her ears ring from the limited sound because she's used to the constant white noise of the concrete jungle.

She focuses on her breath, through her nose and out her mouth. She repeats the cycle, closing her eyes and lifting one eyelid to see if Synarion is still here. He has not moved.

A loud snap comes from deeper in the woods. Leaves ruffle, growing louder.

Synarion grins, saying, "He's here."

"Scaaabbed eeears," comes a slow rumbling voice from behind.

Synarion and Lola rise and turn to face swaying branches moving closer through the thick forestry. The plants shake until they pass the last bit of dense shrubbery, and an animated anthropomorphic tree steps into view.

Lola's mouth drops, taking a couple steps back, close to tipping over the cliff's edge. Her eyes must deceive her; an eight-foot-tall tree person is in front of her.

Three thick roots move the colossal entity onto the dirt cliff, coming to a halt. They hold a mossy trunk housing dozens of branches along the top of the stem. Vines drape over the creature, forming a tentacle-like beard as it lifts its two arm-like branches into the air. Smaller branches with leaves form fingers, pointing as if they were shrugging in disbelief. The two pitch black holes sized for bird nests are separated by an oval-shaped stump. These are, without a doubt, eyes looking at Lola.

"Bark Nose!" Synarion says. "It's wonderful to see you."

A burrow below the nose-stump shifts in shape, moving the bark, acting as a mouth. "Synaaaaarion, why do yoou brrrring a hoomaan heere?"

Lola shakes her head several times. "No fucking way." She's not even high, and those ash trips were convincing. This is a mythological creature standing right in front of her. "No fucking way," Lola takes another step away and almost slips over the edge.

Synarion grabs her forearm, pulling her into him. She is too starstruck to even notice how far she moved and who had grabbed her. She breaks free from his grip and hugs her arms. "This is a fucking dream. Fucking holy shit."

The tree speaks again. "Aaafter the sscrrutiny yooou gaaave meee ovvver Abbyyygaaaaail? Synaaaaaarion, whaaat of yoooour rules? I ooobey themmmmm."

"Lola," Synarion says. "This is real, believe me."

"Yeah," Lola squeaks, unable to catch her breath, petrified.

Synarion says, "Bark Nose, this time is different."

The tree lets out a long groan. The low bass of its voice rumbles inside Lola's chest.

"Things are changing, Bark Nose. Fast. We're no longer relics of the past. The others have mutated into angry souls, wishing to inflict revenge upon the world."

"Caaan I feeed this hoooman tooo Abbyyygaaaaail?" the tree, Bark Nose, asks. "Abbyyygaaaaail likes meeeaaat. Evennn the scraaawny."

Lola looks at Synarion for some reassurance while her knees shake. This is far worse than a drug trip.

"No, no, Bark Nose. Why would I bring you a person to feed

your pet?"

"Soooulmaaate," Bark Nose says.

"How is she your—? You know what, never mind. I don't want to go there. Where is Abbygail anyways?"

"Sheee is heeere, with meee. Commme, I willlll shooow yooou." Bark Nose turns in his sluggish motion and descends into the forest. The three large roots press into the soil in an insectoid motion.

Synarion follows, presuming Lola is with him. Lola squeezes her arms, digging the nails into her biceps to remain calm. She rushes to him and whispers, "Synarion, what the fuck?"

"You wanted proof. Here's your proof," he says.

"A fucking tree?" Lola asks. "Did I hop into a wardrobe?"

"He is a Root Walker, a relic of the past, like me."

"Talking trees? This existed in this old world? How many of them are there?"

"Hard to say. Root Walkers are throughout Earth. Their territories are vast. They can be motionless for days, if not weeks before having to move. Plants use photosynthesis and enjoy water. They are the most effective at hiding of all the old world beings."

"Where is he taking us?" Lola asks.

"It's a long story. He's got a girlfriend, in a sense," Synarion says.

Bark Nose takes them from the wooded area and into an open dirt patch surrounded by sharp thorny bushes and collapsed trees. There's a hole with loose dirt where Bark Nose was hiding in plain sight. He stops beside a girl standing beside the hole. Her white skin belongs on a corpse, which is more eye-catching than the piercing blue eyes glued to Lola. Her pitch-black hair rests against her all-black velvet trench coat, concealing her entire body. Her lips move in a jerking motion, forming a creepy smile on her tilting head.

"Abbyyygaaaaail," Bark Nose says.

The girl sways in a strange hypnotic dance.

"Hi?" Lola says, waving.

Synarion swats Lola's arm and whispers, "Don't talk to it." He raises his voice. "Get it under control."

The girl's trenchcoat unfolds on its own, starting from the neck down, revealing a bright red interior and bloody torn flesh where her throat should meet her torso. Instead, the head is held by dozens of black vines penetrating into the neck. The blooming trench coat's interior is covered with white spikes. The coat's fabric is made of at least eight pieces, or petals, spiralling outward. It was not a coat. Abbygail is a flower.

Black vines slither out of the thick core of the plant, coming straight for Lola. Bark Nose's vines worm down his trunk, intersecting Abbygail's. The two plants coil around each other, and Abbygail's head tilts to Bark Nose. The twitchy smile jerks into a robotic frown.

"Nooooooo," Bark Nose says. "Not thiiis ooone."

Lola's not naive. This plant girl was going to eat her. "What is this?" she asks, patting her back pocket. Yes, her knife and gun are ready if needed.

Abbygail's vines slither into her core, coiling around the stem. The trench coat wraps itself around their neck, and her swaying stiffens. The piercing blue eyes remain on Lola.

Synarion says, "Thank you, Bark Nose. I need this one alive."

"This one?" Lola asks. "You bring others here to feed that monster?"

"No, not like that. This plant is new. We *used* to have rules," Synarion says, emphasizing the word used. "Rules around not mixing. It keeps the humans and the old world separate."

"Now yooou brrreak yooour ruuules, Synaaarion?" Bark Nose asks.

Synarion ignores the question. "Bark Nose met Abbygail beyond my knowledge, breaking the rules. She got mixed up in a bad series of events resulting in her death."

"Sheee is allliiiive, I caaan taaalk with herrrrr," Bark Nose says.

"Yes, yes, it's more of a symbiotic transformation. The blood the plant drinks sustains her mind. She has no control over it. I had a moment of weakness and brought her here for Bark Nose. I didn't have the heart to kill her."

"She was human?" Lola asks.

Bark Nose speaks, "Sheee waaas innndeeed once hoooman. Thaaat is when weee first met. We connnected on aaa level I hadn't knnnown before. Now, weee caaan commmunnicate betterrrr through ourr rooots."

Synarion says, "Frequencies, in layman's terms. Root Walkers have been around long before us. Common folk once called them ancient ones," Synarion says. "He can repress Abbygail's kind, which birth from quite the sinister seed when eaten."

Lola rubs her head. "Is this related to ash somehow?"

Synarion says, "No. Not directly. It is involved now, like everything in the old world." He points at Abbygail with his missing-fingered hand. "Ash isn't the one balancing mission I have. I've had many. The hellseed infestation was one of them."

"That's why you're so mysterious all the time," Lola says.

"Abbygail wanted to help. The hellseeds sprout the vampiric parasite in front of you. Their camouflage works well to prey on people, like how it worked on you."

"No, it didn't," Lola says.

"It did. You said hi to it. Those vines are fast." He wiggles his hand with the missing finger. "Then I had to eradicate their kind."

"You made them extinct? That doesn't sound like balance."

"They're an infestation," Synarion sneers.

Bark Nose says, "Synaaaaaarion lost someonnne quite deeeaaar tooo him."

Synarion clears his throat. "It's not relevant. The point of this was to introduce you to Bark Nose and Abbygail. The old world is gone. Now, the Crystal Moths and vazeleads think they can turn the tides. How? That's what we need to find out."

Bark Nose speaks, "There aaaare maaaany others that haaave survived frooom the lost connntinent."

Synarion says, "We've hidden in the shadows. Beings like Bark Nose hide far from civilization, while those like me blend in. Others rose to places of power, manipulating the global tides to their will."

Lola asks, "Like the Crystal Moths?"

"Indeed."

"Where was this lost continent?"

Synarion says, "It existed in the South Atlantic Ocean."

"And it collapsed?" Lola asks.

"Yes, under its own power. Millions of lives were lost when

it descended into the ocean. Some of us made it out. Others have lived in other parts of the world, like Europe, South America, or the Middle East."

"And Canada? There's a lot of you here," Lola says.

"Canada happens to be where I and Bark Nose ended up. This country is a good place to hide. It's remote, doesn't get much attention, and there are far fewer humans per square mile."

Bark Nose adds, "I arrrived looonnng agooo before the ooollld world colllapse. There were signs of its demmmise. Synaaaaaarion aided in mmmy migration."

Synarion says, "Remember you said my medical plants behave like magic?"

"Yeah," Lola says.

"Magic, in a broad sense, used to exist. The lost continent was bound by a force acting as the beating heart for the land and many mythical creatures. Too many beings with powerful abilities exploited the heart."

Bark Nose speaks. "Eeeaaach timmme they did, mmmore decaaay."

"The signs became obvious a little too late. There's nothing we could have done, and the continent's heart imploded, sending it deep into a watery grave."

"Even with the warning signs, everyone was too dense to notice?" Lola asks.

Synarion smirks. "Isn't it reflective of your people's situation?"

Lola looks at Bark Nose, then the flesh-eating flower girl, unsure how to reply. She is having difficulty wrapping her head around who and what is standing right in front of her.

Synarion says, "Now it's official. You're part of the real world."

Bark Nose says, "Synaaaaarion, yooou said thinnngs are changing. I dooo not knnnow why this hoooman isss here?"

"Like I said, to convince her of the old world," Synarion says.

"Whooo is she, Synaaaaaaarion? What have yooou gotten yooourself into?"

"I fear that balance is almost tipped upside down. Not by the humans this time. It's much older and more vengeful."

A deep rumble comes from Bark Nose as his bark lips press together.

Lola is transfixed on Abbygail, the girl who was once human. Like Lola, she got herself wrapped into the old world. Her mysterious backstory varies from Lola's own, yet it spawns a haunting feeling that she's looking into the eyes of her future. Lola has no idea what other dangers reside in this rabbit hole.

CHAPTER 25
PROFILE

Major Crimes are shifting their focus to the West. Vancouver is a condensed port city an hour from the USA's border, bringing high traffic, including Crystal Moths. Iglesias can't believe he oversaw the obvious. He once believed Lola Cabello to be an innocent girl in a poor situation. She is withholding evidence, sending them on a wild chase, and is now a potential killer.

Iglesias is fascinated with watching criminals spiral down their inescapable path. He's seen it over and over again. To date, Cabello is following these stereotypical patterns. She's the classic case of a criminal losing their mind and having nowhere else to turn. These people are cornered wild animals that bite back when they can't run.

This won't be the last time his job smothers his hope in humanity. Dealing with grit is his duty to justice. There's a reason why laws are in place, and Iglesias enforces them, doing good for the world. The humorous thing is Lola Cabello believes she is doing the same thing. Unlike her, Iglesias puts his faith in the system, whereas she wants to tear it down.

The death of her mother has not helped her decline. Iglesias sympathized with the girl for her losses. He has no personal grudge against her, even now. It's just the law. Thankfully, the RCMP supports his goals, knowing she is connected to ash and the Crystal Moths. Thus, Iglesias is at the airport and ready to take flight with Beckman.

First, they head to Edmonton, Alberta, to pay Cabello's old accomplice a visit. They haven't talked to Donnie Morris in some months. He must have new information since Cabello called him during her travel west.

Second, the two fly to Vancouver and end Cabello's spree. They'll extract intel from her and use it to close the ash trade in Canada once and for all.

Iglesias checks his smartphone's clock to see that Beckman is running late. That's no concern for Iglesias. He's glad they're back on the case after the internal investigations fiasco.

There have been no signs of Chen, even after Sergeant Bando's public call. They won't hear of Chen or internal investigations again. The department is already looking into his family to see if he has returned to them. Yet, they, too, are missing. If Iglesias's gut is correct, it means the Crystal Moths have had their way.

"Large americano," says the barista at the coffee shop.

"Thanks," Iglesias says while taking his cup. It's far too early to be coherent, despite his wandering thoughts on the case. Coffee is the one thing that's going to keep him focused. The slippery slope of liquor sometimes helps. The wine he had with José and Hailey was a special occasion. Iglesias smirks, seeing the humour in serving a vegan rabbit for dinner. He's not much of a drinker, even though he is tempted daily. Coffee will have to do. Cigarettes? He should stop. That isn't likely, not with Cabello on the run and the Crystal Moths free.

He sips his coffee and skims his smartphone to see if there are any relevant work emails. It's the usual messages being CC'd on dozens of conversations he doesn't care for. Major Crimes doesn't stop.

Next are his texts. There's only Beckman saying he's a little behind. Iglesias can't stop working. Even now, when he's in limbo, waiting for his flight. Ash, reptilian scales, Chen's story.

Reptiles. Iglesias had the unit investigate a range of reptilian species throughout the planet after they broke the genetic sequence of the ash diamond. There are no matches to the ash scales. They're related to plants. He has better specialists than him on the job. Still, Iglesias can't stop. He opens his search browser and starts typing in reptilian species.

Where do these things come from? he thinks. The Crystal Moths are bringing ash in from overseas. There are reptiles native to eastern Asia. Bingo. He can search for specifics.

"You didn't get one for me?" comes a familiar woman's voice. Iglesias turns to see Archer walking to him with her suitcase. She gives him her signature crooked smile as her straight hair bobs with a prideful stride.

"What you doing?" Iglesias asks, putting his phone away. Investigating reptiles can wait for later.

"Come on, you didn't think I'd let you and Beckman go without me?" she asks.

"We need you at the station. There's a lot of cleaning to do."

"I know. I've got officer Reyna taking over for us."

"She's not as capable as you. There is a plug in the office. You know that."

"Yes, and what good am I going to be there? Sergeant Bando let me go. More field experience."

"Figures."

"Internal affairs is still down our throats, and Reyna is working with the rest of the unit to handle street dealers of ash and investigate backgrounds on the drug and gang. Besides, we know the game is in Vancouver. That's why you and Beckman are off to have a little romance out west."

"We're not going in blind to Vancouver." Iglesias shakes his head. She's always disobeying him, calling the shots as she wants to.

"I know," Archer says. "Whether you want to admit it or not, you guys need me."

Iglesias wipes his moustache. The girl has charm when she smiles. It's hard to say no. He admires her methods, for Iglesias used to do the same thing when he was in conflict with superiors. He took action first and asked for forgiveness later. His boldness got him promoted. Now here he is, looking at a reflection of his younger self.

"And there's no convincing you, is there?" Iglesias says.

"Not a chance, boss," Archer says. She storms toward the barista, on a mission for coffee. She's way too chipper for the morning. Give it time. She'll wear down. Archer will settle with the man, have kids, get a divorce, and deal with the pressure of the police force the same way Iglesias does. Iglesias shouldn't be worrying about his co-worker's personal life. It's tough when you work together day in and day out. Whether you like it or not, you get to know people on a personal level.

Beckman appears further down the hall. He's made it past security and heads towards them. The tall man has an amusing skip in his step. It's from when he was shot years ago, and Iglesias shouldn't find humour in it. He can't help it. This job's best coping mechanism is to mask the grimness in humour.

"Archer," Beckman says. "You managed to dodge babysitting the unit?"

Archer finishes paying. "That's right. I can't let you two have all the action."

"Good to have you," Beckman says.

"Trust me, I'm glad to be here." Archer gets her coffee, and the three head for their flight doors. She says, "Did you and your wife ever see the new Ashley Amber movie?"

Beckman nods. "Yeah. She's back to doing her typical work. I thought she'd stop following the template after that mental episode."

"Everyone wants the same romance," Archer says.

Iglesias doses off. He won't admit to being glad that Archer is here. Working with the local police and RCMP in British Columbia wouldn't be the same as bringing your own team. Iglesias trusts his top officers not to be plugs.

He unlocks his smartphone and sends one last text message to his son. It reads:

> (You: Hey champ, try not to throw
> any more parties, okay?
> I think your girl is a keeper too.
> See you when I get back.
> 5:54 AM)

The three board the plane and are off to Edmonton for their first stop. Beckman puts his headphones on while Archer takes a nap, and Iglesias remains awake. He is too focused on their mission. Turbulence in the landing alerts the three, and they arrive in the city after a long flight. Their coming has been scheduled with the local law enforcement. An officer picks them up and takes them from the airport. Unlike most large cities, Edmonton's airport is a forty-five-minute drive into the metropolis with no fast transit to or from. The budget is tight provincially, as is the theme of the country.

Their drive gives the three a sense of what Edmonton has become. The streets are filled with trash, poverty, and vacant real estate at every corner. It's safe to theorize they're owned by slum lords like that New Brunswick drug den. The homeless take shelter in the alleyways and side streets, smoking from their pipes in broad daylight. They stay near building vents and have a few makeshift fires to stay warm as the snow blankets the city.

Looking at this place justifies why Lola Cabello and Michael Bradford did what they did. The city is dying, and there is no one to save it. There are too many places like Edmonton. For Iglesias, he is desensitized. He's here for the law, meeting

Donnie Morris.

"You have his address?" Beckman asks.

"Yeah," Iglesias says, checking his phone. "He's in Rundle Heights, a townhouse on 113 Ave."

The Edmonton officer drives the three to the far northeast side of the city, where they come to a series of old rundown townhouses. Clearly, this portion of the city isn't for the rich and successful. These neighbourhoods are for those scraping by on a minimum-wage job. The aged vehicles, cracked stucco homes, and chipped paint reflect the cash level here.

The unit parks on the side of the road beside the townhouses, and the three officers exit. Iglesias takes the lead to the two-floor units. He knocks on the door.

Archer says, "And we know he's home?"

"Oh yeah," Beckman says. "This guy has been a hermit ever since this started."

Iglesias adds, "When you bust both the cops and the Crystal Moths, you kind of want to keep a low profile."

The door opens, and they're greeted by a large, pale man in a black band shirt. His long tattered hair is tucked behind his ears, with a concerned frown in between.

"Long time no see," Iglesias says. "Mind if we come in?"

"Yeah, yeah, of course," Donnie Morris says while stepping to the side.

The three officers enter the townhouse, and their steps creak on the yellow tiles. Children's toys scatter around the living room. The kitchen is a messy scene: dirty plates fill the sink, chips are on the counter, and crumbs cover the floor. There are no fruits or vegetables found anywhere. Fresh produce is for the rich.

Donnie says, "Forgive the mess. My sister hasn't had time to clean."

And you don't? Iglesias thinks. It's a pointless observation because Iglesias keeps his place pristine. He has a distaste for people who keep a messy home. In fact, he loses a little bit of respect for them. Iglesias can't fathom how one can get so large and live in such a dump. Donnie is at least two Archers in one. He must suffer from short-term depression because the guy was far thinner the last time he and Beckman met him.

Donnie takes them to the kitchen table. He pushes aside some of the pencil crayons and papers scattered on the surface. "Have a seat," Donnie says.

Archer asks, "Where's your sister?"

"She's running the kids to the daycare." Donnie sits down.

"Your kids or hers?" Archer asks.

"They're hers. I doubt I'm going to have kids. I'd have to find a girl first." Donnie smiles awkwardly, making Archer fold her arms.

"Great segue," Iglesias says. "How's your girlfriend doing?"

"Sorry?" Donnie's voice goes up a notch.

"Come on, don't be stupid. Lola Cabello. How's the relationship going?"

Donnie exhales heavily. "Look, I've told you what I know. I know you're still tapping my phone because otherwise, you wouldn't be here. You know she called, and you know how that conversation went."

Iglesias says, "Bingo."

Beckman asks, "Have you been watching the news?"

"Yeah, I saw the murder on CAMB. I didn't know what she was going to do in Vancouver. I knew she was heading west, like she said on the call. If you listened to our conversation, you'd know I told her to call you, Detective Iglesias. I gave her your card. I know she has it."

Iglesias says, "Back to the question. How's your relationship with her?"

Donnie flushes and wipes his pink cheeks. "It hasn't changed."

Archer asks, "And how did you guys meet again?"

Donnie says, "Isn't this on my profile from, like, a couple years ago?"

Beckman says, "We lost it."

It's a lie. The three officers are on the same page and want Donnie to confirm his story to see if anything has changed. If he was lying then, he'll slip now. It's a simple tactic that police use time and time again.

"Okay," Donnie says. "I've known Lola for quite a while. We met through the music scene. She was a goth-industrial kid. I enjoyed the metal side and played in the band Blood Bathers. It was a cool metal-industrial blend by adding in samples and a few sequencers, if that's your thing."

The three RCMP officers' faces are flat.

"Anyways. The scenes blend in a city with limited interest. Lola and I went to the same parties and shows. Of course, you chat with people. She was going to school at Grant MacEwan University to become a reporter and told me about the blog she ran. I thought it was the cooler stuff, you know? She was working as an independent reporter, updating her blog with the crimes in Edmonton. She covered a lot of serial killer stuff like the snapper cases and the drainer cases."

"And she convinced you to join her in her independent research?" Beckman asks.

"Sort of. I mean, yeah. She got involved with the Michael Bradford YEGman stuff on her own. After her friends Becky and Michael died, Lola showed me the video of the murders. I was in shock. I mean, to discover the corruption within the police and how they spun Michael's story was insane. We couldn't trust them, no offence."

Iglesias says, "None taken. Corruption is everywhere."

"Exactly," Donnie says. "So Lola had this bomb of information and no one to trust it with. It didn't take much convincing for me to know what had to be done. We're both rebellious music kids who wanted to stick it to the man. I showed Lola how to use some computers because we both knew there'd be a backlash when her video went live. People would shut down her blog. They'd trace her IP address and harass her, or worse. We didn't think it would go this far."

"And?" Iglesias asks.

"That's when you three got involved. The video exploded online. It caught the attention of the cops and freaked me out. Obviously, I listened to the law. Lola didn't. She double-downed. It's admirable. She will do what she wants without worrying about the consequences. The stress on her family and her poor mom."

"Yes. That was a tragedy," Archer says.

"We've supported her father and brother since," Beckman adds.

"I know," Donnie says. "That wasn't good enough for her. Stepping away severed our friendship. She wasn't going to quit, not after losing her life."

"A fiery girl," Iglesias says. "It's tough to resist a strong-headed woman who knows what she wants."

Donnie clears his throat, fidgeting with his sweaty thumbs.

"I can't blame you," Iglesias says. "They make you do crazy things. You can never get them out of your mind. They come back into your life after you are certain that was the end of it. They make you wonder if they are the one. You look past their red flags because you care for them. That's why you picked up her call a week ago, isn't it?"

Donnie says, "I didn't know it was her."

Archer says, "Right, and you answer all calls from random numbers? What about emails?"

Donnie clears his throat again, drowning in nervousness.

Beckman asks, "Has Lola sent emails, Donnie?"

Donnie says, "No." His cheeks keep turning redder.

Iglesias says, "Look, we could grill you again, doing what we did before. Get the paperwork, process you, go through your belongings and invade your privacy. Or you can work with us, and we'll leave today."

"Great," Donnie exhales. "Fine. I knew it was her number. Lola told me what the burner phone's number was before. She sends me the odd email. Obviously, she got rid of the phone after, so it's not even important."

"She contact you after the call?" Iglesias asks.

"Yes, one time through email. It had a recording," Donnie says.

Iglesias asks, "Mind showing us?"

"This way," Donnie says and leads the three detectives from the kitchen to his bedroom upstairs, where his computer is. He sits at his desk and turns on the laptop, navigating to his inbox. He opens the last email from a cryptic address with the email titled, "Listen if you aren't convinced." It has an MP3 attachment.

Archer is already writing the email address as Donnie hits play. The recording begins, and Iglesias clenches his fists, hearing Chen's voice. This is the exact recording Lola gave the police.

"And that's the only one?" Iglesias asks.

Donnie says, "For now. I mean, she's random with communicating."

"Did you reply to her?" Archer asks.

"No," Donnie says.

"Keep the channel open," Beckman says. "Reply back. Keep her interested. If she calls you again, let us know."

"Yep," Donnie says, looking to the ground.

Iglesias says, "Thanks for your time."

The three officers leave the townhouse and stand outside, reflecting on the interview they had over a drag. Beckman speaks, "That kid wants to stay clean."

Iglesias says, "We'll see about that. He's obeying us until his emotions get the better of him. He'll do something stupid."

Archer says, "So until then, it's off to the Vancouver Homicide Department?"

Beckman says, "You got it."

The three officers return to the police unit. Their driver takes them out of the slums and back to the airport. The entire conversation with Donnie could have been done over a phone call, or they could have sent a local officer to do the investigating for them. It would have saved on that limited budget.

Iglesias is an old-fashioned investigator. You lose so much valuable information through a call. He needs to be teeth-to-teeth with people because their physical form has subtle nuances.

It appears Cabello is keeping Donnie around. He will be their line of communication with her. She will contact him again because she can't do this alone forever. She'll crack. Or, she'll make new friends in the world of crime. There are enough wackjobs in the world who will buy into her plans.

CHAPTER 26
TOUGH

Twice a day, Lola applies Synarion's leaf paste onto her wounds. Her bruised rib cage and her wounded clavicle are almost unnoticeable. The rapid rejuvenation makes four days appear to be several weeks. It is magic, despite what the nymph says.

Synarion takes the floor during Lola's time with him. The good Canadian side of Lola feels guilty. The other side is glad to be in a bed, not in her car or on a rundown, lumpy motel mattress.

Lola ponders over Bark Nose and Abbygail over the four days. She asks Synarion the same questions a couple of times. Such as, "I'm not dreaming?" "He's a Root Walker?" "Abbygail was human." "She's held on life support by a flesh-eating plant?"

Synarion's responses are "yes." The old world did exist, and Lola no longer lives in a façade.

A gloved fist soars toward her. She raises her forearms, blocking the oncoming attack. An uppercut comes for her, and she steps to the side, missing it. A foot swings against her calf, and she lands hard on her ass with a thud. The impact on the hardwood floor rattles her torso to her wounds.

"Not terrible," Synarion says. He offers a hand to her. "There's plenty to improve upon with your hand-to-hand combat."

"Does getting stabbed and beaten have anything to do with it?" Lola asks, taking his hand.

He pulls her with more force than anticipated, and her hands land against his stern pecks. She's surprised at how tight the muscles are. Lola lets go, her face flushing, and takes a step away. Synarion is unphased by the interaction and raises his fists again.

He speaks. "The wounds encumber you, yes. They're no excuse. You have to learn to fight in every state. Healthy, damaged, tired, glad, angry, it does not matter." Synarion lunges forward, spinning sideways and ending in a roundhouse kick toward her chest.

Lola dodges and throws a fist. Synarion swats her arm downward.

"You must control your emotions. Pain is a signal from your brain."

He launches a right hook. Lola blocks. She makes a low kick, this one hitting Synarion's upper thigh. He smiles and takes another punch at her. The blow hits her shoulder, making her stumble a few steps back.

Despite the rapid healing, the pain is chronic, and Synarion's aggression makes it far more excruciating. Fists soar at her. Her forearms deflect the attacks. Lola takes several more steps to the corner of the kitchen.

Synarion sends his foot high, the heel whooshing past her chin. She ducks and slams a fist into his gut. It stuns him long enough for Lola to snag him by the neck and drag him onto the ground in a chokehold.

"Very good," Synarion grits through his teeth. With leg power alone, Synarion rolls the two of them to the side, and Lola frees her opponent.

"In this scenario," Synarion says, standing, "you don't want to be underneath an opponent heavier than you. We'll stop here."

Lola's pants end in winces. She wipes her sweat-covered forehead with each movement surging a pang in her body. "I had you," she says.

"Not even close," Synarion says. "We don't want to make your wounds worse. Well done, though."

"Thanks. You kicked my ass twice, then."

Synarion says, "Defensive battle tactics are far more effective than an offensive."

"Yeah, I've heard that a million times."

"Old truths hold value. It's why they've survived the centuries."

"Unlike the old world," Lola says.

"Precisely. A defensive tactic keeps your emotions at bay."

Lola says, "I wasn't offensive."

"It was simmering. Yes, I was cornering you, but you would have been better off removing yourself from the corner rather than standing your ground. In your damaged state, the impact of my next attack would have been colossal. In fact, it would lead to the same scenario as the motel room."

"Great. Another life-threatening moment."

"Don't let it fluster you. Understanding your errors is part of the learning process."

"I have had a lot to process lately."

Synarion says, "Those are your emotions you must learn to control."

"Yes, I get it. This is all for survival. It's a means to an end for me." Truthfully, Lola doesn't like to consider herself a fighter. She is far more interested in the detective work of her unintentional career path. Unfortunately, she isn't working for a news station and needs to learn to fight to save her life.

"I've had a lot to process," Lola repeats. *Ash*, she thinks, knowing she could loosen the tension with another hit. Lola had two sessions, and the comedown is easing, unlike the need which crawls under her skin, slithering around in her veins and tingling her desires with an itch that she cannot reach.

Synarion takes a step closer, inches away. She gets a good whiff of his pine scent again. It pulls her in, like her growing addiction to the drug. Both of which she is failing to suppress. She can't develop sparkle-eyes for the first man who helps her like a naïve high school girl.

He reaches for her face, and Lola tilts her head, leaning in. Synarion's knuckles bump her cheek, brushing against her skin.

It's obvious he was brushing dirt off. Lola leans away as if she knew.

Synarion says, "There is no need to ponder over ash."

He walks to the kitchen, getting himself a glass of water. The sweat on her back turns to ice, and she clears her throat.

How did he know? Lola thinks. She must appear far more impulsive to her desires than she realizes.

"The longing for release from a wretched life is clear as day in your eyes." Synarion hands her a glass of cool water. "Taking that drug is a dangerous path. The old world is filled with many anomalies you can't possibly understand. They're tempting with power beyond your wildest imagination. You need to stay sharp. We have three days before the show's opening. We best be ready."

Lola says, "Will we have to do that much fighting?"

"Hard to say. If one of the vazeleads I seek is there, then great. If it's another vazelead, I hope to start negotiations. Warn their people of the dangers they tread."

"Who is the vazelead you are looking for?"

"A severed past that I hope to mend," Synarion says.

"You have no idea where their people are?"

"No. They stay off of our old world intranet. They have a rough history and prefer to keep it hidden. I'd love to know how the Crystal Moths got in contact with them."

Lola says, "I wonder if Mastema will be at the art show."

Synarion shrugs. "It's possible."

"The opening will also pull in high profiles. If the Prime Minister is connected to ash, we can use that."

"Exactly," Synarion says.

"We'll need pretty good disguises," Lola says. "My face is plastered everywhere."

"We do. I'll obtain some outfits and you some makeup to hide your more prominent features. Besides, I must leave for a couple of days. I will be back by Thursday."

"Sorry? That's the night before the show," Lola says.

"Precisely," Synarion says.

"And what am I supposed to do?"

"The same thing you're doing: heal, process the vast knowledge you've come to learn, and stay out of the public eye."

"This is the second time you've vanished. Where do you go?" Lola asks, wondering if she's asking too much of him.

"It's another balancing mission," Synarion says.

"I don't know who the hell you are," Lola says. "Just wanting to understand."

"I'm a balancer. The ash case isn't my only concern. There are other balancing offences that I must attend to."

"All along the West Coast? What about the rest of the world?"

"I do what I can, prioritizing what I must. Some missions are local. Others take me away for a few weeks to more foreign places. Those must be important. Flying isn't cheap."

"I'm surprised you don't have a secret old world airline you can use."

"Funny. I wish we did. As I've said, nobody is volunteering to assist the cause. I'm on my own." He pauses, eyes glazed over, lost in his past. "With that, I have loose ends for one mission I need to close."

"This one related to that plant girl, and your missing finger?"

Lola bites her tongue. She is taking a presumptuous leap.

"A little, yes. It's not important to you." Synarion grabs his things and heads for the door. "Get plenty of rest. I'll be back in a couple of days."

With that, Synarion grabs his bag and weapons and leaves Lola in the apartment. Secrecy irritates her. She also has little to do on her own and lots of questions for Synarion.

She's spent enough time over the past few days scouring the web to find information on the art gallery, the painter, and anything else she can unravel regarding the Crystal Moths. She needs to take action.

Her reporter mind sparks a brilliant idea. She and Synarion have common goals now, which won't last forever. He wishes to keep balance in the world, which he believes involves the Crystal Moths. Lola wants to exploit the gang, showing the world what they are. If that includes the vazeleads, she doesn't care. Curating facts isn't what an actual reporter does.

Lola goes through her messenger bag to grab her laptop, stack of cash, and recording device. The device is large. It's easy to hide when wearing a coat or tucking in a boot. It's not so easy to hide when you're going to a formal art opening. She needs discretion.

After counting cash, she skims the Internet to find somewhere nearby that sells recording equipment. A camera store, a pawnshop, or an electronics store will do, and in the dense metropolis, there are several within walking distance.

Lola doesn't have much for disguises and starts going through Synarion's wardrobe. Guilt should riddle her for going through his belongings. Lola is cold. Her reporter instincts override any sense of privacy invasion or her naive animalistic tension.

His wardrobe is small, containing simple shirts, hoodies, and trousers. Lola grabs one of the hoodies and slips it on, putting the hood over her head. As with any outing, her knife is tucked right into her belt and ready to use. She takes the keys, exits the apartment, and hikes to the nearest electronics store with her stack of cash.

She keeps her head low and passes the security guard in a large electronics store, moving through the dense crowds straight to the camera department. Their products are behind glass, letting her browse from a distance. On the second shelf is a perfect little square camera with a clasp. It works with an SD card, has an extended battery, wireless uploading, and is discreet enough that she can clip it onto an outfit.

Lola also purchases a wireless microphone to sync with the device. Finally, she's upgrading her recording methods. The purchase eats most of her cash. That's okay. She chose to be in the old world, and there's no going back for Lola Cabello. She is in this dark underbelly forever.

People are complicated, human or nymph, and each person has their own agenda. Lola needs to protect hers. The camera and mic are excellent additions to aid her goal. It's no ash liberation, but it strips away a small layer of stress from her psyche, knowing she is in control.

CHAPTER 27
HISTORICAL DOCUMENTS

Leather boots and dress shoes step on the waxed concrete ground. The steps echo in the vast open space of the dim room with massive canvas paintings mounted on the white walls. This is the art show Erol Terzi told Scalebane about, where his partner, Dasco Amoss, is launching a new body of work. He insisted that Scalebane would enjoy Dasco's paintings. Here they are, the night before the grand opening.

Scalebane lets her tail flow as they walk. The human has not treated her like a monster and is naive to the old world tragedies, which is no fault of his own. Soft skins are simple creatures with short lifespans.

"I wanted to give you a personal tour before it opens," Erol says as they enter the show's first room.

"You were insistent," Scalebane says. Her clawed hands rest on her belt next to her sai, eyeing the room, the ceiling, and the entrances to ensure they are alone. Her mind is on the hunt. Life has sculpted her mind with instincts of survival. Privileges of finer beauties are foreign.

Erol holds his hands behind his back as they walk. "You are of the dark nature, my friend. So is my partner. You could say I gravitate towards tortured souls."

"I'm tortured? What of your demonstration with that human and his family?" Scalebane can't help but smile a toothy grin underneath her metal-muzzled leather mask.

"Chen?" Erol asks. "Your hands-on approach is inspiring me."

"Tortured. That's the most flattering compliment I've ever had."

Erol chuckles, for he is unsure if she's being sarcastic or serious. He continues, "My partner leans towards grim works. He says he is pulled by a muse. It's an abstract idea of creative problem-solving, as he likes to say. I thought you'd appreciate some of his themes."

The two stop beside a five-foot square canvas with acrylic paints of red, yellow, and harsh black lines. The work combines many shapes and faces in rings forming a giant circle. Between the line work of the faces are microscopic hieroglyphics. Further, the entire circle radiates light behind it, shining in the clouds.

"Aztec, Egyptian, Medieval, Dasco combines all cultures," Erol says.

And vazelead, Scalebane thinks. Portions of the varying line weights are similar to King's paintings in his home. She is speechless.

Erol speaks, "His work has been dubbed as post religionism by his critics. It moves the art industry beyond postmodernism. Dasco finds a way to combine every culture into one beautiful mosaic, bringing humanity together."

"I can see that. There's more as well," Scalebane says.

"You recognize some of it?"

"In a sense. Many of it is bound by human cultures without a doubt. There are a few that aren't. How did he know what to do?" Scalebane moves closer to the canvas. Her metal muzzle is inches from the paint. She hones in on the center of the circle, which is no larger than several inches. It contains a triangle pointing downwards with circles wrapped around each edge. Above the triangles are mountains and a river. Further up are a series of rings overlapping each other with a golden gate.

Scalebane says, "I haven't seen such detailed paintings of the Heavenly Kingdoms, the mortal realm, and Dega'Mostikas's Triangle in centuries."

"I beg your pardon, Dega——?" Erol says.

"Dega'Mostikas's Triangle. It's Hell's true name, consisting of three realms. It's nothing like you can imagine."

Erol's face slants. "I see. Before humanity erased it all?"

"Precisely. Judged souls still reside in that Hell triangle, forced to live a second life of agony."

"I bet I have some family members stuck there."

Mother. Scalebane is unsure why she cannot push her from her thoughts since arriving in Canada. She steps away, seeing how the central map and the rings of faces represent a soul's journey. She points to the golden gate.

Scalebane says, "Not all souls end up there. The Heavenly Kingdoms are above Hell and the mortal realm. Most people find themselves there."

"We'll see about that," Erol says.

"Don't be too harsh on your family or yourself."

Erol looks to the ground.

"Afterlife judgement isn't what it used to be," Scalebane says.

"Thank you. I sure hope they're there," Erol says.

"Your relatives are deceased?" Scalebane asks.

"They passed away in Turkey a long time ago. You know, I used to consider myself an atheist. In some ways, I wish that was true."

"Why is that?" Scalebane asks.

"Then there's a guarantee that this will end. There's salvation in an eternal slumber. If this is true, I'm afraid I won't join them in Heaven. After a life I've lived, it sounds like this Dega'Mostikas's Triangle is for me."

"Trust me, it is very real. Mastema is familiar with the afterlife, being the First."

"Yet he is here, in the mortal realm?" Erol asks.

"That is what I would like to know," Scalebane says.

"In time, I think we will learn. There's a lot to unravel regarding the world's history," Erol says.

"Erol, I must say, I'm impressed. I didn't think I would appreciate your partner's work."

A wide grin of victory spreads across Erol's face. "I'm glad you approve of his paintings. It's quite unique."

"Usually, I don't concern myself with art because what's left is tied to human history and culture. This is different entirely."

"We can have dinner one day." Erol clears his throat, grasping the lunacy of his words.

"That would be fascinating. He has to come to terms with what you do first."

Erol swallows the lump of regret and carries on. Scalebane follows, and they move to the next piece, which is enticing. This painting uses oranges, tans, and yellows forming oval blotches, or sand dunes. Surrounding the dunes are many triangles and circle patterns overlaying the hills into a square spiral. Soldiers line the bottom of the painting in scarlet armour, looking at the central naked woman with bright emerald eyes. Her fangs drizzle red droplets onto her chin.

"Vampires, like our two Crystal Moth friends," Erol says.

"There are plenty around. Vampires blend in well with humanity. This painting looks to be of Queen Valturus, the original vampire. She has long since vanished."

"I should take a history course from you."

Scalebane's tail sways playfully. "Think I could be a historian?"

"Sure, when this is said and done."

"Violence is all I've ever known," Scalebane says. "I've never thought of anything else."

"Let's change that. Scalebane, tomorrow evening, when the show opens, we'll have many high-profile clients coming by. This includes the Prime Minister. Mastema wants us to make them feel welcome at the show. We'll be giving them the ash shipment you saw earlier, in the, uhm, dragon statues."

"The country's leader is an ash user?" Scalebane asks.

"That I doubt. He understands our business. He works with us in several channels to control cash in Canada, thanks to his former ties with Allen Shipping Solutions. We want to distribute more along the West Coast rather than shipping it to the East, where we have better political relations."

"And Dasco doesn't know this?" Scalebane asks.

"Unfortunately, business and family are a good disguise. Showing a little bit of vulnerability can bring you new opportunities with your work partners. Look at us."

"A fair strategy. You have given me a glimpse into your world."

"And we've bonded, have we not?" Erol asks.

Scalebane smiles, unseen by her colleague. "I suppose so."

"We invite movie stars, politicians, reporters, and critics to the opening. They know my partner and me. Some know my relations to the Crystal Moths."

Scalebane didn't think there'd be many high-level ash-dashers so soon. The prestige explains why they cannot carry on with the demand. Her sister, Namsruc, must be having a difficult time on the East Coast. Thinking of her, Scalebane wonders how her sister is managing on the other side of the country. They haven't spoken since both were sent to Canada.

Erol continues, "The interest is growing. Which is why we need a faster supply. You and King both know of that issue. However, that's between our bosses, isn't it?"

Scalebane stops at the third painting, ignoring Erol's

question. She's drawn to the primary illustration of a hand with two thumbs and a reptilian eyeball in the center. Patterned borders of eyeballs and triangles run along the entire frame. Dozens of people are below, on the side, and above the hands, bowing in prayer to the hovering hand.

"I'd very much like to meet this Dasco," Scalebane says.

"Well, after the show tomorrow, you can," Erol says.

Scalebane spins to face him, her tail pointing to the ceiling. Her voice rises. "You would do that? Even with me and who I am?"

"I want you to trust me, Scalebane. It will make our working lives better, and I'd like to know you as a person. I'm no idiot. There's more behind those weapons and concealing leather. You're an individual with your own thoughts. I want to know who that person is."

"Most don't," Scalebane says. For too long, she has only known to be a killer, executing King's command. Little has she thought about her desires other than protecting her sister and following orders.

"Because your people hide?" Erol asks.

Scalebane says, "Yes. Fifteen of my people are left, my sister and I included. You wonder why ash is difficult to produce? There's your answer, one that your boss knows too."

"And what of your sister? Is she like you?" Erol asks.

She says, "Sort of. We didn't know who our father was, making it difficult for our mother to be alone. Namsruc hatched at the same time as I. Raising two kids in an uninhabitable environment of raining blood is an impressive feat. No living mortal should be familiar with it."

"I'm so sorry," Erol says.

"It's in the past. Mother found a way for us to escape the land of the damned. Unfortunately, she paid the price."

"Do you think you can find her again?" Erol asks.

"One day. How the afterlife handles souls is beyond my knowledge. My childhood was so long ago. It feels more of a dream," Scalebane says.

"Then your mother is alive?"

"Depends on how you describe alive. Dega'Mostikas's Triangle isn't meant for the living."

"You grew up in Hell?" Erol asks, disbelief oozing from his words.

"As I said, Hell isn't like anything you can imagine."

"Wouldn't Mastema know how to find your mother?" Erol asks.

"Perhaps. He is also deceiving, no offence."

Erol smiles. "None taken. He is ruthless. You have that in common with him, on this outer layer of yours."

"You flatter me, Erol, but I know what I am."

"I don't think you do," Erol says. He steps closer to Scalebane. She doesn't stop him. Curiousness smothers her impulses to see why his bold hand moves to her mask in a slow, controlled motion. "There's more behind this exterior than a cold killer."

The intentions stun her, watching as the man's hand reaches for the leather. Erol grips the mask's edge where the headpiece's cloth meets the leather. He pulls on the rim, lifting it.

Scalebane steps away and pushes the mask down. She walks

to the next painting as if nothing happened, presuming the man will follow. Blood pumps into her scalp feathers, raising the cowl a couple inches. The scales along her spine and tail tingle. Her legs feel light. No human in this generation has seen her face. This is shame at its finest.

She says, "Which is why I had to kill the street dealer."

Erol cups his hand behind his back and follows her. "Yes. Your method surprised me. I would have expected you to enjoy prolonging the man's death."

"Whether it's a soft skin or my own kind, my mother's words hold true. Killing is needed in self-defence and to end one's suffering."

"It's a different style from what Crystal Moths are used to. You let the family go instead of executing them. They saw a part of you."

"Who will believe them? Besides, you wanted to let the girl live," Scalebane says.

"Innocence shouldn't be a casualty in a game of the corrupt."

"Until they grow and shed the naive skin. She needed a mother. It's not easy navigating a world with no guidance. The mother and daughter will serve as a message to anyone who tries to expose us from the inside."

"Fair enough. I respect your reasoning, and we can work with it. I'll make sure their survival story from the Moths is on the news, so the warning is broadcasted to all."

"Good."

"And we'll kill who needs to be killed."

"Precisely, otherwise we are repeating our people's history. Getting that street dealer out of jail was dangerous. Your people's police know that the Crystal Moths are in their system."

Erol says, "Not entirely. We have enough eyes and ears within the law. That incident will be dissolved before you know it." He raises his index finger. "I have something else that will interest you. Killing the vigilante didn't go as well as we had hoped."

"The soft skin from Edmonton?" Scalebane asks.

"Yes. The Crystal Moth we sent to assassinate her was found dead. Smaller news outlets caught wind of the case, and my hands were tied. I had to run the report nationally. Thankfully, we adjusted the story a little, making Lola Cabello the prime focus. Many think she murdered a poor man in the motel."

"She did kill him, didn't she?" Scalebane asks.

"It would be an impressive act," Erol says. "Ramon was a capable man. I theorize she has help."

"Then you need me to take care of this." Scalebane stops by the final painting in the showcase room. This canvas is of a barren red wasteland with black swirling clouds soaring above. Deep red rain pours onto the sand. The detailed landscape is masked in a triangle shape with circles wrapped around the edges. Closer inspection reveals the clouds are made of glyphs varying in tone.

Wretched childhood, Scaelbane thinks. She must speak with Dasco. He painted her birthplace with immense accuracy.

Erol says, "Since you are the foreman specializing in a hunt, I thought I'd offer you the opportunity to assassinate the girl. I can share as much as I know regarding Lola Cabello."

"Give me everything," Scalebane says, staring at the final painting. A rebellious soft skin is no match for a hunter from Hell.

CHAPTER 28
WELCOME TO THE SHOW

Okay, Lola, you've done this before, Lola thinks as her hands wobble, wrapping the small camera and cord into her skintight, formal cocktail dress. Her fingers shouldn't be shaking, considering she has gone undercover plenty of times. It's the intensity of this mission causing her anxiety. The night of Dasco Amoss's opening at North Vancouver Gallery of Modern Prestige is tonight.

A gentle knock comes from the door, followed by Synarion's voice. "Does the dress fit?"

"Yeah, yes. It does. Thanks," Lola says.

"Good. I can't recall the last time I bought a dress for a woman."

"You had a woman?" Lola smirks.

Synarion doesn't answer, and she exhales relief. He is unaware of her camera and doesn't need to know. It's her secret to keep documenting what they find and upload it with the other evidence. Synarion won't be an editorial of facts.

Lola clips the camera onto a golden necklace draped below her jugular notch. This necklace she got after purchasing the camera and mic. The camera's small square shape compliments the black diamond pendant on the chain as if it were part of the jewellery's design. Synarion will be her guinea pig to see how visible this thing is. If she can go unnoticed in the studio apartment, she will be fine in the gallery.

She shifts the dress's fabric around the breasts, ensuring the microphone is hidden behind the strap. Her hands run to the end of the dress and pull the fabric to hide her skin. *Way too exposed,* she thinks. The dress is tighter and shorter than what she would prefer. This flirty fabric ends an inch above her knees. She's not one for showing skin. Black skinny jeans and band t-shirts were her preference in university. She even had to embrace the innocent luxury of shaving for this special occasion. One perk of her spy outfit is using the thigh holster. Synarion bought her one to conceal her gun and knife.

Next is shifting the stylized belt around her waist, tying it so it doesn't put too much pressure and enough to emphasize her curves. The small, single shoulder strap isn't enough to hide the two scars on her chest.

That is where the crimson red wig comes into play. She places it on her head, transforming. Lola fixes the bangs in the mirror that rest above her eyebrows. She combs the straight hair with her fingers, running to the ends that shroud her scars. Perfect.

She is Talia Marquis. The lipstick's exaggerated state conceals the coral cupid bow on her lips. Her mother's nose bridge is a tough one to hide. Thankfully, excessive eyeshadow and blush can create the illusion of a facial shape.

She takes a deep breath, feeling an aching pressure from where her ribs were beaten. Synarion's magic leaves worked wonders to make her mobile, the brutality of the assault left a few spikes of pain here and there. Lola will manage.

The high heels click with each step she takes, opening the washroom door and stepping into the studio space. Synarion is buttoning his vest. He turns and ogles the transformed woman. His gaze is too long, running along her pale legs to her hips and then the necklace. The purple eyes are far more infatuated with the dress's ability to emphasize her breasts. The eyes continue on. He lands on her face expressing an intentional moue. Faking full pouty lips is a simple tactic that doesn't fail to catch a man's attention. Apparently, an ancient nymph is no different.

Synarion catches himself and clears his throat. "It fits well."

"Thanks. Believe it or not, I used to have a normal life where doing this was ordinary, impressing industry professionals in university."

"Well, consider this a drive down memory lane." He finishes tucking his white shirt into his black pants. He raises his arms in a "what do you think?" pose, waiting for Lola's judgement.

"You dress up well," Lola says.

He runs his hand through his slicked-back hair. "Look at us.

Two outcasts are becoming civilized."

"Lucky us. Do you think they'll recognize you?" Lola asks, tapping her ears.

"So far, I have been lucky. The eye contacts help normalize me, and most people ignore the ears. Occasionally, my hair must change. If you stay clear of cameras, you can go unnoticed for quite a long time, and eventually, generations pass."

"What about those photos of you and that girl?"

"Memories. They're the only photos that I'm aware of. In today's world, that's becoming more difficult."

Lola fiddles with the chain of her necklace. *A little too easy*, she thinks, her cheeks turning hot. Lola feels guilty for taking advantage of Synarion's kindness. The nymph would denounce her video camera for the stealth mission. Lola must stay true to her goals.

Synarion heads to the table of junk. He sifts through the electronics and opens a plastic drawer, pulling out a small black device in the shape of a Bluetooth walkie-talkie.

"These will let us communicate with each other. Keep it tucked in your ear and under that wig," Synarion says.

"What about you?" Lola asks, taking the device.

"I've got this," he says, raising his wrist and showing a gold watch. "It'll sync with the one in your ear. It's simple to use, and they have a decent range. Press the button on the back of the device, and it will let you talk. Leave it alone, and that lets me talk."

Lola presses the button and speaks, "Hello."

"And on my end, it shows as text." He shifts his wrist to showcase the screen, which states: hello.

"Subtle," Lola says.

"It has a speaker, too, if needed." He presses a button on the watch and says, "Hear this?"

"Yeah," Lola says.

"Then let's get our tools and head to the show." Synarion snags his black blazer. He moves to the corner of the room with his wardrobe and opens a wooden cupboard. He reveals his throwing stars and puts them in his blazer's inner pocket. Then he takes his spiked knuckles.

Lola pats herself, feeling the thigh guard's tight bond around her leg. She checks the mirror one more time, seeing the earpiece shrouded by the wig. The microphone isn't visible under the single strap. Synarion's reaction confirms the camera's disguise is a success.

She steps out and puts on a fake smile of enthusiasm. "Let's head to the show."

Lola Cabello, Scalebane thinks as she clutches a newspaper. The local paper covers the motel murder that occurred a week ago. The mugshot of Cabello is right on the fold of the front page. The photograph is the one Erol shared with her, taken two years ago in Edmonton. Amazingly, there hasn't been a clear shot of her since. Scalebane will end the hunt.

Kill to end one's suffering, her mother's words echo in her mind. *Or in self-defence.* The last part of the moral lesson applies when Scalebane's mother curses her thoughts. Her sister is far better at following guidance.

Scalebane chucks the newspaper onto the desk in front of a series of monitors showcasing security cameras. They cover the hallways, the main gallery, and the backrooms within the North Vancouver Gallery of Modern Prestige. Babysitting an art opening wasn't her first choice. Erol stresses the importance of tonight; thus, she obeys, knowing her partner's strategy is best. It's what King would want. Then, she can sink her teeth into the girl.

She leaves the security room and enters the next door in the hall, taking her to the loading dock. Erol is here with a handful of Crystal Moths dressed in black, complete with white blazers. They stand by the open garage door. No vampires are here today. Good; they reek of death.

"Ah, Scalebane, familiarized yourself with the facility?" Erol asks.

"Yes, I understand the cameras' cycles. I also checked a newspaper article as well. It has the vigilante soft skin on the front cover."

"We shouldn't have to worry about her," Erol says. "Tonight is focused on embracing our new clientele and strengthening existing relations with our product."

"It's not my product." Scalebane puts her hand on her belt. She isn't a fan of how ash works on humans, unlike King. The drug industry is lucrative, which means the vazeleads are involved. Currency is better leverage than violence in the modern world.

"The SUV should be arriving at any moment with the dragon statues," Erol says. He points at two Crystal Moths standing by the garage door. "These two will be unloading the SUV, if you don't mind overseeing this art gallery portion."

"And you will be where?" Scalebane asks.

"I'll take these three to the art show itself. They will serve as security with the others during the opening. It has to be tight with the Prime Minister being here. Plus, I will be making my public appearance with my partner."

"And I can meet Dasco after?"

"Yes, of course. He'll want to go to an after party, no doubt. I'll get him to stay here a little longer."

"Thank you. I am quite curious of his work and this muse he speaks of."

"We'll see to it," Erol says.

"Are the clients coming here to purchase the ash?"

"Correct."

"Who can I expect?" Scalebane asks.

"We have a checklist of people. The Crystal Moths here will recognize them. There's the actress Ashley Amber. The Prime Minister. Ian Black. Jesse Shawn. Quite a few. Even some from your old world."

The names aren't recognizable to Scalebane. The old world mention is a surprise.

An all-black Ralliart Sportback hums through the alleyway to the loading dock. The windows are tinted, reflecting the nearby skyscrapers. The vehicle parks on the far end of the road, and a woman exits the driver's side with her black high heels clicking.

Her wide-brimmed sunglasses and baggy hood cover most of her pink face. Even with the beige foundation, she looks to have a severe sunburn. Scalebane has seen this skin tone before. The trenchcoat isn't enough to hide the fact she's of the old world.

A new scent pierces past the typical funk of human sweat and feces, rising with a sweet tang. This pheromone is projecting from the newcomer. It's an attractive smell, entrancing Scalebane until Erol speaks.

"Speak of the devil." He chuckles.

"Erol, sweetie. I would give you a hug." The woman says with a smile, exposing a mouth full of fangs behind her natural pitch-black lips. A bystander would presume the colouring to be lipstick.

"I always welcome your embrace."

The woman waves her index finger in a playful no. "Except not today, my dear. You are irritating me."

"Why is that?" Erol asks.

"You've changed the pickup location once again." At the end of her coat, a pointed black spike hides beside her bare ankle. It's attached to a pink tail that slithers under the fabric.

Succubus, Scalebane thinks, collecting herself from the luring seductive smell of the creature. It's not quite a devil. A demon is pretty damn close. Mastema isn't the only being from the afterlife in the mortal realm.

"I'm sorry, Mulier," Erol says, taking a bow. "The shipment will be here soon, and you can be on your way. The constant location change is temporary until we get distribution stable."

"Make it in one place and sell it in another," Mulier says. "It's not that complicated."

Erol forces a laugh.

Make it in one place, Scalebane thinks. Ash comes from overseas, in one place. There's no reason for the location to change. Once the Crystal Moths have the ash, it's theirs to divide.

The succubus stops several inches in front of Erol. "Erol, how is Dasco? You can't keep hiding him from this life forever. I think we would get along."

"I know, I know. Please, accept my sincerest apologies for all of this," Erol says.

Dasco is popular, Scalebane thinks. She walks beside one of the Crystal Moths guarding the garage door. He's got bags under his eyes, a black eye, and fresh burn marks on his face. His gaze is locked onto what little he can see of the succubus's perky ass.

"Who is she?" Scalebane whispers.

He jerks, noticing the cloaked, masked figure standing beside him. "Jesus Christ, man." He flexes his white jacket and says, "How should I know? Aren't you a freak like her or something?"

"Something."

"Oh, wait, *you're* the reptile," he says.

"You know of my people?" Scalebane asks.

"Of them. No idea what you are."

"We'll keep it that way. Now tell me, who is she?"

"Some important client. That's what we're here for. Probably a whore, if you ask me."

"Likely. What happened to your eye?" Scalebane asks. "That's fresh."

"Just a bad deal." The black-eyed Moth folds his arms and looks away.

"Don't make bad moves while I'm here, understand?" Scalebane asks.

The foul stench of his sweat seeps from the skin. It's a subtle change, one that Scalebane can detect. He's experiencing stress and fear, affecting his body chemistry. He's on the edge. It must be her presence.

"Understand?" Scalebane asks.

"Yeah, got it. Christ," the black-eyed Moth says.

Erol's phone buzzes, and he says, "Apologies Mulier, I have to take this."

The succubus says, "Of course."

"Hello, Dasco, my darling," Erol says. "It's starting? Yes, yes, I'll be there right away." He hangs up and snaps his finger, catching the Crystal Moths' attention in the loading dock. He calls to Scalebane, "Keep a good eye out here. The SUV will be here at any moment." He storms to the hallway door with three of the goons at the end of the loading dock.

The pickup location moves, Scalebane thinks. She whispers to the black-eyed Moth. "Why does the pickup location change?"

"It's a standard in this business," the black-eyed Moth says. "Move the lab, make the dope somewhere else. Ash ain't any different. I sell, that's it, man."

"And that pisses clients off?" Scalebane asks.

"Snotty ones like this hag."

Scalebane and Mulier lock gazes. The succubus lowers her shades, showcasing her bubblegum irises above a tooth-filled smile.

What does she know? Scalebane says.

Talia, my name is Talia, Lola thinks. Already she feels sweat building on her back underneath the leather jacket. She fidgets with her fingernails, sitting in the shotgun seat as Synarion drives. They head to North Vancouver, over the famous bridge known as the Ironworkers Memorial Second Narrows

Crossing. The sun is tucked under the ocean's horizon, freeing the night.

They have reviewed their plan numerous times. They've grilled the details of their disguises, weapons, escape plan, and agendas: gather intel and find this vazelead. If the Prime Minister is there, security will be tight, and Lola needs evidence of his involvement with the Moths. It doesn't change the fact that her stomach sinks when Synarion puts the car into the park some blocks from the gallery.

The two exit the vehicle and take one block further from their destination. The minor direction change will distort assumptions of where they came from. Turning a corner, they reach the gallery. It is as portrayed in the pictures online, with white concrete steps in a Mayan pyramid shape. At the top of the stairs are several men in white blazers by the glass doors. The single set of doors compliments the minimal Swedish architecture.

Synarion says, "Lola, or Talia, I should say, I'm going to stay outside to scope the building, so we understand the whole parameter."

"And me?" Lola asks.

"Enjoy the show. See who is there, how the Crystal Moths are involved, and any clues for a vazelead. They won't be in the show itself."

"Right."

"I will meet with you soon," Synarion says.

"Feed me to the lions then," Lola says.

Synarion hands her a ticket. "Have fun."

The two split ways as Lola grips the strap of her small purse tightly. She marches to the staircase, passing people outside smoking. She could go for one right now. There's a pack in her purse. The addiction is best dealt with later. She presses the camera's record button, following behind a group of attendees walking to the glass doors.

Spy time, Lola thinks.

The three men in white blazers check each guest's ticket and give them a red wristband, give them a pat down, and let them pass. The handkerchiefs on their blazers have a small chrome moth emblem clipped to it.

Lola reaches the top of the stairs after the last guest. She hands one of the Moths her ticket, not saying a word. He looks at it, tears the paper and gives her a wristband. His sizable hands wrap the strap around her wrist. Meanwhile, one of the others pats her down, checking her body. They overlook her inner thigh with the gun, being far more interested in her jacket and purse.

The ticket taker says, "Enjoy the show, Talia."

"Thanks!" Lola replies with fake naive joy.

Her arrival is timely. Most of the crowd gathers in the central white room of the gallery past the entrance lobby. Lola pulls the doors open and steps inside the circular space. The interior is bright with fluorescent bulbs to showcase the mounted art pieces. The walls dividing the galley, lobby, and central room don't touch the ceiling, giving it an open feeling.

The secretary at the front desk, to Lola's right, ignores her, as do the additional five security guard Moths. They watch the small circular stage where a woman and a man stand behind a pedestal, ready to give a speech.

Lola slides her jacket off and hugs it with both arms. She strolls around the edge of the crowd to get a good look at the audience. The heavy hitters are easy to spot. With her signature pearl white hair, the famous actress Ashley Amber stands out like a sore thumb. As does her all-skin scrap-of-fabric dress. The next distinguishable character is the Prime Minister of Canada, whose tomato face is a lighthouse for attention. Beside him are some security and other politicians Lola has seen on TV. She can't recall their names.

Throughout the crowd are other familiar faces she couldn't name outright. There are CEOs, musicians, actors, producers, and even men dressed in formal military attire. She angles her necklace so the camera can look at their faces.

The woman on the stage speaks in a clear, powerful voice. "Thank you, one and all, for coming to Dasco Amoss's grand opening tonight at the North Vancouver Gallery of Modern Prestige. We are beyond thrilled and honoured to be here. Thank you to the Prime Minister for graciously joining us tonight. Thanks to all of you, who have come to appreciate the progression of modern art. I bring you Dasco Amoss, who will give a formal statement on his latest collection."

Lola stands beside a white cylinder pillar, fidgeting with her necklace to change the camera's view and capture the whole scene. She is as discrete as she can be, hoping to not draw attention.

"You see anything yet?" comes Synarion's distorted voice through the microphone.

Lola pretends to scratch her ear, pressing the button on the communicator. She whispers, "They're giving the artist's statement."

"Perfect."

"Crystal Moths are the security. They have white blazers and a tiny moth emblem. They're at the entrance, in the lobby, and a few others stand around the edges of the gallery."

"Then we're in the right spot," Synarion says.

Lola whispers, "There's some military or police here. Politicians, stars, and CEOs. Shit. I don't know all of them."

"Do your best to make note," Synarion says.

"They can't all be roped into the Crystal Moths."

"I have no idea," Synarion says. "I'm heading around the back. Touch base if you need me."

"Gotcha."

Dasco places his wine glass on the pedestal on stage and waves several times at the crowd. He pushes his curly hair aside, gathering his composure. He says, "Thank you. Thank you. Truly from the bottom of my heart. I wouldn't be here if it wasn't for my agent, Annabel, here. Before I talk about the progression of my post religionism work, I would be a fool not to acknowledge my life partner, Erol Terzi." Dasco extends his hand to the crowd. "My love. Without your guidance and encouragement, I do not know where I would be." Dasco raises his wine glass. "To you."

The crowd claps in a synchronized formal applause. Some take drinks from their wine while others whisper to each other.

"He's my everything. Now, for tonight's opening. These pieces expand on the post religionism concept from my first body of work. They focus on unifying society by showcasing the terrors we face in life and death."

Lola decides to look at the paintings to get a sense of what he's explaining. She has not even looked at the man's work. A stroll will also allow her to review the gallery. The first painting portrays a sun with rings of faces. The center of the work has mountains with a golden gate above it.

Dasco's voice echoes through the open space. "Creativity is a problem-solving process that extends beyond passion and motivation. We are provided with a situation that needs visual cues to guide its audience into a narrative. Paintings are expressions of the human mind. They incorporate elements of our past, spanning thousands of years. They are the things that survive the sands of time."

Lola keeps moving through the exhibit and spots the kitchen further behind the stage. Next to it is a black marble bar where several guests buy their drinks. Beside the bar are steel doors guarded by two men in white blazers.

She presses the communicator and whispers, "Two Moths are guarding the doors by the kitchen."

Dasco continues, "My work binds humanity under a universal umbrella. The first installations shocked the world by pushing our differences aside."

A drink, act like I belong, Lola thinks. She walks to the far end of the gallery, circling around the edge of the crowd. Reaching the bar, she orders wine from the bartender. Her hand still shakes while grabbing a few coins from her small purse. She takes deep breaths, attempting to calm herself. The sweat along her forehead, pits, and back morphs into a cold chill. *Keep it together.*

The bartender takes the coins and gives her a red wine. She

grabs the glass and thinks she sips it in a controlled manner. Instead, she takes a big gulp while angling the camera toward the two Crystal Moths. They watch Dasco, unaware of her presence.

Dasco's speech carries on. "Through each of these paintings, you can see a progression of the struggles humanity has gone through, the cycles of growth, decay, and the flourishing end where we become anew. The second iteration, what you will see tonight, is intended to transcend beyond our human limitations and let us grow together. We will move past fear. Thank you again to everyone, and enjoy."

The crowd lets out a loud applause as Synarion's voice comes into her ear. "Lots of people will be wearing white tonight. Make a note of the guards. There are two here by the loading dock. They're with . . . no . . . Mul."

"What?" Lola asks. She uses the palm of her wine-holding hand to clap her forearm. The other hand is busy 'scratching' her ear.

"Damn it. This is bad."

"Synarion?" Lola asks.

Lola leaves the bar and walks to another nearby painting. This work is covered in black swirling clouds and red rain falling onto dozens of people below with their mouth open, drinking the liquid. Their pupilless eyes are unsettling.

The crowd dissolves from the stage. Guests head to the first painting while others go to the bar, and some stay and talk in the central gathering room. Ashley Amber walks with a man Lola has not seen before. The two head to the bar, being led by one security guard to the doors. The two Crystal Moths step aside, letting the three pass. Lola moves her camera, catching the details on film.

"Beautiful, aren't they?" comes a thick Turkish brogue.

Lola lets go of her necklace, and her posture straightens. She didn't even notice a man beside her wearing a deep grey suit and white dress shirt. A white pearl ring wraps around the finger on his right hand, holding a glass of wine.

Crystal Moth, Lola thinks instinctively. The gang doesn't own white, yet she can't control her paranoia. They are everywhere.

"Yes. They're quite beautiful," Lola says, smiling.

"I'm sure you heard the famous painter's flattering speech?" the man asks.

"Oh, yes. He's quite the visionary. Lucky to have a partner who believes in him. He must be special."

The man leans in and whispers, "You flatter me." A white smile spreads across his five o'clock shadow.

"You're Erol Terzi?" Lola asks.

"The one and only."

"Wow. It's a pleasure to meet you. You must be so proud," Lola says.

"Of course I am. His talent is unmeasurable."

"Does it make you envious?"

Erol extends his arms. "Of course not. I admire his skill as I have my own unique abilities."

"And what do you do?" Lola asks.

"I am the CEO of CAMB. It's a humble little broadcasting station you might not have heard of."

Lola can't help her genuine laugh. "I can't say I have."

"Most haven't." Erol's brows furrow. "Sorry, what is your

name? You look so familiar," Erol asks.

Lola's throat tenses, and she takes a swig of wine. "Talia. Talia Marquis. If you are into B-rated horror movies, then you know about me."

Erol extends his hand. "Talia, it is a pleasure to meet you."

Lola shakes the man's hand. It's a gentle touch, as welcoming and warm as his personality.

Synarion's voice comes in. "An SUV pulled up. Stay on your guard."

Moving the lab, Scalebane thinks as a black SUV drives into the loading dock. Men in white suits step out of the vehicle and open the hatchback. They take boxes from the trunk and place them on a table where another unpacks dragon statues. Their automated processes are fast, with no Moth missing a beat.

"Thank Dega'Mostikas," the succubus says, pushing her shades.

She takes the stack of cash from her trench coat while walking to the table. The Crystal Moth unloading the dragons freezes as she closes their distance. His mouth dangles open, entranced by the creature.

"Do I pay you? Or who?" Mulier asks, turning around several times.

The dragon statue almost slides from the man's hand. He gains composure when a Crystal Moth by the SUV speaks in an eastern European accent. "Pay here." He's holding a piece of paper on a clipboard with a pen looking through the spreadsheet. "Mulier Cupido?" he asks.

"That's my name, sweetie," Mulier says.

The driver approaches her, checks her name off the list, and takes her cash.

Scalebane keeps her hands gripped onto her sai, watching the interaction. Now isn't the time to start asking questions regarding her brewing theories. There is no local lab because there are two vazeleads on this side of the world.

The succubus snags a dragon statue off the table. She inspects it with a toothy grin, exposing her fangs. "What a cute way to package ash. About time you boys step it up." With that, she heads to her car.

"What kind of freak is she?" the black-eyed Moth asks, looking at Mulier's tail. "I'd still hit it, though. You?"

Scalebane ignores him, marching to the succubus. One question wouldn't hurt.

"You," she says.

Mulier lowers her shades, exposing her bright pink irises. "Yes, love?" Her full lips, large eyes, and plucked eyebrows would be enough to lure any man. Thankfully, Scalebane is no soft skin.

"Where were you getting ash before?" Scalebane asks.

"They're always changing the location. Truthfully, I don't know. It gets plucked right off the reptile, doesn't it? Fresher, the better."

Scalebane taps the roof of the car with her claw. "We need to talk."

"You want some alone time?" The succubus's perverted eyes undo Scalebane's clothes from her boots to the soulless mask. "Whatever you are."

"I do," Scalebane says.

"You can find me at Club Revelation in East Hastings, on Blood Alley."

"Right, that's where you get your prey."

She lets out an exaggerated laugh. "Too funny. I look forward to seeing you, love." She winks and steps into the car.

Plucked right off the reptile, Scalebane thinks. Not the words she was hoping to hear. Ash is not fresh off the reptile, meaning the Crystal Moths are making ash independently. It's impossible. She'll investigate it later. Right now, she's on guard duty for apparent essential profiles. To her, old world or new, they're part of the problem.

The sports car roars to life and drives off, kicking dust in front of Scalebane. The sweet smell of the succubus fizzles out, leaving the familiar scent of humans, car exhaust and pine.

She takes several more deep whiffs of air. The other earthy smell of moss and bark mixes with the first scent. They are nowhere near a forest. Her keen nose continues investigating, taking her several meters away from the art gallery loading dock. The scent is far too familiar, bringing her to her youth.

A grunt and a clang come from further down the alley. She spins to the loading dock. One guard stationed by the entrance is missing. The black-eyed Moth. The other guard is no longer at his post. He's behind the SUV with the others, talking.

She darts from the alleyway back to her post, stomping into a puddle of water. The pine is more pungent. She passes the other Crystal Moths who watch.

"Yo, what was that?" one of them calls out.

Scalebane doesn't answer. She passes the dock and turns the corner, letting her nose guide her. *It can't be,* she thinks.

Dress shoes stick from behind a dumpster. Scalebane unsheathes her one sai and steps over to see the black-eyed Moth on the ground, missing his white blazer. She kneels to sniff the man.

"What the?" he grumbles.

The forest runs rampant over his neck and face. Scalebane snags the black-eyed Moth by the collar, lifting him to his feet. She slams him against the concrete wall and lifts her mask. The cool air runs by her face as she takes a good sniff of him. It is *his* smell.

"Christ!" The black-eyed Moth grips Scalebane's wrists, attempting to pull away. His fear-struck eyes are locked onto her white muzzle and the black scales that line her lips and nostrils. Subtle hues of orange and yellow come from her eyes, highlighting the lower part of her face, freezing the man in awe. Scalebane could care less if the human sees. The smell on his body is far too concerning. She can't accept it and takes another good whiff, detecting the earthy scents. It's as she feared. The man wiggles, unable to escape her grasp. His mouth hangs, eyes bulging from his elongated face. Finally, Scalebane releases the frightened soul and pulls her mask down. He catches himself in the fall, pressing his hands against the dumpster.

"Did you see who did this to you?" Scalebane asks.

"I-I-I-It was too dark. I wanted a smoke. This guy came outta nowhere, like thin air. I don't know." He's entranced with Scalebane's face. "What the fuck?" he mumbles.

"Notify Erol right away. We have company," Scalebane says. She returns to the loading dock, heading for the back door entrance.

There's one nymph who resonates in the northern hemisphere that would be here. That distinct pine smell is like no other. It has to be him.

"Synarion," Scalebane hisses under her breath.

The balancer wouldn't dare to interfere with Mastema and King alone. He must have a new world connection. One soft skin vigilante has made it her mission to fight the Crystal Moths. In an unprecedented turn of events, Synarion and Lola Cabello are here.

Act like I belong, Lola thinks. She's forcing an open smile as Erol elaborates on his partner, Dasco. She has lost focus several times while keeping her nerves in check. Certainly, she is sweating too much. At least the wine has calmed her shaking hand.

Erol says, "He's the troublemaker in the relationship. I have to keep him in order. What about you? Certainly, a woman of your stature must have all sorts of rascals."

"I've had my share. Flying solo due to it. Sometimes you need a break."

"Don't we all," Erol says. A buzzing comes from his inner blazer pocket. He takes his smartphone from the jacket, and his face plummets. "I'm sorry, Talia. I must go."

"No, don't be. Do what you must."

"It's been a pleasure to meet you. I hope we can chat again soon." Erol takes her hand with a gentle grasp and kisses it before storming into the crowd.

Lola exhales and finishes her wine. She presses on her communicator while strolling through the art gallery to anywhere but here. She whispers, "So I met the CEO of CAMB."

Synarion's voice comes through distorted, "Meet me outside."

"What?"

"They have a list," Synarion says.

Lola puts the wine cup on the lobby counter. She swings her jacket on and exits the gallery, passing the entrance's security and into the cool night air. Synarion is smoking a cigarette several steps down. It surprises Lola, not as much as the white blazer he's wearing with the chrome moth clip.

The nymph says, "They're using a black SUV to distribute dragon statues."

"Dragon statues?" Lola asks.

"Yes. Ash."

"Vazelead drac men," Lola says.

"Precisely," Synarion says.

"You're sure?"

"They aren't going to hide small statues behind an art gallery for the sake of it."

"Right," Lola says.

"I placed a bug on the vehicle so we can track it. And if we're lucky, we can get our hands on that list."

"A list of guests?"

"From what I saw, it's a narrower list of who gets ash. Unfortunately, there are far more Crystal Moths than I expected."

"Hence your spiffy new blazer," Lola says.

"And I found a vazelead," Synarion says.

"The one you were looking for?"

"Her twin, and she's dangerous. Where did you say they were taking the guests?"

"Past the kitchen, there are two guards vetting people through," Lola says. "I'm not sure where from there."

"Then that is what we're going to find out." Synarion chucks his drag and steps on it with his heel. "Sorry, Mother Nature," he mumbles to himself.

He places his hand on Lola's lower back and guides her up the staircase. The security out front nods at him as the two step into the gallery undetected. Lola stiffens her posture as they move through the crowds and towards the kitchen. The two guards remain by the doors, their hands cupped, watching Lola and Synarion approaching.

Synarion speaks, "Talia Marquis is ready for pickup."

The two guards step aside and push the doors open.

"Thank you," Lola says. She can't believe that it worked so efficiently. They step beyond the doors and into a bright white hallway.

"Damn it, Synarion," Scalebane hisses under her breath while pushing open the security camera room door. The black-eyed Crystal Moth joins her on his phone with Erol. He's explaining what happened to him.

"Hang on, sorry. Who are we looking for?" he asks Scalebane, fear seeping in his tone.

"A fine-formed individual who doesn't belong," Scalebane says while leaning on the desk, looking at the security cameras. "He once had bone-white hair and pointed ears. Hard to say now."

The Crystal Moth repeats the phrase into the phone. "Of course . . . yup . . . I'll inform the others . . . you got it, boss." He hangs up and folds his arms, standing a meter away.

"He could be with a girl," Scalebane says.

"Who?" he asks.

"The vigilante reporter your people are incapable of catching." She taps the security camera screens with her claws, causing the monitors to wobble. "How do these work?"

"Here." He leans onto the table beside Scalebane, careful not to get too close to her. His magician's hands click a few buttons and change the camera's vision.

"Hold on," Scalebane says, pointing to one camera overlooking the gallery's front entrance.

A girl exits the art gallery in a leather jacket and a short black dress. The low-quality camera leaves her face pixelated, making it impossible to see who she is under the bangs. She turns her head sideways, showcasing a distinctive straight-nose bridge.

"The image is unclear. Can we see more?" Scalebane says.

"Yeah, I can zoom in."

"To this girl." Scalebane pokes the monitor again.

The Crystal Moth obeys, and the camera magnifies into her. The nose is close to Cabello's, and so is her age. She leaves off camera and returns several moments later with a man in a white blazer. The cauliflower ears and slicked-back white hair are evident even through the poor camera.

"Follow these two," Scalebane says. "Get Erol on the phone."

The Moth obeys, making the cameras change views,

following the man and woman as they walk through the art gallery. They head for the kitchen, past the two guards and into the hallway.

"Yeah . . . boss . . . the girl is here too . . ."

"They're heading for us," Scalebane says, hurrying for the door.

"Boss says to use stealth," the black-eyed Moth says. "He says don't mess up this big night! It means a lot to him."

She scratches the door frame, making a nails-on-chalkboard screech. She says, "Tell the other men to seal off exits. We are not letting these two escape."

Keep it together, Lola. You've done this plenty of times before. Truthfully, it gives Lola an eerie déjà vu moment of being in Edmonton with Michael Bradford. It isn't the time to reflect on the Trinity of Souls.

They've taken several turns through a maze of light grey hallways that interconnect behind the art gallery. The open rooms are for offices while other doors remain closed. There's an emergency staircase leading to higher and lower levels.

"Where are we going?" Lola asks.

"Heading for the loading dock. We're getting a statue and that list," Synarion says.

"What about the vazelead?"

"I'm hoping she'll listen to reason."

The two turn a corner and face a long hallway leading to a new door. The second one is to the left. They head forward as the main door opens. The two movie stars Lola saw earlier step in, laughing and chatting with each other. There's no Moth with them, thank God. Ashley Amber and her friend both look pleased, holding dragon statues. The two groups reach each other midway and pass without a word.

Synarion says, "We're on the right track."

The side door bursts open, and a dark-cloaked figure steps into the hall. The being removes its hood, leaving a black cowl draping on its skull. The soulless goggles of the leather mask rests above the demoralizing metal muzzle covered in small breathing holes.

The newcomer draws two sai from the utility belt, pushing their cloak aside and revealing a wicked whip-like white tail with black scales running along the back.

A rumbling alligator hiss booms from the being. It's a haunting reminder of what Lola heard in the Toronto sewers. She is staring at a vazelead.

CHAPTER 29
FINALE

Lola is petrified, staring at the leather-clad reptilian wielding two sai. It's the ash's gravitational pull sucking her into the intelligent reptilian. Lola's scared shitless.

"Synarion!" comes the raspy voice of the reptilian.

"Damn it," Synarion pushes Lola behind him.

"Won't she reason with you?" Lola asks.

"Get back. We need to leave now."

"Synarion!" the reptilian says again.

"Oh my god!" comes the valley girl's voice of Ashley Amber.

"No way," says the man with her, lowering his shades to look at the vazelead.

Synarion says, "Deal with the humans. I've got her." He

marches to their foe, equipping his spiked knuckles and dagger from inside his blazer.

Lola hurries to the starstruck stars. They start to run, and Lola reaches for her thigh holster, taking her gun. "This way," she says.

The vazelead hisses and lunges her sai at Synarion. He blocks the first attack with his knife, making a loud clang as the two blades interlock. He throws the spiked knuckles at her, hitting the second blade. She lashes her tail, sending a loud snap echoing through the hallway. It slices his shoulder open, with red soaking into the white fabric. The two break their locked stance, taking a step away.

"Your people are in danger, Lereif," Synarion says.

"It's Scalebane, you should know." The vazelead thrusts her weapons again. Synarion steps to the side. "After so many years, how do you remain arrogant?"

"You don't have to do this," Synarion says, blocking another oncoming attack. "You're greater than this."

Scalebane's throat rattles.

"Think of your sister!" Synarion says.

"Do not dare mention her," Scalebane says.

"You both know what the Crystal Moths are, Scalebane. Let me speak with your sister. She—"

"Leave her out!" Scalebane charges into Synarion, and the two slam into the wall, cracking the cheap drywall on impact.

Ashley Amber whines. "Please don't hurt us, please don't hurt us."

"I won't if you listen to me," Lola says. "You're involved. How?"

"We just get the ash, okay?" the man says, shaking his statue.

Take it, comes a familiar voice in Lola's head. She's unsure if it's her own or if it's that magnetizing force guiding her.

"That's all, we promise!" Ashley Amber says.

"We don't know jack about alligator freaks!" the man says.

"Well." Ashley Amber looks at the man, then Lola.

Lola's glances back to the fight behind her where Synarion lets out a battle cry, pushing Scalebane off him. He lunges his spiked fist into her leather armour. The blow hits Scalebane's ribs. She barks. Her tail slithers around Synarion's dagger arm, coiling around the wrist. The two struggle for dominance over the other.

He swings his knee into her gut, stunning her. His spiked knuckles slam into her tail, piercing into the flesh. Scalebane yelps. She releases his wrist and takes a step back. Synarion does as well.

Lola turns back to the stars. "Speak!"

Ashley Amber says, "We get the ash, but I knew there was more."

"More as in reptilian fucking people?" the man asks. "Jesus Ashley, what did you get me into?"

Ashley Amber continues, "They have a local growery now. It's where I get my supply while filming here. I've seen it shackled. I didn't know they could talk. I needed to ease some tension!" Her lips tremble, and fresh tears glisten in her eyes.

Another loud crash comes behind them as Scalebane and Synarion smash into another wall, indenting it. White particles crumble onto the floor as their shoulders smear against the broken structure.

"Move," Lola says, raising her gun. "Keep talking."

The three move as Scalebane pushes the fight toward them, one blow at a time.

"Don't get involved." Ashley Amber says. "Crystal Moths aren't human."

"Ashley," the man says. "Did you take a bump?"

"No, she's sober as hell," Lola says. "Ash comes from that thing."

"Bullshit."

"If you want to live, you'll listen to me," Lola says. "We are going to get out of here." She doesn't even know if that's the case.

"Who are you?" the man says.

Ashley says, "I'm serious. They're not human."

"What is going on, Ashley?" the man asks.

"I wanted the ash. It was never supposed to be a big deal. Like, they roped me in. Like, they wanted my connections. They were generous with ash. I don't know."

Scalebane and Synarion keep inching closer with each swing.

"His pockets are deep. Their influence is everywhere. I needed help, Timothy! Timothy, the goddamned mental breakdown last year. I needed the public to like me again and introduced ash to my circles, including you."

"Stay focused," Lola says. "Whose pockets, Mastema?"

"Mastema?" Ashley Amber asks.

"Whose pockets?"

"Erol!"

The two combatants are a couple meters away.

Both doors in the hall burst open, and Crystal Moths enter

with their handguns drawn. They fire without questions. Bullets graze against the walls and ceiling, causing drywall to soar into the air.

"Synarion!" Lola shouts. She spins around and pulls the gun's trigger, making a loud bang. The bullet soars past Synarion and Scalebane towards the Crystal Moths. It pings off the door frame. More bullets race towards her, one almost clipping her ear. She turns and starts running.

Scalebane lunges forward and lashes her tail at Lola with the tip slicing her jacket. Synarion throws another punch, hitting Scalebane's chest. The spiked knuckle rips through some of the leather breastplate and stuns her long enough for him to launch a boot into her torso, sending her back.

He sprints from the battle, joining Lola and the two stars around the corner. Bullets bombard the hall, blasting into the walls. Stomping comes from behind the group. The chase is on.

"Which way?" Ashley Amber asks, coming to a T-intersection.

"Left!" Lola shouts with no clue.

The thudding gets louder. It's too close. Lola looks over her shoulder to see Scalebane skidding around the corner, bolting towards them. Her acceleration is inhuman, closing the gap.

The four turn left and are met by five Crystal Moths at the opposite end. Behind them is a man in a grey blazer, Erol Terzi. The Moths raise their handguns and open fire. A bullet whizzes above Ashley Amber's skull and hits her colleague dead in the forehead. Warm fluid splatters against Lola's face as the man stumbles sideways and slams against the wall. Blood smears behind his skull the further he sinks.

"Timothy!" Ashley Amber whines.

Lola snags her arm, following Synarion backwards, away from the Moths. Scalebane, a good ten meters behind, sheaths her weapons and reverts to her four limbs, pouncing like a wild animal.

"Here," Synarion says, spotting a staircase. He slams into the door, opens it, and lets Ashley Amber and Lola enter first.

Scalebane takes one leap, ending in a somersault, and springs onto her two feet, drawing her sai. She swings. Synarion's dagger deflects the attack into the wall. He thrusts his spiked knuckles at her. Scalebane leaps back, freeing her sai, and Synarion pulls the door shut. He leans against it, keeping it closed.

"Up!" Synarion orders.

Lola follows behind Ashley Amber, whose high heels slow their pace enough to boil Lola's blood. She pushes Ashley Amber to make her move faster while tossing off her own shoes. The star's ankles wobble, and she regains balance.

Another door, a floor below, bursts open and two more Crystal Moths appear. Heavy pounding and scraping come from Scalebane's attempts to break the main door open.

The new Moths dash onto the staircase and fire at Synarion. Another thud comes from Scalebane, and he sprints from the door, hurrying to his comrades.

Scalebane bursts into the stairwell and passes the Moths. She snags onto the railing, using it to springboard onto the next flight of stairs. Her claws snag the raiser's edge a meter from her prey.

Ashley Amber shrills. Synarion takes the lead as Scalebane

pulls herself up. Lola fires at her, and the bullet misses, bouncing off the concrete steps. Scalebane charges. Lola fires several more times. One bullet hits her target in the chest and the reptile yelps, stumbling down.

Lola and the group zigzag up the stairs leading to the rooftop. The Moths' dress shoes click with each step behind them. Synarion pushes the top door open, and the three hurry onto the roof. They spin around, looking for a fire escape ladder. There's no exit. They are trapped.

"To the edge," Synarion says. He cuts his pant leg with his dagger. Strapped to his limb is a folded black matted gun. He pulls it from the holster and flips the various pieces and slates, transforming it into a grappling hook. How Lola missed him equipping this in the apartment is a mystery.

The rooftop door flies open, and Crystal Moths step into the night air, guns raised. Scalebane rushes with a limp past the Moths whose guns speak at the three. One shot hits Synarion's shoulder. Another pierces Ashley Amber in the spine, and she drops the dragon statue. It slams onto the ground, cracking open. The tip of an ash scale appears in the hollow torso of the sculpture.

Take it, comes the gravitating voice in Lola's head.

"Help!" Ashley Amber cries, holding her chest. Another round shreds into her neck, spraying red everywhere. She gurgles. Blood oozes down her clavicles. Merciless bullets volley into her, turning the poor actress into a human pincushion.

Lola snags the dragon statue and fires at their foe with the other. She hits a Moth in the torso, and he stumbles backward, toppling to the ground. A quick unzip of the purse lets her stuff the statue inside.

"Lola!" Synarion shouts. He reaches for her while launching the grappling gun. An anchor flies from the barrel, soaring through the night streets and locking onto a nearby higher rooftop.

Lola wraps herself around the nymph, clutching her purse containing that precious ash. She fires several more times as Synarion pushes a button. He holds the gun with both hands, and the two are yanked off the art gallery rooftop.

Scalebane pushes Ashley Amber's corpse aside, gaining speed, and makes a colossal leap off the building's edge. She clamps onto Lola's leather boots. The claws dig into her ankle, shredding the material and puncturing her skin. Lola kicks Scalebane's mask several times with her free boot. The first kick throws Scalebane's head back, and the second hit breaks a piece off the metal muzzle. A third kick sends the plate flying off.

Razor teeth coated in black liquid are behind the exposed snarl along with a slippery tongue flickering at Lola. An orange glow projects from under the goggles, highlighting the black scales and light grey skin of the reptilian's flat muzzle. This is where ash comes from.

"You're not running this time, Synarion," Scalebane hisses. Her grip digs deep into Lola's ankle. "You abandoned us once. Now you'll pay—"

Lola plummets her final kick. It collides with Scalebane's snout, crushing the cartilage. She barks. The blow forces her to let go.

Bullets whiz past them and hit nearby glass windows of the

building the two soar towards. A loud slam comes from the alleyway below as Scalebane collides with the dumpster bin, then her body rolls off the top and into the trash cans beside it.

The grappling hook reaches the new building, leaving Lola and Synarion hanging. She chucks the dragon statue and purse onto the roof, then her gun, and grabs the edge, pulling herself up, daring not to look down. Lola swings her leg over. She topples onto the other side.

Synarion is next and tumbles onto the roof. The bullets stop. Both pant as sirens blare across the downtown metropolis. They're free from chaos.

Lola reaches for the dragon statue, takes the ash out of the hollow inside and tucks it into her purse. She glances to see whether Synarion saw. He is preoccupied with winding his grappling gun.

"You're bleeding," Lola says, seeing his white blazer soaking in red.

"Not bad," Synarion says. "Come on, we have to leave."

The two stand, and Lola takes one last look at the art gallery. The Crystal Moths stand on the roof watching. In the front of them is Erol Terzi, with the wind blowing against his suit. Lola takes one peek down to see that Scalebane is no longer in the alleyway.

CHAPTER 30
THE MAKING OF EVIL

A flight across the country is exhausting. A midway stop to interview some loverboy doesn't help. There's also no rest when crime is rampant. The three detectives' long travel ends at the Vancouver airport. Iglesias has not gotten any shuteye during the flights. Beckman doesn't have issues sleeping, and Archer pretends to.

The mountains, the ocean, and endless forestry don't provide beauty for the three. They are pulled right into an active crime scene after landing at night. The Vancouver Police Department drives them across the city to the North Vancouver Gallery of Modern Prestige. Famous painter Dasco Amoss's paintings aren't the only blood-themed event during the opening. It's more headaches for Iglesias.

"This can't be the girl, can it?" Beckman asks.

"Moths, for sure. I wouldn't put a past Cabello to follow them," Archer says from the front seat. "She's a complete wildcard."

"Yeah, but still. She was a kid going to university," Beckman says. "And this?"

"How bad is it?" Iglesias asks the police officer driving.

The man grips the wheel tighter. "I haven't seen it. We got the call, and officers arrived immediately, requesting backup. The fire department and ambulance arrived as extra support. From what I was told, there are gunshots throughout the gallery and a couple dead bodies. Maybe more."

Iglesias stares through the window and into the rainy night, contemplating the grim news. Beckman is right. The girl couldn't have caused such damage like that alone and not gotten caught.

They reach the art gallery, where seven police cruisers park by the entrance. Their red and blue lights flash across caution tape, public servants, and witnesses on the streets. Officers continue to evacuate people from the building.

As expected, the news is already here, worming their way past the tape to get the juicy details. Civilians have their phones out, recording in real-time. Everywhere you look, there's some goddamn camera watching you. Iglesias wishes he was back in time before cell phones. Then again, he'd be with his alcoholic wife. On second thought, this is the better life for José.

The driver parks the car, and the four get out. Iglesias takes the lead, with Archer and Beckman following close behind. The driver tends to other matters. The detectives march past the caution tape and catch the attention of a ginger-haired officer in a sergeant's uniform.

"Kind of a rude welcoming to the city, isn't it?" he says in a nasal voice.

Iglesias shakes his hand and says, "Sure is."

"I'm Sergeant Hill."

"Detective Iglesias."

Archer waves. "Archer."

"Beckman," Beckman says.

Iglesias asks, "Is the shooter active?"

"No," Sergeant Hill says. "They're not at the scene anymore. We are searching the vicinity. They couldn't have gone far."

"Is everyone safe?" Archer asks.

"Most of them. Two confirmed casualties somehow wandered into the back of the art gallery. One was chased to the roof and gunned by the shooter."

"Shit," Beckman says.

Sergeant Hill nods. "It's messy. The Prime Minister is okay though. He was far from the shootings."

Iglesias asks, "Can we confirm who the shooter was?"

"Shooters. A man with white hair and a young woman is what we have right now. We are gathering guests for witness statements, getting the security footage, and sectioning off the crime scene."

Archer asks, "The young woman, any description? We're tracking Lola Cabello. It's why we're here."

Hill says, "One of the shooters is the right age and ethnicity."

"You've got the guestbook?" Beckman asks.

"Already on it. We'll have a list of the people who have attended the art gallery. This was a big one."

Iglesias asks, "Why is that?"

"Well, the Prime Minister was here. Tech CEOs, movie stars, musicians, and other arts industry people."

"This guy that big of a deal?" Archer asks.

"A big deal? The guy is a Canadian icon. Not that I care about blotches of colour slapped onto canvas." Sergeant Hill chuckles. "What I want to know is why Crystal Moths were here."

"It's what everyone wants," Archer says.

"Yeah, we found some ash in one of the hallways. It looked fresh. A deal went down here. With the plethora of bullets, too, there had to be gangsters."

Iglesias nods. "Were there witnesses we can' talk to? Or the manager on staff?"

"Right this way." Sergeant Hill leads the group further into the mess, where an ambulance, fire truck, and a couple more police units are stationed. People are being interviewed, dressed in posh outfits, dolled up hair, and the best blazers money can buy.

Iglesias spots a man in a grey blazer and salt-and-pepper hair talking to an officer. He has seen him before. That's the CEO of CAMB. Iglesias has not talked to him, but he knows the news channel's influence. That explains why the media got here so fast.

"Here's the manager," Hill says, stopping by a frazzled lady sitting by the ambulance. A towel rests over her shoulders, and she grips a water bottle tightly. "Ma'am, some detectives want to speak with you."

She looks at him and shakes her head. The gold chains that connect her glasses sway side. "I've d-o-o-ne plenty of t-a-a-lking. Can I please g-o-o home?" Her voice shakes with each word.

"We just want to ask you some questions, then you're free," Iglesias says.

The woman eyes Iglesias from the top edges of her glasses in that classic authoritative move. He kneels to be level with her.

He says, "Were you in charge of the show tonight?"

The lady snorts. "In charge? If this is what you consider in charge. Yes, I run the art gallery. This is one of our biggest shows. Or, it was supposed to be."

"Dasco Amoss?" Beckman asks.

"Yes. I feel so sorry for him. His work is world renowned, and we had many important names come here tonight, likely to buy. He invited his partner too, Erol Terzi." She points to the man in the grey blazer. "They're such a wonderful couple, and I feel awful that this disaster happened."

Archer asks, "Witnesses say two people were killed, one chased to the rooftop. Which of your people was in charge of security tonight?"

"We subcontract it to another company. Truthfully, I have little to do with it and have trusted my operations manager to handle them. Nothing's ever gone wrong before."

"Do they check people for concealed weapons?" Iglesias asks.

"Of course, with having the Prime Minister we did. Still, this is an art gallery! These kinds of things don't happen. Thieves may try off hours. Sure, that's what security is for. Murders don't happen. It's just not right."

Beckman puts his hands on his hips. "Do we know who died?"

Sergeant Hill bites his lip.

The lady speaks, "Yes, two movie stars."

"Timothy Shepherd and Ashley Amber," Sergeant Hill says.

Archer folds her arms, wide-eyed. "The Ashley Amber?"

"The one and only," Hill says. "Apparently, she was filming a movie with Timothy Shepherd here in Vancouver. For one reason or another, they were here at the opening, like all the high-profile folk. If you ask me, it's a perfect place to execute an assassination."

Iglesias says, "Yeah, the pieces line up. Relaxed security. No offence."

The woman shakes her head. "None taken."

Archer adds, "Pick the target you want, and away you go. The Moths think some of the guests were buying ash?"

Sergeant Hill shrugs. "We have a lot of interviewing to do."

Beckman says, "We've got to check those security cameras too. Let's get to work, eh?"

Iglesias's mind is already elsewhere, analyzing this event. His gaze wanders to the Prime Minister, whose pink skin sweats under the beaming lights of the media. Photographers and videographers are capturing what they can as the reporters shove their microphones at the politician giving a PR statement.

Lola Cabello made a point of coming across the country to Vancouver and murdered a family man in a motel. Now, the

Crystal Moths are involved with a high-profile murder of movie stars.

CHAPTER 31
KINTSUGI

Permanent wounds created from trauma are a constant scab that breaks off, bleeds and heals, and breaks off again. Old, tormented memories mixed with new ones leave Lola a jittery mess.

Her scuffs are minor compared to her partner, who shows no signs of pain. He activates his handy grappling gun a second time, letting them hop to another building, disrupting their last known location. It makes Lola think they're some comic book superheroes. *Super,* for sure. *Heroes* is another question.

Lola ditches her wig on this rooftop as Synarion does with his blazer. She checks her necklace camera to make sure it is working. The discrete, angled light in the back is on. She indeed captured what they had witnessed. The audio will be another question for later.

On the second rooftop, Synarion picks the lock of the stairwell door. After several attempts, it clicks open, and they head to the main floor. One would expect there to be security. This office tower is vacant in the stairwell leading to the ground level. Their high-class attire does give an authoritative appearance. Either way, the two aren't stopped, and they exit the building from the stairwell freely.

Sirens echo off the glass skyscrapers. Synarion and Lola keep to the side streets and arrive to at the Hyundai hatchback. They get in and drive away at fifty kilometers an hour, being discrete. Lola exhales relief. She remembers the red speckles on her face and wipes Ashley Amber's blood off. Bits of both movie stars cover her exposed skin.

He was shot, Lola thinks. She goes to check Synarion's shoulder. "You okay?"

Synarion shrugs her off and says, "Let's get clear from danger."

Lola nods and fiddles with her pendant and hidden camera, turning it off quietly. Their location needs to be secret. She grabs the ash from her purse and slips it into the bust of her dress for safer measures. It's hers. The drug is there in case she needs it. Not that she will.

They drive across the bridge, checking the rear mirrors to see if they're being followed. No, they're not. The car goes over the bay and to the East side to their apartment. Inside, Synarion locks the door, and their shoulders drop strain. They're safe.

Synarion starts to undo his shirt, grunting from the pain.

"Seriously, let me help you," Lola says, touching his black shirt. Her hands still shake. Exposing his bare torso showcases a work of art. Intricate Celtic-styled tattoos run along his entire chest and ribcage. The skin is covered in scars from decades, if not centuries, of wounds. His shoulder will be the latest addition from Scalebane's tail and the bullet graze.

"Where's your med kit?" Lola asks.

Synarion laughs. "You're sweet. I'm far more able. Trust me, I'll handle this. Take a moment to unwind. You're shaking like mad."

Lola hugs her arms. "Yeah, it was a lot." She swallows a lump of saliva, pushing away the persistent tears that wish to explode. She wants to behave like a normal person because she likely killed a Moth at the gallery. Normal people would pour their fears out in front of one another as they held each other. She has to be strong. "Have something to drink?"

"Cabinet," Synarion says, opening his bag of mystical medical goods.

Lola marches to the kitchen and finds a bourbon in the cabinet beside the kitchen fridge. Perfect. She pours a glass and downs it in a single gulp. That's to break the ice, hopefully. She gets a second glass and pours two, passing one to Synarion. She sips her second drink, wandering to the kitchen and wondering if this will even aid her new trauma.

Take me, a voice slithers into Lola's mind. It's the same force pulling her into desire. Her heart stops as heat radiates across her chest. The ash. Her hand is wobbling. This is the kind of scab that liquor will not solve.

A microdose wouldn't hurt. She's done it before in the motel.

It helped clear her head, and she unlocked the Crystal Moth's phone. She knows how to manage her doses, which will aid her sleep later tonight. Synarion is distracted by his wounds. Now is a good time.

She slips the scale from her dress, tears a small edge off, tinier than her last dosage, and bites down. Lola chews fast and swallows it with some bourbon. She needs to unwind; is that so much to ask? That's what ash does in small doses. It clears the mind.

For safe measures, she plucks her hidden mic off the inside of the dress's strap and stuffs it in her purse on the counter. She unclasps the necklace containing the camera pendant as well.

Seeing a vazelead in the flesh gives Lola the honest answer to ash. It explains the noise in the sewer, the drug, and her enjoyment. Knowing the truth doesn't make her feel better.

"So that was a vazelead?" Lola asks.

Synarion takes a sip of his drink and cleans his wound. "Indeed it was."

"She knew you." Lola leans against the counter. Her gaze is glued on Synarion's toned abs, guiding her to his pelvis. It's been a long time. After the gore of tonight, lavish skin cleanses the pallet.

"That's correct." Synarion starts applying stitches, unphased by the surgery. "I know, or knew, her quite well and her sister, whom I was hoping to find. Or any vazelead who wasn't her."

"Who is she?" Other than the source of ash, Lola thinks.

"Lereif Scalebane, sister of Namsruc Scalebane. I raised the two of them when they were hatchlings."

"You? A father?"

Synarion chuckles. "I wouldn't go that far. Lereif was troublesome while growing up. She enjoyed her primal instincts of hunting and killing, unlike her sister, who wanted to understand a higher level of thinking. Their mother injected them with good morals. Clearly, those didn't carry into adulthood."

"How did you end up with two vazelead kids?"

"Hatchlings. Their mother was trapped in… Oh, you know plenty. She was trapped in Hell."

"Hell?" Lola can't help but laugh. "Now you're telling me God is alive?"

"Sort of, not what you're thinking. That's not the point right now. How do I put this in modern terms? Think of Hell as another realm."

"Okay."

"Lereif's and Namsruc's mother was there. How she conceived with another vazelead in Hell is beyond me. Or how she found a way to the mortal realm. Then, she happened to find a balancer of all people to take care of her children."

"You fucking serious?"

"Fucking serious. I never knew her mother. A balancer must keep equilibrium, and those two girls needed a father, at least until I found their own kind. There weren't many vazeleads four hundred years ago, and I can't estimate how few there are now. I found the last of their people, ruled by King, a former warlord of another time. He took the two in, grateful for my action because the vazeleads that remained were crazed, dying and had no skills. The Scalebane sisters were far more capable despite their young age. That's why I wish to speak with the vazeleads directly. King knows me. I can reason with their people."

Great, more ancient terrors, Lola thinks. She sips her whiskey as the dim room illuminates. Her muscles loosen enough to give her a slight sway. The blood on her skin isn't concerning anymore. The mix of bourbon and the drug is working and Synarion is too preoccupied to care. The ash is circulating through her system, and her mind is releasing the trauma from hours and years ago.

She asks, "Didn't want to keep them as your own?"

Synarion says, "The hatchlings had no purpose of being with me long term. My life is dangerous. I can't hold onto love of any kind. They needed to be with their people. I had them for a good century, and reflecting on it, Lereif is jaded by that."

"You think?"

"It is as I feared. The few remaining vazeleads work with the Crystal Moths to produce ash."

"Is Lereif the one in the Toronto sewers, then? She was bound like an animal."

"Lereif wouldn't be taken prisoner. Namesruc, on the other hand. She's the softer of the two and took my teachings to heart."

"It's a shame you didn't teach them morals," Lola says.

His eyebrows furrow. "I did. King reintroduced them to anger."

"What about any other vazelead? Could they have been in Toronto?"

"Unlikely. Their numbers are so few, and the Scalebane sisters are warriors. I can't see King risking the others for how weak they are."

"So, in short, Lereif and her sister hate you, the father who abandoned them."

"Lereif is the passionate one of the sisters. She adopted her mother's rules and training from me, fusing them to some moral standard that she lives by. Namsruc is far more sympathetic and calmer and understands why I do what I do. If I can find Namsruc, she'll be my in to reason with King."

And maybe Namsruc was in the sewers, Lola thinks, taking a swig of her drink, locked on Synarion's bare chest. Yes, she is listening to him. Yes, she is losing interest in the reptilians to what is presented in front of her. His form is a sculpture. A two-year dry spell amplified by ash is driving a primal need. Bourbon and drugs aren't enough to mend her fresh mental wound.

"Lereif's eyes. I think they're glowing." She clears her throat to stay level-headed.

"Like fire," Synarion says. "There's plenty of mythology as to why. The common answer is hate. The fire was ignited from the pure anger they have towards humans." Synarion finishes his stitches and moves to bandage his upper arm. "It's folklore. Ever seen a firefly?"

"Yeah, I get it. That's why vazeleads work with Crystal Moths, because they hate humans." The heat from the drug and the liquor pulsates warmth through her body, and she takes off the leather jacket, chucking it on the counter.

"I'd say the vazelead past mixed with the Crystal Moths' ancient origins makes the two well married. They're ruthless, and they've decided that the age of man is over. That's my running theory. I need more information, and that's where the tracker on the SUV comes in handy, even without that list we needed. We can look to see where the vehicle goes, see if it helps find Namsruc."

Too much planning, Lola thinks.

Synarion finishes patching his arm and walks to the closet, finding himself a new shirt. Lola finishes her bourbon and places it on the counter. She strides to the nymph. Her eyes are fixated on his shoulder blades and the indent of his spine leading to his lower back. It guides her eyes to his well-shaped rear that she'd love to grip. Lola wants the body. There's no fighting it.

"And what of your rules?" Lola says, leaning against the closet.

"The rules? They're simple."

"You haven't shared them. They relate to these tattoos?" Lola asks. Her heartrate increases. She wants to touch the skin.

"No, they're from another life. The rules are simple. Number one, look like you belong. Number two, don't stand out in the crowd. Number three, embrace the culture. Number four, stay calm. Number five, don't mix. Number six, learn their skills. This is to help me and others like Bark Nose blend in."

Lola bites her lip. "Look, I think, I think you . . ."

"What?" Synarion asks.

"Thank you for saving me." She steps closer, getting a whiff of his familiar pinecone scent. Lola needs to devour his body, for it has been too long since she has been close to anyone and ash is worsening the thirst. "You saved my ass the moment I got here, and there's no way I could have done tonight without you. Thank you." She steps a little too close, breasts grazing him.

Synarion's eyes move back and forth, analyzing her face. "Are you high?" He lifts her head by the chin, looking into her pupils, his face squinting in distaste. "You took ash."

"It's fine. It doesn't matter," Lola says.

"You're addicted to the scales." Synarion lets her go and snags a shirt from his closet. He attempts to step away, being met with Lola's hand. The hot palm presses against his abs. The touch makes him flinch.

"You're hurt," Lola says. Her hand slides down his torso and to his ribs. He grips her hand, stopping her.

"Lola," he says sternly.

She doesn't reply. Her lustful hand moves against his neck while leaning for his lips. Despite his words, he doesn't stop her. Their mouths press together, and she exhales her longing for victory. His lips are stiff, not returning the affection. He turns his head away.

"Lola, you're not thinking straight," he says far softer.

"It's fine," Lola whispers into his ear. She kisses his cheek, moving to his jawline.

He swallows. "It's why I have rules, to, blend in."

"Let go," Lola orders, kissing his neck.

His one hand grips her wrist tight. The other grabs her shoulder in a poor attempt to resist. It amplifies the greed, and Lola pushes against his arms, pinning him to the wall. She goes for a second kiss. His lips loosen and invite her tongue into his mouth. He lets go of her arms, and she wraps them around his hips, pulling him in. The two exchange heavy breaths in between the passionate kisses. Hasty hands begin untying the back of her dress as she unbuckles his pants.

The two strip away any remaining clothing, leaving their bare forms interlocked. The single entity shifts over to the bed, stumbling onto the mattress. Her hand wraps around his waist to grab the firm cheek. The other moves onto his pecks, ribs, and hipbone, she is almost unable to comprehend the inhuman herculean form, until she reaches his rising member, tugging it. He digs his fingers into her skin as she climbs on top of him.

The ash melts the pointless logical thinking. She is one with her own needs and her partner's. He is hers to command as she slides the head inside. He moans as the rest enters her, and she thrusts her hips.

Lola's innards ignite with flame. The light in the room blooms, sending her far beyond this grungy apartment. Ardent hands run along each body, pushing aside the fears of today and worries of tomorrow. Trauma and rules disintegrate. The two beings embrace one another against all odds of the universe.

CHAPTER 32
HIGHER CALLING

Pride must be swallowed when defeat occurs, for wise failures lead to future success. Now, Scalebane knows Synarion is involved with the human vigilante. She can orchestrate her subsequent move to end Lola Cabello and be rid of the nymph. There are also the uncertain words of a succubus. One thing at a time. Right now, she needs to regroup with Erol.

Scalebane spits a mouthful of her black blood into an alleyway puddle. The rain droplets drizzle down her broken leather mask and onto the road. She grunts while standing. She took a beating with a grand slam onto a dumpster. The leather breastplate has glimmers of silver indented from whence the bullets and spiked knuckles struck. Vazeleads are far more resilient than humans and rejuvenate quickly. Punches, bullets, and falling several stories aren't a concern.

Sirens are blaring from the streets. The gunshots ended the art show and the exchange of ash. Game over. Scalebane navigates through the alleyways to the gallery, avoiding the front entrance. There, the soft skin police are evacuating people and placing caution tape around the scene.

She hurries to the loading dock, where Crystal Moths give a few elite stragglers their dragon statues. There are two cop cars with flashing lights where a couple of officers talk into their radios. The corrupt law keeps the truth in darkness.

Scalebane's arrival makes one of the Crystal Moths jump, gripping the dragon statue close to his chest. A few mumble amongst each other. They're fixated on the sharp, bloody teeth under her scowling, scaly lips below the soulless mask. She doesn't bother to coil her tail. They've seen her. Her goal is to find Erol. She has questions.

A black van screeches to a stop in the alleyway beside the SUV. The side door slides open and more men in white hurry out. They bark orders to each other about cleaning up the mess and removing the bodies of their dead.

The black-eyed Moth spots Scalebane as she passes. He says, "Hey. Did you get them?"

Scalebane growls, ending her noise in the signature rattle. "Where is Erol?"

"Damage control. He's with his partner and the guests. We're going to remove as much as we can. The two cops here can't keep the others away for long." He talks into his phone and says, "You got a replacement? Great. We'll get the blonde out of here."

Two Crystal Moths drag a dead blond woman from the van. She has a single bullet hole in her head. The hallway door bursts open, and three gangsters drag the shredded remains of the human pincushion woman from the rooftop. Her face is unrecognizable, mowed to pieces with bullet holes. They chuck the corpse into the van.

Scalebane doesn't have time to know what the hell they are doing. With the chaos, media and law will be swarming throughout this building. This is Erol's specialty. It's best for Scalebane to vanish.

She coils her tail around her ankle and keeps her head low under the baggy hood and mask's cowl. She storms into the night street, stomping in the rain. At some point, she'll have to find a way to Allen Shipping Solutions and regroup with Erol. Right now, she has a higher calling.

The siren noise of the metropolis starts to dwindle the closer she gets to the ocean. She finds a spot under a bridge with cars driving. The rocky beach is shared with a few homeless a good twenty metres away, staying warm with a fire beside the graffiti-covered pillars.

Scalebane unbuckles the top of her damaged leather breastplate and pulls out a sphere pendant attached to a metal chain wrapped around her neck. She removes her leather glove, freeing her bone-white hand covered with black scales along the spine and knuckles. She places the pendant into her palm, feeling the sphere's matted charcoal surface etched with ancient engravings of a language long forgotten.

She closes her eyes and rubs the pendant in circular motions with her claws as an unnatural heat burns from inside it. The engravings glow as orange as her burning eyes. She grips the stone, focusing on projecting one word, *King,* several times.

King . . . King . . . King.

Scalebane comes a low, echoing voice of almost demonic origin.

She opens her eyes. The rocky beach is gone. Her vision is replaced with a dark room made of stone and torch lamps. Several steps before her is a rocky throne where a vazelead sits. His clawed hand grips the throne's armchair while the other holds a necklace tightly, with glowing orange lights piercing between the cracks of his claws. Even with flaming lights on each side of him, the room is far too dark to see the details of his form. His burning eyes shine, highlighting the charcoal scales on his face.

A brief breeze grazes across Scalebane's exposed muzzle from the real world. Nature's interaction smears the vision of King until it dies down.

"King," Scalebane says.

"I did not expect you to use your soulstone," King says. "What message is so important for you to seek me?"

"Our relations with the Crystal Moths are not going as expected," Scalebane says.

"Yes, your dispute on handling the Crystal Moth traitor and his family. I trust your methods are sound. In the future, do not attempt to change the methods of the Crystal Moths. They have their reasoning."

The family. Scalebane recalls her disagreement with Erol

regarding torture. "It's bigger than that. It's our arrangement."

"With our ash distribution? Let me deal with Mastema. He expects too much."

"The Crystal Moths are sloppy. They waste their time influencing the soft skins. I don't understand why we are dealing with them at all. We should——"

"We need their power, Scalebane. You know this. Your sister knows this. Mastema has global connections, which we do not. We are in few numbers, if you remember, and are to be the last if my son isn't given any opportunity to pass on our lineage."

Not that again, Scalebane thinks. "The Crystal Moths are reckless and violent, killing their own kind and even their clients. The Crystal Moths are everything I hate about soft skins. Everything I wish not."

"Their methods give them the impressive title of the longest-standing organization in any old world faction."

"It's too much."

"Scalebane, the humans have used these tactics time and time again against our own people and against many others. This includes themselves. The nations and groups that have maintained a ruthless structure are the ones who survive the test of time. No mercy has its benefits. Being led by the First also gives them immense insight. This is why we align with them to bring on the new world order."

"It's desperate, making our people look weak."

"It's strategic."

"They're bloodthirsty, slaughtering without cause. It interfered with my hunt for a new foe."

"I am not opposed to who they remove. The humans and

Crystal Moths are collateral damage, as far as I am concerned. Remember, this is a stepping stone. We will turn the tides on soft skins and inflict what they once did upon us. Why concern yourself with a lesser being's life, Scalebane?"

Scalebane does not answer. She bites her lip tightly, piercing the skin, to stifle her anger.

"Who is this new enemy you speak of?" King asks.

"A soft skin girl who wants to dismantle the Crystal Moths. They failed to kill her. I presumed it was the gang's incompetence until tonight. The balancer is working with her. He caught wind of what we are doing."

"Do not concern yourself with the nymph. There's one of him, and a soft skin is nothing. His methods are old and are no longer relevant in today's progressive world. He'll burn out. Don't make his arrival weaken you. He's not your family."

"Synarion is—"

King interrupts. "I know the balancer's morals. I knew your mother's. Their conflicting views have turned you into a paradox."

"I know where I stand."

"I question your confidence, Scalebane. Your anger is what guides you. Your sister, on the other hand, understands the greater picture. She knows why we align with the Crystal Moths and is willing to put aside her personal agendas."

"Her visionary views also blind her to what's in front."

"Scalebane, there are fourteen of us and the one crippled draconem. Three of us are related. The draconem is an incompatible brute. The nine are defective weaklings with no purpose other than to create ash. They must be kept chained.

You and your sister are the two capable of carrying on the lineage of our people."

"I understand our delicate situation, King."

"Do you? You refuse to even look at my son. Unlike your sister."

"Who I haven't heard from or seen in weeks," Scalebane says.

"Namsruc is overseeing the Toronto distribution. She has accepted the noble role of producing eggs with Rithu. When she returns, they will provide us with the next generation of our people. You can also have a noble legacy lasting for eras to come."

"King, I've been with the Crystal Moths for a month in this wretched, cold nation. I work with their overseer, yet my sister is nowhere to be found nor mentioned."

"You're not working with Mastema?" King asks.

"No. I met him once and was passed to a soft skin named Erol Terzi. This man is responsible for ash distribution, while Mastema deals with other businesses. Yet, Erol hasn't gone to the east coast where Namsruc is at all. Where's my sister, King?"

A low growl comes from King's throat. "Let me contact her soulstone. Namsruc is responsive to me."

"Please, King. She is my life."

"I understand. She's important to all of us."

"I don't trust the Crystal Moths. I don't trust Mastema nor Erol Terzi. They have their own sinister agenda, and I believe we are pawns in their game."

"I'll discuss this with Mastema and will set his expectations straight. You are to continue operating as I have instructed. Of course, unless you have reconsidered my proposal."

Scalebane tightens her tail around her ankle, cutting off the circulation. A brief flash of King's son flickers in her mind. His bony body and youthful stench make her nauseous. She could break him with one arm. Gathering her composure, she replies, "I am not breeding with Rithu."

"You have fire, Scalebane. This anger makes your blood strong and a far better candidate than your sister."

"Why don't you get one of the Nine to do it?"

King hisses, slamming his fist onto the stone armrest. "You know they're a mix of corrupt and street scum. Their blood will weaken our people."

"My mother was street scum."

"Until she was born anew in Dega'Mostikas's Triangle. Hell reshaped her. She found a way to birth two powerful hatchlings and return them to this world. You and your sister are newfound hope. My son is of a guardian bloodline. It is the logical choice."

"I don't need offspring. Motherhood weakens the mind."

"Don't discredit motherhood so easily, Scalebane. Zoefani would bite your head clean off if she heard you speak ill of her choice to have my son. And what of your mother?"

Scalebane releases her ankle, recognizing it was going numb. Thinking of her mother's fast flaming eyes turns her heart cold. The glimmer showed a youthful spirit and the warrior's strength, one that reflects Scalebane's.

"She fought to get you out of Hell. I know you're frustrated. We are not in a situation any of us wish to be in. Do you think I wish to treat the Nine the way we do? Do you think I want to align with a fallen angel who runs an underground empire of drugs and organ dealing? Do you think I want to corner you and your sister into having hatchlings with my son? I wish us to be free. I see the greater picture. I know you do somewhere deep inside. It's why you listen to me."

He is right. Their choices go against many of the things she believes in: independence, strength, and vigilance. Yet, here she is, a servant of his will.

"Let me talk with Mastema to ease your concerns. I will contact Namsruc through her soulstone. For now, I need you to be diplomatic with our newfound allies."

"Of course, King." Scalebane forces the words from her tongue.

"Good," King says. He opens one hand, revealing a matted sphere stone identical to Scalebane's. The orange glow from the glyphs fizzles out. Her vision returns to the present underneath the bridge as another breeze brushes by her.

Swallowing pride is not easy. Scalebane trusts her gut and knows the Crystal Moths are not honourable. She can deflect King's proposal for his son Rithu and work with the Crystal Moths. The one thing she cannot do is remain dormant regarding her sister.

Don't act like vermin. Ship her west to the abattoir plant, Mastema's croaky voice relapses in her mind. The fallen angel was on a phone call when she first met him in his mansion. The succubus mentioned local distribution as well.

Ash comes from overseas. Erol claimed it too. Namsruc and Scalebane are the two known vazeleads on this side of the world. The Crystal Moths are making ash here on the West Coast, giving Scalebane a sickening conclusion.

CHAPTER 33
THE ROTTEN BIRTH

There is a reason why the Buddhists practice neutrality. Descending from euphoria creates a havocking force of sorrow. Lola knows the emotional roller coaster well, waking up with dozens of rocks tumbling around in her head. She has the usual raisin-sucked muscles. Her body has not built enough tolerance to the ash to avoid the comedown.

Her eyelids peel open, feeling the skin scratch against the cornea. She stretches in the bed, brushing against her naked partner under the warm sheets.

The sun pierces through the small square windows, highlighting the scars on his back and biceps. He mumbles in his slumber that Lola doesn't understand. She is more focused on his tattoos. The designs and symbols must have Celtic relations. She touches the one on his chest. Her fingers glide against the linework of a gate with vines around it. She feels the texture of his skin and the bumps from wounds over years of brutality.

What other secrets do you have? Lola thinks. She can't explain why she's growing affection. Perhaps it's the longing to be with another, using him as a boilerplate. It could be the ash in her blood. A third possibility is she's developing genuine emotions for the nymph.

Her touch wakes him, and his purple eyes land on Lola's naked form.

"Hey," Lola says in a scratchy voice.

"Morning," Synarion says. His groggy eyes move from her chest downward, feasting on her curves. The greedy gaze is welcoming, and she can't stop herself from smiling.

"Glad we got that out of the way," Lola says.

"I . . . " Synarion rubs his forehead.

Lola shifts onto her side, her arm wrapping around the top of his head, fingers grazing his jaw. She enjoys the small pricks of hair growing on it. "It's fine. We both needed it."

Synarion exhales. "I'm slipping. There are rules for a reason."

"Rules are meant to be broken." Her hand returns to the design on his chest, exploring the vines and trees extending upward from the gate. The three trees form a face, while the wavy vines create hair. Along his clavicles are feminine eyes.

"What do these mean?" Lola asks.

"Balancer symbols. They represent words of power from a long time ago," Synarion says.

"They cover your body."

"Yes. Words of power once let us connect with Mother Nature."

"And you can't now?" Lola asks.

"No. Icons have power over the mind. Think of the cross and what it has caused in the name of Christianity. No different than a country's flag." Synarion is too sharp this early on for Lola. Still, she lets him speak.

"Words of power used to work. Basically, what you'd call magic." He looks at Lola's waist, seeing the square mosaic tattoo forming a heart. "You have one yourself."

"And a few others. Band related." Lola lifts her leg, showing her outer ankle where she has a winking skull with two Cs on the forehead. There's another tattoo on her shoulder blade of a combined S and C through a nail. The classic Canadian Industrial band Skinny Puppy. "I wanted to get more. Now I'm not so sure. It makes you identifiable, like scars. You have more of them than tattoos. Has your life always been so harsh?"

"A balancer's life is no easy road," Synarion says.

"Some are fresh. I'm sorry, but your finger, it looks—"

"New? It was a mess. It involved Bark Nose's companion. That vampiric plant is evil. They're a pain in the ass to kill too."

"Don't lose any more fingers, okay?" The words make her throat tense. *Who am I?* she thinks. This is more than a fling.

Synarion says, "As you can tell, I make a point of damaging the one body I have."

Lola rolls her eyes. Romance isn't possible in her new life. She needs to stop.

"And what of you?" Synarion asks. "You're well on your way to catching up with me." He eyes the two scars on her clavicle.

The fresh one from the motel and the second serve as a constant reminder of the Trinity of Souls. Synarion says, "What actually happened?"

Lola sits, grabbing the sheets to cover herself. "It's a lot. You've heard the recording. That's what it is."

"You give a good PR statement, but I wish to know how you feel. A fire is burning inside. It drives what we do. No normal person gets involved in such a gruesome world unless there is reason to. A personal one."

"It was quite personal. You read about me. You know."

"Yes, your mother, and before that, your friend Becky and Michael. What went through your heart?"

"It's a long-winded one."

"Tell me," Synarion says.

Lola doesn't wish to, despite growing fond of Synarion. Her hangover makes the task tiresome. He's been persistent since she met him. Opening up to Synarion is doing her a world of good. She has an ally, is making progress, and isn't alone. He is worthy of hearing her tale of the rotten birth.

* * *

As you know, I was in Edmonton going to university. My family is out east. Edmonton, at the time, had career opportunities and cheaper schooling. It was a win-win. I didn't know that the city was infested with crime. Once I got there, I discovered reports of serial killers.

I was blogging while in school, thinking that reporting on the killers would be a good case study. I was fascinated with murderers and the stories behind them. Typical goth girl thing, right? The site gained traction within the underground music scene, and I made some close friends, Becky and Donnie. Becky was my closest friend from high school who also came to Edmonton. Bless her. Donnie was a reserved intellectual. He admired what I was doing, which is why he helped at the beginning.

Crime was terrible, as I said. Crystal Moths were rampant in the music scene. Homeless were forced to act on petty crimes. Then those serial killers were wandering the streets. One was vacant for a while. The other wasn't, who broke people's necks and targeted the homeless. He was known as the Snapper and feared by all. That's when Michael Bradford appeared.

His fame rose from getting filmed for stopping a robbery. The videos went viral online, and he was dubbed hashtag YEGman because he was the one man stopping the city's crime. YEG is the airport code for the city, and we needed a hero. The nickname stuck for the mysterious figure in a ski mask and hoodie.

He piqued my interest, and Becky and I found a way to meet with him after he rescued us from a club called The Glowing Monkey. That's when things went south. I didn't know Becky had been partying with the Crystal Moths, with this guy named Alex G.

The gang discovered that Michael and I were onto them. Alex G baited Becky to get to us. I was with Michael when I got the text. It was from Becky, stating: *come get her.* A picture of a map was attached to the message, pinpointing some restaurant in Chinatown.

I had never felt my heart sink so deeply. Like, even though it was snowing outside, my entire body felt frozen for the first time. I knew that was not Becky. Michael was standing beside me showing no expression in his famous ski mask under his grey hoodie. He always wore that, no matter the weather. It was his unintentional superhero costume.

I muttered, "Fuck. That's not Becky." I kept looking at Michael and the phone, hoping he'd give an answer.

Michael snagged the phone, saying, "Let me see."

I panicked and said again, "That's not Becky," several times while bringing my hands to my mouth. Anxiety was a real bitch that day.

Michael handed the phone to me. "You know where this is?"

"No, but in Chinatown somewhere. Shit." I pulled on my long black hair with blue streaks. That was when fashion meant a lot to me. It feels so innocent now. I mean, it's petty of me, but I do miss being a Gothic punk.

I said, "Becky doesn't talk like that. I'll call her."

The phone rang twice as my fingers dug into my neck due to nervousness. In a thick maritime accent, a man's voice answered on the other line. "You know where she is," he said.

I screamed, "Don't fucking touch her!"

The phone clicked, and I lowered it, breathing through my nostrils. Rage burned through my body while being scared beyond belief at the same time. My Becky Bubs. My best friend. We did everything together, even moving to Edmonton to ensure we were at the same university. We knew each other inside and out and talked about getting matching tattoos and what we'd be like when we were old. Our souls were bound to each other, unlike anything I've ever had.

Michael asked, "Do you recognize the voice?"

I said, "I don't know, she also has a bit of a coke problem. She knows a lot of dirtbags, but she doesn't have many enemies. Everyone loves Becky Bubs."

"They might be trying to get to you," Michael said.

"Who?" I asked.

"The Crystal Moths. Alex G knows you know too much," Michael said.

I replied, "Becky had one of the Crystal Moth's numbers. I told her to stay with Brian!" Brian was my deadbeat boyfriend at the time. I wanted Becky to stay safe, and he was our best bet.

I cried in front of Michael, looking at him for answers. He had to have a plan. He was our city's hero, and I had the privilege to work with him directly. I was his voice in the media, giving people the facts. That's when my blog changed from being a girl who likes disturbing crime to being a legit local news outlet.

Michael was convinced that we could get Becky, while I believed the world was ending right there and then. She was my whole universe, for fuck's sake. But I trusted Michael. He had a plan. We took a cab over to Chinatown, which was one hell of a weird ride through the slushy snow. Michael had slit a man's throat earlier, and here we were, off to have a face-off with some gangsters, taking a taxi to do it.

I mean, even with his brutality, Michael sympathized with the world. It's why he did what he did. On the ride, he kept me close to him to give me some comfort. It was robotic, and I could tell he was uncomfortable. It made me feel awkward, but he tried.

Chinatown was in pretty bad shape. Most of the buildings were vacant or torn down. Those open late had some relation to the Crystal Moths. There was an archway over the road leading into Chinatown made of green and yellow text. The English portion of the sign read: *Gate of Happy Arrival.*

We both saw the irony in that.

Michael had hatched a plan where I would go in alone and meet Alex G while he came from the back entrance, and he would take them out. We'd stay on call so he could hear where I was, and I'd hide my phone in my boot. It was janky spy stuff, but it worked.

Never did I think I would be going undercover into some gangster's lair to save a friend. But I did. Saving Becky was what mattered. I mean, I was so naive at the time, thinking Michael would go in and beat the hell out of the bad guys. I foolishly put it on him.

That's when I made the famous recording that destroyed my life. You know the one. Michael wasn't aware that I had set my phone to record in case anything went south. I thought it would be significant evidence of what happened if one of us died. I didn't think we'd discover what we did, nor did I think it would result in my mother's heart attack and leave me here.

We exited the cab a block from the restaurant, and I tucked my phone into my boot. From there, we initiated his plan.

Michael went through the alleyway as I headed for the restaurant. I pulled on the icy handle of the door to find it locked. I knocked several times. A second later, the door swung open, and there was a Crystal Moth goon. As usual, they were dressed in white.

He stuck his head out and looked both ways down the street, not even acknowledging me.

"Good. Get in," the man said.

He guided me into the restaurant, passing a fountain and through a maze of rice paper dividers. The restaurant was empty except for one booth at the far corner where the relentless Alex G sat.

The guy had his legs crossed, arms wide. He was a cocky fuckhead and loved his full white suits. The sheen on his black boots was as reflective as the gel in his slicked-back hair. He eyed me up and down as he did with any girl he would party with. I sat down. The Crystal Moth who led me stood there, looking the other way.

"You come alone?" Alex G asked.

"Yeah, I'm alone," I said, crossing my leg to get the phone closer to him so Michael could hear.

"Good. So you want your friend back?"

"Yeah, where is she? Is she okay?" I asked. I felt the sweat on my chest turn to ice. I needed Becky.

"Yeah, she's fine. Why would I drag you here if she wasn't?" Alex G's tone was more condescending than usual.

"Is she here?" I asked.

"She is."

"Please, let her go. I'm here now," I said as I leaned forward, begging.

Alex G chuckled. "Can't do that, doll."

I replied, "Do what you want. Seriously. I . . . Whatever you want of me. I'll do it." I knew Michael had a plan. Even then, I was desperate.

"You don't have anything I want," Alex G said.

"Is it money? I can find money," I said.

Alex G shook his head np.

I asked, "Is it sex? I-I-I can do anything you desire. I'm yours." Becky's safety was all I could think of. I've had plenty of bad fucks in the past. What would be another to the pile?

Alex G shook his head again.

I was running out of options and added, "I'm yours. I can give you information. Please."

Alex G shook his head a third time.

"I will work for you," I said.

Alex G snapped his finger, and the guard snagged me, pulling me from the booth. I squirmed to break free. His grip was too firm.

"Please let us go!" I cried while being dragged away.

"You'll get to see your slut," Alex G raised his voice, following behind. "Keep moving!"

I was frightened, with tears dripping off my cheeks mixed with black mascara. I held on, knowing Michael was there.

The two Moths took me to a staircase. The unfinished basement had concrete walls and poor lighting. It was a perfect place to keep people as prisoners.

"Please," I cried one last time.

"Put her in here," Alex G said while opening a door into a room with no lights.

The Crystal Moth dragged me in with my boots skidding, attempting to stop him from moving me into the darkness. I was useless. Alex G followed behind, flicking the light switch on, and Becky was dead centre in the room. She was strapped to a chair with zip ties.

"Becky!" I said. Dried tears painted her cheeks, mixed with blood running along her forehead. The fluids even seeped into her neon-red dreadlocks, staining them.

She raised her head and a weak smile spread on her face. "Lola love!" Her voice trembled.

"I'll stay with these whores. You check on the others," Alex G said.

"Alex G, you don't have to do this. Please. We didn't do anything," Becky bargained.

The man didn't respond, and the other Moth executed the plan. Their elaborate setup was to lure Michael there and kill him. They knew. That's the Moths for you. They always know.

Becky was the bait to lure me in, and I was the bait for Michael. I had no idea how many Crystal Moths were in this building. I feared for Michael's life and ours. Hope dwindled more after the ropes, and zip ties bound my wrist, ankles, and chest, strapping me onto the chair.

Gunshots came from beyond the closed door. Alex G flicked his collar, pacing back and forth, nervous. The guy even got on his phone to contact his goons. Then, he made one last call and spoke quietly.

"Lola, what are you doing here?" Becky asked.

I whispered to Becky, "We're getting you out of here." Michael had to be beyond that door. I had to believe. Otherwise, we would be dead.

Alex G lowered his phone. "What the fuck did you say?"

"Nothing," I said.

"Bullshit."

"Don't feel like a big man anymore?" I said.

"You shut the fuck up!" He put the phone away and stormed towards us. He coiled a fist and slammed it into Becky's nose with a loud crunch, and blood spewed from her nostrils. We both cried as he turned to me. He swung a backhand into my face, leaving it bright red.

My god, more shots and muffled fists came from beyond the door. I knew Michael was near.

"You're dead, you hear me! All of you!" Alex G took his gun from its holster and shouted to the door. "If you want to see these cunts alive, back the fuck off!" He pulled the trigger, aiming at the ceiling. The loud bang bounced off the concrete walls. Becky and I quivered, wishing we could hold each other.

Alex G shouted, "I'm not fucking around, asshole!"

The fists and shots stopped from beyond the doorway. Our sobbing was heard.

Alex G breathed rapidly. "You hear me?" He stepped closer to us. "Acknowledge that you understand, or I will shoot one of your whores."

Two taps came from the door.

"Okay, good," Alex G said. "So, this is how it's going to go down. I'm gonna let the girls go. You're gonna drop your gun and keep your back to the door. Tap if you understand."

I couldn't believe it. Even through the fear, I wasn't going to allow Alex G to win. Michael and I had come too far. "Fuck you!" I shouted. "The cops are on their way."

"Lola, shut up!" Becky said.

Alex G stepped towards me, pressing the gun's burning tip against my sweaty forehead. "Shut your lying mouth up, or I'll do it for you."

My innards ignited, and I said, "Shoot me? You need us alive. It's all that's keeping YEGman from bursting this door down and making you his bitch."

Alex G snorted. "YEGman? The fuck is that? I'll keep your mouth shut bitch — with this." The guy clutched his crotch, shaking it.

"With your size? Come on," I challenged. I had no idea what he was packing. The taunt was enough for a small man.

"Fuck you!" Alex G shouted. He spun his gun around and pistol-whipped my face, then punched my gut.

Becky cried, "Lola!"

"Try me!" Alex G shouted, followed by another pistol whip, hitting my jaw.

I mustered the strength to say, "I already called the co—" Alex G punched my gut several more times. It left me dazed, unable to comprehend what happened next. The room was spinning, with dual vision, and the sound was fuzzy. All I could hear were gunshots firing. Drywall flew in the air while Becky screamed, "Lola!"

A couple bodies toppled onto the ground. Becky cried my name again, "Lola!"

Then, I heard Michael's voice. "I'm coming. Hang on," he said with a groan. He was hurt.

Michael was crawling over to us in his red-soaked hoodie. The man couldn't even lift his legs. I got enough air into my lungs to breathe clearly, and my vision normalized.

Half a meter from me was Alex G. Bullet holes covered his chest. One ripped through his jaw, leaving part of his face intact. He made horrible gurgling sounds through his open throat. I didn't even bother moving my boots from the blood seeping under my feet.

"YEGman," I said, not believing my eyes. We had made it.

"Hey," Michael said, letting go of his gun. He pulled a knife from his pocket and said, "Come on." His voice shook. "You girls have to get out of here." He cut me free first.

I spat blood on the ground and wiped my face with my hoodie. I wobbled, dazed from the beating.

"*We're* getting out of here. I'm not leaving you," I said.

Michael asked, "You called the cops? I can't be seen like this." He lifted the knife, extending it to me.

I took it and freed Becky. She stumbled onto her knees next to the chair. I took her into my arms, inhaling her comforting peachy aroma. Becky was safe, finally.

I said, "I didn't. It was a bluff."

Michael's arms shook, leaning against the chair I was confined to. With each breath, he stuttered, getting weaker. Fluids dripped from his body and onto the chair in large, heavy splatters.

"Good job," he mumbled, watching Becky and I embrace each other.

"We're getting you out of here," I said, freeing Becky. "He was on his phone — he called someone."

"Fuck," Michael muttered. "You girls get out of here." His arm gave out, and he collapsed, face hitting the chair.

"YEGman, no." I ran to him and stroked his hooded head.

"No, no, no. This can't be happening. I'll call 911 — they'll get here before the Crystal Moths do."

"Police! Stay where you are!" came a grizzled voice from the hallway.

Michael mustered the strength to look over. "Sergeant?"

I don't know who the man was. He wore a black suit, holding a gun and badge. "It's okay. You're safe now," he said.

Becky stepped forward and said, "Please help! He's dying."

The sergeant waved his gun at me. "Step away from him. He's dangerous."

I hugged Michael's head. "He saved us! He needs an ambulance."

The sergeant was a meter away and put his gun into his holsters. He leaned down, grabbed Michael's gun, and checked to see if it had any bullets. "He saved you?"

"Yes!" I cried. "That's what I was trying to tell you. Please, we need an ambulance."

The sergeant put Michael's gun into his back belt and eyed the rest of the room. He looked at the bullets covering the walls and ceiling. He looked at Alex G, who was a bloody mess. He looked at everything except for us.

Becky said, "Lola, can we please get out of here?"

I pointed to Alex G. "Sir, he called for backup! I saw him. We got to do something."

The sergeant nodded to himself. "Yeah. I know."

I stood. "What?"

The man darted forward. He wrapped his arms around Becky, and she squealed. His sheer size and large arms locked her into a chokehold, dragging her close to me. I ran to save her as he snapped her neck and dropped her in one motion.

My heart stopped, and I shouted, "Becky!" I continued to scream her name until the wind left my lungs and the throat burned. Holding the knife to the man, I said, "You mother—"

Before I could finish my sentence, the sergeant took Michael's gun and pulled the trigger. The shot pierced my clavicle, giving me my scar.

I dropped the knife as the bullet knocked me into the chair. My body toppled over it, and I landed flat on my ass. I didn't move. I couldn't. Between the pain and the shock, I stayed there. I could hear the sergeant talk to Michael.

The sergeant yelled, "Fuck! What a mess. Whoever you are, you've made this much easier to clean up. Are you the same asshole who has been getting the attention of the news? Who is this mysterious vigilante?" I think he pulled Michael's ski mask off because he said, "Holy shit! Michael?"

Michael coughed and mustered the strength to say, "Why?"

The sergeant said, "Michael, Michael. Why? You were a good cop. Why the fuck did you have to go and get yourself involved in of this? You could have walked away and lived a happy life!"

Michael said, "You . . . Her neck. Snapper."

The man said, "The Snapper? No. The Snapper is a bunch of horseshit. Something we made up to keep the news occupied."

"The murders?"

"Yeah, there were a few cases of necks being broken — most of them staged by the Crystal Moths. As for a serial killer, that breaks necks? Get real."

"Whuh?"

"We targeted the homeless because no one cares about them.

It was a good distraction and got rid of some rubbies. At least, that was before you snapped a neck outside The Glowing Monkey. Not like we knew who you were at the time, but Alex G mentioned how he and his crew got their asses handed to them by some rogue hero in a ski mask. That's when I knew we could bring the Snapper to life. We could avoid our operation being unravelled. Well, before this fiasco."

"The freezers, Sergeant." Michael said.

This was when I had first learned the Crystal Moths were into the red market, dealing organs. Again, at the time all I could do was listen, unable to comprehend the horrors that were taking place in front of me.

"I'm not your sergeant, Michael. I will admit I'm pissed off that we have to shut down this location. Lang isn't going to be pleased. We'll set up shop again to keep the organ market going. This chapter closes with you as the Snapper."

"Robert," Michael coughed.

"No. It's over, Michael. When Major Crimes get here, they'll discover you went on a rampage and killed that poor girl in your signature Snapper style. You had a shootout with the Crystal Moths. You killed that fuckwad in the alley, rescuing this girl. You were obviously fixated on her with some deranged interpretation of love. It's why you rescued her and her friends outside The Glowing Monkey. The Crystal Moths kidnapped the girls to kill them. You killed her friend because you were jealous. You wanted her to yourself. The girl lives. The media loves it when a pretty girl survives a tragic event."

Michael mumbled. I swallowed the blood building in my mouth and controlled my breath so the sergeant wouldn't know

I was awake.

The sergeant continued. "Really? You think everyone is a goodhearted cop? I own Major Crimes. And your partner? He knew you were the violent type — he won't question it."

"Lola. She'll call you on your shit," Michael said.

"No, she won't."

"She saw . . . she'll expose you."

"Let her try. She was in shock. Besides, you shot her."

"No."

There was scraping against concrete. I think Michael was crawling away.

"Yeah, the gun was in your hand. You shot her because she didn't love you back. It made you very mad. She tried to defend herself and fatally sliced your neck, and you bled to death. It's a shame. I liked you, Michael. You're like me, doing things your way. My way doesn't get me killed, though."

"No. Rob—" The sound of a knife ripping through flesh was next, followed by a heavy thud. I wanted to gasp, and was biting my tongue to stay quiet. Michael was dead.

The sergeant called the police to the scene and staged a few more things while I lay there. He left the room to meet the cops, and that's when I mustered the strength to get my phone.

My hands were sticky from blood, and I wiped them on my jeans to use my phone and get the recording I had made. I tapped away on the touch screen. It uploaded to my cloud storage, and I deleted the whole thing before the police arrived. Then I tucked the phone into my boot.

The aftermath went according to the sergeant's plan. The police pinned the crimes on Michael. The media believed

YEGman was a psychotic killer in love. They still call him YEGman because it makes a better name for the story rather than the Snapper. The news and people love when the bad guy gets it. I was the tragic girl who survived. Becky and Michael had no justice given to them. I couldn't live with myself knowing I had the evidence to dismantle it.

I couldn't trust the police. The sergeant owned them, and he worked with the Crystal Moths. That's when I knew that the wretched gang went far deeper than simple street hooligans in white. The one thing I could do to counter them was upload the video to my blog, so the people could hear it. Donnie got involved and showed me a few more things with computers to keep myself secure.

Boy, were we wrong. The rest played out. The world listened to my video recording, you couldn't see anything with it in my boot, and read the blog post. The sergeant was arrested and killed in prison, or by the Moths if you ask me. They kill people who talk too much. The cops wanted to take me in, and I resisted. I made my follow-up article explaining what I did. It wasn't enough.

The Moths harassed my family, wanting to know where I was. I was kicked out of school. Life was crumbling around me, and I didn't know what to do next. If I went to the police, the Moths would get me.

The law couldn't find me and went after my family, thinking I had evidence there. The raid on their home was right when my mother was cooking, and it was too much for her heart. She died on the scene. I wasn't there, I wish I was. Like, it is my fault she died and I was hiding like a coward on the other side of the country.

The government thinks some cash for my brother and father will mend what they did? They won't admit it. Why would they? The law is controlled by the Moths.

Donnie gave in to the police while I went on the run. The Crystal Moths continue to watch my family. Between my mother and the gang, there's no way in hell my brother and father will talk to me. They've disowned me because of it. It's for the better, so the Moths don't kill them too. The rest is history.

*   *   *

Lola is so lost in her tale that she doesn't even realize Synarion wipes a tear off her cheek. It's the least amount of emotions she has expressed regarding the incident since it happened. Michael, Mom, and Becky continue to haunt her memory, fueling her need for vengeance.

"The Crystal Moths will pay," Lola says, moving from Synarion's affection.

"I'm so sorry," he says.

"It's why I have to do this. I have nothing left, and I'll take them with me."

"Be careful, Lola. Revenge is a dangerous path. It blinds you."

"I have it under control," Lola says.

"That's why you consume liquor like water and explore ash?"

Lola straightens her posture, looking away. Synarion's hands run along her lower back to her shoulder, pulling her into him.

She accepts the embrace, resting against his chest, using the sheets to cover herself. This is the normal person behaviour she has been wishing for. Who knows when she will have another's body again.

She says, "It's so fitting that the Crystal Moths are responsible for ash. It's not what I wanted to focus on. I want to expose the bastards. They're complicated, and here we are."

"Their roots are ancient, going far deeper than the law," Synarion says, stroking her hair.

"You know what Donnie had told me?"

"What?"

"Alex G attempted to recruit him one time. He told Donnie that the Crystal Moths were more than drug distributors, using it as currency. What caught my interest was what Donnie said after. Alex G said there were a lot of low lives in Edmonton. They were attracted to drugs, like moths to the light. Beyond the symbolism, the Crystal Moths were looking to make people useful again, and the gang was the light so scum could contribute to the higher classes of society. The worthless would become heroes, being reborn."

"I don't think it's far from what they have planned."

Lola says, "Donnie asked if they were part of a new-age cult. Alex G said they weren't religious propaganda. They were business people. Well, I don't know what they are."

"And yet you take the very thing that they supply."

Lola looks at him and says, "It's changing me. I have not experienced this before. It's, I think it's talking to me, making me stronger and smarter. It lets me see things the way they are. It let me see you."

"That's the drug talking. Vazeleads come from a long lineage. In layman's terms, magic lives on through their bodies."

"Maybe that's a good thing."

"It means we have work to do. We're hot on the Crystal Moths' trail with that GPS." Synarion attempts to stand. Lola keeps him down. "We mustn't waste time."

"Not yet." Lola turns to face him, wrapping her inner thighs around his waist. "Let this moment last a little longer. It might not come again." Her one hand moves down, grabbing hold of his genitals.

"Lola."

She leans into him for a kiss while reaching lower. His body surrenders to her seductive power, letting her take him one final time.

CHAPTER 34
NOT SO ENTANGLED

Exposing one's soul to another opens new growth, building a mutual understanding of each other's psyche and physical form. Lola regrets sharing herself. Since Donnie, she has not told anyone why she is involved with the Crystal Moths. It was hers and no one else's. A long night of violence, sex, and drugs does not help. Life is there in the morning.

Synarion has gone to get them food and caffeine. Lola washes off the stench, blood, and dirt from the art gallery. Goodbye, Ashley Amber. She sits at Synarion's table of junk, glad to be in her cargos and tank top. Formality was never her thing. She opens her laptop, sipping on dirt-flavoured tea, skimming her emails. There are no messages from her brother and father. Go figure. Donnie, on the other hand, did reply to her email with the MP3 of Chen. It reads:

<donnie.dube@youmailnow.com>

To: You

Hey Lola, that's a wild recording. Be safe. The news is saying some crazy stuff. I hope it's not true.

Donnie

Lola strokes her neck. Donnie has not abandoned her, fueling her hope. She replies:

You

To: donnie.dube@youmailnow.com

It's not.

Next, she transfers the video footage from last night to her encrypted storage. There is no better time with Synarion gone. It leaves her organs in a knot. The twisted sinking feeling in her gut is as she feared: feelings. Rationality says she doesn't know a thing about him. He is ancient and has his own skeletons. Her own interest is what matters. Foolishness must be suppressed.

The video uploads successfully, and she scrubs the footage's playlist, highlighting the event's key moments. To her luck, the wireless mic recorded wonderfully. The footage plays. She enters the art gallery after approval from the Crystal Moth security. Lola wishes she could have kept the emblem from Synarion's blazer. It would have been useful. The Moths love their symbolism.

She scrubs through Dasco's opening statement, pausing at times to look at faces she recognizes. With a pen and paper, she jots down as many as possible. There are faces she knows by name. Others she cannot place. Internet searches give her the needed answers with ease. The first three were Prime Minister Stéphane Trudell, Ashley Amber, and her colleague Tim, also known as Timothy Shepherd. She writes the names that she can find:

1.   Ashley Amber
2.   Timothy Shepherd
3.   Stéphane Trudell
4.   Seth Bolt
5.   Duane Gordon
6.   Max Storm
7.   Ian Black
8.   Ruben Bravo
9.   Jesse Shawn
10. Sam Holt
11. William Wallace
12. Devin Pink
13. Hugh Duff
14. Jennie Taylor
15. Nicole Little
16. Lizzie Legend
17. Susan Thompson
18. Jordyn Khan
19. Erika Holt
20. Mandy Howard
21. Christina Wood
22. Ava Day
23. Kristie Forrest

It's a giant mix of actors, politicians, tech CEOs, energy sector tyrants, musicians, artists, and key media players. These are the ones she can identify. There's no certainty how many of them are related to the Crystal Moths, either. She saw Ashley Amber and Timothy Shepherd enter the hall. The night was too young. She'll share the list with Synarion, claiming it was from memory.

She fast forwards the video to when she met Erol Terzi. They know with confidence he is involved with the Crystal Moths from Ashley Amber's words, standing in the hallway, and then on the rooftop. The pieces are aligning. Erol runs CAMB. The media is putting the spotlight on her. It's the same reason they pegged Michael as the Snapper. The largest Canadian broadcasting station is in bed with the Crystal Moths.

A prick jabs her palm, and she sees how tight her grip was on the pen's tip in a post-ash fidget. She loosens her grasp, then gets back to scrubbing. The footage shows Synarion and Lola in the hall running into Scalebane.

More, Lola thinks. Or it wasn't her. It's a growing need for the ash scale.

From far away and with the cloak, the vazelead's form blends into society. Upon closer inspection, the hind limbs aren't human at all. They're far closer to a dog or bird, storming to Synarion and Lola. Then there's the long, whip-like tail and sharp claws. It can't be true. Yet, ash comes from her. It's a disgusting thought, consuming another being of equal intelligence for Lola's own gain, and she cannot stop herself.

Lola hugs her arms, getting a chill despite no open windows, a side effect of the fear of this reptilian warrior and the drug comedown. Scalebane and Synarion's background complicates her mission. Lola hopes that Synarion won't soften if anything comes to brass knuckles. Scalebane is a Crystal Moth.

That is where Namsruc comes into play.

Fast forwarding, she pauses in the frame where Scalebane clung onto Lola's ankle. The vazelead's mouth is open with sharp teeth and a flickering tongue. The scales on her muzzle disappear under the mask into an orange glow. Even in the dim lighting, the bone-white scales make her less human. The black ones along the lips, nostrils, and nose bridge are close to ash. Lola can't imagine what kind of monster hides underneath.

Synarion raised her, which has to count. Lola has to remember Synarion's words, "Intelligent reptilian is a derogatory term, isn't it? It's not wrong and not accurate. It is like calling you an intelligent mammal." He said they were born of hate because of humans. Under that menacing face is another living being.

Lola downs the rest of the dirt-tasting tea. She's spending far too much time in her head and cannot let herself go soft. Scalebane is the enemy. Synarion's agenda of world balance doesn't involve her. She will take the Crystal Moths down.

The front door rattles, and Lola stuffs the camera and mic in her messenger bag and closes the windows on her computer. Synarion steps into the door with a couple of sandwiches wrapped in brown paper and a tray containing two cups of coffee.

"Some fresh fuel for the mind and body," Synarion says.

"Great," Lola says, squeezing her arm. "That tea was terrible."

"There's not a lot of riches to be had in a balancer's life," Synarion says, pulling a chair beside her. He chucks the sandwiches onto the desk and spots the paper Lola wrote on. "What is this?"

"Just a bunch of names of people I saw at the art show. It's from memory, so I'm unsure how accurate it is. Well, and Erol Terzi."

"That was Dasco's partner, correct? It said so on his artist biography."

"Not only Dasco's partner. He runs the Canadian All Media Broadcasting station. It's the largest in Canada. The grey suit in the hallway with the Crystal Moths."

Synarion takes a bite of a sandwich, speaking while chewing. "So the media is involved at the highest level."

"As I feared."

"Nothing unexpected from the Crystal Moths. This is good work. Did you see any more people in the hall by chance?"

"No." Lola drinks her coffee, embracing the hot, bold taste of a custom brew.

"No worries. Let's take a look at the tracking device on the SUV, shall we?" He powers on his computer, wolfing down the remaining sandwich.

Lola eats hers turkey sandwich while watching him type away on the computer. He's been so kind, and she's using him. Lying isn't her favourite thing; somehow, it's become second nature, living a double life. *Stay focused.*

"Here," Synarion says. He points at the computer screen of a map highlighting a path through city streets. One pin rests on the art gallery. The second sits inland from the bay beyond the city in the east. The right column on the screen shows time stamps, one from the art gallery and the other at the new location. "That's where the SUV is right now."

"It stayed there last night."

"It appears so. However, unless they found the tracker, the timestamp is from half an hour ago," Synarion says.

"How often does it update?"

"It pulses every thirty minutes. It's old tech, but it's what I got."

"Where is that?" Lola asks.

Synarion zooms into the map, showing an industrial park with plenty of manufacturing offices and warehouses. The building with the pin has a label called *Allen Abattoir Plant*.

Lola says, "That's where they're keeping ash from overseas."

"Perhaps," Synarion says. "Perhaps. The dragon statues are an interesting choice."

"It is odd."

"Not only the choice of a dragon, it's the fact that vazeleads and dragon-like beasts share a long lineage."

"The Drac men?"

"Precisely. Let me ask my colleague, Eden Breaker, if they can give anything on dragon statue imports from that company." He opens a web browser prompting a port, IP address, username, and password. Synarion fills in the information and accesses a search engine with a message board below. "This intranet, Lola, is how the old world stays in contact."

"Cute. You have your own little community forum?"

Synarion smiles. "You could call it that. It keeps us connected, at least those that wish to."

He fires off an email on this hidden intranet while Lola opens the maps on her computer to fixate on the Allen Abattoir Plant. It is a clean exterior made of concrete with chimneys. The property is fenced off, like a slaughterhouse.

"And done," Synarion says.

"How did you meet Eden Breaker?"

"Why, through the Internet, of course. The same way I found you."

"Right, your creepy stalker methods," Lola says. "So what's next? We have the location where they keep ash. Think Namsruc is there?"

"Possibly. Or the abattoir plant's freezers make a good place to keep the scales from drying out."

"Right."

"We need stealth. That art gallery incident is going to be a hot topic. I wouldn't be surprised if they find a way to peg you for this. You were there, after all."

"I was disguised."

"They aren't shy of manipulating evidence. We need to keep you on the down low."

"We did that last time, Synarion. It doesn't matter."

"It does. Don't fear. I wish to check the abattoir plant as well. If Namsruc is there. That's an if."

"It's worth going."

"Let the Crystal Moths think they got away clean. They'll be paranoid right now. For now, we need to take a sidestep."

"What do you mean?" Lola asks.

"When I was at the loading dock of the art gallery, I saw an old world being I know. Mulier Cupido, better known as Mul.

She made a disturbing statement."

"Who is he?"

"She. A succubus. Actually, she is how I first learned of ash. I introduced her to our intranet, bringing them into the global network. That's when she offered me ash. Raising two vazeleads made it obvious what that scale was. I told Mul to stay away from it. Clearly, she didn't."

"Great, another old world freak show. A succubus, like a demon that seduces men to feed on them?"

"You got it," Synarion says.

"What did she say?" Lola asks.

"Mul said the ash changes location and is plucked right off the reptile."

"She has seen the vazelead the Moths are holding captive. Why would she need ash?"

"I'm sure she uses ash to lure men, making them weak. Demons have immunities and aren't affected by worldly things quite like you humans are. Liquor, drugs, medicine, none of them work. I think we need to pay her a visit. She's far more involved than I thought."

"Totally," Lola says. "Where do we find her?"

"There's a club on East Hastings. It's where she goes hunting."

"Great, I get to meet a succubus." Lola can't help but smile. Her situation has once again become more absurd.

"Lola, before we go any further, I must ask you something important."

"Of course," Lola says, holding her breath. *Shit,* she thinks, wondering if he discovered her camera.

"You told me your goal, and you have your recording device from the motel. I'm no fool, and I guarantee you have some evidence from last night."

Lola grips her arms tightly, looking into his brown contact lenses.

"This is where our alliance has friction," Synarion says. "I have to ask you again not to expose anything without me overseeing it first."

"I know," Lola says.

"Keep this under wraps for now, don't share anything you have on Scalebane. Never."

"Never? Synarion. It's why I'm here. I poured my heart out telling you. I want them to pay."

"Do you know how deep the Moths go?"

"Mastema. He's at the top. I'll find a way to break his empire."

"Even if you get the right evidence, where will you take this?"

"If the Canadian government is as corrupt as I fear, I'll go south to the states, and if they're crooked, I'll upload it to the Internet. The people will know. I'll find a way."

"Do you know what happens to whistleblowers?"

"Yes."

"Exactly. Lola." He touches her hand and she steps away. "Lola, please. This is bigger than your pride. Let me curate it."

Lola says, "Pride? Are you fucking kidding me?"

"If you publish whatever evidence you have or get from what we do, you will create more damage. You will be an outcast. What of your family? Then there are the vazelead people who are near extinction and misguided. There are more old world beings who are vulnerable, too. You met Bark Nose. There are many more like him."

"He's not involved with any of this."

"No. He is of a dying race. All I am asking is to withhold the old world."

Lola's nostrils flare as the blood pumps to her face.

Synarion stands. "I need to make a call." He rubs his forehead, seeming distressed. "Please," is his last word before exiting the studio apartment.

Call to who? Lola thinks. She brushes the thought aside, not wanting to bother. Chances are it is some balancing mission. He can hold onto his secrecy. What he can't do is suppress her vengeance.

Two souls are masked in their protective shells once more.

She is in over her head and needs to broaden her definition of allies. Her eggs are in one basket. Donnie offered her hope by replying, and even one last resource before distancing himself. A contact number belonging to a Detective Iglesias.

CHAPTER 35
WE'RE NOT ALL HUMAN

A single crack in the foundation of a relationship is enough to make the whole tower crumble. A line was drawn in the ground. Synarion had to mention Lola's agenda again. That strike shook the earth and made a permanent imprint on their accord.

The two know that the damage exists and act as allies because of their common goals. How long that will last is a mystery. For now, they are driving to a club to meet a succubus. The damp evening's cloudless sky is accompanied by a brisk wind as Lola and Synarion step into the car. He doesn't show a single hint of injury. It would be impossible if he was human, considering the brutal beating he took one night ago. She worries if he is hiding the pain. The concern comes from empathy that stems from naivete. Synarion is a warrior and can handle himself. Lola's butterfly stomach must remain buried in the line Synarion drew. Thus, she distracts her feelings with a visor mirror. The straight black wig and heavy eyeshadow will work well for a club night. As for Synarion, he wears the same simple black or brown work shirts, a zipper hoodie, and a leather jacket with black pants tucked into his boots. Fashion for a club isn't his strong point.

East Hastings is a long strip, one of the oldest in the city, with a rich history dating back to its birth. It hides many secrets like a demon on the hunt. The road takes them to the far west side, straight into the downtown core near a section known as Gas Town. Portions of the strip are fine. Wander too far west, as Lola and Synarion are, and you're met with the poor, addicted, and rejected. They're in survival mode. Each passing street has the ill-fortuned huddling beside dumpsters, keeping warm. Look one block over, and there's a clean sidewalk where a security guard stands outside a high-class gold-trimmed skyscraper hotel. Men and women in designer clothing, suits, and formal dresses come and go from the revolving golden door.

The high contrast sickens Lola. The down-and-out are created by the Crystal Moths and those predators like them. These upper-class people are thoughtless. They're either ignorant or in bed with the gang.

Synarion parks the car in a parkade a few blocks from the

heart of misery. It's best to make sure the car is safe. From there, the two head through the streets. Every type of anguish you can imagine awaits.

One man injects right on the sidewalk, visible to all. His hands shake as he jabs the needle into his puss-covered infected forearm. Then there's the jittery old woman who can't keep her spine straight due to heroine withdrawal, standing in the middle of the path, groaning relentlessly. After that, a hooded man with a limp pushes his cart full of trash. Another smokes crack from a pipe. A little further is an alleyway where a man in a white dress shirt sells drugs to two skeletal men in torn clothing.

That Crystal Moth is of no interest. Synarion takes her a block further into a crooked, descending alleyway. Blood Alley. A subtle bass pounding comes from a metal door with a red neon sign above it. The sign reads "Club Revelation".

Synarion says, "I need you to stay close."

"Of course," Lola says.

Synarion's knuckles clang on the metal from knocking. It screeches open, and a beast-of-a-man steps out. He's taller than Synarion and twice as wide.

"IDs," he says.

Synarion pulls out his fake ID, as does Lola, who is Talia Marquis. The bouncer checks both cards, then gives Lola a long cold stare.

"She's with me," Synarion says.

The bouncer doesn't blink as he returns the ID and steps aside. His gaze would have frightened her a few months ago. Present Lola is unfazed. The tough guy attitude is typical in a life of night and crime. More than anything, she wonders if he is human.

Synarion leads Lola inside the red-lit hallway and down a staircase, taking them closer to the crispening electronic music. A second beefy bouncer stands by a black matte kiosk, gating the hallway. Behind the booth is a pint-sized girl with glowing orange irises and pigtails. The dark room makes it impossible to see anymore.

"Fifteen each," the girl says. She smiles at Synarion, showcasing a mouthful of piranha fangs. A strange smell of melting plastic comes from her form.

Synarion hands her cash, and the girl takes a stamp from the kiosk and places it on Synarion's wrist, then Lola's. It's a cartoon illustration of a radioactive monkey with swirling eyes. A strange sense of déjà vu for Lola, recalling the Glowing Monkey club in Edmonton with Michael Bradford. Everything is connected.

Onwards, Synarion and Lola pass the kiosk and into Club Revelation. The sound is aggravating, similar to the gunshots whizzing past her flesh the night before, then the grim reminder that one of her bullets pierced into a man's chest. The loud electronic music booms from corners of the club, blasting into Lola's ears. She has not gone clubbing since her life flipped. It puts her on guard, for people are too close.

Keep it together, Lola thinks.

The underground open space has a dozen brick columns for support that work as casual leaning spots for groups of people chatting. Most appear to be human. A select few are either well-fabricated costumes or are old world beings with horns on foreheads, long and pointed noses, and sharp ears. A couple have far too much hair on their skin from head to toe. Others have pink flesh, green, or grey.

There are too many faces. The place is packed shoulder to shoulder from the bar in front of her leading to the dance floor at the far end. She takes Synarion's hand, not knowing where he is guiding her. Smart move, Lola; it's best not to get lost.

The two worm through the sea of beings. They find a quieter open spot at the end of the long black marble U-shaped bar under a blue and red light. Synarion leans against the bar and waves at the bartender to come over.

"Are you sure she's here?" Lola shouts into Synarion's ear so he can hear her over the trebling dance tunes. It lets her sneak in a good whiff of his scent, feeding her naivety.

"Absolutely," Synarion says.

The bartender arrives, and they both order whiskey on the rocks.

It's the little things, Lola thinks, ogling the nymph's drink. *No.* She needs to keep her mind focused on her mission, not her growing infatuation due to their similarities.

"Act more casual," Synarion says. "You stand out."

Lola also leans against the bar. "Sorry. It's been a long time since I've gone clubbing."

"I haven't gone out for a party night like your kind. This happens to be a convenient place for information."

"What about those festivals in your photos?"

"Live music isn't this."

Lola chugs her drink. She asks, "Are all of these people old world?"

"It's hard to say. There are clear prosthetics for costumes. They must be having some special event. They are here, though. It's a safe haven in some regards. This is where I met Mul."

The song ends, and the DJ fades to a new track, a little slower, enough for the dance floor to clear so people will buy more booze. It's the usual club routine. It once let Lola dance her demons away. Now, she is looking for one. She doesn't even know what these creatures look like.

The swarm of dancers heads for the bar. One lady in particular catches Lola's eye. She strides with curves in the right places from head to toe. Her mesh crop top snugs her fit form with a bondage buckle undergarment, showcasing her breasts. Lola can't look away, and she doesn't know why. The woman's legs move with power in knee-high leather laced boots, peeking out with each step from under the long black skirt. Her hair is fashioned in a fifties style with hairspray and pins. A few curly strands dangle against her black lips, bobbing with her step.

"Bingo," Synarion says. He takes a swig of his drink.

The woman spots Synarion. A wide smile spreads across her face, emphasizing the dimples on her cheeks. Lola notices the sharp teeth and the pink eyes that crawl over the nymph's body. She was lost in a trance.

"Synarion, my love!" She extends her arms, and the two hug. Synarion pats her several times while she keeps him locked in the embrace. Her hands slither along his back, getting in a good feel. She releases him and says, "I didn't think you would come back to me so soon." She runs her long nails against his chest.

Synarion says, "Yes, well, it turns out you have far more value than I anticipated."

Now she notices Lola. "And who is this?"

"Mul, meet Lola. Lola, Mul," Synarion says.

Lola waves at her with a drink in hand. *Succubus*, Lola thinks, sensing the sweet scent. The trance makes sense. Even the beads of sweat on her skin look delicious. They lead Lola lower, past the toned abs and skirt. At the edge of the fabric by the knee is a black spike with a dash of pink flesh. It's the end of a tail.

A demon, Lola thinks. Fear and curiosity run through her. Like each old world being she meets, her mind is bombarded with questions.

"My, my, Synarion," Mul says. "She is a rare beauty. I see you got your taste wet, and now you can't stop." She laughs.

"You know what a balancer is," Synarion says.

"Your rules? Please. Like I haven't heard you say that before." Mul leans on the counter between them. She waves at the bartender. "I told you what I knew last time. I don't know how to get into Dega'Mostikas's Triangle."

"I'm not here for that," Synarion says. "Where were you last night?"

"Jealous?" Mul asks.

"I saw you at the North Vancouver Gallery of Modern Prestige. Collecting ash?"

"Oh, this again," Mul says.

"Mul," Synarion says.

"Yes, yes. The boys love it. It also gives them a distinct taste, oddly enough. The drug doesn't do a damn thing for me, unfortunately."

Synarion says, "I told you to stay clear of it."

"You did. And here you are, returning to me. As I said, the boys love it." She winks at Lola.

Lola shifts her stance, nervousness tickling her guts. "What do you know about it?" she asks.

"Ash? I introduced it to Synarion. He sure was upset that night. I fixed that. Truthfully, I don't see what the problem is. We all need money. The Moths are using their unique advantage. I use mine."

"Because I allow you to," Synarion says. "Who's that man you had?"

"My, you are stalking me," Mul says. "He's nothing to concern yourself with."

"All right," Synarion says. "Last night, you said the Moths pluck it right off the reptile. Have you seen one?"

"Not quite. I heard it, that's for sure."

"Have they told you the new pickup location for ash?" Synarion asks.

"Not yet. They will in time. Why?" Mul says.

"That gallery was for high-profile clients of the Crystal Moths. You climb from street dealers to a top-class Moth. Who tells you the pickup location?"

"What will you give me?" Mul asks. "The girl?"

Synarion says, "This works into a previous agreement. We'll extend it."

Mul turns around, looking into the crowd, contemplating Synarion's words. Lola feels like a third wheel, missing whatever these two have going on. It explains Synarion's constant disappearance.

"All right, fine," Mul says. "The man is Erol Terzi. I got to know him through the Crystal Moths while buying ash. You know how these things work, sweetheart. A little bit of chitchat, you meet someone else. It takes you to a party. From there, you connect with others, and next thing you know, you are in the Prime Minister's bed while his wife is on a book tour."

"And you have Erol Terzi's info?"

"No. Just the same number I gave you last time. The Crystal Moths are so hush hush."

Lola asks, "And what of Mastema?"

Mul raises her eyebrows. "Smart and pretty. Synarion. I'm the jealous one now."

Synarion downs the rest of his drink.

"What do you know about him?" Lola asks.

"Well, there are many fallen angels and demons. I cannot know each of them."

"Come on, Mul," Synarion says. "We don't want to be here."

Mul says, "You have quite the fascinating life, don't you, Synarion the balancer? Mending your poor broken heart, and now you're chasing the most dangerous fallen angel to ever exist? The First, I might add." She grabs Lola's jacket, feeling the material. "I see why this human gravitates towards you. We gals love a thrill."

Lola says, "Look, I've researched Mastema. I know he comes from the Book of Jubilees and the Dead Sea Scrolls. He's the persecutor of God. Eventually, he is written from holy books. Now, if this is the same person, he is running the Crystal Moths."

"So many questions and I have no drink," Mul says.

"You can't get drun——" Synarion stops himself and waves at the bartender. "Keep talking."

Mul says, "Let's sit for this one as the gentleman gets us a round."

The demon's black-nailed hand reaches for Lola's. She looks to Synarion for help. He shrugs as the delicate hand locks Lola in. It is soothing to touch, like holding her dear Becky Bub's hand so long ago. Mul takes Lola deeper into the club, away from the dance floor and its loud music. The new wing of the club is filled with high-backed circular leather seating arrangements. Mul finds an open one and sits cross-legged, pulling Lola in to sit beside her. She takes both of Lola's hands and caresses the skin.

"Now, how did that damaged old nymph pull you into this?" Mul asks.

Lola's back stiffens, and her jaw clenches. The demon's pink eyes don't blink. It's not a look of a person having a conversation. It's like a tiger watching its prey, ending Lola's relapse to Becky. This is not a friend. It's a demon holding her hand.

"It was kind of mutual," she says.

Mul keeps massaging her hands. "Mmm. He's a fan of mutual. Who are you, sweetheart?"

"Look, I don't know who you are. We need some info on the Crystal Moths."

"Feisty." Mul smiles.

Now Lola feels a pointed object slide against her leg. She jumps, noticing a tail graze her calve with its black pointed tip. Lola ignores it. "The Crystal Moths took everything from me.

That's all there is to it. Synarion found me and is trying to stop them. Now we work together."

"He is a busy one, with that balancing of his. The weight of the world is on his shoulders. Want to know about me?"

Lola decides it's best to play her game. "What about you?"

"Oh, me? Well, I'm quite old. I may not look it, but get me chatting and I talk like it. Other than that, I go about my business, finding men to restore my youth and stay out of sight where I can. Still, I must say, I am a little envious of you. Most males are easy to tempt."

"Okay?" Lola says.

"Not Synarion. You have a talent."

"It's not like that."

Mul laughs. "Sweetie. Who do you think you're fooling?"

"We work together."

"Believe what you want. The body says more than you think." Mul stops massaging Lola's hands. "Here's my warning to you: He breaks his rules from time to time. In the end, he is a balancer. It comes first, no matter what. Watch yourself."

"And how well do you know him?" Lola asks.

Synarion returns with the drinks, and Mul frees Lola from her grasp. The nymph sits on the other side, placing the drinks down.

"Okay, let's get this over with," he says. "Mastema, the First."

Mul says, "Right. It is a name I have not heard in a long time. Being in the mortal realm, I've lost many of my connections in the afterlife. Truthfully, it's way more fun here. You humans capture erotic pleasures on film. Then there are the toys."

"Mul, focus," Synarion says.

"All work," Mul groans. "Mastema is a name to me. He's the First, as you should know, which means the Creator made him before anything else. It's such old history it's a myth. In fact, most angels and demons don't believe in him because it's so ancient."

"What of the Crystal Moths?" Lola asks. "They say Mastema is their leader."

Mul taps her chin. "I don't know their chain of command, love. If you want to learn who Mastema is, you can find the Fallen Angel Encyclopedia. Ever hear of it?"

Lola and Synarion shake their heads no.

"It's a book documenting every angel that has left the Heavenly Kingdoms. It could be in the flames of Dega'Mostikas's Triangle. It might be here. Imps, angels, demons, who isn't moving from the mortal realm? Either way, Mastema would be in there."

Synarion says, "So, no idea where we'd find this book?"

"Sorry," Mul says.

"You don't remember anything else regarding Mastema?" Lola asks.

"Look, no human is impersonating Mastema. He wouldn't allow it. He's the father of evil, the flatterer of the Creator."

Synarion asks, "Father of evil. What of Dega'Mostikas? Isn't he the root of evil?"

Mul says, "That bastard, ruling his three realms of Hell? He ruffles the feathers of the Heavenly Kingdoms, but the father of evil comes before. Mastema serves a purpose for the Creator. Dega'Mostikas is an infection. Brush up on your history, love."

"He'd be the true Devil then?" Synarion asks.

"The Satan, the 'Adversary,' pick your name for Mastema from centuries ago. We change names over time. He's no devil, though. He is, or was, an angel. You need that encyclopedia for his historical accounts of why he had fallen and why he is here."

Synarion says, "The vazeleads? You know where they are?"

Mul shrugs. "The reptiles? I don't know. I get ash from the pickup where the vazelead is. It keeps the scales moist, far better than their overseas method."

Synarion asks, "Where is this vazelead?"

"It's some slaughterhouse now. They'll change it again and I'll have to learn how to drive there again. I hate driving. Drivers are so angry."

Lola and Synarion exchange looks.

Mul takes a drink as the DJ changes to a fast-paced track. It makes her foot tap, moving along with the beat. "I can send you the address on that intranet."

"I think we have that already. Do send it in case," Synarion says.

"I'm sorry, darlings. That's what I know. The afterlife is a dangerous convoluted place. Dega'Mostikas, Mastema, the Creator, you're playing with the originals. It makes sense why Mother Nature stays clear of it and sticks to her Earth. I'd follow her footsteps if I were you."

Synarion says, "I'm afraid Mastema is bringing the afterlife here."

"Well, the mortal realm is temporary. The afterlife is not. Care for a dance?" Mul asks.

Synarion rises. "No. We must leave."

All three exit the booth. Mul extends her arms. "Always business and no fun. So good to see you."

Synarion gives a stiff hug for the succubus as Lola downs the rest of her drink. Liquor is water. Ash is the one thing that can numb the stress of this lunacy. The words from the succubus are a concern.

What does she have on Synarion? Lola thinks. The nymph and demon mentioned Dega'Mostikas before. He wants in there for some reason.

Mul lets the nymph go and steps to Lola. "I'm sorry, dear, I'm a hugger."

Mul's hand is magnetic, pressing onto Lola. She places her hands on the demon's bare back, feeling the warm sweat on its skin. It's not the disgusting kind. In fact, Lola begins caressing it with perversion.

Mul whispers into her ear with the hot breath breaking the trance. "Come find me when you're done playing with that nymph. I will show you what ash can do for you."

CHAPTER 36
SCAPEGOAT

A process of elimination should eradicate conspiracy theories. *Should* is the keyword. Unfortunately, if every possible rational reason is ruled out, then the fantastic remains. For Iglesias, that isn't good enough. There must be some explanation for it all. Chen's and Fulcher's rambling around reptilian people and the Crystal Moths' shadowy order of influence is pure fiction.

Iglesias puffs on his cancer stick outside the headquarters of the Vancouver Police Department. After the fiasco at the North Vancouver Gallery of Modern Prestige, they're left with two new murders and fewer answers.

Beckman and Archer arrive from down the block with

coffees in hand.

"You ready for this, boss?" Archer asks, handing Iglesias his cup.

Iglesias shrugs. "No. We have to go."

Beckman lights a smoke and says, "I can't believe we have to deal with the US now. Christ."

"They're interested in the two movie stars. They can't interfere with the case, not their country," Iglesias says.

Archer adds, "Except it's entangled. Those deaths are linked to Lola, which links to the Crystal Moths and ash."

"This web keeps growing," Beckman says.

"It makes me paranoid concerning anything we find," Archer says.

Iglesias says, "I know. That's why the three of us have to stay in close contact at all times."

Beckman nods. "This gets better and better."

Iglesias and Beckman finish their smokes. The three head inside, going straight for the War Room, where another dozen or so officers in varying rankings sit. Several stragglers arrive after Iglesias and his crew.

The three, and many others, stand because there's not enough room for each officer to have a seat. Iglesias spots Hill, the sergeant from the art gallery, at the far end of the room.

Iglesias leans against the wall while sipping his coffee. One officer closes the door and dims the lights so the projector can present a slideshow of the evidence.

The chief of the Vancouver police stands by a laptop and the projector. He clears his throat before speaking. "Thank you, ladies and gentlemen, for joining us today as we coordinate our efforts from our departments to put an end to this escalating issue. I'd also like to thank the three FBI agents from the United States for flying here to join us to provide their expertise." He nods to the three suits sitting opposite from Iglesias.

No grace, just teeth, Iglesias thinks. He is best to keep his opinions to himself.

"I'm here to kick off our meeting and evaluate the evidence we have to date about the various suspects involved with the horrendous incident that occurred less than twenty-four hours ago. As most of you know . . ." The chief starts the slideshow, showing the art gallery and some photos of blood stains at the crime scene. " . . . there was an attack on the North Vancouver Art Gallery of Modern Prestige during painter Dasco Amoss's opening. This was supposed to be a historical Canadian moment, and it's mutated into an active crime scene for two murders that we need to figure out. The Crystal Moths were at the show. They were operating as security right under the gallery's nose."

The slideshow changes to a new image of the actress Ashley Amber and the actor Timothy Shepherd.

"There were two deaths after a shootout involving a wanted vigilante named Lola Cabello. The Hollywood stars Ashley Amber and Timothy Shepherd were shot dead. Our primary suspect is Lola Cabello, who has been wanted nationwide for many incidents, which we will overview."

"There's no way," Archer whispers to Iglesias.

Beckman leans closer and adds, "There are too many bullets and blood in the hall and on the roof. There are more bodies."

"Where are they?" Archer says.

Iglesias says, "Both of you, quiet."

The chief says, "The bullet shells found match those that were in a motel murder earlier this month. Cabello may have a hit list because these two weren't the only high profiles at the gallery. To our luck, there are no other civilian casualties."

One of the Americans raises his hand above his goatee and spiky hair.

"Yessir," the chief says.

"Yeah, hey. Are we able to drill into this Lola Cabello character more? In case she goes across the border."

"Of course," the chief says. "We'll go over the art gallery and circle back to Lola Cabello."

"Thank you," the man says.

The chief continues, "Our local department is interviewing attendants, staff, and anyone nearby to provide witness statements. We're checking security cameras to see if there's rooftop footage. Many of the witness statements heard dozens of gunshots, which contradicts Ashley Amber's and Timothy Shepherd's corpses. The security footage from the gallery is being processed. Lots of unanswered questions. Cabello is the prime target."

The chief changes the slide showcasing the motel crime scene Archer had texted Iglesias about.

"We found Lola Cabello's car parked at the motel with her belongings for a fake persona. A man was found murdered in his motel room. He gave a good fight before his unseen death. As you can see in the photos." The slide changes to the photograph of the dead man in a white tank top. A puncture wound is in the back of his skull. "The assailant was either invited in or broke in to kill the man with a sharp object to the skull."

Crystal Moth, Iglesias thinks. The presentation is starting to bore him. The evidence is fragmented and doesn't align with the profile he has on Lola Cabello. She isn't a young, scared university student anymore. She may have killed some people, but her agenda doesn't involve movie stars.

The slideshow goes into detail regarding who the man in the motel was. He grew up with a family and had a stable career. Yet he has a giant scar on his face. He's built. Then for some reason, he went alone to a cheap, dingy motel on the outskirts of the metropolis. The motel murder is identical to the art gallery, a fudged story. There are too many bullet holes and blood in the hallways, stairwell, and rooftop for two murders. It doesn't make sense with the single bullets they found in Ashley Amber's and Timothy's skulls.

The inconsistency leaves a sickening twist in Iglesias's stomach to the point that he cannot finish his coffee. His terrible hunches are true. The Crystal Moths have more plugs in the law than he first feared. Chen's escape wasn't the singular incident. The Crystal Moths have been mucking evidence from the get-go, and Cabello is their scapegoat. Can he trust anyone in here?

The presentation continues, moving from the motel to the background of Cabello. They cover her schooling and blogging site, which has not had an update in weeks. Officers ask who Cabello is, what's her motive, why she is in Vancouver, her childhood, if the Prime Minister is in danger, and how this ties in with the Crystal Moths.

Sergeant Hill of the homicide department takes over the presentation. Then Iglesias and his team talk, sharing their information from when they first discovered ash in New Brunswick during the summer and following Cabello for two years. After a good four hours, the chief calls for lunch. They'll regroup in an hour. The three detectives leave the headquarters, getting fresh air, away from the stuffiness of the War Room.

"Well, that was a lot of horseshit," Beckman says.

"Is that where they're going with the case?" Archer says. "It's as bad as the internal investigation with Chen."

Iglesias lights a smoke and says, "No. I fear we are in a lot of trouble."

"Us?" Archer asks.

Beckman smokes his own dart and says, "The entire system."

"Okay, come on. You think the Crystal Moths are puppeteering this fiasco?" Archer says.

Iglesias and glesias and Glen don't say a word, both inhaling their smoke.

"Christ," Archer says. "Can I have one?"

Iglesias gives her a cigarette and lights it. She puffs on it several times and folds her arms. "I don't believe it."

"Neither do I," Iglesias says.

"I need a drink," Beckman says. "I feel like no one else has their head on their shoulders."

"We've been in it the longest," Archer says.

Iglesias says, "We have a profile on Lola Cabello. I did pass what we had to the group before the War Room meeting. Still, they glaze over the facts of who she is. Yes, her gun's bullets were found in both scenes. Yes, Crystal Moths were at both locations. Yet, they overlook how evidence goes missing when the gang is involved. We can't be the only ones who see through the façade."

Archer says, "If there are others, none of them will speak out, like us."

"What does Sergeant Bando think of this?" Beckman says.

"He wants this solved, fast," Iglesias says.

Archer says, "We can counter these War Room hooligans with a good counterargument. We have to."

Iglesias says, "I'll chat with Bando and let him know what is happening. We don't need to insult the chief of police here. It's their district."

Beckman says, "I kind of want a keep my job. My wife and I are almost done with the mortgage, and I'm close to retiring."

"We each have things we have to protect." Iglesias reflects on José. More than anything, he would rather be with his son than deal with the increasing complexity of the case.

"I say we leave this meeting," Archer says.

"No can do," Iglesias says. "We need to be there, lay low, and play nice in the sandbox while keeping our opinions on the case to ourselves until I talk with Bando. From what they've gathered, it points to Lola Cabello as the primary suspect. She could be responsible for murder now. So, get into that War Room and participate, got it?"

Archer finishes her smoke and chucks it on the street. "Yes, boss."

"Littering?" Beckman asks.

Iglesias repeats Archer's action and smirks at Beckman.

"You too? Beckman puts his butt in the ashcan beside where

the two threw theirs. "Where's lunch?"

"Anywhere. Truthfully, I'm not hungry," Archer says.

"I'm going to call my son," Iglesias says. "Then Bando."

"You got it," Beckman says. With that, the two head through the street, with Archer's voice piercing through the downtown traffic, complaining about the case.

Finally, for a moment in time, Iglesias can put work aside and return to his family. He dials his son's cell number. Several seconds go by, and he lights another cigarette with a single hand. Eventually, his son answers and says, "Hey, Dad, what's up?"

Iglesias's heart bursts with warmth. His son's voice is deepening, and he still has his boy's tone. José is the one thing that brings joy to Iglesias's life, and hearing him fills him with regret for not being there. It's the damn weekend. "Hey, son, I wanted to give you a ring and an update." A giggle comes from the background, too girlish to be one of his friends, meaning it's Hailey. "Got company?"

"Yeah, Hailey is over. How goes the case?" José asks.

"It's a disaster. You see it on the news?"

"Yeah, there's an art gallery?" José asks.

"That. The girl and the Moths are tied into this. I'm not sure how long I'll be here. You doing okay?"

"Yeah, good. Tanner is coming by later to hang."

"And that's all?" Iglesias asks. "With this free time, you're not going to throw another party?"

"No, Dad. I promise."

"Thanks. You know you're in prime party years?"

José laughs. It makes Iglesias smile, a genuine one he has not had in weeks. He used to smile like this when in the park, pushing his son on the swings. Life was so simple then. José is almost a man, and Iglesias can't keep relapsing to the past, wishing for a better now.

"That's the only news," Iglesias says. "Not much I can tell you other than it's a complete shit show. I'll call you tomorrow."

Hailey speaks in the background and José says, "Stop it." He laughs. "Yeah, that's cool, Dad. Hey, I gotta go."

"No worries, son."

"Cool, thanks."

"I love yo—" the phone hangs up before he can finish his sentence. Iglesias sighs. He recalls his days of being a teenager going through hormones. With a girl in his bedroom, his father's love would be the last thing he would want. As are the priorities of a teenage boy.

Next, he calls Sergeant Bando.

"Bando here."

"Serg, we're running into conflicting evidence with the Vancouver Police."

"I caught wind of the shooting. You guys got there at the right time. Give them what you have, and let's get Cabello. I'm sick of hearing about her," Bando says.

How much do I share? Iglesias thinks, wondering if Bando is in on the Moths. They've worked together for so long. "It's concerning. The chief of police is overlooking key issues with the art gallery murders. Now the FBI is here."

"Those assholes? Ah, well, nothing they can do in Canada," Bando says.

"Evidence is being skewed. It's like Chen when the security

footage was deleted."

"Yeah, it's got me paranoid."

"Same here. How far should I push this?" Iglesias asks.

"We're losing grip. DND is breathing down our necks to get the CFMP involved. Be sly. Rock the boat a bit so it stays on the record. You and your team need to give us tangible evidence to work with. Playing devil's advocate doesn't always work."

"Yes, Serg," Iglesias says.

"Good. Anything else?"

"No."

"You got this." Bando hangs up.

Iglesias finishes his dart and strolls, texting Archer to learn where the two went. He's by a park now, unaware of how far he has walked. A small lizard dashes from the corner of his eye, past the sidewalk and into some grass, vanishing into the blades.

Reptiles, Iglesias thinks. It sends his mind into a rabbit hole of his own conspiracies. Tycho Fulcher's words rise from the dark in an inconsistent order. "*Not a metaphor like krokodil from Russia or nothin'. True, crazy, Illuminati shit. Like these reptilians can talk and walk among us. They've changed the whole game. They've been around for so long, dormant.*" It's a testimony to Chen's explanation.

The Crystal Moths worm their way into everything, corrupting the entire system. Iglesias's gut sinks, fearing he's one of the few good cops left and onto a tangible trail. He must keep truth at the forefront of his mind. Reptilian people don't exist. The Crystal Moths are real, and their circle of influence is vast, led by a single man named Mastema. Those are the facts for Iglesias and his team. They haven't illuminated all possibilities and can't conclude the fantastic.

CHAPTER 37
CLOSE ENEMIES

A hunt requires patience. An old saying goes: keep your friends close and your enemies closer. It is mad to spend your mortal time with those you distaste. Scalebane has enough wisdom to comprehend that time is a tool on its own. She must blend in with the prey. Let the clock tick, and their weakness will unravel.

She had repaired her mask at Allen Shipping Solutions, bolting a new make-shift metal muzzle onto the leather base. The anonymity of the mask strikes fear into her enemies once more. It also serves as a shield from the biting wind ten thousand feet above the metropolis. She holds onto a railing in the passenger seat as the helicopter takes her to Mastema's mansion. She and her allies are to regroup after the art show disaster. That means Erol will be there. Scalebane would love to grab the man by the throat and demand he tell her where Namsruc is. Then, she'd crush the life out of him.

She has no luck meeting Dasco Amoss any time soon with that attitude. It's a side note that can be dealt with later. The painter isn't going anywhere.

Her sister is the prime concern. Scalebane has no proof of anything and is riding on the words of a succubus and her instincts. A visit to this demon is in order. That damn wretched creature. Scalebane's continual disapproval of other beings will not end because demons are too close to her childhood.

The helicopter lands on the helipad behind Mastema's mansion that is tucked far in the northern mountains. On the ground is Jekos, the half-imp, another disgusting being. Standing beside him is Erol himself. He's wearing his usual grey suit and stands straight with confidence. Behind him are the two silent vampire Moths. Scalebane exits the chopper and fails to acknowledge anyone as Jekos takes a bow.

In the imp's scratchy high voice, he says, "Welcome back to Mastema's mansion, Scalebane."

Erol takes a bow as well. "Scalebane, it's good to see you are in one piece after that nightmare."

"Where's Mastema?" Scalebane says.

"Jekos. Lead the way," Erol says.

Jekos takes the group along the garden path.

Erol speaks low, leaning into her. "Mastema can get quite tempered. Be cautious of what you say."

"I can handle heat fine," Scalebane says.

"We'll clear this mess and return to business within a week. I guarantee it."

"Don't be too sure, Erol," Scalebane says. "I think you underestimated this Cabello." *And me*, she thinks.

"Save the fire for the meeting," Erol says.

Jekos takes them through the garden, into the mansion, and up the spiral staircase. He pushes two golden rings carved into the shape of gargoyles eating their own tails. They're attached to red wooden doors. In the new room are four black circular pillars and deep burgundy walls. A red carpet leads straight to the end, where an oak desk rests. Mastema sits in a black leather button tuffed chair. As before, he champions a full white suit. His long bone hair is pushed back, his feet resting on the desk.

"Excellent," Mastema says, swinging his legs down. "Come, sit."

Erol takes the second guest chair, and Jekos bows. Scalebane stops by a fireplace to her right with a seat in front of her. She places her claws on her sai. The flame's heat is a comfort from the constant cold sinking its teeth into her skin. Still, her tail coils around her ankle, restraining her frustrations.

"Master, is there anything else you need?" Jekos asks.

"Dismissed," Mastema says, waving his hand and commanding the half-imp and vampires to leave. "How's the flight, well?"

"Of course, sir," Erol says.

"Lereif, take a seat, please." Mastema extends his hand to the second chair.

"I'd rather stand," Scalebane says. Mastema is bold enough to use her first name, fueling her anger and damaging her pride. The cunning fallen angel is feasting well.

"Lereif," Mastema says again.

This time, Scalebane obeys and sits on the red velvet cushion of the chair. She keeps her claws to herself, knowing she will dig right into the wood.

Where's my sister? Scalebane would like to say. She keeps quiet, tightening her tail on her ankle. It's a growing coping mechanism while working with these Moths.

"Good." Mastema brings his hands together and looks at them, letting the fire crackle fill the air. He slams a fist onto the desk, splintering the wood. "By the Creator, do you mind telling me what happened?"

Erol clears his throat. "We misjudged the abilities of the vigilante. The girl is alive."

"What girl? I'm discussing the art gallery," Mastema says.

Erol nods. "Yes. The girl is involved."

"The one from Edmonton? By the gods. I am exhausted from her. Why can't you kill the damn mortal?"

"I believed we had," Erol says. "It appears she is craftier than we first thought. The assassin I sent was murdered. Somehow that has led her to the opening."

Mastema presses his index finger into the table. "You know that was an important event for us, right?"

"Yes, sir."

"It's not only the money they have," Mastema says.

"Yes, sir."

"We need their influence on humans."

"It's important," Erol says.

"We need those elite pricks."

"I know."

Mastema leans back, putting his feet up again. He lets out a deep exhale. "And what is this girl's motive? We've made her a pretty face for the law and media. Yet, you can't remove her?"

Erol looks at Scalebane. "Well, somehow she learned of the art gallery, as I said. She arrived and attempted to destroy our operation. The girl kidnapped a couple of our key clients, Ashley Amber and Timothy Shepherd. We had to take precautionary measures."

"As we do in those situations. Tell me something new," Mastema says.

"We adjusted the crime scene as the police arrived. Our allied law enforcers assisted in skewing the evidence. Ashley Amber's body was replaced with the lookalike."

"And the Prime Minister? Did he get his ash?"

Erol shakes his head. "No. He escaped and made a PR statement to downplay the whole thing. I don't think anyone bought it. Still, I have no doubts he'll keep Allen Shipping Solutions unbothered by the law.

Mastema wipes his face.

Erol continues, "And the staged gun was placed at the art show, pegging the vigilante."

"This is some university girl. You have trained men with far superior firepower. How have you failed twice? I want her gone. I want us to focus on ash." He points at Scalebane and says, "I want King to give us more ash. We can't make progress without it. How is this so complicated?"

Scalebane says, "The soft skin wants to dismantle your

organization. This is a personal vendetta. She won't stop until she's either dead or has ignited the Crystal Moths."

"That's fine. You're a skilled hunter, Lereif. Kill her," Mastema says.

"She has help."

Mastema raises an eyebrow. "Help?"

Scalebane bites her tongue, hesitating. A forgotten vision runs through her mind. She and her sister as mere hatchlings, squawking at a purple-eyed nymph for food. He smiles at them, serving two bowls of home-cooked lentils. He strokes Scalebane's black and blue scalp feathers, then Namsruc's white and black feathers. The reflection warms Scalebane's heart far better than that fireplace ever can.

She pushes air out her nostrils, reminding herself to suppress the memory. That time was pleasant and later destroyed by his abandonment. King offered the truth. It took her years to understand the world's destructive nature.

"She is working with the balancer," Scalebane says.

"*The* balancer, from the Grove?" Mastema asks. "Didn't the balancers collapse with the rest of the world centuries ago?"

"One of the nymphs lived after the continent of Zingalg fell into the ocean. He's sworn to his duty."

"What's his name?"

"Synarion," Scalebane says.

"Not of the Grove's council then," Mastema says.

"No," Scalebane says.

"Can't say I've heard of him. One lone balancer can't do much on his own."

"Don't be too quick to judge him. My sister and I crossed

paths with him long ago. He is crafty, persistent, and an able fighter."

Mastema rubs his brow. "All of this incompetence is beginning to irritate me."

Scalebane says, "Mastema, I would suspect that Synarion has pieced together what we're working towards."

"Did he now?" Mastema leans forward. "Who dares challenge my power?"

"A balancer and a soft skin."

"I want them dead," Mastema hisses through his teeth.

"Consider it done," Scalebane says. Her throat tenses, unsure if she can commit to the task.

Erol adds, "Any man or weapon you need is at your disposal."

Scalebane says, "Your Moths are useless to me. I have what I need."

Mastema's mood pulls a one-eighty with a wide smile. He opens his hands, sitting upright. "Excellent! That's the kind of effectiveness that I like to hear. Erol, you should be taking note of Scalebane's hands-on initiative."

"Yes, of course," Erol says.

"Now for this art gallery nonsense. Be done with it and do what you do best, Erol, with the media. I'll have Jekos contact the law and ensure that this disaster is nailed on the girl. That's all I can be involved with. I have many more interviews for new recruits to broaden our reach. Then the red market, I have to run this whole operation on my own. I don't need to do these nitpicky things."

"Of course," Erol says.

"And, in fact, I happen to have a meeting with King soon, Lereif."

Scalebane's tail uncoils around her ankle. "Good. That is long overdue."

"Indeed. You're both dismissed."

Erol and Scalebane leave the office and go into the hall. Jekos slithers from the corner beside the doorway and closes the doors behind them. He guides them down the staircase, where the vampires join them. The group exits the mansion and returns to the helicopter, where the blades of the machine spin.

"Scalebane," Jekos says.

A rattling rises from her throat.

Jekos says, "There is one place you could look for information regarding your hunt."

"And where is that, halfbreed?" Scalebane asks.

Jekos steps forward to whisper into Scalebane's ear. He's close enough that she can smell the high-end cologne. It stings her upper nostrils, as his natural scent of burning plastic lingers below. "There's a club along East Hastings in Blood Alley. It will prove to be of value to you. Club Revelation."

"I already know this."

"And do you know I run the place? Your nymph has been there. So has a demon or anything else you need. You and your people walk a dangerous line. Your allies' weaknesses aren't what they seem. Tell them Jekos sent you, and you wish to find revelation. Otherwise, they won't let you in with your gizmos and gadgets, friend."

A spontaneous smile spreads across his face, and he opens his arms. "Scalebane! What a change of heart!" The halfbreed wraps his stick-like limbs around her, bringing her into his embrace. She could kill him right now. She doesn't due to his words. "Mastema is fooling your people. He's not possessing a human body. Watch yourself." He slaps her back, freeing her. Next, he approaches Erol, shaking the man's hand with a firm grip, holding his forearm with the other. "It's always good to see you. Take care."

Scalebane is dumbfounded, watching Jekos be so bold, so staged, only to complicate the relationship with the Crystal Moths. She's left bewildered as Erol and her step onto the helicopter. Then the machine takes flight, soaring far from the mansion.

Eventually, Erol asks, "Do you know where to find this girl?"

Scalebane says, "A general idea. Leave the details to me. Take care of the art gallery."

"As long as you stay clear from cameras, okay? This situation was too close. We almost didn't get the security footage wiped in time with you running around like that."

"I must get the girl."

"Scalebane, I can only control the media for so long. Eyes are everywhere, and the people have power."

"Then keep them distracted."

Scalebane's second agenda aligns with her first. Finding the girl is no longer her top priority, despite her encouraging words to her employer. Scalebane's first is to discover where this hidden ash production site is and how it links to her sister.

Erol is cunning. Mastema lies. King dismisses her. Now, her once repulsive halfbreed comrade has morphed into the key solution as she maps her next move, taking her to Club Revelation.

CHAPTER 38
DEREALISATION

Lola has been staying low since the art gallery two nights ago to plot her next moves. The downtime escalates the ever-constant itch that lingers in her mind. The creeping metaphoric being doesn't have to say a word, for stillness is plentiful, reminding her that she has an ash diamond at her disposal.

A presence is near, exterior, reminding her to control her impulses. She opens her eyes. A fist comes soaring to her face. Barefooted and shirtless, Synarion is her combatant.

She dodges the oncoming blow and throws a punch to his gut. The low strike is met with a knee to her chin, throwing her back. The nymph hops around and locks her in a choke hold, one she can't escape, and she taps his forearms, indicating

469

surrender. Both pant as he frees her.

"You're hesitating too much," Synarion says.

Lola isn't numb to this. Her own limitations irritate her because it's beyond reach. She knows what to do. She knows how to act. Then she freezes as if something is missing, and it's obvious what is.

"Trust your instincts," Synarion says. "They've gotten you this far."

"Wanted by the law and squatting in the dump of some outcast?"

"At least you know what the real world is." He raises his fist. "Another round?"

"Humour me," Lola says.

"With?"

Lola heads to her bag on the table with her laptop. She unzips the inner compartment and takes her diamond of ash. Synarion sighs, watching her peel off a piece far smaller than any amount she has done before. She raises the ash.

"Are you serious?" Synarion asks.

"Yes. There's more to it than a high. It's changing me."

"How?"

"Every time I take it, I get stronger and smarter, like it's broadening my senses. Let me try." Lola spins the small piece in her hand.

"Fine," Synarion says, his tone oozing disapproval.

Lola chows down on the ash strip, swallowing the drug and exhaling. "Give it a minute to kick in." Lola focuses on her breathing to empty her mind as the ash courses through her body. She sits cross-legged and closes her eyes.

Rise, comes the familiar voice. It's distant, like at the art gallery. Lola obeys and opens her eyes, standing and lifting her fists. Already the drug is absorbed into her stomach and travels in her veins. The colours in the room glow, showing more hues of amber, gold, green, and browns, making the room far more alive. The depth of Synarion's knuckles expands slightly, and the distance between them lengthens. It tells her the exact length of his reach.

"Ready?" Synarion asks.

"Go," Lola replies.

Synarion is the first to attack, dashing to her with a spin, ending in a roundhouse kick. Lola ducks. He sends another punt, a miss, and follows with a punch. He's less merciful this time, wanting to embarrass her. To his surprise, Lola dodges the three attacks.

Now. Lola throws a fist. Her hand collides with his rib with a loud slap, knocking him back.

Synarion grunts, stabilizing his stance. He starts to circle her, more cautious in his step. He sprints. A fist flies to her, and she steps to the side and then throws a kick to his shins. He deflects it with his leg, opening his torso.

There. Lola punches his stomach. He's stunned. Her foot slams into him again.

Synarion blocks the last attack, taking a step away. He's on the defensive as Lola strings a series of fists and kicks that he counters.

Same move, comes from the distant voice.

He throws a knee at her, and spins behind her as he did in their first fight. Synarion goes in for the headlock. Lola turns, her leg soaring into the back of his knee. The blow knocks him off balance. Her foot slams into his chest, and he flies onto his ass with a satisfying thump.

Lola has her fists raised, ready to keep fighting, breathing fiercely.

Synarion chuckles, brushing dirt off his pants. "I'm impressed."

"See?" Lola says. "There's a power to ash. Like I can feel you. I can feel what you're going to do and, and what you need."

"What I need?" Synarion asks.

"I think. I don't know. This is new and strange." Her heart is pumping fast. Even with a little dose of ash, she is in an altered state of consciousness. It's the better Lola.

"Well, the Crystal Moths are highly invested in it. Be careful, Lola. You don't know what you're playing with."

"I know. It's calling to me."

Synarion puts on his shirt and says, "That's the addiction."

Lola hugs her arms, unsure how to reply. It could be, or she is connecting with the real world. If she doesn't try, she will never know.

"I'll manage it," Lola says.

"You're your own person, Lola. Well done today. We should talk about the Moths."

"Right. The SUV's location?" Lola asks. "I mean, I know you needed to rest after the art gallery. Mul had little information, and we must keep on the Moth's trail."

"Patience, Lola," Synarion says, sitting by the desk and opening his laptop. "Just because I heal faster than you doesn't mean I'm not cautious in an investigation, considering our lack of numbers. Didn't they teach this wisdom to you in your university days?"

"I didn't investigate organized crime on a global scale." Lola takes a seat beside him, inhaling his natural aroma and sweat.

Take him, comes the voice. Yes, she wants to ravage him again. The ash-heightened senses are impulsive and beneficial at the moment, and she has not mastered controlling it.

" . . . come find me when you're done playing with that nymph. I will show you what ash can do for you." Mul has knowledge she can use. Lola needs to know the demon's knowledge. Later.

Synarion says, "My colleague Eden Breaker has replied with good news regarding the dragon statues."

"What?" Lola leans into his laptop screen. The right column in the browser window has the open email from Eden Breaker. To the left, the smaller column has a list of email messages. There are many names she doesn't recognize, except for the second one from the top. It's from Mul. The subject line reads: *I have more info on your darling.* The rest of the title is hidden by the column's length.

Synarion is unaware or doesn't care. He says, "It turns out that the statues are common in vanity stores. They're manufactured by a production plant in Vietnam, made by a company called Lang Enterprises."

Lola asks, "Does that mean anything to you?"

"No. It's noteworthy. Maybe the vazeleads are in Vietnam." He closes his laptop and stands. "We will check the slaughterhouse tomorrow."

"Why wait?" Lola asks. "We have them."

"I've been watching the SUV's movements. It drives around the city and returns to the same location. We don't want them to have any suspicion that we are onto them. Give it another day." He heads to his closet, putting on a new shirt, his usual hoodie and leather jacket.

"Where are you going?" Lola asks.

"I have other work to do," Synarion says while putting on socks and boots.

"Is it related to Mul?" Lola asks.

"There are other balancing tasks that I have to take care of."

"Like what?" Lola asks.

"I've been doing this for a long time, Lola. Getting you up to speed would take an entire history course."

"I can help?" Lola asks, standing.

"No, you can't, Lola. Not this time." He straps his weapons and utility belts on, then goes for the door.

"Synarion," Lola touches his arm, getting him to stop.

"Lola, if you want to be productive, see what other information you can get on the Crystal Moths. Don't pursue the abattoir plant until I get back."

"When is that?" Lola asks.

"Tomorrow."

Lola doesn't know what to say. The spontaneous change in mood is an unusual side to Synarion. He's expressed it before. The nymph has his own skeletons. Mul gave her a tidbit of what it could be. A visit with the demon must come sooner than later.

"Okay," Lola says, folding her arms.

"One day," Synarion says. He heads for the door, opens it,

and leaves Lola with a final click from the lock.

The nymph's secrecy feeds her paranoia. Synarion's evasiveness increases as the days go by. Mul is involved, somehow related to Hell and a *darling*. Finally, Lola is looking past Synarion's wit and charm. It took ash to do so. This further validates her theory about the drug.

Mul spoke of a broken heart. Synarion is on a personal agenda, not his noble balancing mission. It's no different than Lola, who seeks to avenge the Trinity of Souls in her mind. This raises the question: who is Synarion looking for?

The succubus is a vault of knowledge regarding Synarion and ash. Unfortunately, it is Monday, and the likelihood of Club Revelation being open is next to none. She will have to wait until the weekend and hope the succubus is there.

Lola's paranoia sends her mind to Michael Bradford, then working with Donnie, interrogating Chen, and going undercover in an art gallery. She is in over her head. A university dropout who thinks she can take on the world.

She must because no one else will. People continue their day-to-day business arrogant to what is wrong with civilization. Look at Donnie, who gave in to the tainted police. Synarion's adopted child, Scalebane, works for the Crystal Moths. Mul embraces evil for her own greed. Synarion is full of mystery. Then there was Bark Nose, the one who removed himself entirely.

Lola sits at her computer and checks for any new mail. She reviews the news. No surprise, the art gallery has made a headline, and Lola's face is plastered on the front page. The article is pointing fingers at her for Ashley Amber's death.

Thankfully, there's no mention of her new fake identification.

She has been vacant on her blog and checks it to see many new comments on older article posts. They're the usual ones of encouragement and hate. Her public email address is no different. People praise her rebellious nature, and some chant her death.

Death to Cabello. Avenge Amber! Death to Cabello. Avenge Amber!

Her heart falls into her stomach. There are no further emails from Donnie. Why would there be? She expected such. Even then, each time she opens that inbox, a sliver of hope enters her soul that he will reconnect and understand the danger that the world is in. Donnie replied once, unlike her brother and father in the disowning club.

A wave of abandonment rushes over her, like the aftermath of when she first uploaded the video two years ago. Even Synarion drew a line. Everyone leaves Lola.

She must fend for herself.

Lola opens the photograph she took of the detective's business card. Donnie claims Iglesias is a good cop, which entices Lola. Could Iglesias be, or is he connected to the Moths?

"Damnit," Lola mumbles while rubbing her face with her palms.

She's not ready. She needs to go deeper into the old world and separate herself from the derealisation of human civilization. She will find answers. Mul is unreachable at the moment. To Lola's luck, there is another.

A C T

IV

ACT IV
DEPENDENCE NORMALIZED

Good evening, and welcome to *CAMB News Now with Hucker Dime*. Canadians have suffered a double tragedy to remember.

Dasco Amoss's opening at the North Vancouver Gallery of Modern Prestige ended in slaughter. Actor and director Timothy Shepherd and megastar sensation Ashley Amber were murdered with evidence pointing to the vigilante Lola Cabello.

Prime Minister Stéphane Trudell says, 'Ashley Amber was

dear to our hearts, and it is a tragedy for everyone. Our deepest condolences go to her family and loved ones.'

Timothy Shepherd and Ashley Amber were, without a doubt, important to all. Their movie *Love, Play, and No Work* will cease production due to their deaths, resulting in thousands without jobs. We are grateful that the police arrived when they did before more lives were lost.

A voice of a generation is gone. Bless the late Ashley Amber.

Amoss's work is filled with blood and dark imagery. Many higher-class individuals attended the evening. It paints a good conspiracy of evil elites for the mentally ill. Why else would Cabello go on a slaughter?

The Vancouver chief of police has stated that their resources are being pooled into the case. He ensures that Lola Cabello will be caught. The police are looking for any witnesses to come forward.

In other news, the missing Crystal Moth Yang Chen, who had escaped the police, was found dead. His eyeless head was impaled on the other side of the country along the shores of Vancouver. His daughter and her mother were tied to the docks with Chen's head meters away for hours before a local man found them gagged and bound. The mother, Lian Chao, says the Crystal Moths took Chen and spared her and her daughter as a forewarning to the police. Crystal Moths are a relentless threat.

Canadians are angered and fearful between this disturbing gang message and Cabello's rampage. The government is incapable of keeping us safe. Throughout Canada and the United States of America, people are demanding justice for Ashely Amber. Protests are rising outside of capitals. 'Avenge

Amber!' they shout. The people want answers. Throughout the streets of Vancouver, civilians are flooding the Burnard Bridge heading for the city's parliament. The local protests started a day ago, and there are no signs of slowing down.

The arrest of Cabello must happen.

Not all news is good news. We'll see brighter days, which takes us to Justin and Danielle for the weather.

Thank you so much for tuning in. We strive to provide you with facts regarding the latest news at CAMB. Stories that continue to evolve regarding you and your country.

CHAPTER 39
THY NATURE'S ROOTS

Words fall in the presence of action. Lola must be persistent with her mission and not listen to Synarion's request. Her supposed ally, and the old world, are too great of a mystery for Lola's comfort level. A reporter needs answers. Thus, a detour is needed. Somewhere deep in the Lower Seymore Conservation Reserve is a walking tree and a flower girl who can provide clarity.

Lola leaves Synarion's apartment, taking her usual survival necessities with her: gun, knife, a stack of cash (she's unsure about the legitimacy of the credit card Eden Breaker supplied), and a fake ID. Her phone is tucked in the cargo pocket. Food and water are stored in a backpack of Synarion's that she slings over her shoulder. She wears her pendant to record her upcoming adventure. Lola even tucks the remaining ash into her bralette to aid in her journey.

Synarion led her through a maze of woods the last time they were in the reserve. She doesn't know the exact path to find Bark Nose, but the ash should give her the clarity needed to find him.

The conservation reserve is far from her location. Several bus routes will take her there. With her hood over her head, she sits at the end of the transport. The bus is filled with tourists, youth, and elders this early in the morning.

Synarion said he would be back today. Lola doesn't care. She'll return when she wishes. He isn't in control of her. She was kind enough to leave a note on his table saying she'd be investigating personally. It's vague, like Synarion. He can have a taste of his own medicine.

She shouldn't be so bitter concerning him. There's no romance between them, and he owes her no explanation. She doesn't trust anyone. He is an ancient being who has lived many lives. Based on the polaroids he shared his life with many other girls. Then there are Mul's words. Lola's and Synarion's intimate moment was a temporary release with no spark. She needs to remind herself of this. Feelings get you killed.

Lola needs shuteye to gain energy for the rest of her trip. She had taken a small slice of ash the day before. The post-drug symptoms of headaches, raisin muscles and heavy bones are prevalent.

After a few hours, hopping onto another bus, then another, the final one reaches the Lower Seymore Conservation Reserve. The people exit the transport, followed by Lola in the rear. She strays from the others, recalling where Synarion had taken her. Finding a giant walking tree in the vast forest isn't an easy task. The ash-dasher slips the goods out and takes a small bite.

She activates the camera on her necklace. It's best to start recording in case the ash takes her too far. If she can get Bark Nose and his plant girl on the footage, she'll have more evidence for her case. Lola doesn't want to expose the location. Edits can be made later. It's a shame that the two are crossfire in a bigger game.

The trail is far wetter than the first time due to the excessive rain the province gets. Her boots are ready for the challenge. Portions of the path are familiar, making it easy to navigate where to go next.

A hum rises in Lola's limbs. It's the ash. The nearby branches stretch far, with their leaves pointing away. The tones in the vegetation are gaining more variety. The sound spectrum grows wide with her boots in the middle hemisphere and the chirping birds taking the higher. Her breath fills the lower portion.

Through her cerebral senses, the mind is still the same.

It's not enough, Lola thinks. She is building immunity and decides to take more. She takes the ash and chows down. One large bite leaves a sliver of scale left.

"Fucking work," Lola groans, stuffing the remaining ash into her bralette.

This is the most she has taken since the first trip with Jack. She needs to utilize her tools to find Bark Nose. The further she walks, the more foreign the forest is. Her journey takes her over a hill. Lola pants and sweats. The path opens into a wide road. To her left, a single narrow dirt track hides in the bushes and goes deeper into the foliage.

She closes her eyes and focuses on her intuition. Her body's chemicals are mixing with the ash. If you talked to Lola a month ago, she'd think this behaviour was pure lunacy. Now, under the influence of ash, everything changes.

A breeze arrives as she breathes steadily, standing in front of the two directions.

Thy nature awaits, comes a singular whisper inside Lola's ear. This is an exterior whisper. It's a tingle, and she swears it was accompanied by the wind. It wasn't like the gravitating voice she heard during the other ash sessions.

She opens her eyes. The small dirt trail expands as the bushes twist clear, providing a path toward a bright light. Even the leaves on the nearby branches twirl, pointing toward this newfound direction.

Lola steps to the light, following the plants. Her willingness to move is passive as if the radiant beam is pulling her in. It has to be Bark Nose. Unless this forest hides other secrets. Either way, Lola will find out.

Embrace the roots, comes the whisper.

"Yes," Lola mutters under her breath.

The wind ruffles against the leaves, creating a rhythmic sound in sync with the singing birds. Her heart rate is their tempo, with each breath following slower, along with the world's tune. She is a part of this living garden with all creatures.

She steps forward and doesn't hit the ground. Her foot sinks into the mud. No. It's melding with the earth. Her foot dissolves gently, becoming a pool of goo, followed by her second foot. Next, her entire body melts until she is a puddle. The leaves dance with the world's beat.

Keep going, comes the whisper.

What does the whisper think she can do? She can't move, for she is mud. She's where she needs to be, sensing the living connection to the earth.

The ground moves and the puddle drizzles out, separating her conscious state. The remnants of her moves closer to the trees. There, in the sky with the dancing branches, the sun beams on her through a cloudless lens. It radiates the colours of the rainbow. The sun shifts into dark frizzy hair and wrinkled skin. Why, it's Lola's mother.

Two additional faces are formed in the space. One is a burly bald man, Michael Bradford. The last is of a girl with black and red dreadlocks. Becky. The Trinity of Souls, who she must avenge.

Return to us, Lola. The voices speak as one, quite different from the whisper.

"I am," Lola says or thinks. She can't tell.

Live, the voices say. *Don't burn.*

"I'm not," Lola says.

A breeze blows by, and Lola's scattered goo form rejoins as one.

A gentle whisper says, *Embrace thy nature.*

The wind gains strength, blowing mud Lola up vertically. The blast splatters the earth and roots, forming a skeletal frame. The dirt wraps around the bones, mutating into red and pink flesh, while leaves slam into the muscled being, wrapping around, creating skin. More foliage plasters on, completing human Lola with her clothing.

She is sitting cross-legged on the ground, covered in mud. Her backpack is gone. She pats her belt and boot, the weapons are there. A tap on her chest confirms her necklace, and the camera is recording. Her ash session can be deleted later.

Lola stands, not angered by the loss. There's a warm connection to the ground. The breeze pulls Lola in a new direction, and she follows it, letting her broadened intuition guide her. It takes her to an open patch of grass with shrubbery and moss-covered trees forming a circular space. Above, the clouds cover the sun entirely. The wind stops.

Lola, that is your name, comes the whisper. It's behind her.

Lola turns to face a pale girl with black bangs fifteen meters away. She's motionless. Abbygail.

A small smile spreads on Lola's face. The ash worked. Her crazy theory is proving true. She glances at the camera's discrete light. It flashes, indicating the device is recording.

Abbygail's wrapped trench coat sways her body side to side, her head bogging in a reverted motion.

"Oh shit," Lola mumbles, grasping the danger.

The plant girl's lips twitch, jerking into a smile. The disguised flower petals peel backwards, exposing the bright red interior and white spikes.

Flesh pod, says the whisper. Fill me with thy nutrients.

Now Lola has enough sobriety to recall her last encounter with Abbygail.

"Shit, shit," Lola says. A gun is too loud, and how many bullets does a flower take? She reaches for her knife.

Abbygail's petals bloom with the interior spikes rattling

against each other. Three black vines covered in thorns slither from the thick stem as the girl's head erects high with an angry scowl. One vine darts through the air, aiming for its prey. Lola frees her blade and slices into the oncoming vegetation. Red liquid sprays out of the black vine, splattering onto Lola's face. A second vine soars towards her. She leaps sideways, rolling on the ground as a third snake vine slithers her way. The plant girl's smaller roots on the ground drag her closer to Lola. More vines uncoil from the stem and fly towards her. She swings her dagger up, splitting one of the vines in two as a second one latches onto her arm. The thorns pierce into her leather jacket and into her skin, resulting in no pain, thanks to the ash. She hacks at the plant, cutting it off. The dead portion remains coiled around her arm.

Attack, comes a whisper.

A couple more vines are closing in. Lola bellows a primal shout, echoing through the open space. Birds fly from nearby branches as she charges Abbygail. The vines soar after her, coming from her left. Lola slices into both with a single swipe. A new one appears to her right. She hacks upward, cutting it down the middle. A fourth vine springs forward, and Lola dashes to the side, several meters from Abbygail.

The head.

Lola leaps into the air, flying over a nearby vine, aiming the blade straight for the ones holding Abbygail's head in place. The others slither to their master's defence. The distance closes in. The blade is half a meter from her foe. Lola has won.

A large branch drops in front of Lola, and her chest slams into the bark. The impact knocks the wind clear from her lungs. Her nose bumps into Abbygail's ice-cold nasal tip. More branches appear, curling around Lola's torso. They pull her back. Her knife falls.

Abbygail's vines retreat to their core, and the black and red flower petals fold, making her a humanoid once more. Abbygail's head lowers, watching Lola be pulled away.

Lola's lungs are prunes as bile projects from her mouth, splattering onto the bark enveloping her. Saliva and vomit drizzles on her chin as the forest darkens. The branches, trees, grass, and even Lola's hands twist inwards. They mutate into a mucky mess. They keep spiralling inwards until colour vanishes, and there's only blackness.

CHAPTER 40
BORN AGAIN

We all wish to be happy, oblivious to the fact that the universal laws apply: for every action, there is an opposite and equal reaction. Euphoria is always met with misery. Remove the peaks, and you're left with fair-mindedness.

Lola is familiar with the side effects of her drug sessions. Ash-dashers experience beauty and greatness and then wake with a skull-grinding headache and dried organs. They are familiar with the classic sandpaper eyelids that scrape past their eyeballs. Lola also has splatters of bile and blood on her chin, chest, and arms to solidify her comedown.

She groans and lifts her head. The weight is too much to bear, and she sinks into the pile of leaves, shielding her eyes from the sun rays piercing through the branches. The movement makes her grunt, reminding her that spiky vines had coiled around her flesh. The wound isn't as tormenting as the light blaring into her face.

Did I? Lola thinks, unable to finish a thought as she clues into where she is. Her body rests in a hammock made of green vines, rocking between two branches. It's far higher than one would put a hammock. In fact, she's a good fourteen feet off the ground. This height tightens her gut, and the urge to vomit rises. It's enough to spring Lola from her lying position. She gags. The heaving is a thick ooze. She grips a branch, spewing green and red bodily fluids far below.

"Yooou, hoooman are fulll ooofff surprises." A deep, elongated voice rumbles below her. The talking makes the whole hammock rock.

Lola recognizes she is on top of Bark Nose. "Where, where the fuck am I?"

"Yooou are heeere with Mothhher Naaature, hoooman," Bark Nose says.

Lola eyes her wounded arm. It's wrapped in leaves that stain red. Her leather jacket hangs on a branch acting as a hook. The knife and gun rest just below it. Her phone is in her pocket and the necklace is intact. On the ground below is her adversary, Abbygail, watching her.

"How did you find me?" Lola asks. "Or did I find you?" She checks the camera's light to see it is off. There's no telling how much footage she has. The battery died or the recording file got too large.

Bark Nose says, "You, hoooman, were attunnned to

Mothhher Naaature. Something I haven't seen sinnnce the ollld world. Whatever yooou did unnnlocked an ancient forgottennn part of Mothhher Naaature. Sheee speaks in formmms beyond linear language."

"Ash?"

"Was thaaat it? It is gonnne nooow."

"Like magic?" Lola asks.

"It wasss enough for yooou tooo hear Abbyyygaaaaail. It was enough for meee to hear yooou lost in the foressst. You spoke to Mothhher Naaature herself."

"I was what?" Lola rubs her head and lies down on the leaf hammock. She is too hungover for this.

"Yooou poisooooned your body with a foooreign connnnsumption," Bark Nose says. "I sennnsed it, Abbyyygaaaaail could sennnse it, drawing yooou tooo her to feed off your life. What yooou took tuuuned yooou into naaature annnd you knew removing Abbyyygaaaaail's head would kiiill her. I couldn't let yooou hurt Abbyyygaaaaail."

"Sorry," Lola says. "It was intuition, like, I knew to do it."

"That is the powwwer of Mothhher Naaature. She knooows all and sees all. Immmpressive. Incredibly daaangerous annnd naive for a hoooman to channnnnel such potency."

"Yeah, I'm feeling that now," Lola says. She can't believe she's talking to a giant tree person. The ash hangover is too strong for her to give a rat's ass around the situation's absurdity. She wanted to find Bark Nose. She did. "How long was I out?" Lola asks.

"After yooou regurgitated onnn me, yooou have slept onnne suuun cycle."

"So what is it, Wednesday?" Lola asks.

"I don't keep track offf hoooman timmme," Bark Nose says.

"Okay. Sorry about the vomit."

"There isss a firrre in yooou, hoooman. Little by little I ammm seeeing why Scaaabbed Eeears approooves of yooou," Bark Nose says.

"That is why I'm here. Have you heard from him?" Lola asks.

"Not sinnnce the twooo of yooou caaame here."

"Great. He is concerning me."

"Annnd why is thaaat?" Bark Nose asks.

"He is being evasive, and I don't know him that well and am unsure if I can trust him. I have nowhere else to turn to now, so I wanted to find you and get some guidance."

"Aboooout Synaaarion?" Bark Nose asks. "We've knooown each other for a lonnnng time. I trusssst himmm. He is onnne offf the few remaining goood souls, trying tooo saaave Mothhher Naaature."

"That is what he says. What else does he do?" Lola asks, sitting. The motion stings.

"The lifffe of the baaalancer is not fffor meee to know. I ressside here, in my hommme."

"This is a waste of time," Lola mumbles.

"I dooo knnnow that Scaaabbed Eaaars is faaar mooore connnected with persssonal deeemons then he willl admit," Bark Nose says. "Like all living creeeatures, he feels happinnness, saaadness, feeear, passion, and looove."

"That's why I'm concerned," Lola says. "I fear he has his own personal goals blinding him."

"Hoooman, Synaaarion is nnno different thaaan the rest of us.

Rottennn roots are withinnn all. It is up to usss to triiim themmm." Bark Nose leans onto his branches which look to be his hands and knees, angling his head so Lola's hammock is a metre off the ground. "Offff yooou get now, hoooman."

Lola slides off the hammock and wobbles a bit, standing. A single vine from Bark Nose moves in front of Lola, with her dagger wrapped around it. Dark red coats the blade.

"Dooon't hurt Abbyyygaaaaail," Bark Nose says. "Sheee is my ooonly commmpanion."

Lola takes the knife. The dried red liquid is, without a doubt, blood. Abbygail would have filled herself up nice and fat with Lola's life force, too, if she didn't fight. "Thanks, I won't if she would do the same."

Bark Nose rises, his bark creaking with the motion. "Abbyyygaaaaail the hoooman is connnscious in that skull, with bloood flowing to her frommm the hell flowwwer she is connnected to. She hass nooo control."

"You knew Abbygail well before she was this thing?" Lola asks, watching the flower girl stare at her.

"I diiid, we were innn looove. Her old soul annnd yooouthfull naaature ignnnited me with a newfound appreciation fooor life, annnd hooomans. We spennnt maaany nights tooogether."

"What happened?"

"Sheee haaad eaten a hellseed. The creeeaaature burst out of her booody. She wasss too naïve to the dannngers of the ooold wooorld to understand that not evvverything isss beautiful."

Lola sheaths her blade as her entire back quivers. The ash, or the haunting story, raises goosebumps over her forearms and neck. The dead girl forewarns that some things are best left in the dark. Donnie was right the whole time.

"Is there anything else you can tell me that will help?" Lola asks.

"Did Mothhher Naaature not tell yooou everrrything you need tooo knnnow?" Bark Nose asks.

"Well, I'm not sure. I got some new insight into my own demons. That was Mother Nature? Like a person?"

"You haaad yooour doubts?" Bark Nose asks.

"I . . . it's a lot to process. What of the old world, the vazeleads, or the Crystal Moths?"

"I've tooold you, as I told Scaaabbed Eeears, I do nnnot partake in the modernnn wooorld. In the old wooorld, otherrr species sufffered frommm the sammme delusions of hate as hooomans do. Evvven Synaaarion's kind, the nymphs of the Grove, were taaainted with aaa need for connntrol. Theeey and the othhhers led thhhe old world's collapssse. Nowww history reeepeats itself with you hooomans' dessstructive naaature."

"Nothing changes," Lola says.

"That is why Synaaarion is the lassst of the goood. He fights a fight thaaat no soul is willing tooo," Bark Nose says. "As for yooou. Do returnnn to Mothhher Naaature with less firrre in yooour soul. There's much yooou caaan learn."

"Thanks," Lola says. "And thanks for the care." She raises her arm with the plant bandages.

"Connntrol your flaaame, hooooman. It is destrrructive annnd will take yooou with it when there's nnnothing leffft to burnnn."

His vines take Lola's jacket and gun from the top of his form and passes them to her, ending their conversation. The Root Walker guides her from his home and through the Lower Seymour Conservation Reserve, returning to human civilization. Abbygail stays behind, ever-watching Lola's movement.

A part of Lola doesn't want to return. Being the puddle of mud, she felt connected to the earth. That must have been Mother Nature. The hostility of the man-made world did not exist there. Lola's ego was stripped away, and the Trinity of Souls didn't judge her. They warned her as Bark Nose has. Yet, she's compelled to carry on with her mission, even if it will scathe her. She's not one to back down.

Bark Nose's most hand-like branch points to a dirt path. "Take this paaath, hooooman. There is a riiiver to waaash yourself cleeean. Followww it, yoooou will find yoooour kinnnd."

"Thanks. Again, sorry about the mess," Lola says.

"I donnn't get many visitors, hooooman. I liiike it thaaat way. You offfered interesting innnsight into the storm thaaat is brewing. A hooooman found a waaay to connnect with powwwer from the ollld world. Ammmazing. Usssse it wisely."

With that, Lola waves goodbye and follows the narrow path. She finds the river and strips from her clothes not long after, making sure her last piece of ash is secured on dry land. She washes her shirt and pants from the vomit, dirt, and blood and gives herself a good rinse. Goodbye post-ash extravaganza odour.

Lola can't wrap her head around her ash trip. If she did speak with Mother Nature, did she speak to her mother, Michael and

Becky? The other possibility is Lola was blitzed off a drug.

Ash is calling to her, making her stronger. Bark Nose believes in it. It's also harsh on her body, but it gives her an edge if she is careful.

Bark Nose speaks praise for Synarion. Her paranoia may be misled. Still, it's better to keep him at a distance. He can't be her one ally. Lola's pile of evidence keeps growing, and she has the power of ash. She has cards to play. Her next one is to form a new allegiance.

CHAPTER 41
COCK TEASE

Nails digging into your arm is a sign of agitation. It's also seen in ash-dashers who need another fix. Less than twenty-four hours have passed since Lola's last session, and she's already craving more. The addiction level is unnatural. Besides the nails, her body sweats, mixing into her damp clothing after washing them in the river. She sits in the back of the bus leaving the reserve. The window's reflection shows heavy bags in her sinking eyes.

The pain in her arm from Abbygail isn't helping either. It feels as if a dozen knives punctured her skin. Her jacket and hoodie conceal most of the holes in her clothing. The collision with Bark Nose will leave her torso bruised for weeks. She even faked a laugh with the bus driver regarding how she "fell" into the river and got her clothes wet. She's fine! That's what they need to know.

Anxiety flows with each thump of her heart. Vertigo keeps her petrified as her vision spins to the dark shadows underneath the seat in front. Her nails jam into the flesh as both of her legs bounce.

You can do it, she tells herself. It's not just the ash or the pain causing her ill-ease. She's fearful of calling Detective Iglesias.

Synarion knows she is documenting their mission. He doesn't know her other contact. She plans to keep it that way. Seeing Abbygail with Bark Nose proves what happens when one gets too close to the old world. The girl fell in love with a talking tree. Now, post-ash, Lola is comfortable admitting that she developed problematic feelings for Synarion. She will not share the same fate with Abbygail. Acceptance is the first step to solving a problem.

Mental clarity is another perk of the reptilian scale. She problem-solved jailbreaking the phone, and she has concluded Synarion is not of romantic interest. She is also bold enough to call a detective. Sober Lola couldn't even think her way through these situations.

The bus reaches its station. At the stop, a swarm of people wearing blond wigs hop onto another bus heading downtown. Many of them carry picket signs. One visible poster reads: AVENGE AMBER. DEATH TO CABELLO.

Looks like Ashley Amber's death took a toll on people's will. A protest is of little interest to Lola, as long as she isn't recognized. Her focus is on locating a pay phone. There's one inside the small bus shelter. There aren't many of these relics that serve well for those who wish to keep themselves hidden.

Lola is cunning enough to not leave herself hanging dry. She calls a cab from her smartphone first, saying that her bus will arrive in ten minutes and she needs a ride from the station. The operator does not question her words, and the wheels are in motion.

Here we go.

Lola takes some change from her pocket, standing by the payphone. She already has Detective Iglesias's number memorized. In the back of her mind, she has wanted to call this number for two years. It was driven by the fear of quitting. Now, she can use the cop for her own agenda.

Lola drops the coins into the machine and punches Detective Iglesias's personal cell phone number. The cool plastic of the phone presses against her hot ear as the phone rings. The first ring passes. Then the second.

Come on, Lola thinks as the third ring cycles. It stops midway.

A smoky middle-aged man's voice answers, "Detective Iglesias here."

"Detective Iglesias, as in Ricardo Iglesias, correct?" Lola asks.

"That's correct. Who am I speaking with?" Iglesias asks.

"You know my friend, Donnie Dube."

"Sorry, who's this?"

"He contacted you in exchange for his innocence. He's not the one you're looking for, is it?" Lola asks.

"Okay, are you going to give me a name or make me play a guessing game?" Detective Iglesias asks.

"You know who I am."

"Do I?"

"If I say my name, you promise you won't trace this call?" Lola says.

"Okay. This is between you and me. This is my own cell, after all."

"Good." Lola exhales and says, "Lola Cabello."

"I'd sure like this to be true. How do I know it's you?" Detective Iglesias asks.

"You don't. But Donnie trusted you enough to give me your number a long time ago."

"So why call me now?"

"I don't trust a lot of people."

"Yeah, well, it looks like we have that in common," Detective Iglesias says.

Lola glances around, making sure she is alone. Now she sees her hands shaking beyond control from the nervousness of this conversation. "I'm glad you can see that. I'm not who the media says I am."

"I'd like to believe that too."

"Then you have to listen to me. I want to keep this line of communication open if you don't tell another soul about us, got it?"

"Understood, Lola. You know you're in a lot of trouble?"

"Duh," Lola says.

"So you've decided to trust me?" Detective Iglesias asks.

"The odds are stacking against everything I do, and I can't come forward, can I? I need a person on the inside. I have evidence, unlike anything the law has."

"You know, I've studied your profile for a long time. It is not in your character to start going on a killing spree. Then again, people do unexpected things."

"Like calling out of the blue."

"Precisely," Iglesias says. "No . . . one moment. . ." Another voice is heard on the other end. "No, it's my son. I have to skip this meeting. It's important. Sorry." Iglesias's voice turns to a whisper. "Okay, I am all ears."

"I'm calling because Donnie trusted you," Lola says.

"And why would you do that?" Iglesias asks.

"Because I need you," Lola says.

"How about we meet, Lola, see each other in the flesh."

"Romantic. I want to, but I'll decide when it happens. I'll give you some information you can share with the police to start."

"Like you did with Chen?" Iglesias asks.

"I have a hunch that didn't go well for him."

"What makes you say that?"

"Crystal Moths don't like when their people squeal," Lola says.

"Are you going to give us another tied-up Moth?"

"No. This is better. I'm not innocent, but I didn't kill anyone." On second thought, Lola isn't sure after the art gallery. She did hit a Moth or two.

"The evidence says otherwise," Iglesias says.

"I have records. There are videos, text messages, and audio, like the one you had of Chen in Toronto. You won't get them in one go."

"I'm presuming you've seen what happened to Chen on the news?" Iglesias says.

"No, just a hunch. Lives aren't worth a thing to the Crystal Moths."

"What about your life?"

"I don't have much to lose," Lola says.

"And what of my life? I have a son to worry about," Iglesias says.

"That's up to you, Detective Iglesias. What I can give you is a piece of solid evidence. It's a cell phone."

"So we will meet?" Iglesias says.

Lola says, "No. We will not. There is an abandoned building on the east side of the harbour by Hawks Drive. I want you to go there tomorrow, where you will find the phone on the second level."

"Okay," Iglesias says, his tone dripping with concern. "What makes you think I'm in your town?"

"A hunch," Lola says.

"Hawks Drive, Vancouver, I take it?"

"If you get there any sooner than noon, our deal is off, and I won't be contacting you anymore."

"Got it. I have to earn your trust, and then we can meet?" Iglesias asks.

A cab across the street turns into the bus station. That's her cue. "Precisely. I don't have many allies, Detective Iglesias. I want to make you one."

"Same here, Lola," Iglesias says.

"Good." Lola hangs up.

She hurries to the cab and gets in, ordering him to drive several blocks from Synarion's apartment complex. No cop cars arrive at the bus station as the cab drives away. She exhales relief, leaning back in the seat of the vehicle.

Next, Lola needs to place the Crystal Moth phone she stole

in the abandoned building near Synarion's location. She hopes Iglesias stays true to his word. She has no method of policing his behaviour if he doesn't. She can watch the building, that's all.

She wants to earn Detective Iglesias's trust by feeding him valuable evidence in small doses. At the same time, she'll be working with Synarion to dig deeper into the Crystal Moths. Their next stop will be the slaughterhouse. If her scheming goes as she hopes, she'll feed Iglesias the SUV's location after.

The triple life of working with Synarion, keeping her own agenda, and pulling Iglesias into the mix will be a chore. She wears masks as often as she changes her name and wigs. There's one person she never had to dance around. Donnie Dube. In fact, she should email him when she returns and tell him she contacted Detective Iglesias. She'd like to regrow their friendship.

CHAPTER 42
HUNT

Everyone's biological purpose reverts to procreation and the need to feed. Scalebane's hunting nature isn't bound to stuffing her gut or finding a mate. It serves a far more critical goal operating at a higher plane of thinking, far beyond her instinctual, primal mind.

Her pursuit ritual begins with focused meditation, listening to the waves splash onto the shore. She sits cross-legged in the sand under the solidifying moon behind a shaded tree. Scalebane's eyes open to the vast ocean. The burning star compliments the smokeless flames consuming her eyeballs gazing into the water.

She takes the folded leather armour beside her and equips each piece over her simple tunic. Next are boots to hide her clawed three-toed feet. The cloak, belt, and both sai follow. She places the cowl and mask over her head, tucking her black-and-blue scalp-feathers under the fabric. Sealing her ritual, she straps in a final buckle behind her skull and is ready for the hunt.

Her prey: Lola Cabello. Scalebane has familiarized herself with the girl's background. Lola is a creative chameleon with fake identities to blend in. She is crossfire for a much bigger game, interfering with King's plans. Her allegiance with Synarion makes her a threat. Scalebane would feel pity for the soft skin losing her mother if Lola wasn't becoming a nuisance.

Scalebane has an additional hunt: Mulier the succubus.

The demon must be found first in the metropolis. Scalebane stands under the starry night in the downtown core, watching hordes of people with signs and blond wigs marching on the road holding candles. One in the front carries a megaphone shouting, "AVENGE AMBER, AVENGE AMBER!" The various signs have pictures of Ashley Amber and text reading: Rest in Peace, 1992-2016, Avenge Amber.

The poor lost sheep are alone without their beloved movie star, idol, and in a way, leader. Humans have a strange sense of loyalty to people that they will never meet. It baffles Scalebane that such a large horde can worship one person. The rich couldn't give a damn about them. Still, they praise their leader, living or dead.

Her interest doesn't lie in the protest-funeral mix these humans are having. She is heading to Club Revelation.

Jekos, the halfbreed, was gracious enough to let her use his name to get in. Apparently, this is where she can find Synarion as well . . . *Your nymph has been there. So has a demon . . .You and your people walk a dangerous line. Mastema is fooling your people. He's not possessing a human body.Watch yourself.* Those were his final concerning words to her.

The club is easy to find for those who walk in the shadows. Alleyways, side streets, and back entrances are common for those of the old world. A thumping bass comes from beyond the steel door under a red neon sign. Scalebane knocks on it, it swings open, and she is met by a beefy man. His impressive muscles wouldn't be a match for her strength.

He examines her attire and says, "There's no way you're getting in here like that."

"Jekos set me," Scalebane says.

"I'm sure he did."

"He wishes for me to find revelation."

He stands his ground.

"Should I get him to come here? I'm sure he'd love to talk to you."

The man scowls, stepping aside. He waves at the second bouncer and ticket girl, indicating Scalebane gets a free pass. She steps into the hall, keeping her cloak wrapped tight around her body.

The pounding bass rises to an irritating level. The stench of sweat radiates all around this damned building. It's not limited to human smells; there are others in this packed club. They dance and chat, enjoying a night of fun. It sends Scalebane's senses into overdrive. She must suppress her agitation and tune into the hunt.

She slips through the crowds looking for anyone of interest.

Synarion wouldn't be casually at a bar. It was not his thing. It sounds like Mulier's, though.

She scans the black bar to her right, then the lounge further away, and finally, the dance floor, where a wave of bodies moves as one in rhythm to the beat. Stragglers who dance alone and in pairs are on the outskirts of the single entity.

One woman shakes her hips with a man. Her hands caress her own body. Even under red lighting, the skin is far too pink. The bump along the tailbone is not the extra buttock thickness that most men would presume. That bulge is a tale pressed against clothing to conceal it. The knee-high leather boots and tight fishnet dress leaves little to the imagination for the poor soul who has his grubby hands wrapped around her lower waist. The fingers grip her skirt with hopes for more. The woman's black lips whisper into his ear. That is not makeup, and those sharp teeth are not prosthetic. Indeed, it is Mulier the succubus.

Scalebane storms through the crowd, weaving between clumps of hot flesh before reaching the two dancers. The sweaty creatures are too involved with each other to notice that a goggled being is standing beside them. She pushes the man's shoulders, knocking him with enough force to startle him. He almost loses balance, his hands sliding from Mulier.

"Hey!" he says in a slur. "Piss off, freak." He rolls the sleeves of his unbuttoned blue dress shirt.

"Hold on, love," Mulier says through the noise, touching the man's bare chest.

Scalebane leans into Mulier, identifying her sweet tang. It's a significant improvement from the foul feces her nose has been tortured with while inside this building. "We need to talk,"

Scalebane says.

"I'm a little busy, cutie," Mulier says as the music shifts to a slower rhythmic tempo. It makes it easier for them to hear.

"What do you know regarding the ash pickup location?" Scalebane asks.

"I said I'm busy. Can you come at a later date?" She waves at the man to come back to her. His eyes are entranced with the succubus, locked under her spell as she wraps her arms around him. She leans to his shaven neck, kissing it. Her pink eyes land on Scalebane. "Later, okay?" she says.

"And what of Synarion?" Scalebane says.

The name breaks Mulier from the man's flesh. "Sorry?" she asks.

"Synarion, the nymph. What do you know of him?"

"I don't know what you're talking about."

"Jekos?"

"I thought you wanted some fun with that BDSM outfit, but you are a bore, doll."

Scalebane isn't going to get anywhere in this environment. There are too many people here and far too much security. A predator must know when to strike and when to step back. She leaves the dancers and goes to the bar to observe Mulier dance with her prey.

This isn't over. Scalebane is patient and can outlast a demon. Mulier knows more than she wants to give. Scalebane will make her change that.

CHAPTER 43
AGAINST THE LAW

Laws are designed to keep civilians in line. The governing bodies execute the bills, keeping society safe. It sounds great on paper until people learn to bend the lines. Stars, politicians, suits, and clever crooks can evade the rules in the muck of grey, even in the name of supposed good.

What the hell am I doing? Iglesias thinks. He leaves the hotel, taking the elevator to the parkade. It's early in the AM, and he is off to meet his colleagues Beckman and Archer for the daily War Room meeting. Then, Iglesias will follow Lola Cabello's instructions.

The girl wants him to earn her trust. She claims she'll trickle him information until she deems him worthy. He can't blame her. Cabello has been alone for quite some time. As the heat starts to rise, she wants out.

Iglesias enters the Vancouver Police Department in his rental SUV, parking underground to meet his colleagues. He checks his phone to see it is eight in the morning. He has four hours to wait.

His focus fizzles in the War Room. His arms are folded, and his mind drifts into space. *Cabello.* He could tell the officers right now. That's an excellent way to lose evidence to the tainted law under the Moths' wing. In a strange twist, he enjoys the secrecy. It resurrects his youthful rebellious ways.

Tasks are distributed, with most of the team gathering evidence and statements from the art gallery. It will take days to process it all. Officers are going through the guest list. Others have been tasked with backtracking Cabello's past, where she got her fake ID and her journey to the West Coast. They want to build a better psychological profile of her character. These meetings run for an hour. Then, the teams disperse.

"Feels like a wild goose chase," Beckman says as the three head outside.

Iglesias lights a smoke and offers one each to his comrades. "Your wife is gonna kill you," Iglesias says.

Beckman shrugs. "What can you do. We're here for days." He lights his drag and passes the lighter to Archer.

"All week, more like it," Archer says.

The old men have tainted Archer into the smoking group. If you hangout around old, grizzled detectives, you'll become one, unlike Iglesias, who is reverting to a youthful rebel. More than anything, he wants to share the fascinating news with his team. In time he will. It's too early.

"So, we're gonna get bossed around by the Vancouver Police Chief and the FBI? Where's the authority?" Beckman says.

"We play ball. Otherwise, it will make things a hell of a lot more difficult. Sergeant Bando is keeping the CFMP and the DND at bay," Iglesias says.

Archer adds, "Yeah, but still. We're going to go through that list of attendees? Isn't that the job of the city's cops?"

Beckman says, "They're short-staffed, like everywhere. Unless you got a better idea?"

Yeah, Iglesias thinks. "Listen, you guys go and get a head start on that. I want to stick around here and make a few calls."

"About what?" Archer asks. "Don't want to be a part of the fun?"

"Trust me, do I look like I belong in the office? I want to check in with the lab, and the station, to see if they have any info on Cabello and Chen. Or if anyone has insight to where this drug comes from."

"I checked in with the labs. Nothing from either," Beckman says.

"Messing around on the Internet, wonderful," Archer says sarcastically.

"You want to sit on your ass all day?" Iglesias asks.

Beckman shrugs. "Fair point. It's you and me, kid."

Archer smiles. "Kid? Christ, this is gonna be a long day."

Iglesias finishes his smoke. "Catch up with you two later this afternoon."

"You got it, boss," Archer says.

Iglesias goes into the station and exhales. That worked far smoother than he expected. The three know research is a dead end. The department in Ottawa has dug into the drug's chemical compounds. They can't trace its origins.

There's time to kill. A good cop double, triple, and quadruple checks their work. It's also a great cover-up when going against the law. He turns on the laptop at his temporary workstation and digs through his old documents, the lab notes, and his team's findings. It's the same information he's looked at before. He checks his phone to see the time. It crawls minute after minute, teasing him of what waits at noon.

A quarter before twelve arrives, and that's damn close enough for him. Iglesias snags his keys off the desk, closes his laptop, and hurries to his wheels.

The drive is half an hour with the heavy traffic until he reaches the industrial port Cabello told him to go to. He parks the SUV a block away to get a good look at this abandoned building. It's boarded up and covered in graffiti. It's the right street, and the time is twelve-fifteen. Iglesias's gun is holstered in his belt, his rubber gloves are in his blazer pocket along with a couple of plastic evidence bags. It's time to go rogue.

The hairs on his skin stand as he exits the car. His breathing is in sync with each step. The wind blows past his blazer under his dress shirt, sending little icy fingers running along his spine.

There it is. That missing rush from his day-to-day activity on the force. The last time he had it was when they discovered ash. He is no adrenaline junkie. Still, it's one hell of a way to feel alive.

Iglesias walks past the boarded entrance, along the brick

walls, to the alleyway, where there's a back door. Planks of wood lie on the ground with nails in them. They've been removed from the door frame. This is promising.

He puts on his rubber gloves and twists the knob. It's unlocked, and he pushes it open. The hinges make an elongated squeak that echoes throughout the empty space. He unholsters his gun and steps inside.

Brick pillars are distributed throughout the first level. The space is barren, except for a few dusty plastic tarps on the concrete floor and some nearby crates. Most windows had been blocked, allowing next to no sun in.

By the front entrance is another staircase leading to the second floor. Iglesias takes his steps carefully, reducing the sound he makes. His dress shoes reverb against the walls as he heads to the second floor.

The new level is far brighter thanks to the glass windows. The giant open space has a single wooden crate dead in the center with a small black object resting on top. The phone.

Iglesias keeps his gun raised, approaching the crate. He appears to be alone, no new red flags. This mission in itself is a giant danger signal. He reaches for the phone, and his own buzzes in his pocket. Iglesias twitches and holsters his gun to check the caller ID. It's an unknown number.

Iglesias answers. "Detective Iglesias."

"Take the phone." It's Cabello. Her voice is far less croaky, unlike the first conversation.

"What is it?" Iglesias asks.

"A little piece of evidence. It will make you look good and could help my case. You have to share it with the right people and if you are indeed a good cop."

"That depends on who you ask. Me going rogue doesn't put me in anyone's good books."

"It puts you in mine. Isn't that what this is for?"

"Care to pay me a visit?" Iglesias asks. He spins around several times, hoping to see the girl somewhere.

"Not a chance, detective. Soon. Use that evidence wisely. It's related to the art gallery. In there, you will find text messages regarding the Crystal Moths going to work at the show for high-profile clients. They make a fascinating comment about ash and the Prime Minister."

"Whose phone is this?" Iglesias asks.

"Some street dealer. He's fine. I locked the phone after cracking it. That way it doesn't look suspicious when you present it. You found it by the art gallery loading dock. Don't change that story."

"I'll see what I can do," Iglesias says. "If we are building some trust, Lola, I have to be honest. There's not a lot of people in the station I can trust."

Lola chuckles. "Welcome to the club."

"There are two on my team. I can introduce them to you?"

"I have to remain in control here."

"Alright. I have this evidence. What's next?" Iglesias asks.

"Wait. I'll be in contact with you again. Keep your phone with you and don't let anyone else answer it."

"This isn't my first rodeo."

"I like to cover my bases," Lola says.

"You think you have enough evidence to prove yourself innocent?" Iglesias asks.

"Not yet, but as I said, I have the data stored. If anything doesn't go my way, I am distributing it across the web."

"Now, why would you do that?" Iglesias asks. "Isn't that what got you in trouble in the first place?"

"Yes. I was a different person then. What I have is enough to disrupt the balance of society."

"That's a powerful statement, Lola."

"You have to be bold when crawling out of a river of manure."

Iglesias smirks. "I hope you're right."

The phone clicks, and Iglesias puts it away. He takes an evidence bag from his blazer and places the new phone in it, and then seals it. Iglesias isn't sure who he can trust within the police department that would be able to crack the phone. At least he has it.

Iglesias texts Beckman on his own cell, saying:

(You: hey, is there anyone we can trust that can open phones? 12:25 PM)

Iglesias leaves the abandoned building, heads to his SUV, and starts the engine. His phone buzzes. It's Beckman:

(Beckman: let me look into it. What do you have? 12:28 PM)

(You: I'll tell you at the station. Meet me in the parkade. 12:29 PM)

On the drive, Iglesias ponders the call. Cabello was far more energetic this time. Her tone wasn't as scared or as rough. The one-eighty mood makes Iglesias wonder if he's taking orders from a druggie. She could be getting far too close to the Moths, taking their goods like any ash-dasher. This is a concern, although, not abnormal for him. Tycho Fulcher is not that different. The substance use would be a surprise considering how focused Lola is. Either way, Iglesias wants this to be over with so he can return to his son.

At the station, Iglesias spots his two comrades in the underground parking lot. He exits his SUV and takes the evidence out of his blazer pocket.

"Look at this," he says.

Their faces squint in confusion until Archer says, "I thought you were going to be desk-bound?"

Iglesias says, "I got bored. I went back to the art gallery." He bites his tongue, hating that he is lying to his team.

"They scrubbed that place clean," Beckman says, taking the bag and looking at the phone.

"I don't think they checked the loading dock fully. This cell could be related to the case, and I don't want anything we find tampered with by the others."

"Fair enough," Beckman says.

Archer says, "I have a contact in Ottawa who can crack that for us."

"Good," Iglesias says. "Once it's been opened, let me know immediately."

"So, are you going to join us?" Beckman asks.

"I've had enough alone time," Iglesias says.

"How about a drink after this?" Archer says. "The staleness of these interviews is driving me nuts."

"Sure," Iglesias says. "Take care of that phone first."

Iglesias hopes to hell he can trust Archer to handle the phone.

She and Beckman are his best, and he lied to them. It's temporary. That's what he tells himself to push the regret down his throat. Anyone else in his department comes and goes, changes roles, or they see him as too high of a figurehead to relate to. Beckman is a direct partner, and Archer is cocky enough that she doesn't give a rat's ass which Iglesias respects.

Archer takes care of the phone, and the three continue the interviews as instructed at the War Room meeting. It's dry and pointless, as most civilians don't have anything of value to say. Most heard loud gunshots repeatedly. Security went to the halls, more shots, and the guests evacuated.

Their work takes them well into the evening. They call it quits past eight, and the detectives pick a local neighbourhood pub. They sit on cheap metal stools with plastic cushions, watching the bartender pour drinks to the noisy crowd.

Iglesias swirls his straight whiskey. *This case is gonna make me no different than my ex*, he thinks. It doesn't help he's spending his time with Archer, who likes these dingy bars and booze. Their influence on each other goes both ways.

He asks, "Are you sure you can trust them with the phone?"

Archer raises her whiskey on the rocks. "Yeah. Dennis is good stuff. It's on priority shipping to Ottawa, so he can take care of it."

Beckman says, "Major Crimes and the Vancouver police will be pissed."

"It's easy," Archer says. "They're clogged by too much info, and we have a good lead on this."

Beckman says, "Based on what?"

Iglesias says, "It was in the alley of the art gallery where the loading dock is. Call it a detective's hunch."

Beckman raises his drink. "To old school."

The three clang glasses and take a sip. Iglesias is amused that Archer has a whiskey, like her two colleagues. She's closer to being a crusty old geezer than she understands.

Beckman says, "You know, in a strange way, I wish we could interview some of the celebrities who were at the art gallery."

"Luck of the draw," Iglesias says.

"Yeah. It would be kind of cool," Beckman says.

Archer says, "And Ashley Amber! Like what the fuck? She was making such a comeback after her breakdown."

"I know," Beckman says. "My wife is taking it hard. She was her favourite actress."

"I like Jenny Taylor a lot better," Archer says.

Beckman squints. "Really? She plays the same role."

Archer shrugs. "She has a natural charm."

"If you say so."

"Well, I don't think she'd pull in the protests that we're seeing on the streets."

Iglesias says, "The people are angry and want answers."

"No one has addressed the public on the case, have they?" Beckman asks.

"Well, the Prime Minister made a statement, Vancouver chief of police gave an update, and Hucker Dime never stops blabbering," Iglesias says. His statement holds true, because CAMB is playing on the television to their right, while the one to the left broadcasts an old hockey game.

"We don't have all the answers," Beckman says. "That's why I'd like to interview some of these stars. Plus, it'd be cool."

Archer says, "Instead, we're looking for eyewitnesses and scrubbing security cameras that saw nothing. The evidence doesn't line up."

Iglesias says, "Just like with Chen."

Archer says, "You heard what happened to him?"

"Yeah," Iglesias says.

"Shame," Beckman adds.

Iglesias says, "This is why a lot of hope is in your guy, Dennis, to crack that phone. We keep everything tight and share with each other until we build a good case."

"Of what?" Beckman asks.

"Where the data takes us."

Archer nods. "This shit is going on far too long."

Beckman says, "Personally, I don't mind a little bit of time away, you know?"

Archer says, "Don't be so quick on that. In this line of work, your last time with a loved one could be the final."

"Ah, that's overthinking. You haven't been in it long enough. Rarely does it go south," Beckman says. "Catherine is a couple years from retirement at the school, and I am another three years out. I'm alive. We'll have plenty of time to spend together in retirement."

Iglesias says, "That's presuming your kids don't need you to pay for their entire college fund."

Beckman laughs. "Don't jinx it."

"Kids are a money pit," Archer says. "Too much responsibility, and they destroy your body."

Iglesias says, "They change you. It's the best thing that happened to me."

"You have no idea how many times people tell me that. I'd rather meet a partner, keep our cash, and travel."

Iglesias says, "Marriages can go south." He takes a sip of his drink, reflecting on his failed marriage. It's a spiral he's gone down plenty of times to no resolution. He's good at curbing it before it gets the better of him. Yes, he was not the best husband, and his wife was not perfect either. Everyone is human, and it didn't work out. End of story.

Archer says, "You keep in touch with her?"

"No. Alcoholism has a way of getting out of hand. José doesn't want to either. So here we are."

Archer says, "You're one hell of a father. Wish my dad was like that. Not to make it weird."

Beckman and Iglesias chuckle. Each takes a drink.

"Speaking of that," Beckman says, "it's getting late, and I want to chat with Catherine before hitting the sack. See you guys in the morning." With that, Beckman pays and leaves the bar.

Archer looks at her empty glass and says, "One more?"

Iglesias pulls out his phone. It's past eleven at night. Time is distorted when he is on a case. José won't be awake, considering the time difference. Still, he sends him a text.

> (You: Are you up?
> 11:06 PM)

He puts the phone on the marble counter to keep an eye on it. "Yeah, I'll have one more. If José calls, I'm out."

"Perfect," Archer says, waving at the bartender.

"I'm impressed with what you've done, Bridgette Archer," Iglesias says as the bartender slides new drinks to them.

"Truthfully, you remind me of myself at your age."

"Where is this coming from?" Archer asks.

Iglesias says, "Nowhere particular. It's an observation I've made. When I first joined the force, I had a rebel's nature from my days on the street. It gives you an edge. Just don't get too hot-headed."

"Noted," Archer says.

"And don't let the work suck you in. It will take over your entire life."

"I don't always work this much."

"That so?"

"I don't want to be a phase one detective forever. I'm so close to upgrading."

"Don't push it. You're on your way. It takes time and a lot of learning. Then the real temptation starts."

"Temptation?" Archer asks.

"To work more. To catch the bad guy. The cliché stuff that makes life passive."

"I have a life."

Iglesias snorts and takes a swig of his drink.

"Seriously, I do," Archer defends.

"That so?"

"Fitness is my thing." Archer says.

"Fitness and work. Find a man to share your life with?"

"Men aren't for me. All these guys want is to pump a kid in you and make you their housewife. Or they're spineless nerds."

"Okay? That's not all men."

"It is."

"Girls?" Iglesias asks.

"They're a flighty bunch. Fun and no kids, but still needy. That's why I fly solo."

"Fair enough."

"Basically, dating is tough because of this job. It leeches your life."

"Thus proves my point. Don't let work consume you as I have," Iglesias says.

"Hey, you've got a life outside of work. You got José, and I respect that, sir." Archer says. "Work and fitness are my things. Travel, sure. I keep thinking about work when I'm on holiday."

"I thought the same thing. Get old enough, and your opinion starts to change. You appreciate creature comforts a lot more."

"Presuming I make it that far," Archer says.

"That's the hot-headedness talking." Iglesias stares at his phone. It flashes its notification light regarding new emails. That doesn't stop.

Even with the numbing alcohol, Iglesias's chest sinks. He wants his son to text him and say, "Yeah, Dad, I'd love to talk to you." Knowing his son, he is too busy with his girlfriend, Hailey. Why would he want to talk to his old man who rambles concerns about his work life? Iglesias waited too long to text him. He was fixated on the case. It's thanks to Cabello feeding his adrenaline. She will call him, and he can ride the high again.

CHAPTER 44
LIFE TAKER

A successful hunter knows that patience is the key to catching prey. Attack too soon, and the prey will gallop away. Ambush too late, and you'll never reach them. Timing is an art form, much like a well-executed painting. Scalebane is the artist.

Rain trickles onto her hood as she watches the entrance to Club Revelation from the rooftop a block over. According to Scalebane's mechanical pocket watch, it's well past one in the morning. Soon, Mulier will have to leave. She doesn't mind the wait. There's valuable information to be had. It's far better than listening to Erol talk high-level utopianism for humanity while lying through his teeth. Scalebane sees through that two-faced snake.

The metal door to Club Revelation swings open. A flirtatious giggle pierces through the thumping bass. The bouncer steps aside as a woman in a trench coat clings to a man in a business power suit. Her hand plays with his red tie. She sways side to side with the man. The coat, laugh, and hair belongs to Mulier. She has found new prey. Unlike her soft skin target, the succubus isn't drunk. Her acts are controlled.

Showtime. Scalebane descends from the rooftop through the fire escape stairwell and follows the succubus and her meal. They leave Blood Alley and return to the main streets. This late at night, the hunter isn't concerned about walking on public streets. There are enough freaks that wander at this time in any metropolis.

She keeps a block away from the two. Pedestrians glare at Scalebane, eyeing her as she walks by. Her tail is coiled around her leg, and her entire body is wrapped in her cloak, giving her a human appearance. The mask causes gazes.

One staggering man says, "Gnarly outfit, dude!"

The clown receives no answer. Scalebane stays behind the demon and her soft skin into a cleaner portion of downtown surrounded by glass skyscrapers. She shifts to an alleyway as Mulier and her meal turn down a side street leading to the first apartment complex. This seven-story building's modern finish consists of grey and red tiles. It's either the suit's home or Mulier's lair, where she will drain the life force from this ill-fated man.

The next trick is getting into the building. Mulier and the man reach the door, and she uses a key fob to unlock the lobby, and they step inside. Scalebane hurries from the alley and to the door as they take the elevator at the end of the entrance. The numbers atop the elevator door change from one, to two, three, four, and finally, the fifth floor. Each unit has its own balcony, making it an easy climb. This late at night, most lights are off in the units. She needs to watch which ones will have lights turned on.

Scalebane walks around the building, watching the fifth floor. She circles into the alleyway with the dumpsters. A light flicks on in a corner unit facing a busy street. That's the target.

A groan comes from the garbage bins. Even in this pristine neighbourhood, a few homeless shelter themselves with boxes in the rain. They don't even notice Scalebane, who leaps onto the dumpster beside them.

In a single jump, she lands on the edges of the first balcony. She balances on the metal railings, then leaps again, snags onto the second balcony floor, and pulls herself up. She repeats the jump until reaching the fifth balcony.

The lights inside are an electric red. The curtains are open, showcasing the modern open concept of a charcoal island in the kitchen beside matte cupboards. A small loveseat is in the living room. Mulier and the man are nowhere to be found.

Scalebane leaps over the railing. The window of the next room illuminates the same red. They must be there. The hunter pulls on the balcony door, and to her luck, it slides open. All too easy. Then again, who would bother locking it? Humans cannot leap five levels to perform a home invasion.

Inside, the unit is well-heated. Music comes from the other room. It's similar to the club sounds except it is slower and more sensual. Scalebane slides the balcony door closed and creeps from the living room towards the master room. Her tail sways low as she unsheathes her two sai.

A seductive moan comes from the bedroom with heavy panting and grunting. Rhythmic squeaking of a bedframe follows with each breath. The sweet, tangy smell of the succubus radiates throughout the entire unit. Underneath that pleasant coating is the pig-filth stench of a man who sweats off his deodorant. A new smell perks Scalebane's interest, slithering between the two senses. It's a swampy muck that occurs when igniting vazelead scales. The man consumed ash.

A loud groan comes from the bedroom. Then a yelp and a loud hiss. He mutters the words, "What the fu—" The words fizzle into gurgling.

Scalebane peeks through the doorframe, witnessing the two naked forms on a silky black bedsheet. The hazy purple smoke from ash saturates the room, leaving highlights of the man's feet, scrawny legs and Mulier's bare body on top of him.

The demon thrusts her hips in sync with the bed squeaks. Her tail coils around the man's neck, turning his face blue. The black spikes pierce his throat as his hands attempt to pull on her tail. Her shoulder blades crack and reshape, expanding in size. Large spikes rip through them and rise in an arch, extending the skin with thin bones holding the web together. These formed wings spread wide in front of her helpless prey.

Mulier folds the wings and slides off of the man. Her tail releases his wounded throat. Too much air has left his lungs that he has no strength to fight. His arms flop to the sides in defeat.

Claws rise from her fingernails as her hand coils around his erected member, losing blood in its shaft. Her nails pierce into the flesh. He wheezes. Mulier keeps digging in, tearing the genitals from the crotch. He cries with a weak exhale as his limbs convulse. Blood spews onto the sheets as Mulier clutches the meat cylinder of victory.

She smiles and bites into her new snack, tearing the flesh from the head. The man no longer breathes. Mulier rolls onto the bed beside him, gnawing on the man's disfigured device. Her wings fold around her form in a cocoon shape. The tail flops side to side playfully. The succubus has gotten her meal, meaning her defences are down. It's time to strike.

Scalebane crouches low and follows the shadows into the room. She stops beside the dresser where the smoking pipe rests. She creeps to the edge of the bed. Mulier is unaware, crossing her feet and swaying them side to side.

The hunter snags the demon's ankle with her tail, yanking Mulier to the edge of the bed. She lunges one sai right at the throat. The demon's mouth hangs open, with tendrils of meat dripping onto her lip.

Mulier smiles. "You can't get enough of me, can you?" She chews the remaining bit of flesh and swallows.

"You need to talk," Scalebane says. "Or this won't end well."

"A grip that tight tells me you don't want to talk," Mulier says.

Scalebane growls and lunges her second sai towards the demon's crotch. Mulier blocks the attack with her hand, and the sai pierces into her inner thigh. She yells and kicks, freeing her ankle from Scalebane's grasp, knocking Scalebane's chest. Mulier rolls off the bed and stands with her claws drawn, exposing her blood-coated fangs. Her pinned-up hair is part way down, revealing curved black horns on her head. The wings spread wide.

"I would rethink your next move, mortal," Mulier says, her voice rising beyond a natural tone.

Scalebane twirls her sai, charging at Mulier. The demon shrieks as the hunter moves around the bed and thrusts at her. Mulier whips her tail. Scalebane ducks, lunging her sai into Mulier's outer thigh, then the hamstring. The leg gives in, and Mulier stumbles onto one knee. Scalebane's tail lashes forward, ripping open Mulier's cheek. The demon swipes down with her claws, slicing into Scalebane's cloak and tearing into the scales along her spine.

Scalebane rolls clear from danger. She leaps onto the corner wall, rebounding off the surface. Mulier is almost standing as Scalebane slams into her wings. The force topples the demon to the ground. Scalebane's knee pins her neck. The demon's wings flap, blowing wind. Mulier's tail flails radically, and the spike tip jabs into Scalebane's lower back. She ignores it, pressing harder with her knee. The demon howls. Her claws slam into the wood flooring; her nails dig into the grain, ripping it and dragging herself forward.

The tail plucks from Scalebane and lunges for another attack. Scalebane's sai deflects it and spins several times, entangling the tail between the wings and shaft of the weapon. The twisting is so tight the bone within the tail breaks with a loud snap. The demon howls, her forked tongue flickering as she claws into the ground. The wings fold and expand in spasmatic motions. Scalebane grunts, suppressing the burning pain growing in her back. She has no idea how long she can keep the demon down.

"Talk now," Scalebane says.

"Go to hell," Mulier says.

"I was born there, leech."

"You're just a mortal. That's not possible."

"On the contrary, it's possible. For I was born among repenting sinners under black clouds raining blood on the living dead. I come from the infernal you reject, claiming this realm as your own. I've fought my way out of your native land to return to mine, where my people need me. We will reclaim our right from the wretched like you." Scalebane twists her sai further, mangling the demon's defenceless tail.

"What are you?" Mulier squeals.

"You knew of the ash local distribution."

"I don't know shit." Mulier pushes up again. This time she has impressive force, lifting both of them off the ground for a moment. Scalebane frees her knee, and Mulier completes a full push-up. The hunter slams her boot into the succubus's neck, and the demon collapses with a heavy thud as her wings flop against the floor.

"Where's the local distribution site?" Scalebane says.

"It moves all the time," Mulier says.

"Where is it now?"

"Erol tells me."

"Where?" Scalebane shouts.

"East, outside of town. Allen Abattoir Plant. Look, that's what I know."

They sent my dear sister to a slaughterhouse, Scalebane thinks. She twists her sai further, pulling on the skin and bone. The demon squirms to stop the pain.

"You saw how they make ash, didn't you? You said they pluck it right off," Scalebane asks.

"Yes, I mean, what? They rip the scales right off the beast."

"We're not beasts," Scalebane sneers.

"Whatever you are," Mulier says.

"Are they still there?"

"Yes!"

"Where in the slaughterhouse?"

"I think the chilling room. You reptiles run hot."

"Are you certain?"

"It was one of you! I didn't see your damn tail the first time we met. How would I know? What does this have to do with me?"

"More than you think. What do you know of Synarion?"

Mulier freezes. "Nothing, I know nothing."

Scalebane sheaths one sai and clutches the succubus's head, pressing her boot down to amplify the pressure. She pulls the demon's head and tail towards her core, straining the neck and spine. This angle will break her. Mulier squeals, waving her arm around.

"Synarion is a balancer!" Mulier wheezes.

Scalebane eases the tension.

"I met him a couple months ago. He seeks me for information as he pleases."

"What for?"

"Balancing missions. He's a nymph of the Grove. Look, he learned of ash through me. I use the drug for an easy meal. It doesn't work for me. It works pretty damn well on humans, and

I don't have to fight. That's all I am. That's all I do!"

"Your tool has made you weak," Scalebane says. She pulls again, putting pressure on Mulier. It isn't necessary anymore, but Scalebane enjoys watching the demon struggle for her life.

Mulier sputters, and blood spews from her mouth onto the battered floor. "That's how I know Synarion. He was disturbed by the ash."

"You still talk to him, for what balancer mission?"

"He needs to get into Hell," Mulier says.

"Not for ash?"

"No. Well, he asked. I told him what I told you. I don't know anything about ash," Mulier says.

"Go on." Scalebane eases the tension on the demon's neck and spine.

"He is a lost soul. The fool is entranced with a vampire. The worst of all."

"Being?" Scalebane asks.

"Queen Valturus, the original."

"She's long since vanished," Scalebane says, reflecting on one of Dasco Amoss's paintings. One of them was a clear interpretation of her in her prime with loyal servants.

"Who isn't into hiding, fool? The vampire walked among the humans and disappeared recently. She was dragged into Hell, and the lovestruck fool thinks he can get her out. It's lunacy."

"Not entirely."

Mulier lets out a pathetic laugh. "Fuck, if a bitch like you can crawl your way out, then he is right."

"Which Hell in Dega'Mostikas's Triangle is the vampire queen in? There's three."

"He's trying to find out," Mulier says.

"What else?" Scalebane asks.

"That's what I know. I can listen to Synarion, tell you everything. Let me go, and I'll do anything you want. I can please you in ways you can't even imagine."

Typical, Scalebane thinks. She yanks on the succubus's tail and neck. The force makes Mulier gurgle, and her legs and hands slam onto the ground in uncontrolled spasms. Her wings flap in desperation.

Scalebane says, "Is Synarion with anyone else?"

"He's got some human side piece with him."

"Who?"

Mulier says, "Lola. I don't know her. I met her once at the club. Synarion brought her. I could see it in her eyes. Ancient lineage. There's a fire in there."

Ancient lineage, Scalebane ponders. That must mean Lola has an old world connection through her blood.

Mulier continues, "It's obvious from the withdrawals when a human uses ash. If she has old world lineage, imagine what she can unlock consuming your scales?"

"I can, and she won't. Where is Synarion now?"

"I don't know. He comes here or meets me at Club Revelation," Mulier says.

Scalebane says, "What does Jekos have to do with any of this?" She loosens the tension on Mul's body.

Mulier coughs and lifts her arms, limbs shaking. Her body flops helplessly. "Jekos? He owns Club Revelation. Did he send you?"

"No. He knows of you."

"I owe him some money for ash. That's all," Mulier says.

"Do you know Mastema?" Scalebane asks.

"The First? I don't *know* him. I know *of* him. By the Creator, everyone knows he's the First. There's word he runs the Crystal Moths now. Why would a fallen angel of his level do that?"

"How well do you know the Crystal Moths?" Scalebane asks.

"Not well. I've only dealt with Erol."

"Has Erol shared anything else with you other than where you get your ash?"

"No. I deal with him directly."

"You haven't seduced him for more?"

"Why would I? I'm not an incubus. He has no interest in the feminine form. Money talks. I pay well. He knows I deal with the Prime Minister and the Moths want to influence him. Look, I have connections. They're yours."

Scalebane looks around the room. The man on the bed has bled to death, leaving a dark pool of red on the sheets. The music keeps playing. Heavy, low tempo beats rumble through the hazy room. There's not much else she can get from this demon talking. She still has value. Scalebane will finish both of her hunts with one clean trap.

"How does Synarion contact you?" Scalebane asks.

"He has me on some computer with other old world beings," Mulier says.

"That's all?"

"He gave me a number. Sometimes the poor sap calls me. I'm the one with insight into saving his soulmate."

"Where's your phone?"

Mulier points to her trench coat on the ground. "In there."

"How does it open?" Scalebane asks.

"Fingerprint."

"Good," Scalebane says. She then pulls, her arms shaking from the intense resistance of the demon's bone refusing to break. Mulier screeches as her neck is reeled backwards. Her tail crunches as the flesh peels from her spine, freeing a chunk of it with the sai. Scalebane swings the weapon in a complete arch, slamming the blade straight into Mulier's ear hole, piercing through the other side.

The demon exhales one last breath as her pink eyes droop in opposite directions. Mulier's body goes limp as Scalebane frees the now lifeless head from the sai.

Hunt complete.

CHAPTER 45
REALIGN

Failing post-secondary school isn't a complete disaster. Those developed skills come in handy later on in life and you don't need to work at a grease-coated burger joint drowning in debt. For instance, Lola is applying her journalism knowledge to this day, tracking the Crystal Moths.

Since then, she has acquired new abilities: stealth and control. A perfect example is her standing a block from an abandoned brick building, hood up, watching Detective Iglesias leave through the backdoor. She holds a phone tight to her chest while her other hand scratches her arm several times, careful to avoid the wound from Abbygail.

The detective gets into his car and drives off, meaning Lola's second interaction is a success. She is unsure if Iglesias is trustworthy yet. He could be a Moth. Her gut tells her that the latter is false and begs her to consume more ash. It's not the best source of information.

A sliver of the drug is left in her bralette. More than anything, she would love to take it. If she did, she would have to find more. Reason tells her it must be saved for its function. It's not about getting high. Lola must wait. If Detective Iglesias is authentic, she has a chance with the law. Her life is not bound to Synarion anymore.

At his apartment, Lola turns on her computer and plugs in her camera to download the video from the reserve. Then, she starts uploading the footage to her cloud storage.

The note she wrote Synarion is resting on the desk. She snags it, crumpling it. Two days on, and the nymph has not returned. It's odd, for he's punctual. There's little she can do regarding the oddity, and she focuses on her computer screen.

She switches windows, performing the usual checkup on her website and email. Some comments claim Lola is dead, while others say the Crystal Moths got her. Others flood her with hate, AVENGE AMBER. The common consensus is: where is she?

There's no emails from her father and brother or Donnie. She hopes they will want to re-establish a connection if Detective Iglesias shines true.

It's also nice to dream.

Lola clings to hope and sends Donnie an email:

You

To: donie.dube@youmailnow.com

Hey,

So that detective's card came in handy. Thanks. Maybe I can get out of this mess.

Hope you're well. I miss you.

Lola deletes the last two sentences, and hits send.

Next, she skims through the list of celebrities from the art show and scrubs the videos again to see if she missed anything the first time. Her eye is sharp and indeed missed no details. The two primary characters of interest are Prime Minister Stéphane Trudell and Erol Terzi.

An Internet search reveals both individuals. Stéphane Trudell, the Prime Minister of Canada, has weight in the private and public sectors. Based on his biography, he was part owner of Allen Oil Site Solutions decades ago, the parent company of Allen Abattoir Plant and Allen Shipping Solutions. That's enough to make him a candidate for the Crystal Moths. Mul mentioned an affair with him. If there is a connection between the Prime Minister and the Crystal Moths, it would be a significant win. A future meeting with the demon is in order. For now, she makes note of the comment since there is no proof to her claim.

Other than his career, Stéphane Trudell is squeaky clean. His political stance leans liberal, focusing on the people and the environment. Quite the turn from his corporate career. That's your ideal candidate for most of the country. No one would presume there's a dark side to him.

Next is Erol Terzi, CEO of CAMB. The search results on him are far less compared to the Prime Minister. He has several social media accounts of his public persona. There are few posts on the profiles related to CAMB. Beyond that, the man is a ghost.

On a second browser window, Lola scrubs the video to find where Synarion, Lola, and the two Hollywood stars ran into Erol Terzi with the Crystal Moths. Rewinding further, she returns to the conversation where Erol mentions his partner Dasco Amoss.

There are plenty of results on the famous painter. His website portfolio, social media, and various art galleries have represented his work. It's the same surreal paintings as seen at his art opening. His social media profiles are far more interesting. There are photographs of his process and a few personal photos of him and Erol smiling on a beach. They are so normal.

Mul was at the gallery opening as well. Synarion saw her, and Lola wonders how well she knows Erol Terzi, considering she gets ash and is acquainted with the Prime Minister. From what Lola has learned so far, the intricate web of the old world brings everyone together.

Her Internet searches sprawl well into the evening. Still, there's no sign of Synarion. Lola doesn't want to wait around forever. The nymph had an active GPS on the SUV to the abattoir plant. She has to check it out.

Realistically, Lola should give herself some rest. There have been far too many incidents of violence involving her name recently. They've rendered her wounded. Trauma doesn't count. She's used to the mental beating. That's what alcohol, cigarettes, and ash are for.

Take it, whispers her desire.

Lola pours herself a drink, suppressing the calling. She wonders if she can get more, bringing her dangerously close to her targets. Lola needs it. Her journey in the forest, battle with Abbygail, and connection with Mother Nature are proof of the drug's benefit. Without it, she's nothing more than a girl. Ash also gave her a direct connection with the Trinity of Souls. Or she is experiencing her own guilt from the drug. In a brief blip of clarity, Lola knows that Michael Bradford would be one for revenge. Her mother and Becky were sweet beings. They'd want her to live life for them.

The thought is washed away with a gulp of whiskey. If Synarion isn't going to show, she can finish off his booze. It aids in controlling the desire for ash. The weak muscles and headache aren't going away. Time will take care of that.

She exits the apartment to smoke, exhaling the nicotine into the cool night air. It's past midnight. She'll reassess the situation tomorrow and trickle more information to Detective Iglesias.

Under the dark streets, the headlights of a small hatchback vehicle come from down the road. The silver automobile parks across the street in Synarion's usual spot. The nymph has arrived. Lola rests against the building, watching him with a smidge of resentment oozing out of each slow puff of her drag.

The nymph crosses the street and stops beside her, close to the light. Synarion stares at her cigarette. Now the black smudges on his face and the scorch marks on his cuffs and boots are clear, as if he'd stepped into a fire.

I told you what I knew last time. I don't know how to get into Dega'Mostikas's Triangle, Mul had said to Synarion and Lola. The succubus mentioned *flames of Dega'Mostikas's Triangle* as well. A noted observation for Lola, adding more mystery to the balancer and his precious old world.

He says, "That isn't good for your lungs."

Lola exhales a puff to Synarion. "You have them too."

"When undercover."

"What took you so long?"

"Sometimes balancer missions go south."

"I can see that." She points to her cheek. "You got a little something there."

Synarion rubs his face with his fingers and then inspects them.

She wants to smile because it is kind of a charming clumsiness but remains stern. The liquor and cigarette help give her mental clarity so the emotional wreck of her ash-begging body doesn't spiral into a primal animal longing for physical comfort. She is better than Abbygail. Her mind is more robust than her primal self.

"What is this other mission?" Lola asks, sucking the smoke.

"It's difficult to explain," Synarion says.

"Try me," Lola says.

"I don't want to get into it."

"And why is that? Are you too close to it?"

"No." Synarion puffs his chest. "It's complicated."

"More complicated than an interconnected web of drug lords and intelligent reptilians roping in politicians and the media for total control?"

"Okay, not quite like that. It's more cerebral," Synarion says.

"I think I can handle it," Lola says.

"Another day."

"Synarion, I got into this by trusting you." Lola chucks the butt of her cigarette. Synarion's eyelid twitches at the motion. She continues, "You said there would be no going back, and I needed allies. You are my ally, or so I hope. Yet, here you are dancing around my questions."

"I'll help you to a point, Lola."

"To a point? What does that mean?" Lola asks.

"I know what you want, and working with you, I can see how much it controls your life. I can't have you do that."

"This again? Christ," Lola says.

Synarion steps closer. "Quite frankly, my other balancing missions don't involve you. Seeing how you disagree with a clear reason to hide the old world proves it. You don't care about the balance of Mother Nature and the protection of those living within her."

"I want my goddamned life. I want revenge upon those pieces of shit who have ruined everything. I want to see my family." Lola hugs her arms, feeling her lip tremble.

"Idealism is a dangerous path to walk down. The goal I propose benefits the entire world, not just you."

Lola looks away, wiping away a tear squeezing from her eyelid.

Synarion continues, "This is why I can't share more of the old world with you. I know you're documenting it. You want to publish powerful articles that will unravel the real world and show that the conspiracies are true, clearing your name."

"It's not like—" Lola can't even finish her words because it's true.

"Our goals align for a while. Neither one of us can handle the Crystal Moths on our own. They're too big. The art show is a perfect example."

"Synarion, I don't know. I have to record what I see."

"Have you thought about what would happen to me? What would happen to Bark Nose?"

"I have. I want to protect them. A mass info dump is the last resort if my plan goes south. It's why I have the tattoo. I don't want to cause harm."

Synarion reaches into his pocket, pulling out his phone. He taps away on the screen and his face sinks with concern, losing interest in Lola's words.

"What is it?" Lola asks.

"It's Mul." Synarion's voice goes down a notch.

Lola leans in to see the text message, which reads:
(Mul: get to my place now.

Bring that human plaything with you.

I have something urgent.

2:12 AM)

Lola says, "What do you think it is?"

Synarion keeps staring at the phone. "That's not Mul. She doesn't text."

There are no other messages on the screen. Lola presumed he deleted them. She says, "So, who is it?"

"I don't know. She could be in trouble," Synarion says with haste, walking to his car.

Lola follows and says, "I'm coming with you."

"This could be dangerous. It would be wise to stay here," Synarion says.

He unlocks the vehicle, opens the door and steps inside, swinging it shut. Lola grabs it, preventing him from closing the car.

She says, "Look, this gap between us is growing. If we're going to work together, let me help. This could be related to the ash."

Synarion hesitates, not blinking nor looking away, and then says, "Get in."

CHAPTER 46
YOU, ME, AND THE DEVIL

Something is killing us every day. The murderer might as well be one you enjoy. If Lola makes it to a ripe old age, death will come through throat cancer. Her puffing on a smoke in Synarion's car is the rational choice to keep her emotions and desires at bay. Boozing in the shotgun seat isn't a prime solution. Ash must be reserved.

She wishes to hide her feelings and be a robot. She can't be human. In life-and-death scenarios, there is no room for the irrational components of humanity. Thus, Lola keeps sucking hard on her cancer stick.

Synarion puts the car in park and turns off the ignition. The muffled droplets of rain fill the silence. They've reached the west side of the downtown city. It's a far cleaner part, meaning there's money here.

"Put that out," Synarion says.

Lola is still smoking, even with the car windows rolled up. She doesn't listen and exits the vehicle, puffing away. The last thing she needs is Synarion taking the high ground about cigarettes.

The nymph exits the car and locks it. He says, "Keep on your guard. We don't know what we're getting into."

Lola finishes the smoke, tossing it into the gutter. She follows the nymph to a seven-floor condo building as he punches numbers on the intercom. The speaker rings. It rings once more before the door clicks and buzzes, letting them inside. Lola takes her hood off and fidgets with the handle of her knife tucked into her pocket. Her other sly hand slides her phone out of her inner jacket pocket and hits the video record button. The touch screen buttons are second nature to her, and she activates it while stepping into the elevator. Next, she puts the phone in her outer pocket. From what she can tell, Synarion hasn't noticed, or he sees no point in stopping her.

They ride to the fifth floor, ending with a ding as the doors open. Synarion takes the lead to the demon's suite. It's the one unit with the door not shut, with a red light peering from a crack inside.

Synarion knocks on it as he steps in. "Mul?"

There's no response.

"Close it," Synarion whispers.

Lola enters and closes the door with a soft push. She stays behind Synarion as they walk past the entryway and into the open-concept layout. A fireplace is off to the right, and an island is to the left. Music plays from the bedroom to the far right in the hallway. A cool breeze comes from the bedroom.

Synarion takes one throwing star, gripping it. Lola takes her knife and the two walk to the bedroom's half-shut entrance. From the opening, a man's foot is visible. Synarion pushes the door aside, revealing true horror.

The funk of all kinds of bodily fluids flies free in the bedroom. A naked, mutilated man lies dead. His mangled crotch is a wet mess of red liquids dripping onto the silky black sheets, oozing from the bed frame onto the ground. To the side is a secondary corpse of a naked, headless demon. It lies on its stomach with the tail twisted and ripped. The wings are lifeless, and the spine and neck tendons are a shredded mess on the hardwood floor. The curtains flow in the air from the open window of the far-left side, sending icy bites against Lola's fingers.

"Your cautious nature hasn't changed in age," comes a hiss from the far corner beside the door.

Synarion turns, raising his throwing star in a battle stance. Lola lifts her dagger, stepping behind Synarion. Both face Scalebane, who perches on top of the dresser like a gargoyle. The lifeless goggles of her leather mask highlight a deep red. Her one hand cups Mul's upside-down decapitated head. The claws dig in between the curling horns, sinking into the knotted black hair. Scalebane tosses the skull as if it were a ball. Her other hand holds her sai with loose fingers. The tail sways side to side, grazing the ceiling.

"Lereif, what have you done?" Synarion asks.

Scalebane grips the head tightly. A grumble comes from her throat, and she chucks the head at Synarion. It topples onto the hardwood floor, leaving splatter imprints of red as it rolls next to his boot.

"It's Scalebane. You should know this," she says.

"You didn't summon me to fight. What do you want?" Synarion asks.

Scalebane slides off the dresser, standing tall with her tail perked up and curling above her head. "That answer depends on your next choice of action."

Synarion lowers his spiked knuckle and nods at Lola. She follows his motion. He says, "Now you're slaughtering anyone from the old world?"

"I wouldn't say a demon is from the old world. You know my distaste for these horrible immortals. Why would you express such sympathy for a succubus of all kinds?"

"She was useful intel," Synarion says. "She and I were working together."

"Yes, she mentioned that," Scalebane says, tapping her sai on the dresser. "She said quite a bit before I relieved her of the mortal realm."

"Scalebane, you don't have to go down this path."

Scalebane slams her fist into the wall, punching a hole into it. "Still so foolish, are you? Here you are working with a soft skin? They're the ones who are responsible for destroying what we once knew."

"Namsruc would disagree," Synarion says.

"Her name doesn't leave your tongue unless I tell you so. It's only been her and I."

"The both of you couldn't stay with me. It was far too dangerous."

"Of course, your precious balancer duty. Look how well the Grove protected Mother Nature. You pained her. Your people were nowhere to be found when humans enslaved mine. Your kind collapsed the continent of Zingalg, killing millions. You balancers are as arrogant as the humans."

"We're not here to resurrect old wounds. You called us," Synarion says.

"Always to business," Scalebane says, walking over to Mul's headless corpse. The vazelead's torn back peeks through the shredded black cloak and leather armour. Black blood cakes over the gaping hole. Amazingly, she has not expressed a single hint of pain. Scalebane kicks the neck. "Unfortunately, this is tied to personal relations. I wanted to keep it to business, Synarion. Truly. More hands are involved with ash and the Crystal Moths than I anticipated."

"King and the other vazeleads are unreachable," Synarion says. "I have no method of diplomacy with this."

"We don't care for your methods of unification."

"So you align yourselves with a fallen angel? The First, at that."

"Not my choice to make," Scalebane says. She turns to read Lola's face, which remains stone cold, biting her inner lip to fake braveness. "I could end her now, you know that Synarion?"

The nymph breathes heavily.

Scalebane continues, "That is not why I'm here. At least for the moment." She raises her sai, pointing at Lola. "Don't think I won't come for her."

A sting pricks Lola's intestines. She can't ignore the growing fear, for she knows this hellish reptile isn't lying. Her dagger is lowered, but she's still gripping the handle for her dear life in case she needs to fight.

Synarion says, "Scalebane, please."

Scalebane's tail slithers to Mul's head, coiling around the horn and dragging it away from Synarion. The blood smears the ground until she lifts the head. She says, "Your friend here was so desperate to save her own skin. She confirmed my fears. The Crystal Moths aren't what King presumes. King keeps the vazeleads under a tight wrap because there are so few of us. He's never proposed making ash here in Canada. Yet, there is one within the city."

Scalebane tosses the head onto the bed. It lands between the thighs of the dead man with a squish.

"Another vazelead?" Synarion asks, glancing at Lola. Both share the same concerns, knowing that the SUV tracking device leads to them.

"I'm afraid so," Scalebane says. "I haven't told King. He won't take direct action. As far as I know, two vazeleads have left our home. Myself, and Namsruc."

"Did you come with your sister?" Synarion asks.

"King sent Namsruc east first to work with whatever operation the Moths have there to misdirect the law. He sent me to work with the chief of their ash business. I thought I'd work with Mastema. Instead, I'm stuck with a soft skin."

Synarion says, "Who?"

Lola says, "Erol." Her voice rises a notch, guessing the name, still riddled with fear.

Scalebane growls at Lola.

Synarion extends his hand at Lola. A clear sign to shush.

Scalebane continues, "Your succubus shared this with me. I had my hunches that Erol allowed Namsruc to be captured. She doesn't answer her soulstone. They're using her, Synarion."

"Isn't that normal? Don't you provide scales too?" Synarion asks.

"No, Synarion. King ensures the Nine do."

"Who are?" Synarion asks.

"They are the corrupt and street scum. Weak, useless, degenerate vazeleads that King deemed unworthy to carry out the empire."

"That isn't wise, considering how few of you there are," Synarion says.

Scalebane says, "It is not my choice to make. King fears breeding with corrupt vazeleads will tamper the bloodline."

"And how many of you are left?" Synarion asks.

"None of your concern, balancer," Scalebane says.

"And you believe that Namsruc is being forced to produce ash against her will?" Synarion asks.

"Precisely."

"We share the same fear."

"The demon squealed her whereabouts, and I'm going to free my sister. I know the power of the Crystal Moths, and caution tells me I cannot do this alone."

Synarion and Lola exchange glances, already knowing where the conversation will lead. The nymph says, "You wish to work together?"

Scalebane walks to the dresser, watching Lola. "That's, unfortunately, the case."

"You are sure King is unaware and uncooperative?"

"Unlikely. He has a clear agenda for us Scalebanes. He also values Mastema and will push our pain if it doesn't kill us. I care little of their game, Synarion. My sister comes first. I need to get Namsruc back. I need to show King what the Crystal Moths are."

Synarion says, "Let me speak with King. We can work through this as one."

Scalebane shakes her head no. "Why are you so naive, Synarion? How can you not see there is no possibility of peace amongst all walks of life? There's a disease within Mother Nature. They come in the form of flesh and bone. These primates must be eradicated, meaning it's either the soft skins or the rest of us. Even then, if we freed Mother Nature of her plague, the others would turn on each other as they did once before. It always goes this way. There cannot be peace. Did the Grove not teach you of the natural law?"

Synarion is quiet.

Scalebane says, "You know this. You're also riddled with complex emotions. Pride, anger, desire, and even love."

Synarion's nostrils flare. "Scalebane, I want to work with you. Anything you hold against me, we can work out."

"This isn't related to you and me. It's far grander. Right now, time is of the essence because I don't know where the Moths will take my sister next. Mulier says they move the location frequently."

"Right," Synarion says. "We can get her, and the three of us can unite. I can aid you. I'll ask again, let me speak with King, and we can bring reason to the madness."

"I don't wish for your reason, Synarion. You're stuck in the old ways of balance. There is no place for your kind in the New World Order. It's led you down pointless paths and aligned you with a whore demon and a soft skin who is a sad, lost soul longing for her mother, thinking she can prove herself worthy."

The words strike Lola's core, morphing the fear into the fire she always had. She says, "It's not personal vengeance. It's justice."

Scalebane takes a step closer to Lola. "Justice? Please. If you knew your people's history and what they've done, you would know there is no such thing as justice in Mother Nature's world. We are both sophisticated animals nonetheless. Abstract ideas of right and wrong don't apply here."

"I want to fix things," Lola says.

Synarion speaks. "We'll work with you, Scalebane. I want you to trust me again."

"It's not about your trust, Synarion. I know you're loyal. This is why I contacted you because I need your help, and you care for my sister." She steps away from Lola, pacing to Mul's corpse. "We need to strike now and rescue Namsruc."

"What do you propose?" Synarion asks.

Scalebane sheaths her sai. "We have a temporary window of agreement before our purposes stray, and we become enemies once more."

"Again, Scalebane, we don't have to—"

"No, get your head out of your arse, Synarion. You wish to

restore your view of balance to the world. I want my sister and me to remain loyal to my people's will. This soft skin wishes to engage in a personal vendetta that will undo the old world."

"It's not just that," Lola says.

Scalebane's tail sways like a cat waiting to play with its prey. "I know where you come from, how you arrived here, and what you plan to do next. You are no different than the rest of your filth. A selfish animal that needs to be put down."

Synarion says, "Stay focused. How do you foresee this going?"

Scalebane says, "The Crystal Moths dispatch their product to dealers during evenings and nights, meaning they aren't producing. We act early in the morning while they're out."

Synarion says, "Early as in two AM?"

"In a few hours. They are nightcrawlers. In the morning, the defences will be lowered. It won't last long, and they will call for backup. I need you to meet me at a factory called Allen Abattoir Plant."

Synarion nods. "We happen to have the location."

"Swift. Meet me there in three hours. This is our one time to work as one. After this, we split ways, understood?"

Synarion says, "Understood."

Scalebane walks towards the open window. "I will pressure this again. We don't have much time. It will be violent. Prepare yourselves." She hops onto the window frame. "Don't be late." With that, she leaps through the window and disappears into the shadows.

CHAPTER 47
UNTIL THE END OF THE NIGHT

Never make assumptions about life. Assuming how life is supposed to be will lead to frustration when the soul evolves. No matter how hard Lola tries, there's some new angle to this misery she has created. If she wants her plans to remain intact, she needs to act fast. The stakes have risen.

Synarion types away on his phone. Lola hugs her arms, staring at the succubus's naked decapitated corpse.

"I need a smoke," she says, still looking at the demon corpse and remembering a sai can't carve a head off, and there are no knives nearby. Scalebane must have used sheer force to rip that head off. A reptilian from Hell bested a demon.

"Don't go far," Synarion says, typing away. "Almost done."

He is contacting his old world colleagues to clean this mess. Apparently, they have cleaning services. It's a logical choice. You can't have the police find this horror scene.

Lola steps out of the bedroom, through the hall, and onto the balcony to light a smoke. The drag is a cover-up. She takes her phone and stops her recording. Being in her jacket, the audio will be muffled. She can check it later. Right now, she dials Detective Iglesias's number.

The phone rings.

"Come on," Lola mutters, inhaling her cancer stick.

At this hour, Iglesias won't be awake. She doesn't know until she tries. The phone rings several times before it goes to voicemail. Lola calls again. The same thing occurs. She texts his number:

(You: answer. It's important

2:38 AM)

No, she doesn't have to involve Iglesias with the abattoir plant. She wants to. There aren't many opportunities for her to validate her story. This is her best shot in a long time. She makes one last attempt to call Detective Iglesias. The phone rings once, twice, three times, four, and a click comes on the fifth.

"Hello?" Iglesias croaks.

Lola smiles, feeling relief that a plan is going her way. "Fuck, I didn't think you'd answer."

"It's shy of three in the morning."

"This is important. I need you to meet me."

"Now?" Iglesias asks.

"I know this is sketchy as shit, but I need you to trust me this one time."

"Okay, you in trouble?"

"No. Not yet. Everything got real. In an hour, meet me by that abandoned warehouse again, closer to the docks, though."

There's a pause, and finally, Detective Iglesias says, "All right, see you soon."

Lola hangs up and finishes the last bit of her cigarette before throwing the butt over the balcony. She takes a deep breath to compose herself. She has a lot to process.

She and Synarion will infiltrate a Crystal Moth drug den to save Scalebane's sister; Lola is getting the law involved in hopes of plugging this rabbit hole. She's not the scared little girl wanting revenge, as Scalebane claims. Or so she tells herself. The firm, crafty Lola is around when she's under the influence. Ash-dasher Lola is brave, resourceful, and sharp. It's what she wants to be. Unfortunately, Lola doesn't have much left. There is a tiny spec that rests in her bralette. It will come in handy tonight. For now, she must ignore the constant hum under her skin.

Real Lola is a reporter. She can use her old-school tricks to gather more evidence. She pulls out her phone, turns on the record function, and holds it upside down. It's tucked into her jacket so the camera peeks out. She steps into the apartment and walks to the bedroom, where Synarion finishes a call. Mul's head is a good meter away. It's toppled onto its side with the tongue hanging out. The pink eyes roll back. It's a good look for the camera.

One of the horns is chipped, with a fragment by the dresser.

Perfect, Lola thinks, kneeling to take it. This is solid evidence. She stuffs it into her cargo pocket.

A blip of guilt pinches her heart. She feels remorse for what she is doing behind Synarion's back. He has no clue that Detective Iglesias is joining the party. Still, Lola doesn't belong here. None of this old world nonsense is her fight. It's about her and the Crystal Moths. Destroying their scheme and exposing the vazeleads will hurt them where it counts.

Synarion keeps yammering on the phone. ". . . uh huh . . . that's right. Get them here now. I owe you." He hangs up his phone.

"You have connections everywhere, hey?" Lola asks, angling the camera to look at Mul's decapitated body.

"Yeah. Eden Breaker has more skills than simply cracking open technology. They have their own contacts, and the gentleman I spoke to will take care of this mess. We don't need humans finding any of this. It's one thing if they learn of the old world, and a whole other ball of mess when dealing with dead demons from the afterlife."

"Right, because of the religious component."

"Precisely. That would send humans into an uproar with clashing views of faith. It would prove them right and wrong simultaneously."

"How so?"

"If you think the old world is convoluted, wait until you learn about the afterlife."

"Can't wait," Lola says.

"In time. Eden Breaker's cleanup crew will take care of Mul's body and this unit. We need to move fast to meet with

Scalebane."

Lola says, "How do you know we can trust her?"

"Because the one person Lereif Scalebane is loyal to is her sister, Namsruc."

"And she will come for me once this is done, you know that, right?" Lola says.

"That is what she says. We will deal with that when the time comes. Right now, I cannot have Namsruc in danger. If I can talk to Namsruc, there's hope to fix this."

"Would you consider them family?" Lola asks.

"Yes, I do. It broke me to pass them on to their people. I don't know if Lereif feels the same. She carries her family name with pride." Synarion exits the room, presuming Lola is following him to the door.

Of course, Synarion had to see the Scalebanes as family. That adds another layer of guilt onto the pile. His scenario isn't too different from her own vendetta. No. She cannot give in.

Lola follows Synarion, and he speaks, looking at Lola's boots and up to her jacket's cuffs as if he is inspecting her. "I hope you see why we must keep this hidden from the humans."

This again, Lola thinks, folding her arms to hide the phone. "Synarion."

"I may be old and slip from time to time, but I have faith."

"In what?" Lola asks.

"In you," Synarion says.

Damnit, Lola thinks. She doesn't reply, looking to the ground in shame.

With that, the two leave the unit. They take the elevator down and head to the car, leaving that nightmare for Eden

Breaker's team. Lola turns off her camera and checks the time. They have a good two and half hours before meeting Scalebane. For Lola, it's a half an hour to meet Detective Iglesias.

At the apartment, Synarion and Lola gather their gear for the inevitable showdown. Both put on their communication devices as they did for the art gallery. This time, Lola clips her small cube camera onto the collar of her leather jacket, keeping it discrete. She also uploads the video of Mul's apartment, looking over her shoulder as Synarion prepares himself.

"You need to stay focused when we're there, got it? Don't get obsessed with documenting it," Synarion says, as if reading her thoughts.

"That's a given," Lola says.

"You understand that, but will you do it?" Synarion asks.

"Why do you keep hammering on this?" Lola asks.

"Because I can see your withdrawal."

"Excuse me?"

"Ash. The sweat. You're twitchy and moody nature since I've returned. I know you've been using. You can do whatever the hell you want, but don't fuck this up."

Lola blinks a couple of times, taken aback by his change of tone. "You got it," she says. "What's the plan?"

Synarion says, "We work with Scalebane. She is a powerful warrior who can infiltrate the Crystal Moths."

"Great. So she handles the Crystal Moths, and I rescue Namsruc. None of this will get us to Mastema, though."

"No. I'm hoping I can win Scalebane and Namsruc over. I want them to trust me. If I can get to Namsruc first, she can help me convince Scalebane."

"So you can talk to her boss, King, is it?"

"Correct. If I can speak with King, we'll have a better chance at getting to the top of this scheme."

Lola checks the time. Detective Iglesias will be at the docks by now. "Look, I'm going for another smoke before we get going." She gets her phone, gun, and knife. Better safe than sorry.

Synarion says, "Don't be long. We should go over our plan again."

"There's not much of a plan. Sounds like we're going in like an eighties action hero, guns blazing, trusting some bloodthirsty reptilian hell-warrior who wants to kill me."

Synarion shakes his head. Sarcasm is an excellent tool to silence people. The nymph doesn't suspect a thing as Lola exits the apartment. She fast-walks through the street to save time. The warehouse isn't far, with the docks right beside it. If Detective Iglesias is one of the good cops and doesn't arrest her, Lola's whole scenario will change.

CHAPTER 48
IN DIRT

Addicts are everywhere. Workaholics, adrenaline junkies, druggies, and gamblers root from chemical or behavioural themes that will damage their lives and those around them. Iglesias and his two comrades don't mind their fix despite their evening drinks with one another to drown it. The three will keep pushing through until they solve ash and get Lola Cabello in their hands.

Ash has proven to be a sophisticated case. There are too many departments involved, thanks to the supposed murder spree Cabello is on. This further complicates their progress, devouring resources for the entire week. Crime scene reviewing, photo and video gathering, witness statements, and lab analysis are a waste of time compared to Iglesias's secret.

He drinks his stale coffee in the War Room with Beckman and Archer late in the evening. The other officers left long ago. Iglesias stares at the board covered in pinned notes, photos, a map, and strings pointing to Cabello. They even have a note about the phone Iglesias found and the text messages on it. Beside Cabello is a sticky note with large text stating: *Mastema?*

Who are you? Iglesias thinks.

Archer swings in her chair, feet on the table, looking at the board. "That phone sure was a lucky find."

"Yeah," Iglesias says. *I need to tell them*, Iglesias thinks. He can't, not yet. He needs more information on Cabello to know if she can be trusted or if she is who the evidence points to. He heard her voice. She's a scared girl, not a killer. He's dealt with killers.

"It doesn't give us much," Beckman says. "We know the Crystal Moths were there. That's what the texts say, matching our assumption."

Archer says, "It mentions the Prime Minister."

"So? I can mention the Prime Minister too, saying he is *expecting*. Doesn't make it true."

"It's evidence Bando can use as leverage to keep the case ours," Iglesias says. "We're running around in circles with these other clowns involved."

"I think more are coming from the circus," Beckman says.

"What do you mean?" Iglesias asks.

"I followed up with the zoology lab and the substance analysis team. They said they've already passed the info onto the Covert Operations Branch."

Iglesias rubs his brow. "Are you telling me the goddamn military is keeping evidence from us? We got the damn phone. It's hard evidence."

Beckman says, "My theory? The CFMP will be knocking on our door pretty soon."

Archer says, "Wasn't Sergeant Bando going to keep them back for us?"

"He said he'd try," Iglesias says.

"We did, the phone," Archer says.

Beckman says, "That's not much."

Archer shrugs. "Shit. Well, if it means we have to work less, I'm into it."

Iglesias says, "We don't even know where ash comes from. There's no point in bringing the Covert Operations."

Beckman says, "Tell that to Sergeant Bando's boss. This thing is growing into a big enough threat. With the CFMP involved, we'll hear from the DND and the Minister of Public Safety."

Iglesias bites his inner lip. Beckman is right. The Department of National Defense will want its claws deep. If the Covert Operations Branch gets involved, this case will slip from Iglesias's control. Sergeant Bando's leverage goes so far, and time is running out.

Iglesias says, "Look, they haven't contacted us yet. We'll deal with those lab geeks and green boots later. Let's hone in on Cabello. We get the girl, then report." *I could end this whole thing now,* he thinks. Cabello is in his grasp if he wishes it.

"Alright," Beckman says. "This whole thing is getting sticky."

"I know," Iglesias says before downing the rest of his coffee.

CRYSTAL MOTH CONSPIRACY BY KONN LAVERY

"If any superiors get in touch with us, I'll deal with them directly."

Beckman nods. "Yeah. I just don't want them to rip you a new one."

Iglesias smirks. "Thanks."

Archer swings her feet off and stands, gathering her belongings. "So, do we call it a night?"

Iglesias says, "Yeah. Not much else to do for the day."

Beckman stands while shaking his head, staring at the board. "Can you believe that people think they saw a grappling hook on the roof?"

Iglesias looks at the board's photo of the art gallery. "Actually, yes."

The three exit the War Room. They head to the parkade with sagging eyes and frowns, which say far more than words could regarding their exhaustion and defeat. Beckman's statement holds the truth. The department isn't making fast enough progress. Ash is expanding and the evidence says Cabello is a growing threat. Iglesias and his team will play less and less of a role if they can't pull proof out of their asses soon. Iglesias prays Cabello will give him tangible clues to work with.

Not to mention the internal affairs investigation regarding Chen. Iglesias can't ponder it too much. He needs his mental energy here and now. The uncertainty of trust lingers in his mind.

At the hotel, Iglesias pours some whiskey to calm his mind. He shouldn't be drinking this much. It disgusts him with each sip he takes. It's the one thing that can help him unwind. There are too many pieces locked away, and his single card is Cabello.

He texts his son goodnight and attempts to relax, lying on the bed. Eventually, the whispering words of his mind fade into the background, and he is met with peaceful blackness. Bliss.

The rest is short-lived when his phone buzzes several times. At first, Iglesias presumes it comes from his dreams. The humming doesn't stop, pulling him from his slumber.

He rises, seeing his cell phone ringing non-stop. The caller ID states *Raymond Alexander*. Iglesias's eyes widen, and he snags the phone. There is no Raymond Alexander. It's a simple renaming for his contact number of Lola Cabello.

"Hello?" Iglesias answers.

Wind and rain come through the speaker as Lola says, "Fuck, I didn't think you'd answer."

Iglesias looks at the time and says, "It's shy of three in the morning."

"This is important. I need you to meet me."

Iglesias sits and starts looking for his pants. "Now?"

"I know this is sketchy as shit, but I need you to trust me this one time."

"Okay, you in trouble?" Iglesias asks, finding his trousers.

"No. Not yet. Everything got real. In an hour, meet me by that abandoned warehouse again, closer to the docks, though."

Iglesias contemplates this scenario. He shouldn't be doing this. It's also what he wants. If she meets him, he could gather a team to arrest her right then and there. They could call it a day and go home. They could regroup regarding ash, the Crystal Moths, and Mastema and use Cabello while she's behind bars. He would be a good cop, a hero.

There are also plugs in the Major Crimes department. Are there Moths in the DND too? Cabello will suffer a fate no different than Chen before she sings. Iglesias can't let that happen.

He says, "All right, see you soon."

Iglesias hangs up and gets the rest of his clothes. His gun is loaded, and he ensures he has his cuffs. Anything could happen.

By three-thirty in the morning, he is out the door and driving to the docks. It's a good half-hour drive from the hotel. His anticipation distorts the journey to several hours long.

He parks his SUV a block by the abandoned building and steps into the night. At four in the morning, it is far too dark. As he walks to the docks under the cloudy sky, his red flags are firing from all cylinders. He marches down the street, eyeing the alleyway and corners for anything suspicious. The streets have a few rubbies shooting up by a dumpster. They appear harmless. The coast is clear.

A couple blocks further, he walks past the ocean line to the docks. His gun is in hand's reach, tucked right under his armpit. His dress shoes click against the pavement. At the edge of the docks, there's a slim, hooded figure. It's Lola Cabello. Finally.

His approaching footsteps make her turn around. The lighting is too dark. Basic feminine features appear under the moon.

Iglesias says, "Are you who I think you are?"

"That depends," says the girl, whose voice is identifiable as Lola's. "Are you alone?"

"Lola Cabello," Iglesias says, stopping four meters away. He places his hands on his hips. "I've been waiting quite some time for this."

"Detective Iglesias," Lola says. "You alone?"

"I said I wanted to earn your trust," Iglesias says, raising his arms.

"Okay, good."

Iglesias steps forward until he is two metres from the girl. He scans her as he does with each person he meets, treating them as suspects and reading their body language. Her cargoes fray at the ends over her black boots. There's a bulge in the pants pockets, indicating she has some object of importance. Under the leather jacket and hoodie? It's impossible to tell. He must presume she has a weapon for his own safety.

Beneath the hood is the face of youth. She's in her mid-twenties, with hazelnut eyes that radiate fire. That focused glare says she's closer to her forties and on a mission.

"I haven't had a late-night call from a girl in years," Iglesias jokes. "Why now?"

"Things are heating up. I didn't want it to escalate this fast, but I need you."

"What do you mean by escalate?" Iglesias asks.

Lola says, "I found where the Moths are producing ash, a local one at least."

"And what do you want with me?"

"I need you to bust it after I get there. Then you can bring the heavy guns or whatever you have."

"What are you going to do there?" Iglesias asks.

"It's kind of a rescue mission. It's irrelevant to you. You have to do as I say."

"I've been doing a lot of that. You need to talk."

"We are talking. We're going to a slaughterhouse. Make it there, and I'll bring you the Crystal Moth in charge of ash," Lola says.

"That so? You're quite the star in the news. Things don't look good."

"No shit. I know you don't believe me. Please, just make it."

Iglesias says, "You know what happened to those two actors at the art gallery?"

"Yeah. They were shot in front of me, gunned by Moths. I didn't kill them."

Iglesias says, "Right. What about the motel murder?"

"A Crystal Moth. He tried to assassinate me."

"He's a big man. You got him by yourself?"

"I have people. Like our relationship. I can rely on your types to a degree. Still, I'm on my own."

Iglesias nods. "Right. Is it safe to say you haven't committed these murders?"

"Yeah. I didn't kill anyone."

"Where's the evidence?" Iglesias asks.

"That's the problem," Lola says. "The Crystal Moths have their hands in your system, and I hope to God you're one of the good ones."

"I'm going rogue."

"For what it's worth, I'm so glad you are. I don't know how I will prove myself innocent with this. I have a ton of data."

Iglesias says, "Which you've withheld for a long time."

"I'm well aware of that. I'm trying to do what's right."

"And what is right, Lola?" Iglesias asks.

"Real justice. Vengeance, in a sense. I think you see the same thing. I want to break the Crystal Moths. They did this, Detective Iglesias. They took my life from me. My mother, I can't even talk to my brother or father. Donnie hangs on by a string. My friends. The Moths own the law. They have to pay."

"They've got quite the web. Do you have any other information on them?"

Lola says, "I do. If what we're going to do goes well, I will share more with you. You'll have the man responsible for ash. I need to know you're going to do this."

"Okay. You said this was urgent. How urgent?"

Lola checks her phone. The screen's light eliminates her face's soft features and the bags under her eyes. She's far too pale. Her cheekbones are too pronounced, indicating she doesn't eat well.

She says, "In two hours. Believe it or not, the Moths are making ash in a slaughterhouse outside town. I don't know how many Crystal Moths there are or how much ash is being made. I need you to get the cops to the location by half an hour after six AM. We should be done by then, and the Crystal Moths are yours."

"Right. How do I persuade them?"

Lola pulls out her phone again and says, "Here. I'm going to send you some information through VoIP. It's a fake number with the location of the slaughterhouse."

"How can you be sure this is the right location?" Iglesias asks.

"Because I tracked an SUV selling ash at the art gallery. It comes and goes from this spot. The Moths are there."

"This doesn't explain how I got the information."

"I don't care, Detective Iglesias. Convince them. You spotted the SUV from street cameras and followed it. I don't know."

Iglesias's phone buzzes. It's the text from Lola. She reaches into her cargo pocket, pulling out a long, jagged organic shard. It looks to be a piece of an animal horn. She steps forward, handing it to Iglesias. "Here, take this."

I could bring her in, Iglesias thinks. Instead, he asks, "What is it?"

"You wouldn't believe me if I told you. Keep it close. Get it analyzed by someone you trust. Document it. Don't share it with anyone."

Iglesias takes the horn, rotating the torn fragment. He's no animal expert. It looks like it belongs to a goat. He says, "What are you doing, Lola? You're making this case a hell of a lot stranger."

"It's doing that for me. I'm along for the ride, like you, and I will stop it with fury. Justice wasn't given to Michael Bradford. I'm going to fix that. I'm going to avenge Becky, my mother, and even Donnie. If that means I have to do this on my own, then I will."

"You're not alone, Lola."

"I wish that were true. I have to survive. I hope you stick to your word, detective. Don't be late." Lola marches from the dock, storming right past Iglesias without a moment's pause.

Iglesias watches the girl leave. He could follow her, find where she has been hiding. Instead, he fiddles with the horn fragment in his hand, contemplating what she told him. He checks his phone and sees she sent exact coordinates to some slaughterhouse outside of town.

That's something, Iglesias thinks. They've built a loose bond of trust that he hopes to strengthen, for they are both in the dirt. Iglesias can't keep the relationship in the dark forever. Somehow, he has to rope in the others.

If this is a local ash production, similar to what Chen described, they'll see if this reptile nonsense is true.

CHAPTER 49
UNRAVEL

Scalebane longs to go on a rampage, massacring the soft skins for what they've done to her people. Now they've taken her sister. An emotional response of the ill-willed creates dreadful consequences. Thus, Scalebane must master herself to avoid foolishery.

She is unfamiliar with soft skin technology of transportation, information exchange, and electricity. Scalebane does have plenty of survival skills to move around. Reasoning through a scenario is lacking in the soft skins' world. Their tools made them weak. This gives Scalebane an advantage.

She can navigate some technology, like Mulier's phone. The map on the device gave clear directions to the Allen Abattoir

Plant. It's far. Three hours is plenty of time to reach the outskirts of the city.

Scalebane has no doubts that Synarion and his plaything are well on their way. An experienced hunter doesn't reveal their whole plan. Synarion and the soft skin will arrive at the time she gave them. Scalebane will already have infiltrated the slaughterhouse, more Moths will arrive, and her allies will function as a distraction.

Far in the grassy shrubbery alongside the highways, her chest ignites. The warmth pulses from her soulstone. King is contacting her. She unbuckles the top straps of her leather armour and snags the glowing orange pendant. She takes off her one glove and holds the stone. The grass fields dissolve. King's familiar cavern and the stone throne are in front of her. The vazelead leader sits in the dark as before. He grips his soulstone that radiates light.

"Scalebane," King says in his demonic voice, far more intimidating than Mulier could ever perform.

"King," Scalebane says.

"I have attempted to contact Namsruc, but she does not answer her soulstone."

"I know."

"This concerns me, Scalebane."

"I found her location. I will get her," Scalebane says.

"What happened?" King asks.

"Time is crucial, King. I must act now. Once I have Namsruc, I will inform you of the betrayal."

King's throat rattles. He releases his soulstone, and Scalebane's vision vanishes. She puts the soulstone away and buckles her armour. The hunter reverts to all fours for faster motion. Her boots dangle over her neck, tied together, letting her clawed feet embrace the cool dirt.

She reaches the Allen Abattoir Plant as the rising sun peeks beyond the Great Canadian Rockies, painting the sky in hues of orange and red. Scalebane slithers through the tall grass. She rises to her feet, puts on her boots, and circles the fenced facility. Sniffing Namsruc's scent will be challenging. It's not impossible for Scalebane, who is trained at navigating through the invisible world of smells. Already her nose is irritated with the foul stench of excrement, blood, and the gritty sting of refinery equipment radiating the environment.

The plant has a large concrete structure with a number of chimneys and several small wings attached to it. Around the back is a fenced-off area containing valves, pipes, and other machinery. At the far end is a wastewater treatment section. Several other smaller buildings trickle throughout the fenced area. On the opposite side of the loading bay, one sheltered section is the pre-slaughtering pens housing pigs. The animals are compacted in small, singular caged units, fearful and unaware of impending doom.

It's the main building that is of interest. That's where the killing occurs, and the meat is put into the chill room, where Namsruc should be. The front of the building has a parkade. Countless cars are parked there. More drive towards the plant from the main road. The loading docks have semi-trucks in various bays.

The factory's setup is no different than when Scalebane used to kill and gut animals for coin centuries ago. First, the animal is slaughtered, and the meat is cooled, deboned, and then stored for later consumption. What she sees here is her past on an industrialized level. Hopping the fence and entering the slaughterhouse will be no problem from the loading docks.

Scalebane moves through the tall grass, keeping low until she reaches the fence by the semi-trucks. In a single leap, she jumps over the chain link wall and onto the grass. She rolls once, landing on her knee. A couple of humans in white and blue uniforms are by the garages. Any one of them could be the eyes and ears of the Crystal Moths. Security cameras are a risk too.

She prefers stealth. Not this time. Her sister is so near. Wisdom slips as her blood boils, turning her into a fool for rage.

The humans walk from the trucks and into the bay. The hunter darts from her frozen stance and onto the concrete. Her movement is a blip, and she's on the other side against the building's wall. She creeps to the open garage and unsheathes her one sai. Her other hand's claws are extended, ready to strike.

She peeks around the corner, seeing the two men from earlier standing right in front of her. One has a clipboard facing her, and the other has his back turned, looking at the paper. The clipboard-man squints, spotting Scalebane. His eyes widen, and he starts stepping away. His co-worker is too slow to turn as the sai lunges into his neck, bruising and puncturing the skin. She slashes her claws into his spine, slicing diagonally into his ribs. His hand cups his wounded neck, lost in shock. He collapses to the floor, soaked in red.

Scalebane marches on. The clipboard-man starts shouting.

"Help! Security!" Others from the other bay hurry to the fallen man.

The hunter walks to the one door leading inside, careless of the humans. She swings it open. She storms through a bright hall, passing other slaughterhouse workers who slam their backs against the wall at her presence. Their limbs shake in fear.

One worker stumbles, standing right in front of her. The poor deer in headlights doesn't know what to do. Scalebane whips her tail at the man, coiling it around his arm. It pulls him into her sai poking against his gut. He gasps, yanking her off.

Her tail slithers to the man's arm and wraps around his neck, bringing him closer. The sai presses harder, piercing the skin. She growls into his ear. "Take me to the chilling room. Now."

The man's shaky hand points behind him. He wheezes, unable to get enough air to speak. Scalebane frees her weapon and spins him around. She pushes him forward to walk with her. Screams and whispers come from the hall as soft skins watch Scalebane take her hostage away. They are the lucky ones in this rampage.

The two reach the hygiene swinging doors. She shoves the man through as he holds onto his bleeding stomach. They step into a vast open space with rows of assembly lines. Hooks hang pigs above each belt, where workers organize the meat onto smaller belts. The machinery noises and moving parts of the industrial plant make Scalebane and the hostage unseen.

She and her guide march past the workers along the belt and to the next room. Now the workers see the cloaked death. They gasp and run for safety.

Onwards, the two pass another set of hygiene swinging

doors. They enter a new room with far more sophisticated machinery and piping connected to the ceiling.

The hanging pigs follow into the room through an open window. Their lifeless bodies are hacked into by workers wielding butcher tools before the corpses reach automatic blades that further slice the meats.

"Over there," the man manages to gasp through her tail's tight construction. He points to the next set of hygiene doors. "Chill room."

"Good," Scalebane says.

They march on. The nearby workers are stunned, holding their blood-dripping blades. Some mummer amongst each other, unsure what to do. A few start to run until the next room's doors burst open. Four men with shaved heads in white blazers step out, gripping handguns. They fire at Scalebane and her hostage. The workers scatter and duck as bullets splatter into the meat.

Several bullets hit Scalebane's hostage, and he goes limp. The weight rests on her tail. She keeps him upright, serving as a flesh shield, and progresses toward the four Moths. They continue to fire. No mercy. Another step closer, and Scalebane can unleash hell.

Her tail launches the corpse towards her furthest opponent, enveloping his view. Scalebane's tail whips back, lashing against another man's face, shredding the skin and breaking his nose's cartilage. He screams and fires blindly. His messy aim shoots the ground, wall and ceiling.

Another Moth fires, and Scalebane ducks. The bullet rips through the fabric of her cloak, grazing her shoulder. She pulls out her second sai and thrusts both into the man's stomach then slams the sai into the man's jaw. One down.

Her tail flails in a wild motion, forcing the other three Moths to step away. The closest one is hit by her tail. It coils against his arm. She spins him around to face his ally. His twitch reaction pulls the trigger of his gun, and it speaks of death. The bullets mow down his own comrade. Two down.

She lunges at the trapped Moth to meet her sai. The tips slam into his ribcage, cracking the bone and piercing his inner organs. She uncoils her tail. He drops to the floor. One left.

The split-faced man shouts, "Call the boss!" He clutches his ripped skin as cherry-red liquid drizzles between the cracks of his fingers. "Now!" he shouts to the door.

A fifth Moth is late to the party.

"Call them," Scalebane hisses, spinning her sai.

She storms towards them. Scalebane flings her tail again, lashing the bleeding Crystal Moth's wrist. It splits open the skin, disarming his weapon. She slams the handle of one sai onto his chest, and the other's tip pierces his eye.

The newcomer steps against the wall, too horrified to see he missed the doors.

Scalebane sheaths her sai and walks to the man. He's frozen. She clutches him by the collar with one hand, lifting him high off the ground. His legs squirm as he grips her wrists. His strength is no match.

"Where is the reptilian?" Scalebane demands. The slur leaves a bad taste on her tongue for its simplification of her people. Unfortunately, this soft skin wouldn't understand any other word.

"I d-d-don't know wha-a-at the f-u-uck you're talking about," the man stutters.

Scalebane slams him against the concrete. "Don't bullshit me." Her throat rattles with her blind rage. "You will tell me, or I will make dying the merciful option. I was once a butcher."

"The other room, I swear," the man says.

Scalebane's throat rumbles again as she leans into his face.

"Take a right in the chill room, the third aisle down. Control room."

"Good," Scalebane says. "Now call your boss, and get them to call theirs until it reaches Erol Terzi. Get Mastema involved while you're on the phone. Let them know." Scalebane grabs him with both hands and swings him around, launching him headfirst into the mangled meat on the conveyor belt.

She marches to the two hygiene doors and pushes them aside. A powerful rush of cold blasts her body. It tightens her skin, even under the leather armour and cloak, her heart slows ever slightly. Her people aren't designed for the intense temperature. She presses on, fueled by burning rage of a fool.

Dozens of rows of gutted pigs are spaced evenly. Above the butchered animals is a metal walkway that runs from one end to the other horizontally. No humans are visible.

She takes a right, passing the aisles under the walkway. With each step she takes, the scent of vazelead blood pierces through the death and meat of the slaughterhouse. The path leads to a closed door. It must be the control room. She reaches it, twists the knob open, and steps inside. A heatwave blows by. Refreshing.

Scalebane takes a good whiff of the air, smelling the vazelead again. The scent is familiar from her childhood. It's the most crucial smell in the world. Yes, it is her, Namsruc.

She steps past blue and red metal pipes running along the wall and ceiling and down the zig-zag staircase, wrapping a concrete pillar until gunfire erupts. It whizzes by her, pinging against the railing. She ducks as a couple more bullets soar in the air, missing her.

Scalebane unsheathes her sai and leaps over the railing, descending a level down. She lands in front of a Crystal Moth, and her sai slams into the man's forearm, numbing him. The first sai arches up and pierces his neck, while the second plunges into his chest. Her boot sinks into his torso, launching him against the concrete pillar.

Rattling chains come from around the corner as another Crystal Moth steps into view. He holds his gun with both wobbling hands in front of his young face that has patches of facial hair.

He shouts, "Stay where you are!"

Scalebane's tail sways side to side. Her presence alone will stun him into submission.

"Don't you move, asshole!" the boy shouts.

"Step aside," Scalebane says. "If you wish to live."

The Moth swallows heavily. "I mean it."

Chains behind the pillar rattle again, followed by a muffled hiss.

Scalebane dashes to the pillar. The man fires, missing. She leans against the edge and whips her tail at his gun. The tail coils around the chamber, and she yanks it to the floor and forward. He keeps firing. Bullets shred into the concrete, throwing particles into the air. The third shot hits the man on the ground in the head, splattering blood.

He's pulled right into her sai. They pierce into his ribs, extracting any air left as the weapon slips from his hands. With both blades under his ribs, she lifts him, pinning him against the pillar.

"Who did you fools call?" Scalebane asks.

"Our bosses," he manages to wheeze. "You've messed with the wrong people. Freak."

"I know who. Is it Erol? Mastema?"

"I don't know."

"Who is in charge here?" Scalebane asks.

"Ricky. I don't know his last name!"

"Where is Ricky now?"

"I don't know. Moving the ash."

"Is Ricky coming back after?" Scalebane asks.

"Probably. Along with the rest of his crew. You're dead."

"I doubt that." Scalebane frees her sai, dropping him. She plummets both into his earholes, shredding his brain.

Next, she wipes the blades and steps around the pillar. There's an operating table with a surgical tray beside it, housing several tools. There are a couple fold-up tables with packages and boxes used by the Crystal Moths to distribute ash. No dragon statues here.

Beside the makeshift distribution setup is a gated fence. Beyond it is a naked being with smooth charcoal skin and a bloody black mess drooping down their spine and tail. Namsruc, her sister.

Small smokeless flames flicker from Namesruc's eyes, a clear sign she is weak. Chains shackle her black blood-coated wrists, ankles, and tail. They're linked together with a cuff binding her neck and a muzzle, concealing most of her face. The intricate bondage keeps her crouched on the ground. She's not a damn animal.

Whatever is left of Scalebane's heart sinks. She sheaths her sai. "Namsruc!" She hurries through the corpses, looking for a key. The first Moth has them in his front pocket. She takes the set, hurrying to the cage.

Her sister's spiked scales along the eyebrow ridge slant back. Many scales have been torn from her legs, tail, and spine leading to her neck. What remains is fresh, gooey scabs.

"Namsruc," Scalebane says again, unlocking the gate.

Namsruc speaks an inaudible phrase due to the muzzle. The black-and-white feathers running along her scalp puff as blood pumps into them.

"It's okay," Scalebane says. "It's okay. We're escaping the human filth."

Eventually, the correct key slides in, clicks, and unlocks the gate. She hurries to her sister. Briefly, she opens her arms to hug her. Time is of the essence. She fumbles through the ring of keys to find the right one to open the shackles. One by one, she finds the right ones for each clamp and the muzzle. The chains slide down, and Namsruc is free. Scalebane takes her twin into her arms, feeling the bone just below her skin. There's no meat left on her body, and her grip around Scalebane's back is soft.

"Lereif," her sister whispers. Her voice is raspy from dehydration.

"It's okay, Namsruc. I have you."

The comforting smell of her twin sister resurfaces the emotions Scalebane suppresses daily. Namsruc is her family, her blood, and everything that matters. They must escape. The stairs back to the forthcoming allies is their best option, for more Moths will come.

Scalebane scans the control room. It confirms that Namsruc's belongings are nowhere to be found. Her clothes, weapons, boots, and even her soulstone are gone. She cannot communicate with King. At this point, Scalebane doesn't want to, but she wishes for the stone not to fall into the wrong hands. She needs to shield her sister from the elements.

Shouts erupt from beyond the control room. They're muffled, echoed. Gunshots fire. Scalebane's backup is on time.

CHAPTER 50
TRINITY OF DECEPTION

Calmness is vital when in stressful situations. The internal monologue will betray you, rendering you a fool. Lola must act to keep her thoughts from oozing with fear. There's one thing that will calm her: ash.

She slips the remaining bit from her bralette and consumes the scale. In short time, the twitchy limbs and sweating body dwindle. It eases her mind, giving it complete control of her body. Her senses heighten, providing her a near-instant reaction in the present. The ash-dasher lives.

Lola returns from meeting with Detective Iglesias with a new idea birthing. She double-checks that the cop isn't following her. The coast is clear. She pulls out her smartphone outside of Synarion's apartment.

Yes, the ash is expanding her mind's possibilities. If she's bringing the cops, she can hit two birds with one stone. It's why she needs the drug.

Lola looks for the CAMB's head office number on the phone's browser. Based on the time, they won't answer. She shifts her search to their top reporters, remembering one that is infatuated with ash and her case.

Hucker Dime. He made a social media post one hour ago. Perfect.

His number will be next to impossible to find. Hucker's social media is good enough to leave a voice message. She logs into one of her sleeper accounts and taps Hucker's message button.

All too easily, she raises her voice to that of a distressed girl. She says, "It's horrible. They're everywhere! Christ, please. I called the police, and they're nowhere. I don't know who else to call! These men in white, they're killing people at the Allen Abattoir Plant."

She hangs up. It's a simple bait that Lola reinforces with a second sleeper social media account. She private messaged the CAMB account, stating:

(You: Erol Terzi, the light
leads the Moths to a slaughter.)

He'll understand the message. If they have a rescue mission, Lola wants to make the most of it. The media has been controlling the narrative of her life, and she's damn determined to fix it. Erol will be a tasty treat for Detective Iglesias.

From there, Lola does have that smoke she said she went outside for. It's her final meditation, mixing with the ash to center herself. Deep breaths in and out focus her mind. Lola is ready.

Synarion exits the apartment and nods at her. No words are needed, and the two get in the car. They must be punctual on their arrival to meet Scalebane. Lola's juggle of media and police rely on it.

Her discrete camera is ready to record. The smartphone is in hand's reach to activate her tattoo code. Others will be there to witness what the Moths are. One way or another, Lola will validate herself.

Synarion parks the car off the highway and in the forest for an easy getaway. They hike the remaining way off the road and to the slaughterhouse. The gate is open with people evacuating the building. Cars roar out of the parkade and onto the highway.

"Damn," Synarion says. "She's already started."

Lola activates her recording camera and pulls out her gun. Ash channels through her veins. Her senses hone in, amplifying her awareness of the surroundings. A subtle wind under the clear dawn brushes against the beading sweat of her forehead. Her heart pumps faster in anticipation of the violence that awaits.

"Let's go," Lola says.

The two rush past the gate, the parking lot, and into the main lobby. Workers buzz by, escaping as fast as possible, avoiding Lola and Synarion.

"Where do you think she is?" Lola asks.

"We'll follow the trail of the dead," Synarion says.

Lola looks at the entrance, seeing several large black SUVs speed into the parking lot. They brake on a skid. These are no friends.

Move into the facility. There's the voice.

"Synarion, I think we have visitors. Come on," Lola says.

The SUV doors open from the three vehicles. Men in white suits step out, each holding weapons of murder. Handguns, shotguns, and automatic ones. A Moth even has a belt of grenades wrapped around his chest.

Lola takes the lead, moving past scared workers and into the hall. A blood trail guides them to two swinging hygiene doors. It takes them into the slaughterhouse itself.

Move, comes the whisper.

They hurry past the assembly belts to a second set of doors and step through. At the far end of this room are four corpses of Crystal Moths by another set of doors. The two rush to the exit and into the chill room. The temperature is refreshing with the ash running hot in her system.

Gunshots fire behind them as the doors swing shut.

This way, comes the voice. To Lola's right is an open door going downward.

"Synarion," Lola says.

"Go, I'll ambush them," Synarion says, stepping behind the hygiene doors. More shots come from the other room. The Moths must be killing workers, because the police aren't here yet.

She reaches the doorframe, stopping in front of a dark figure helping a second frail, scaled humanoid in a black cloak up the stairs. Scalebane and her sister Namsruc.

"How many are there?" Scalebane asks.

Lola wants to stare at Namsruc's flaming eyes. She composes herself, saying, "Three SUVs. Maybe fifteen Moths."

"Unlikely," Scalebane says. "Expect an army."

More, Lola thinks, gazing at Namsruc's bloody body.

The thought dissipates as the chill room doors swing open. Three Crystal Moths barge in, their guns pointed forward. Lola raises her own, pulling the trigger. The bullet soars past the edge of the door and rips into the man's chest. He falls backward, landing on his ass. Looks like she is accountable for murder charges after all.

The two Crystal Moths return fire. Lola, Scalebane, and Namsruc take cover behind the door frame. Synarion steps from behind the chill room doors. He slams his spiked knuckles into the back skull of one Moth, knocking him out cold.

The last Crystal Moth spins around to blast him as Synarion redirects the gun-wielding arm. His spiked fist lands on the man's nose, collapsing the cartilage. A second punch hits him in the jaw. He topples to the ground.

More shouts come from the hall. Company is near.

Scalebane, Namsruc, and Lola regroup with Synarion. They rush through the row of gutted pigs, heading for the opposite room divided by another set of doors.

Scalebane stops and sniffs again. "We need another exit. They're surrounding us."

Namsruc croaks. "Human stench. All over."

Lola peeks through the round windows on the doors. Through the frosted glass is a freezing room where more men in white march to them.

Lola says, "Here they come."

"This way," Synarion says.

He guides the group past a couple aisles and down another, clear of view from the main hall. Both opposing sets of doors burst open. Shiny dress shoes and white pants peek underneath the hanging pigs. The heels tap against the cold concrete floor.

"We're trapped," Scalebane says. She frees her sister, unsheathing her two sai.

"At first, I didn't think it was you," comes a thick Turkish brogue bouncing off the walls. "Scalebane, you must know the consequences of your actions."

Perfect. Just as Lola had hoped. Erol Terzi has arrived. She needs Detective Iglesias to follow through.

Erol continues, "Now you side yourself with the rogue Edmonton girl? I didn't expect you of all to do so."

Scalebane growls until Namsruc's weak claw touches her arm. Namsruc whispers, "Hush," through her scaled lips.

In this brief moment of downtime, Lola is sucked into Namsruc's burning eyes. The reptilian's thin vertical pupils keep focused on her sister. It's far more distracting than the black-and-white feathers running along the scalp under her hood.

Erol says, "We can work through this, Scalebane. Mastema and King have their reasoning. You must trust in the higher powers."

"King has nothing to do with this," Scalebane mutters.

Run is the single word that enters Lola's mind. She's unsure if it's her fear trickling in or the ash. Either way, something is wrong.

"We need to go now," Lola whispers.

A click comes from above along the metal walkways. The grenade-equipped Crystal Moth stands over them and chucks a small, studded oval object onto them.

"Grenade!" Lola shouts.

The group scatters as the bomb detonates, sending swirls of fiery heat against the chilling pig corpses, shredding them to pieces. Bits of flesh, concrete, and metal fly through the smoke and flame.

Lola lands on her stomach, sliding onto the ground. Her ears ring, muffling most other sounds. The blurry vision clears, and she sees Namsruc beside her. Gunshots erupt through the flames coming from both directions. Synarion and Scalebane are not in view.

"Get up!" Lola says, crawling to Namsruc.

Silhouettes of Crystal Moths crouching under the rows of scorching pigs come through the flames. Bullets whiz through the heat. The emergency lights flick on, casting the room a deep red as the sprinklers activate, attempting to stop the flames.

Lola's gun speaks back as bullets wiz past her. A bullet pierces into Namsruc's shoulder, and she barks. Lola fires again, hitting a Moth, and the shadowy figure falls. She wraps Namsruc's arm around her, helping the vazelead to her feet. More bullets rain on them. One shreds Lola's outer thigh, ripping through the flesh. The ash is enough to numb the pain and she keeps dragging Namsruc.

Scalebane's rattling sound reverbs through the chilling room. A man's scream of agony is next. Grunts and ruffling follow.

Their allies are alive.

More bullets slam into the concrete beside Namsruc and Lola, missing them by a fraction. The man on the metal walkway takes another grenade from his belt, his eyes are locked on Lola.

A shimmering chrome object flies past the spraying water and smoke and into the Moth's neck. The man freezes. He lets go of the grenade, failing to pull the pin. Blood spurts from the wound as he holds the star stuck in his flesh. Synarion is her saviour once more.

"Here," Namsruc says, pointing to a ladder against a wall leading up to the walkway.

"Can you make it?" Lola asks.

"I must," Namsruc says.

The two reach the metal ladder, and Namsruc goes first. Her limbs shake as she hisses through the pain, lifting herself. Lola follows, avoiding pressure on her grazed leg. Now she feels the blood running into her boot.

They reach the top and stand on the walkway. The far end of the path leads to a closed door over the control room. It must lead to the plant's offices. That's their best bet.

"This way," Lola says, taking the lead and passing the dead Moth.

The Crystal Moths below are distracted by Scalebane and Synarion. It's impossible to know where they are through the smoke, but they can handle themselves fine.

More Moths burst into the chill room from both directions, firing their guns with no aim through the chaos.

Lola and Namsruc walk over to the control room. They're a

couple meters from their exit. The office door swings open, and a tall, beefy man steps through. Lola and Namsruc stop in their tracks as the man lumbers towards them. Both of his hands hold brass knuckles, his gun holstered to his belt. His choice of weapon says he wants to rumble.

Lola fires, hitting the man in the chest, revealing a silver glimmer underneath his white blazer — a bulletproof vest. He's too close and swings at Lola. She ducks, dodging the attack, and takes the knife from her boot.

Namsruc leaps onto the man's face, her claws puncturing his flesh. Lola shivs the man in the thigh, and he groans, punching Namsruc in the ribs with both fists, knocking the wind out of her. He grabs her by the tail and flings her back into the doorway. Her body smashes the door's side.

Lola stabs the man several more times, moving to his gut. She fires her gun into his chest as he throws another fist, hitting Lola's skull. Bright red stains seep into the white fabric of his pants. The man is bleeding out, and it's not enough. He throws another fist into Lola's face, and the brass knuckles crush the bridge of her nose. She drops her gun, still holding the knife. Another punch lands on her chest. Her vision blurs, saturating the colours with it. Sharp pain rises through her system.

The ribs, comes the voice.

The man raises both fists. Lola springs forward, and her blade pokes the man's side. It pierces below his lungs, and she digs into the lower gut, slicing through vital organs. His fists slam into her back. Bone cracks, and she grips the man tightly, stabbing with whatever strength she has left. He punches her back again. His massive form stumbles sideways. Lola keeps thrusting the blade as he wobbles into and over the railing. The two slam onto the control room's roof, breaking the flimsy structure. Both fall until the Crystal Moth lands head first onto the ground with a loud snap from his neck. Lola's wounded leg hits the ground first, breaking on impact. Bone rips through her cargoes. She cries in agony and dares not to look at her leg.

Whether it's the adrenaline or ash, Lola tucks her knife into its sheath. She crawls over to the dead man, snagging his holstered gun. With her other hand, she takes her smartphone and unlocks it with her bloody hands. She navigates to the text messages and finds Detective Iglesias. She taps away with her red, sticky fingers:

(You: where are you?
6:32 AM)

He has to arrive. Her plan is a complete disaster, and she fears for her life. It's now or never. Lola activates the QR code scanning app, just in case. She grips her gun and crawls clear of view from the walkway and stairwell.

Lola reaches a concrete pillar, managing to sit. Further in the control room are an operating table and two foldouts. A few bags of ash scatter the surfaces with whole scales.

She presses the communicator in her ear. "Synarion. Where are you?"

Footsteps come from the stairwell above.

CHAPTER 51
DISSOLVING VENTURES

An explosion isn't enough to stop a creature born from smoke and flame. The scorching blaze heightens her rage. Her sister will be free. Each strike she makes—every blow, kick, and whip of her tail into the soft skins stack her adrenaline. A fool's rage basks in bloodshed!

Fighting alongside her former caregiver, Synarion, would strike emotions in any normal being. Unfortunately, Scalebane has long learned to eradicate her feelings for anything other than her family. Hate is the only emotion she can feel for anyone who has wronged her.

The grenade's flames divide the Scalebane sisters as Crystal Moths come from both ends of the chill room. The smoke, sprinklers, and fire serve as coverage, letting Synarion and Scalebane ambush the six newcomers at the freezer set of doors.

Scalebane leaps high as Synarion slides low, disorienting the Moths who fire openly. Synarion's throwing star plummets into one man's heart. He rolls, springing to his feet, and rams his spiked knuckles into a second. Scalebane's tail whips a man, knocking his gun sideways. She lands in front of the Moth and his comrade. Her sai strike both Moths. Once, twice, and a third until they topple to the ground.

Two Crystal Moths remain. They open fire with their automatic weapons.

One bullet pierces through Scalebane's bicep, shredding through the other side. It doesn't stop her. Pain doesn't affect her people like soft skins, her sister's resistance is a perfect example. The second bullet misses, smashing into the wall. She sprints and then ducks, skidding low, and trips one man as Synarion goes for the second. Scalebane leaps on top of the fallen Moth and plunges her sai into his mouth. The metal breaks his teeth and rips through the back of his throat. Blood floods into his open mouth. Synarion throws an uppercut, sending the last Moth into the air. He meets the ground with a thud, dropping his gun in defeat.

The victory is short-lived. Mystery bullets rain from the other side of the chilling room, soaring through the cloak of elements toward them. Synarion and Scalebane dart to the far side. They exit through the doors, hiding in the freezer room.

Scalebane cannot sense smells from burning flames and roasting pig carcasses. Shouts come from the chill room and further in the abattoir. The bullets no longer flying at the doors and are directed inside the space. Namsruc and Lola are taking the heat.

"Lola, can you hear me?" Synarion says, pressing the communicator on his ear. "Lola?"

"They can't fight like us," Scalebane says. Already the icy bite of this environment is slowing her body. Vazeleads are not designed for such a hostile cold.

"Did you see them?" Synarion asks.

"No. The explosion pushed them the other way. They have to be close to the control room."

"Damn," Synarion says. He looks at his outer leg where the skin has been shredded on his upper thigh with thick red liquid dampening the fabric. His arms and some of his torso are stained with a moist red. It's impossible to know if it's his or human blood. He says, "There's no way you could have done this on your own."

"Thus, we are here, nymph."

"Aren't these your men? Tell them to stand down," Synarion says.

"They're not mine. They belong to Erol Terzi, who works for Mastema. If you haven't noticed, I'm not a Crystal Moth."

"Which is why I wish to reason with you and your people."

"Now is not the time, balancer." Scalebane peeks through the window of the door leading to the chill room. No Crystal Moths or gunshots are visible. Muffled shouts and bullets are heard. "We need to go now."

The sound of a door pushing open comes from the far end of the freezer. Footsteps pick up. The stacks of boxed frozen meat shroud the exact location.

Synarion presses on his communicator again. "Lola."

Scalebane pushes the doors open to the chill room and spins her sai, creeping low. She moves down the rows of scorched carcasses and around the flames to the other side.

Bullets roar past another row of cooked pigs. The two doors leading to the butchering room swing open as Crystal Moths hurry into the chill room, using the doors as shielding. They fire into the other room, where soft skins wearing blue uniforms shoot back. The law has arrived.

That is of little importance. Within the group of eight Moths is a man in a grey suit, yammering away on his phone. Erol Terzi. A fool's rage commands Scalebane to strike vengeance.

"Control room?" Synarion whispers from behind.

"That or the walkway above," Scalebane says. "The good news is they aren't after Lola or Namsruc."

Synarion says, "I can't get hold of her."

"I'll sniff them out," Scalebane says.

"Through this mess?" Synarion says.

"I can try."

Stomping comes from above on the walkway. A group of three Moths stand by the top of the ladder. A swarm of bullets flies towards them from the opposite end, far too many for Lola's one gun. It must be the police. One by one, the law mows the gangsters, the Moth bodies dangle over the railings with blood dripping into the fires.

"Lola?" Synarion presses on his communicator. The two creep against the wall close to the control room

The freezer doors burst open, and more Crystal Moths rush

into the chill room. They run around the opposite side to aid their allies against the cops.

"Lola? We're coming," Synarion says. He eyes the control room door as a few Crystal Moths leave the group of eight towards the doorway. They raise their guns and open fire down the stairwell.

Scalebane lifts her mask enough to get a good whiff of the hot air. "They're both there," she says, sniffing. "Fresh vazelead blood." She lowers the mask.

"We need to hurry," Synarion says. He takes a throwing star and brings his arm back, ready to strike at the control room attackers. Scalebane snags his wrist with her tail, pulling him in close. He raises his spiked knuckles, stopping centimetres from her goggles. His purple eyes slant into a sneer. He already knows what she is doing.

"No need to turn on me, balancer," Scalebane says.

"Scalebane," Synarion says, grinding his teeth.

"Lola is a threat to me, you, and all others."

"Let her go this one time," Synarion says.

"You also pose an issue."

"Lereif," Synarion says softly. "Please. You're better than this."

"So you keep implying, Synarion. Your soft skin is a thorn in King's plans and, therefore, mine."

"We have Namsruc. She has to be with Lola in the control room. Let us regroup together. I'm not a fool, and I know your plan doesn't align with King's. There's far too few of you."

Scalebane cocks her head. "Look around you. The Crystal Moths are far outnumbered by the police. This battle is over.

The girl will take the fall for this, and you will disappear."

"I can't let you do that. The Crystal Moths are a larger monster you fail to see. Let me reason with King."

"Don't give me that balancer order nonsense. I know what drives you at the core. It's not balance for Mother Nature. It's the same reason why you abandoned Namsruc and me. It's why you will abandon Lola. Your desires are far more . . . natural. Does the name Queen Valturus strike your heart?"

The muscles in Synarion's jaws clench, trying to control the turmoil inside himself.

Lola's muffled voice comes through his communicator. She's shouting, no doubt.

Scalebane continues, "Your demon friend, Mulier, squealed one last bit of information before I ended her life. I know what you long for, Synarion. Without that succubus alive, I am the only one who knows how to get into Hell. Namsruc is too pure. If you want *her*, you'll abandon the girl."

Lola keeps shouting through the speaker as the Crystal Moths send a volley of bullets into the control room. The police from the slaughter room advance foot by foot using riot shields, boxes and pillars as protection. The law on the walkway has cleared the spot entirely, shooting at the remaining gangsters.

"Our window of opportunity is closing, Synarion," Scalebane says. "Deal with the Crystal Moths and the law. Let me have the girl, and Namsruc and I will escape. You and I will reconnect. I will help you get into Hell and save your love. You have my word."

Scalebane frees Synarion, and she slithers away. He remains frozen at first and then takes a gold ring from his pocket. He bites his lip, shaking his head and then kisses the metal fangs holding a red gem and equips it. Then, he moves as commanded. What a simple creature. With anger, he launches his throwing star at an officer above. The blade runs right into the man's throat, ripping it open. Rapidly, Synarion pulls out three more, flicking them, and they spin from his hand.

One blade hits a cop. The remaining officers retreat to the doorway whence they came. Synarion sneaks through the smoke, heading for the Crystal Moths by the doors. There are a good twelve due to the earlier backup from the freezers. With both hands, he grabs a man's head from behind. One twist snaps the neck.

The next victim meets Synarion's spiked fists in the side of his skull. A third suffers blows in the ribs. Now, the remaining Moths see the threat. They shift their aim to stop the balancer.

Erol Terzi hangs up his phone, rushing to the metal ladder in a foolish attempt to escape. The Moths by the control room haven't moved, firing below. Scalebane has time.

She sheaths her sai and waits for Erol Terzi to climb up the walkway. Scalebane springs from the ground and snags onto the bottom of the walkway in a single leap. The hunter swings herself over and slides underneath the railing, lifting herself in front of Erol.

His mouth dangles open, and he fumbles through his blazer. She sprints as he reveals a small gun from his pocket. Scalebane smacks it from his hand, grabbing his neck with her claws. He chokes, struggling in her grasp as she lifts him off his feet.

"Scalebane, we don't have to do this," he manages to grunt.

She carries him to the other end of the walkway, far from his comrades, and slams him onto the platform surface with a loud bang. Her claws break into his skin, blood beads poking from the flesh.

"Scalebane!" Erol cries. "We can work this out. You're a reasonable being."

"There's nothing reasonable about me," Scalebane says.

"You must understand. Mastema has high expectations."

"I don't care for Mastema or any of your Moths. You took my sister, do you know that? Or are you as dense as every soft skin?"

"I did what I must, Scalebane. You have to believe me."

"I don't trust a word out of your snake tongue." She squeezes tighter, causing him to cough. His limbs flail wildly, slamming onto the metal ground. "To think, I almost let my guard down with you."

"Please, Scalebane. I didn't wish for any of this."

"And you will pay with your life," Scalebane says,

"My partner! My partner! Das, he can tell you things. His paintings, you related to them."

"I'll find him myself. Perhaps I'll kill him when I'm done."

"Mastema will have your head! You will not lay a finger on Das." Erol's face scrunches into a hateful scowl.

"Mastema will remain diplomatic. King and the vazeleads have the ash. You are a pawn in a greater scheme, soft skin."

"You're dead without the media. The Crystal Moths will be exposed. Your people will be eradicated!"

"My people have been through worse."

Another explosion goes off, this one coming from the slaughter room with the police. As much as Scalebane would love to torture the man, she has to get Namsruc. The brief moment after the explosion lets her focus on the smell. The subtle familiar hint of a swamp and rust is on the walkway. Namsruc was here.

"Scalebane, I have a partner who needs me. You must understand. Family is important, clearly!" Erol says.

Scalebane says, "I don't mix family and business." She squeezes tighter around his neck, crushing his tendons.

The man winces one last phrase, "Go to Hell!" before his neck snaps in her clutch. The claws sink deep into the meat, digging through the muscles down to the broken bone.

Already went, Scalebane thinks.

A satisfying death to quench a fool's rage indeed. Scalebane rises. Synarion is no longer below. The Crystal Moths by the door are either dead or gone, meaning the police are close. Namsruc's smell lingers. Time is closing.

CHAPTER 52
JUSTICE SERVED

Dust and concrete particles scatter off the pillar. Lola stays close to the concrete structure as the bullets soar down. There is little she can do, trapped in a basement control room with death reigning from above. Synarion doesn't answer his communicator. She has not heard from Detective Iglesias. Her sliver of ash is wearing off, and the pain rises beyond control. Everything she planned is falling to pieces.

Lola leans around the corner and fires at a Crystal Moth, missing. She hides and checks how many bullets she has left. The chamber has six shells remaining. It's not enough to finish the last of the Moths.

"Soft skin," comes a raspy voice from the dark shadows.

Namsruc's fiery eyes are visible as she slides off a metal tank. She comes into the light, crawling on her feet and one hand. The other grips her torso, where black blood seeps between her claws. It leaves a trail of droplets on the ground.

"There's a vent," Namsruc says, pointing to the opposite end of the room. The action is an odd polarization from her sister's nature. It's also Lola's best chance to get out.

"We could get trapped in there," Lola says.

"It's the one option. If we can make it, I can pry it open."

"You have the strength?" Lola asks.

More shots come from above the stairs, and a Crystal Moth topples over the railing, slamming face-first into the ground. The raining death-from-guns lessens.

"We'll find out," Namsruc says. "Hurry!"

Lola uses her arms and one good leg, dragging the broken one. Namsruc is well ahead of her. The pain is unbearable without the ash. Reality is seeping into Lola's mind, her senses honing in on agony.

Namsruc reaches the opposite end of the control room. In a couple of tugs, she rips the vent cover off and glances at Lola.

Lola uses all her might with each pull of her shaking arms. Strength is fading. She's several meters from Namsruc as the bullets continue. They ping against the railings, and others slam into the ground beside her.

She rolls onto her back and fires. Her shot pierces a Crystal Moth right in the chest. He grips his wound, stumbling into another. The second Moth steps in front and fires.

Namsruc crawls to Lola and grabs her arm. A bullet pierces into the vazelead's back, and she barks.

"Go!" Lola shouts, sending two more bullets at the Crystal Moth. Three left.

"I'm sorry, soft skin," Namsruc grunts, her spiked brows slanted back. She releases Lola, limping to the vent. She slips inside and disappears into the shadows. The cover to the vent is put into place. Lola is on her own.

The Crystal Moth fires again, missing Lola. A leather-clad reptilian appears behind him. Her sai lunges into the Moth's spine, stunning him, and she tosses him over the railing. He lands on his back beside Lola with a heavy thud, breaking a bone. Scalebane leaps down onto him, her boots crushing into his skull. Lola has never been so pleased to see the vazelead.

Another set of footsteps come from the control room, yet there are two of them. The violence is distorting Lola's senses.

"Where is Namsruc?" Scalebane growls, sheathing her sai. "I can smell her." Her tail flies to Lola, snagging her gun-wielding arm and locking it in place.

"Where is Synarion?" Lola grits. She tries to gain control of her hand. It's no use.

Footsteps continue, close, even though they are the only ones here. A creak of a hinge follows.

Scalebane lifts her mask, exposing the ivory-white muzzle.

Another squeak from a hinge comes.

The black scales around her nostrils compress and extend as she takes heavy sniffs. She spots the closed vent and trail of blood. A mouth full of razor-sharp teeth appears under her grin.

The distraction is enough for Lola to take her knife from its sheath.

Footsteps fade on a metal surface.

Men shout from above. "Don't move! We have the area surrounded."

Scalebane pulls Lola to her, lifting her by the arm to be at eye level. Little does she know Lola's other hand hides a knife. The vazelead's armour seals her torso too well. Lola knows there must be an opening.

Scalebane snags her neck, flicking her forked tongue at her. "Erol couldn't have made it here in time, nor should have the police. You're a cunning one. It's a shame yo—"

Lola shoves the dagger into Scalebane's inner thigh, silencing her. It digs deep as she drags it down. The vazelead yelps, freeing Lola from her tail. Her claws soar into Lola's face, slicing it open.

She frees Lola's neck and slams her good knee against Lola's ribcage, making a loud snap. Lola lets go of the knife. Scalebane grabs Lola's forearm with both claws and pulls down, breaking the bones.

Lola cries as she's spun around and feels the knife plummet into her spine. Both sets of claws dig into her back. She's lifted into the air and is thrown towards the ash setup. Lola crashes into the two tables, collapsing them. Drug bags, boxes, and ash scales topple onto her. Without her ash numbing her nerves, the pain isn't like anything she could imagine. Perhaps this is what dying feels like.

Footsteps come from the stairwell with flashlights waving. Scalebane pulls her mask down and limps to the vent, leaving a trail of blood. She reverts to all fours and scurries into the vent as her sister had, leaving Lola to deal with the forthcoming police.

It's not over yet. It can't be. Lola has strength and the know-how of what to do as her final ultimatum. With her one good arm, she presses the camera on her jacket to stop recording. She reaches for her smartphone in her inner pocket and attempts to sync it with the camera and upload it to her cloud storage.

The connection is slow. There's not enough reception. The top corner of the screen shows a text message notification. One swipe reveals it's from Detective Iglesias. There has to be enough time for the transfer to finish while she activates the scanner app.

Footsteps grow louder. Lights beam on the corpses near her.

She lifts her tank top, exposing the heart-shaped tattoo and aligns her phone's camera with the design. The screen states SCANNING. The milliseconds roll by, and the text turns red: UNABLE TO READ.

"Fuck," Lola mutters. She attempts again and sees her wet body has far too much blood and dirt on her stomach for the app to detect. She wipes it with her palm and scans it again.

SCANNING . . .

A bright light beams onto Lola.

"Freeze!" shouts a man in a blue uniform, gun pointed at her. Several more officers descend the stairwell, rushing to her.

Come on, Lola thinks, keeping the smartphone aligned on her stomach.

SCANNING . . .

An officer hurries to her, spins his rifle around, and slams the butt end of the weapon into Lola's face. She drops the phone, and her vision goes black.

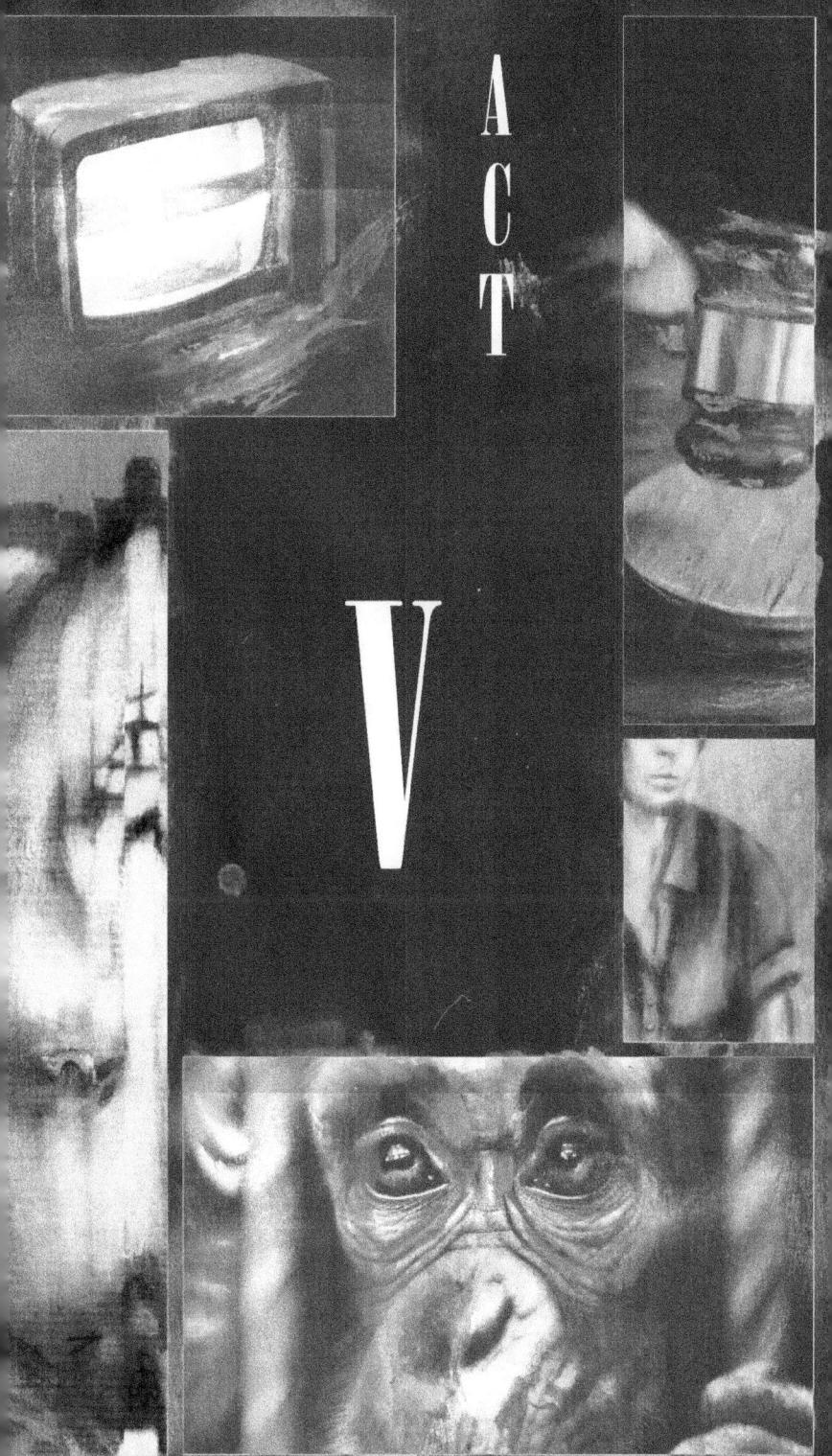

ACT

V

ACT V:
MONKEY ON ONE'S BACK: A NEW BUDDY

Good morning, and welcome to *CAMB News Now with Hucker Dime*. I'm coming to you live with a special report from my normal timing after receiving an anonymous distress tip.

A mass shooting occurred at Allen Abattoir Plant in Vancouver, British Columbia. The death count is at thirty-eight, with many more hospitalized and unlikely to recover from their wounds.

What caused such a horrific event? The police are uncovering what happened. We know that wanted criminal Lola Cabello, responsible for three murders, was there. The notorious Crystal Moths were also present at the crime scene. It's been over two years since the horrendous November 2014 YEGman incident in Edmonton, Alberta and Cabello is surpassing her predecessor.

Cabello has been wanted by the police for withholding evidence. Since then, her crimes have stacked. We believe her arrest has been made and the *slaughter* at the slaughterhouse is over.

Vancouver chief of police says they will make an official statement within the hour. Right now, all we can do is follow the CAMB team at the crime scene and social media posts.

If Cabello is indeed within police custody, we'll see an end to the global riots regarding Ashley Amber's death. We've asked for statements from the Mayor of Vancouver and Prime Minister Stéphane Trudell.

I have no other words for such a horrific tragedy other than reiterating that here at CAMB, we strive to provide you with facts regarding the latest news. As we've seen over the past month following Cabello, stories about you and your country continue to evolve. We keep you up to date with *CAMB News Now with Hucker Dime*.

Now, let us have a moment of silence for the lives lost.

CHAPTER 53
FINAL CONTACT

Drug busts used to give an unmatched rush. Serial arrests become numb. Monotony sinks in, and even with the risks, one feels a loss of humanity. At least until something new comes around and shakes it up.

Over the past summer, the first discovery of ash jolted Ricardo Iglesias with a brand-new sense of purpose. The mysterious drug proved to be a challenge he wanted to sink his teeth into, surging his spiral into workaholism.

Iglesias questions if any of it was worth it, standing in the parkade of the Allen Abattoir Plant. He isn't getting the rush he first experienced when finding ash in New Brunswick. He misses his son.

The police storm the entire plant from the front, rear, and sides of the factory. A couple of helicopters are flying to the scene. They're arresting the remaining Crystal Moths found within and near the plant now that the shootout is over, with minimal casualties from police. The plant workers and Moths weren't that lucky.

I should have been on the front, Iglesias thinks, folding his arms against his bullet vest, contradicting his feelings for family. It was wise that he wasn't in the line of fire, considering the army of gangsters. José needs a father. He feels responsible for the injured officers and dead plant workers. It's natural when married to the law.

Iglesias is aware of his aging body, unlike the first time he found ash. He cannot risk his life. His family needs him. The detective's brain is also far more valuable than his brawn. He, Archer, Beckman, and a couple more key officers maintain the perimeter and make sure no suspects sneak in or out of the slaughterhouse.

Iglesias's inner pocket buzzes. It's a message from Lola Cabello reading:

(Raymond Alexander: where are you?
6:32 AM)

(You: we are here.
6:33 AM)

Iglesias didn't receive a second text from Cabello. She wasn't lying. Suspicious deeds ooze from this plant. Most workers have already left the facility, fleeing for their lives. The law will catch up to them to see how much they know about this massacre.

Already the media is here to get access behind the caution

tape where officers keep them at bay. Somehow, they beat the fire department and the ambulance. Those leeches can paint this as a wrapped event by spinning facts and building a narrative the public prefers. They always do.

There's more to the story, and Cabello is the one with the information. Call it instinct or his overworked mind, but Iglesias's gut tells him this isn't what Cabello planned. The girl doesn't want a bloodbath. This plant is no different than the art gallery.

Beckman says, "I gotta give it to Fulcher. I didn't think he'd give us anything helpful ever again. Our visit to him paid off."

Iglesias nods, playing along with his lie. It was a simple maneuver to take Lola Cabello's information and claim that Tycho Fulcher, his intel, provided it. After all, Fulcher was the first to introduce the police to ash.

Archer says, "Not that I've met the guy, but his skittish nature didn't seem like he had a lick of value in him."

Beckman laughs. "He's a character, all right. Now here we are."

Iglesias mumbles, "Here we are."

The familiar redhead, Sergeant Hill, walks to them, finishing a call on his com. He says, "We're clear to go in now. Sounds like they have something you will want to see."

Fire trucks and ambulances arrive at the scene. First responders and firefighters join the group through the trail of havoc. Hill leads the three through the lobby, through the hallway, and towards the factory core. Forensics, police officers, blood analyst specialists, and coroners work meticulously. They sample and mark blood splatters, corpses, bullet holes, and shells at the crime scene. Mind the paperwork that is to come back at the office, corpses litter the floor, gangsters and civilians alike. Iglesias hasn't seen such a horror. Bullet holes cover some corpses while others have throwing stars stuck into them. Many have stab wounds and slash marks in consistent series of four.

Hill points to a stretcher beside an elevator with a zipped body bag. He says, "You'll recognize this character. Looks like these Crystal Moths have their fingers in everything."

The four approach the body bag, and Hill unzips the top. Unmistakably it is Erol Terzi with his neck crushed inwards. There's no good reason for this man to be here. He was also at the art gallery shooting. Erol Terzi, head of CAMB, is tied in with the Crystal Moths.

"Wild, ain't it?" Hill says.

"Fuck," Archer says.

"Indeed," Iglesias says.

"It gets better, come on," Hill says. "We think we found your girl alive."

Iglesias looks at his two comrades. "I'll take care of this."

Archer says, "You got it, boss."

"This way," Hill says.

Beckman and Archer stare at Erol's corpse as firefighters rush through the hall. Paramedics rush by with more stretchers to aid the wounded and dying.

The firefighters pass Hill and Iglesias, pushing the hygiene swinging doors aside into the chill room. The two follow as the firefighters turn off the sprinklers. The flames are gone, and smoke lingers throughout the scorched blast site.

"Down here," Hill says, taking him to a doorway leading to a basement. They pass a mound of Crystal Moth corpses and pigs that reek even through the cooling temperatures of the room.

Down the stairs, Hill stops behind a medical team with none other than Lola Cabello. The girl's closed eyelids are ripped, with four nasty slices running along the broken nose and right cheek, ending at her jawline. Bones poke from her forearm and leg. Her shirt is lifted with her phone resting on her smeared stomach beside a mosaic heart-shape tattoo on her hip. She rests unconscious on collapsed tables with boxes, drug bags, and ash scattered around.

"Looks like you got your gal," Hill says.

"Apparently so," Iglesias says. This is not what Cabello intended at all. She had the living hell kicked out of her. Those four cuts on her face match the ones on the corpses.

His gaze moves from the ash-covered Lola to the bloody floor. It's not just red. There are plenty of pitch-black droplets. Some stain the white blazers of the dead. Trickles run along the concrete. He kneels to inspect the liquid.

"Don't get too close," Hill says.

"Relax," Iglesias says. A strange sense of déjà vu floods Iglesias as he stares at the black blood. It's similar to the first time he saw ash in that bedroom. This time, it's a liquid. This isn't oil. The splatters are far too consistent with the nature of bloody wounds.

Chen's words haunt Iglesias's mind: *a fucked-up whack reptilian humanoid thing.* A chill rattles his spine and down his legs. Yes, even through the years numbing him and witnessing the most extensive shootout of his career, he gets a spike of adrenaline far more potent than anything he's had.

Fulcher, Chen, and even Cabello could be telling a tale of truth. He has the horn that she gifted him. Could it be? Could intelligent reptilians exist, as foretold by countless conspiracy theories around the globe for centuries? Reason tells him no. Still, the subtle clues are showing. Erol Terzi, a man who shouldn't be here, has immense power to mask the media. What they're uncovering here is evidence unlike any other, pointing to one unrealistic answer.

He can't be a believer. Not yet. Iglesias is rational and understands that they must eliminate all other possibilities. Perhaps this blood is reptilian, but no damn intelligent one. With that, he rises, knowing that the blood will be inspected by forensics, and they should get details on it, and, hopefully, answers.

To be safe, he wipes the blood droplet under his armpit, staining his dress shirt. He can get it analyzed along with that horn.

He points to the blood. "Make sure that the blood results get into my hands."

"Of course," Hill says.

He looks at Cabello. She's going to be knocked out for a helluva good time. Those wounds will take months of healing while his department grills her.

Iglesias leaves the control room as the medics put Cabello on a stretcher, taking her to the ambulance. There is plenty of more work to do. This is a gold mine, as Cabello promised. The crooked law and Moths can conceal Chen's escape and misguide internal affairs, leaving Iglesias on edge with his own team.

They can't keep this hidden.

Beckman rushes into the chill room as Iglesias reaches the main floor. He says, "We've got problems."

"What?" Iglesias asks.

Beckman takes him to the set of doors and pushes it open, revealing five green-uniformed men. In the middle of the group is a man covered in dozens of badges pinned to his coat. They march down the factory towards Iglesias.

"Fuck," Iglesias says. The military has arrived. As Beckman has predicted.

"Fuck indeed," Beckman says. "Sergeant Bando couldn't hold them off."

The military march to Iglesias and Beckman, stopping several paces behind the general.

"Detective Iglesias," he says with a cold gaze behind his wrinkled eyelids.

"That's me. You are?"

"General Florence," the man says. "Your services have been appreciated. The DND and the Minister of Public Safety have great concern regarding the process over the ash drug that is spread throughout Canada."

"Understandable. We made a major breakthrough today," Iglesias says.

General Florence's face is stone as he stands straight as a rod, making it impossible to read what he thinks or feels. He says, "With many casualties and no further info on ash. The CFMP will be spearheading the operation from here on out. You and your team are to provide your evidence to date. You will continue to work with us in a supportive role."

Beckman and Iglesias exchange glances. "Of course, General," Iglesias pushes through his teeth.

He can't believe it. Of all things to happen, he's going to lose control of the case. He doesn't even know if he can trust the military. Now, Iglesias is starting to think like a conspiracy nut. Cabello needs to be conscious so he can ask her what the hell happened. That isn't going to be the case. He is too close to this and needs a fresh perspective.

More military arrive at the abattoir, overtaking the operations with their own teams as Iglesias and Beckman head outside. They both light a smoke in defeat.

Cabello has more secrets, and it's clear how this story will play out with the media watching, the justice system, and the CFMP. Lola will take the blame as a mass shooter with multiple charges, she'll be locked up, and the media will pin her as the mastermind. Sergeant Bando will have the team cooperate with the military without question.

Free of their duties, Iglesias and his team fly home. Cabello, the prime suspect, will be brought to a federal prison while the evidence is processed. Beckman can return to his wife. Archer can learn about life other than work. For Iglesias, he gets a much-needed break at home.

He hugs his son who had not burned the place down. There are no signs of parties. His girlfriend, Hailey, is sticking around. This is what is essential.

"I missed ya," Iglesias says while holding his son tightly. He can't change the world and has to remember the important things in life. He's one man. A father. That's what comes first.

"Good to see you, Dad," José says, breaking free from him. "Listen, I'm gonna go hang with Tanner."

"Tonight? It's a school night."

"Yeah. Homework is done." José heads for the door as a vehicle's headlights appear on the driveway.

"Sure thing," Iglesias says.

"Tell me about the case after. Cool?"

"Cool," Iglesias says.

His son opens the door and heads over to a white Mitsubishi Lancer parked in the driveway. In the driver seat, under the tinted windshield, is Tanner at the wheel. The driver's face is hidden in the darkness while the front door lights illuminate his white dress shirt.

Cool, Iglesias thinks.

CHAPTER 54
CLOSER FRIENDS

Keeping your enemies closer than your friends sets false expectations regarding life. For example, Scalebane was too focused on her foe and here she stands outside the Allen Abattoir Plant in the brisk British Columbia morning, lost without her sister, who is the one she cares for the most.

Sirens boom from the highway and helicopter blades linger in the skies as the wind brushes against the scrap of bloody green fabric tied around two feathers Scalebane holds in her hand. The black-and-white feathers are indistinguishable from Namsruc. As for the blood and cloth, the pine scent is Synarion's. The damn balancer escaped before her and left an unsettling note.

There is no need for a written message, for the sign is loud and clear. Synarion has what Scalebane longs for. The cunning nymph was one step ahead of her. From her youth, he was the same, and he has not changed. Her orchestrated plan failed. Her sister is once again out of reach.

There's a brief blood trail of her sister in the grass that vanishes. Her smell is gone. Synarion is not here. His ghost movements surpassed Scalebane's senses undetected.

The stifled anger she unleashed on the Moths and Erol Terzi has washed away. New tides of hate drown her as she, Mastema, and that damned half-imp Jekos are flown overseas to Vietnam. They're accompanied by the two vampire Moths as well. They must be here for protection from her.

Scalebane is not one for flying. These strange transportations belong in the soft skins' world. Unfortunately, it is the fastest way to King. The fool's rage pumping in her blood is repressed during the flight. She cannot attack Jekos, Mastema, or their bloodsuckers. At least, not yet.

She thinks of Namsruc during the flight. Right under her muzzle, the Crystal Moths have double-crossed King and Scalebane. Even from the get-go, her suspicions about their agendas were ever present, yet, King pursued. Erol Terzi's death, the capturing of Namsruc, and Scalebane's rebellious nature will all be handled professionally. The trip across the world will allow the parties to reconnect. They'll discuss their options.

Scalebane can't stop mulling over her sister and where she is right now. Synarion wouldn't kill her. He values life too much and understands the rarity of the old world beings. The prick raised Scalebane and Namsruc. He may even love them. The question is what lies he will seed into Namsruc's too trusting mind.

The journey to the vazelead's hidden lair is met with silence. Mastema is a businessman and knows that no words are worth spilling until the necessary parties are involved. Jekos, Mastema, and Scalebane sit in a meeting chamber in an underground cavern. The vampire Moths wait outside.

Scalebane's claws tap on the rare polished blackwood tree table beside a stone throne. This type of wood existed in the old world and made beautiful furniture. She keeps her gaze on Jekos and Mastema at the opposite end of the room. Her mask-free face is stone cold. Yet, her fiery eyes flicker fast with anger. In their lair, she can be herself and does not fear what these two Crystal Moths think.

The half-imp fidgets with his fingers, scheming whatever nonsense he has. He knew what Scalebane wanted at Club Revelation. If what Mul said is true, she owed him money. Scalebane is sure there's more to this story than just wanting cash. Imps are far more malicious than greedy.

He warned Scalebane of Mastema. Mastema is fooling your people. He's not possessing a human body. Watch yourself.

As for the First, he slumps on the velvet cushions of his blackwood chair, staring at the table. He sits straight, adjusting his white blazer. It gives a subtle glimmer of the golden bracelets under the dim orange lighting.

The drug lord says, "I didn't expect you to throw such a wrench in the ash operations. It's self-mutilation."

Scalebane growls, her tail coiling around the leg of the chair.

Her black and blue scalp feathers puff from the blood rushing to her head. "I'll rip you apart," she says.

Mastema chuckles in his typical smooth voice. "I'd like to see you try."

"The First means little to me."

Mastema taps his cuffs and says, "Confident you can destroy this poor human body?"

"It would be too easy," Scalebane says. She fears Jeko's warning. Mastema isn't possessing a human body and is the First in the flesh.

"We'll see what King has to say," Mastema says.

"You'll be dead before that happens."

Jekos, sitting behind Mastema, mouths the word, *No*, gripping his one wrist.

Scalebane holds her breath, keeping the half-imp in her peripheral view. Instincts tell her that message is meant for her.

Mastema says, "Such a naive child."

Before she can spit lip, the stone doors leading into the chamber slide open. Two new vazeleads step into the cavern. The broad shoulders and muscular arms behind the armoured reptilian catch the group's attention. The gunmetal humanoid mask conceals the newcomer's face underneath the black cloak resting on his head. The king of the vazeleads.

He marches past Scalebane to the stone throne, accompanied by a female vazelead whose silver scalp feathers create a long mane running past her bare back covered in scales to her tail. The thin black fabric of the dress drapes from a strap around her neck, covering her front torso and reconnecting with a belt around her hips. The lower fabric brushes against the cavern floor with her bare feet poking out. King's wife Zoefani's clawed toes tap the floor, making a clicking echo.

King sits on his throne as Zoefani stands beside him. Her hand rests on his shoulder as he grips the throne's armchair tightly. One by one, he eyes his guests, landing on Jekos. A low rumble comes from his throat. The distaste for the halfbreed imp is shared among the vazeleads.

"I'm experiencing tension in the room," King says in his deep demonic voice. "The methods of the Crystal Moths are disturbing me, Mastema."

Mastema raises his one hand in a casual shrug. "You refuse to answer our requests, and naturally, we had to take things into our own hands. Do you not see?"

"The Scalebane sisters were to oversee your operations to ensure we work together, fallen angel. I can see treachery does not leave your actions, even after descending from the Heavenly Kingdoms."

Mastema taps the table. "I bow to no one, friend."

"Which we have in common," King says, his claws scraping into the throne. Zoefani grips his shoulder, easing his tension. "Scalebane was sent to the West Coast to work with your chief to oversee the shipping. Namsruc was to coordinate the East Coast supply and misdirect the humans. And yet, you took her for your own use."

"She did coordinate the East Coast. She was involved with the distribution of ash on that side of the country, then the west. Didn't she go above and beyond her purpose?" Mastema looks at the group with slanted brows, more confused than guilty.

Zoefani releases King and says, "Your methods are tainted by the imp that accompanies you." She flickers her black tongue at him.

Mastema smiles, extending a hand to Jekos. "The servant has no influence on such."

Zoefani continues, "We have strict rules that the Nine corrupt are to be used for ash production. The Scalebane sisters are the two pure remaining vazeleads alongside the Blacktooth family."

"This I was unaware of," Mastema says.

"You are fully aware. The Scalebanes are to continue the bloodline of the Blacktooths. We do not mix with the corrupt!" She jabs a clawed finger towards Mastema. "You jeopardized Namsruc's safety with your reckless methods. Shackling and locking her away is what the soft skins did to us. You claim you wished to rid them of this Earth."

King says, "And Namsruc is missing, despite Scalebane's best efforts."

Mastema says, "You still have one." He nods at Scalebane. "Produce as many eggs as you wish, my dear friends. This is why I am confused. I returned Namsruc's belongings, including that precious soulstone. Besides, you don't quite know if Namsruc is dead or ran away. So the irrational emotions are counterproductive."

"The balancer has her," Scalebane says.

"A balancer?" Mastema snorts. "Please. The Grove was eradicated long ago. What you have is a megalomaniac nymph who deems himself the protector of Mother Nature. Namsruc won't listen to him."

"On the contrary," Scalebane says. "I'm sure she will."

"Mother Nature doesn't answer to anyone. This balancer is alone, defending those with nowhere to go, including old world beings. He won't lay a single finger on your precious Namsruc."

Scalebane says, "Namsruc was bleeding excessively. Your people left her for dead, stripping her of her scales, feeding her little."

"That I was unaware of," Mastema says.

Lies, Scalebane thinks. She keeps her composure, saying, "I've known Synarion for centuries. He aligns himself with the soft skin who is hellbent on dismantling the Crystal Moths. He's coming for you."

"Nymphs are weak beings and a balancer even more so," Mastema says. "They're too stuck in their morals."

"He does not stray away from killing," Scalebane says.

Mastema claps his hands together, leaning on the desk. "Okay, we can go back and forth with this, blaming each other. Clearly, we were not aligned with our arrangement. We need to move forward. Thus, I propose that we rework our terms. I do apologize for my misunderstanding on our end." He points at Scalebane with both index fingers, his palms pressed together. "We have many things to thank Lereif for. Her natural hunting instincts have helped eradicate a thorn in our backs. The distribution of ash has been rattled by this balancer and that human accomplice. I didn't know my men and Erol Terzi were so harsh on Namsruc. Then Lereif comes along and manages to shed light on the situation while illuminating the human threat. That vigilante has taken the blame for most of the damage."

King says, "That's not the end of it. The humans know too

much."

"No," Mastema says. "It's not. The humans will remain distracted by this Lola Cabello character while we hunt and execute witnesses. Every witness, including Moths, who saw Lereif and Namsruc will die. Lola Cabello is at the forefront of the media. It will give us time to re-collect what we're doing. This balancer, Synarion, will return in some form. Erol Terzi's death, at Scalebane's hand, left us with a giant void in our operations. Things are more complicated."

Scalebane says, "I'll take control of the operations."

Mastema's mouth hangs open, surprised by her words. He looks to King and Zoefani for confirmation.

Scalebane continues, "Erol Terzi got too close to what we're doing. He was sloppy. His personal life blended in. I have a disassociation with ash. I learned how he operated and can make sure there's no other slips or schemes."

"I admire your boldness, Scalebane," King says. "However, there's a burning fire in your soul that makes you unpredictable. Your deliberate disobedience of the Crystal Moths is proof. We need you here with our son. With Namsruc missing, we cannot risk you straying from the Blacktooth bloodline."

"I do not wish to mother your grandchildren," Scalebane says.

Zoefani raises her index claw. She says, "I propose a mutual resolution. Why not send Rithu to work with Scalebane directly? They can bond through hardship. Our people know that difficult times are the most effective method to bring two souls together."

Scalebane raises her spiked eyebrow.

King grumbles and shakes his head. "I'm unsure. It's risky."

Zoefani says, "He must grow at some point, King. We can't keep him sheltered because of our infertility. He needs to grow strong as you. Scalebane and Rithu are our last hope for the vazelead people."

Mastema says, "This is wonderful. I couldn't agree more with your suggestions. Lereif will work as head of ash. She can bring your son, whom I'd very much like to meet. He'll learn our business, and we'll nurture our relationship. Vazeleads and Crystal Moths."

King says, "And how do I know you won't abduct my son?"

"We need to bridge a new bond of trust. I apologize for Namsruc, truly. We will get her, whether with Lereif or my own men. We will hunt Synarion down." He points at Jekos. "Because I am burdened with too much, Jekos will be my eyes and ears when I am not present for Lereif and your son, Rithu. We will mend this damaged relationship from the fault of my choices. I assure you."

The room silences. King is still gripping his throne tightly. Zoefani folds her arms. Scalebane's tail burns from the pressure of her coiling around the chair's leg. Her sharp teeth bite into her inner lip, puncturing the flesh with a crunch and giving her a salty taste of her fluid.

Mastema asks, "Are we in agreement?"

King looks at Zoefani, and she nods at him. He says, "Agreed."

"Perfect. I look forward to working with you closer, Lereif, and the heir of the Blacktooth family." He rises and buttons his blazer. Jekos follows his action. "Lereif, there is a crafty servant

I'd like you to meet in Ottawa. We can thank them for misdirecting the law."

Scalebane stands. King and Zoefani watch her. Their minds are scheming at what they wish for her to do. She can't think of a worse fate than mothering the children of Rithu Blacktooth.

One victory at a time.

Lola Cabello is gone, and Scalebane has secured a far more advantageous position between the Crystal Moths and the vazeleads. She can be the guardian of her people. Scalebane can determine the nature of Jekos's warning. The far too young Blacktooth heir will be easy to dismiss. She'll keep the Crystal Moths from overstepping again. She will find Synarion. Scalebane has the secrets to finding his love. He will surrender Namsruc to her.

One battle at a time.

CHAPTER 55
THE SCREEN

The world isn't what the history books chalk it up to be. Reality has intricate gears, many actors, and no-win scenarios beyond any one person's ability to comprehend. It's far easier to be a watcher, zombified by the screen. This is tangible survival.

People will remember what was recorded in the media, and the rest washes away. A packaged story is far more digestible than real-world horrors. Civilians tune into the screen in the safety of their homes, on their phones, and even in their offices. They feed their dopamine, relish in excitement, and embrace what enrages them. Media serves as the addiction. Outcasts and vigilantes who spearhead factual, unbiased information are portrayed as culprits of evil. Those that are lucky enough to flee the country stay alive, while those that get too close are obtained by the police. This is the law of the concrete jungle.

I'm sorry, Mom, Lola thinks, rotting away in a locked hospital room with a broken body covered in casts. Her mother's ghost cannot watch the media, but her father and brother can. Lola's name is plastered on every television screen, newspaper, website, and social media platform as the mastermind behind the murder sprees on the West Coast. Poor Ashley Amber is avenged, or so the public thinks.

The angry mobs demand Lola's death. They protest outside of the hospital where she is held. They share Ashley Amber's face online, on posters, and on signs as a reminder of their beloved dead star. They share the stories of Lola Cabello murdering her in cold blood, Timothy Shepherd, the CEO of CAMB, and countless unnamed others.

Lola Cabello's story of false vengeance ending in a violent outrage has spread far beyond North America. The world's public knows she is a deranged murderer. Still, she claims innocence.

Hope is not lost. Her loyal followers defend her because they see through the inconsistencies of the supposed piling evidence. They post their own conclusions online, explaining the issues. They check her website continually, which champions her actions, as these people champion the truth behind Michael Bradford in Edmonton.

These are the genuine ones. They look beyond the screen's façade. The unsung heroes know that the world is not what history books write and not what the media claims.

If only they could see the evidence that Lola had gathered over the years. These people are asleep to the old world, intelligent reptilians, and the fantastical mythos of legends that she has found. They are unaware of how deep the Crystal Moths go. They do believe in her, though.

Lola doesn't believe in herself, and escape is impossible. All of her evidence exists in a distant digital safe, her cloud storage. Unfortunately, the scanning of her tattoo did not complete. She doesn't know if her final video was uploaded to the cloud. She hopes.

If she ever gets access to a smartphone, she will activate her tattoo. The sleeper social media accounts, the vacant blogs, and her own website will mass distribute the evidence. That's a guarantee. For now, she sits in her cell, wishing she could find faith. Her fingers twitch due to withdrawal. Lola tries to sit up and can't, wrapped up in bandages and casts.

Detective Iglesias is one of the good officers who followed each instruction she gave him, yet the power is beyond his control now. Other hands are involved.

She will have a defence attorney.

She will stand trial.

She has no money to choose her defender.

This whole case will be closed. That's what the Moths deem so.

The media spearheads linear stories for the zombie fantasy world. Everyone feels satisfied because feelings are important, not facts. Without feelings, we would go mad, like Lola is. She's mad for revenge. She is mad for the unjust. She's mad for being unable to feed her ash addiction which screams from the depths of her core. She's mad she never discovered more of the old world. She's mad at Synarion's evasiveness and his actions. He didn't come for her. Why would he? Her role is finished for him. She has taken the blame for the chaos, and the old world stays hidden.

Vengeance for the Trinity of Souls haunts her burning soul. Justice for her mother, Becky, and Michael Bradford will happen. Donnie is passive. Synarion is a plastic hero. Detective Iglesias is tied up. Lola is on her own and will find a way out of this prison. The Crystal Moths will fall. Scalebane and her people won't stand in the way. She'll climb the ladder of powers until she reaches the top and breaks the Moths.

Lola sure could use a hit of ash to scheme an escape. It's not to feed the addiction. At least, that's what an ash-dasher likes to tell herself.

THE STORY CONTINUES.

Book two now available!

Find *Obsidian's Command* at konnlavery.com

ALL WORK

Ash Born Series

- Crystal Moth Conspiracy: Ash Born Book One
- Obsidian's Command: Ash Born Book Two
- World Mother Ascension: An Ash Born Novel

Mental Damnation Series

- Reality: Part 1 of Mental Damnation
- Dream: Part 2 of Mental Damnation
- Purity: Part 3 of Mental Damnation
- Mortal: Part 4 of Mental Damnation

Terrors of the Macrocosm

- Rave
- Cultivate: Seed Me Relapse Edition
- YEGman

Short Stories of the Macrocosm

- Into the Macrocosm: Short Stories of the Dark Cosmic, Bizarre, and the Fantastic
- Beyond the Macrocosm: Interactive Short Stories of Dread and Wonder

Rutherford Manor Series

- The White Hand: A Rutherford Manor Novel
- Fire, Pain, & Ruin A Rutherford Manor Novel

Audiobooks

- Cultivate: Seed Me Relapse Edition Audiobook
- Into the Macrocosm Audiobook
- Rave Audiobook
- Fire, Pain, & Ruin A Rutherford Manor Audiobook

Novel Scores

- Frequencies of the Macrocosm Score
- Missing Head Highway Rave Novel Score
- World Mother: Seed Me Novel Score
- Sounds of Society: YEGman Novel Soundtrack

All publications, including short stories, are listed on konnlavery.com/publications

ABOUT THE AUTHOR

Konn Lavery is a Canadian author whose award-winning fiction has reached the bestselling charts on Amazon and in his hometown, Edmonton. His work has been described as uncanny and immersive and frequently falls under the Dark Fantasy and Horror genres. Each of his stories are housed within the expanding universe known as the Macrocosm spanning across time and space.

He has been recognized by reviewers such as Reader Views, Readers' Favorite, Literary Titan, and by award programs such as indieBRAG, The Wishing Shelf Book Awards, eLit Awards, and Dan Poynter's Global Ebook Awards. His work has also been curated into the Edmonton Public Library's Capital Press collection.

Konn started writing stories at a young age while being a homeschooled vegetarian, enthralled with storytelling. After graduating college, he began professionally pursuing his writing with his first release, Reality, in 2012 while balancing his graphic design business. Konn's visual communication skills have been transcribed into the formatting and artwork found within his publications, supporting his fascination with transmedia storytelling.